The Reluctant Captain

Michael Tefft

Copyright © 2014 Michael Tefft

All Rights Reserved

Cover Illustration by Emilee Jayne Smith

ISBN: 978-1507710081

Chapter 1

"Bloody hell! Is that really four bells?" cursed Malcolm. Lieutenant Commander Malcolm Robertson, Chief Engineer of the Her Majesty's Airship Daedalus, was up to his elbows in the main drive motor. Malcolm always tinkered with the engines to get the last bit of efficiency. Tearing down an engine while wearing his dress uniform was a first, even for Malcolm.

Malcolm had not meant to make engine adjustments in his dress uniform. He merely meant to stop by and ensure that his assistant Mr. Frye had everything under control. Upon entering the engine room, he heard a telltale vibration alerting him that something in the motor was out of synch. It was subtle to be sure, but Malcolm knew that if left too long, it might cause bigger problems. It was a minor adjustment; it would only take a moment.

The engine room bustled with noise and activity. Malcolm worked on the center of the three large motor casings. The mighty motors thrummed as they turned the three propellers used to push the Daedalus through the sky. The steady hum of the engines was the soundtrack to the activity in the engine room. Crewmen monitored the control panels for each engine, noting the temperature, revolutions and oil pressure from the gauges on each control panel. Another mate manned the engine control levers, matching the speed indicator with the speed relayed from the bridge. The smell of diesel permeated the air. The Air Service had used diesel since the days when the airships were filled with hydrogen and the danger of an open flame made coal too risky. For that, Malcolm was grateful, as he no longer had to shovel coal like he had when serving on the coal powered steam ships of the Royal Navy.

"Aye," replied a hesitant Mr. Frye. He was young, not long out of his engineering courses. His yellow hair and sharp blue eyes gave him a perpetually cheery countenance. "Aren't you supposed to be taking mess with the captain at four bells?"

"Yes," hissed Malcolm. "Just give me a moment. I've almost got it adjusted.... there." Malcolm pulled his hands out of the engine and they were covered with grease. He instinctually went to wipe them on his overalls, but caught himself when he realized that he was wearing his dress uniform. "Mr. Frye, fire it up and let's see how she's running now. And could you get me something to wipe this grease off my hands?"

Mr. Frye sent one of the mates to find a rag while he went over to restart the engine. The engine started immediately and as Frye gradually increased the power, its purr crescendoed into a low roar. Malcolm concentrated for a moment, his brows knit together in a scowl as he listened to the engine. He listened for the telltale vibration and after a few seconds more, nodded his head in approval before yelling, "Where the bloody hell is that rag?"

A nervous mate showed up and pressed the rag into Malcolm's hand. "Thank you," Malcolm said. As he wiped, he examined his hands. "Damn," he thought to himself. "I'm going to have to go back to the cabin to get this grease off."

"Mr. Frye, you have the engine room. If you need me for anything, anything at all, come and get me," he urged, hoping that Mr. Frye would get the hint and save him from dinner with the captain.

"Oh, Commander, I wouldn't want to deprive you of such an opportunity. The boys and I have everything under control here," he replied mischievously. He liked Malcolm, but couldn't help but enjoy a little fun at Malcolm's expense.

"Thank you, Mr. Frye. I'll have to find some way to pay you back for your... helpfulness," he said playfully.

"I'm sure you will," Frye replied. "Sir, you better get going, the captain will have your head if you're much later."

"Bloody hell, you're right," Malcolm cursed as he half-ran to the engineering bulkhead. "Remember, get me if you need anything.... I mean anything," he said, placing special emphasis on the last word.

"Aye, sir," Frye replied. Malcolm hesitated at the door taking one last look around the engine room. He sighed wistfully, wishing he were spending the evening here rather than in the stuffy officer's mess. In fact, he decided, he would rather shovel coal on a leaky old destroyer than go to the captain's dinner.

"Sir, you're going to be even later...." urged Frye.

"What? Yes, right. Carry on." And with that, Malcolm turned and closed the bulkhead to the engine room. Malcolm half-ran, half-walked down the hallway, still rubbing at the recalcitrant grease on his hands. He gave half salutes to all of the crewmen who saw him and stopped to salute. To each, he muttered a hasty "Carry on," and hurried down the hall.

Malcolm reached his room, Spartan by even Air Service standards. To the right of the door was a simple desk that was actually more like a table with drawers attached. A sea of paper and journals covered its surface. A single bed was attached to the left wall so that it could swing up and be secured out of the way. A built-in dresser bordered the door to his left. A shaving kit, a comb, and several jars of some sort of cream lay on its top. To the right was a closet filled with his uniforms. Other than the shaving kit and the sea of paper, there was almost no indication that anyone lived in this room.

Malcolm took a towel out of a drawer, quickly opened up one of the jars, scooped out a liberal amount of the cream, and slathered it over his hands. After a few seconds, he wiped the cream off his hands, its soap-like scent reminding him of his mother and home.

Home. He hadn't thought about his home in a very long time. Malcolm's home was the tiny village of Kilmacolm, some fifteen miles west of Glasgow, the great ship and airship building heart of the British Empire. His grandfather was a blacksmith, serving the local farming community around Kilmacolm. When the railway connected Kilmacolm to Glasgow, the little village became flooded with people seeking to live in its modest homes away from the noise and crowds of Glasgow. The train now made living in Kilmacolm and working in Glasgow a realistic proposition. Soon the young men who used to work the farms around Kilmacolm were drawn to the money available working at the shipbuilding companies. Malcolm's grandfather's smithy got less and less business. Seeing the future, Malcolm's grandfather gradually turned his trade to repairing the new steam-powered contraptions, as he called them. With his knowledge of metalworking and his smithy, he could fabricate many parts himself, allowing him to repair machines others deemed hopeless. Malcolm's grandfather's reputation as someone who could fix anything grew and he was often called to assist the railroad. While the wave of industrialization around the country made it easier to buy something new when a device broke, the frugal people of Kilmacolm went to Malcolm's granda to repair their new devices.

Malcolm's father George had no desire to run the repair shop. George assisted his father since he was old enough to hold a broom and hated it. George saw the comparatively big money in shipbuilding and went to Glasgow to earn his way. Shipbuilding was hard work—12-hour shifts of welding and riveting. It was hot, sweaty, dangerous work. Malcolm's father had many burn scars to show for the long hours. For Malcolm's father, the chance to make his own way was worth the risk.

His mother Kate worked as a housekeeper. She was often not home to take care of Malcolm, so she sent Malcolm to assist in his granda's shop. At first, Malcolm could only clean the shop. Gradually, his granda taught him the names and functions of the tools in the shop. He became his granda's assistant, passing him tools, and holding the contraption so his granda could get at the repair work. By the time Malcolm reached ten, his granda's health began to fail. His eyes dimmed from too many years staring into the fire of the hearth and his hands began to shrivel into claws from arthritis. His infirmities did little to stop Malcolm's granda; his mind and ears were still sharp. He could tell if a machine was running correctly by the vibrations it made. He taught these skills to Malcolm who soon became the old man's eyes and hands.

Malcolm rose every day before dawn, going downstairs to his granda's shop and organizing anything his granda would need for the work of the day before leaving for school. Many days, his hands and school uniform were dirty from work begun on repairing some device left at the shop. After many notes from the school regarding Malcolm's disheveled appearance, Kate developed her special grease-cleaning cream that helped to make sure that at least Malcolm's hands were clean before school and she prevented him from ruining at least some of his school uniforms.

Malcolm smiled as he recalled this period of his life. It was the perfect life for an inquisitive boy who liked to know how things worked. By day, he studied composition, arithmetic, and science. He excelled at math; the algebra problems were little puzzles that he just had to apply the right knowledge to solve. But science was his first love and he easily mastered the subject. Years of tinkering showed him how sciences were applied; now he understood why machines worked the way they did as he began to grasp the laws that governed them.

When Malcolm was thirteen, his granda caught pneumonia. As the days wore on, it became apparent that little could be done but to ease his suffering. One night, his father told him that the end was near and he should go to say goodbye to his granda.

As Malcolm opened the door to his granda's bedroom, he saw his granda was failing. His skin had a gray cast and Malcolm could hear the wheezing in his labored breathing. His granda's eyes were closed. He hesitantly entered the room and whispered, "Granda?"

At the sound, his granda's eyes shot open. "Malcolm, my boy. Please come here. I want to talk to you." Malcolm hesitantly brought a chair next to the bed and sat down. Granda reached over and grabbed hold of Malcolm's hand.

"Don't cry, laddie," he said. "I'm an old man and I've lived a long, full life. I'm finally going to join your gram. But before I go, there are a few things you should know. The first is that when I'm gone, your da intends on closing the shop, getting rid of all me junk, as he likes to call it, and rent it out to a proper storekeeper."

"He can't sell the shop. I'll quit school and run the shop!"

"No, you won't, laddie. Your da is doing the right thing. You're a bright boy; you shouldn't be hanging around Kilmacolm scratching out a piss poor living fixing everyone's broken things. You should be designing ships or discovering some new scientific theory. You're a bright boy and you can do so much more. That's why I told yer da to close the store. I want the money from that sale to be used for your education. Go to college. Promise me that you'll go."

"I will Granda," he said, fighting the lump that was rising in his throat.

"But," his grandfather added mischievously, "if there is anything in the shop that you'd like to keep, you best smuggle it out before your father gets around to selling the shop." This brought a chuckle from Malcolm and temporarily kept the tears from welling in his eyes.

"And there's one more thing. There's something I want you to have," Granda said as he groped on the nightstand next to the bed. "Ah, here it is." He pushed a golden pocket watch into Malcolm's hand. "The railroad gave me this for helping them fix one of their locomotives. I fabricated a replacement part for their engine. It wasn't fancy, but it got them to the depot where they could repair it properly. The bloody watch stopped working about a year after they gave it to me. I could never get the bloody thing to work. I want you to have it. If there's anyone that can get that bloody thing working, it's you. When you get it working, think of your old granda and all you learned in the shop."

"Thank you, Granda. I'll not forget," Malcolm croaked in response.

"Good boy. I never told your own da how proud I was of the man he became. I probably should have; maybe we wouldn't be at each other's throat all the time. But I'll not miss the chance to tell ye I'm proud of you, Malcolm Robertson and me only regret is that I willna get to see the fine man you'll grow into one day."

"Oh, Granda," Malcolm half-sobbed as he reached over to hold his granda. Granda feebly returned the hug.

"Alright, Malcolm, me lad. It'll be fine. 'Tis life. Could you do me another favor?" he asked conspiratorially.

"Anything, Granda," he said, wiping the tears from his face.

"In me dresser, in the third drawer down, you'll find a scarf all wrapped up in a ball. Bring it over here." Malcolm obediently went to the drawer and returned after a moment with the scarf. It felt oddly heavy for just a scarf.

"Let me have it, me boy," Granda said. Even with hands nearly crippled with arthritis, he expertly unwound the scarf until, much to Malcolm's surprise, he held a small flask.

"Now, here's me true medicine. Whisky is all I need to make me feel better." He unscrewed the flask and took a long draught. After a sigh of pleasure, he pushed the flask to Malcolm. "Here, laddie. You're nearly a man. It's about time you embraced your heritage."

Malcolm raised the flask like his granda when Granda warned, "You best be careful, if you haven't had it before." Malcolm, wanting to show his granda he was a man, took a big swallow. The liquid fire washed down his throat and he was sure that he no longer had a throat or even a stomach, just a gaping pit of fire. His eyes filled with tears and he sputtered as he tried to breathe.

Granda laughed, "I warned ya, laddie. You have to sip it. This isn't beer. This is a real drink. Now, try again. This time go a little slower and try not to drink the whole flask in one go." Malcolm did and this time, to his amazement, it tasted like something other than liquid fire. He could taste hints of honey and even nuts. It still burned, but this time it felt warming, and not like a raging inferno.

"Much better this time, eh? You have to sip it slowly. Now give me that flask back before your mother catches me. She'll have me hide if she catches us drinking. Best not trying to rush my inevitable demise," he sighed as his placed the cap back on the flask and hid it under his pillow.

"I'm feeling tired, laddie. I think it's time I got some rest. Would ya turn off the lamp on the way out?"

"Yes, Granda," he said. Before he turned the lamp off, Malcolm looked up. "Granda?"

"What?" he replied groggily, sleep already beginning to overtake him.

"Thank you," Malcolm said.

"Thank you for what?" Granda murmured.

"For the watch, the whisky. For everything."

"You're welcome, laddie."

Malcolm turned out the light and as he reached the door, he whispered, "I love you, Granda."

"I love you too, laddie," came the whispered reply, the old ears still as sharp as ever.

Malcolm wiped the tears from his eyes and left the room. The next morning, Malcolm's mother told him that his grandfather had passed on that night. And true to his granda's words, his father set about to sell the shop that very day. Malcolm made away with a set of wrenches that had been his granda's favorite.

Malcolm caught his reflection in the mirror above what served as his dresser. Twenty years had passed since that young boy said goodbye to his granda. The man who returned his gaze had a strong, square chin and bright blue eyes. His was a strong, dependable face that some might consider ruggedly handsome. His black hair, although longer on top, tapered abruptly to a shaved area just above his ears. As he wiped his mother's cream from his hands, he smiled as he thought of her insistence of giving him several jars of her homemade concoction. She knew that her son would be right in the machinery and forever covered in oil or grease. He noticed how calloused, blistered, and rough his hands were compared to the other officers of the ship.

Suddenly, he broke out of his thoughts. The other officers, hell and blast! I've got to be at dinner, he thought. When he was satisfied that his hands were reasonably free of grease, he checked his granda's pocket watch. He was five minutes late. Damn it to Hell, why did the captain have to have these damn dinners on the first night of departure? There was always so much for the airship's engineer to do.

He looked at this reflection, straightened his uniform, ran his fingers through the hair to arrange it in a somewhat presentable fashion, and hurried out of the room to meet his fate.

Chapter 2

"Where do you suppose our engineer could be found?" drawled Commander Arthur Bromley. "Do you think he'll arrive all covered in grease or will he come smelling of that foul concoction he uses to remove it?"

His joke brought a chuckle from several of the other officers in the room, with a few notable exceptions: Captain Archibald Collins, Ship Surgeon Doctor Edward Jenkins, and the young Gunnery Lieutenant Charles Saxon. The officers began to gather around the table in preparation of the evening meal. Wherever one looked in the officer's mess, one saw mahogany and brass polished like mirrors. The brightness was subdued by the deep burgundy and browns of the upholstered chairs. On the wall behind the head of the table directly behind the captain's chair was a large oil painting of the Daedalus made for the occasion of its christening.

"Perhaps, unlike others here," Doctor Jenkins said looking squarely at Bromley, "his duties require constant attention."

"Yes, yes," said Bromley disgustedly. "We all know how hardworking our chief engineer is, but he is an officer after all. He doesn't have to get his hands dirty doing the work. That's why he has an engineering crew."

"So, when you're wounded, I should leave you to the tender mercies of my assistants rather than 'dirtying my hands' with actual work," Jenkins suggested pointedly.

"No, that's different. You're a doctor; it's your job to attend to the wounded."

"And Robertson's job is to attend to the ship. Mark my words, there will come a day when you're glad he spends so much time doing the dirty work," Jenkins remarked.

Bromley snorted. "I think our Mr. Robertson is in love with the ship. You never see him looking for companionship when we have shore leave. He's always in his bunk reading technical journals or tinkering with some contraption or another."

"Perhaps he's more interested in bettering himself than chasing women," retorted Jenkins.

"Well, that's just it, isn't it?" Bromley replied sarcastically. "It wouldn't be very hard for him to improve himself. He is a stupid jock after all. He already has rank far exceeding his station. How does he think he could possibly be an officer like us?"

"Not all of us have been privileged to have been born with a silver spoon in our mouths," retorted Jenkins, in a tone of anger. "Some of us have to work for what we have. I, for one, am very grateful that our so-called jock works as hard as he does. On more than one occasion, he's saved everyone on this ship. Did you forget Constantinople?"

Bromley's face immediately reddened. "I have not forgotten, Jenkins," he said coldly. Bromley had been the commander of the watch as they approached Constantinople. In order to reach the city ahead of schedule, he had ordered Robertson to run the engines at full all night. Robertson strenuously objected, telling Bromley that running the engines for that period of time would cause them to seize up as they had not had a proper retrofit in months and were scheduled for such in Constantinople. Bromley insisted, to the point that he threatened to throw Robertson in the brig for insubordination. Robertson relented, but insisted that the log clearly state he was against the order, but following it nonetheless.

As Robertson predicted, first the starboard engine seized up, followed by the port engine and ending with the main engine itself. The heat from running the engines at top speed for several hours had caused the engine chambers to warp just enough that the pistons refused to move, despite Robertson's attempts to cool the engines. Malcolm tore the engines apart without waiting for them to cool and received several nasty burns for his efforts. He had opened the engine room windows as well as the service bay doors in order to have as much cool air circulate in the room as possible, in the hopes of cooling the overworked engines.

It was Malcolm himself who made an improvised forge using a welding torch as the heat source and reshaped the combustion chambers so that the pistons could move. They weren't perfectly aligned and it caused much sputtering, and it was Malcolm himself who manually adjusted the fuel flow so that the engines would continue to fire.

Bromley received a rebuke from the captain as a result of this episode. Malcolm, despite his near insubordination, received a commendation for technical expertise for allowing the Daedalus to complete its mission to Constantinople only slightly behind schedule. Bromley resented the fact that this uncultured jock had been right and made Bromley look like an idiot in front of the captain and crew.

Captain Archibald Collins, sensing that Jenkins's rebuke would provoke a much stronger response from Bromley, cleared his throat. "Whatever the state of our chief engineer, the issue is not his heritage, station, or technical acumen. The real issue is that he's delaying our meal." Captain Archibald Collins locked his steely gaze on both Doctor Jenkins and Commander Bromley. Jenkins nodded slightly, understanding the captain's silent order to disengage from his verbal confrontation with Bromley. Bromley was much slower to take the meaning of the captain's gaze and several awkward seconds passed before Bromley, too, nodded his acquiescence.

"Well said, Captain," ventured Lieutenant Charles Saxon. "I, for one, will be glad of a meal and look forward to finding out more about our mysterious mission that had us leave in such a hurry."

Captain Archibald Collins nodded to Saxon. "In due time, my young lieutenant. Until then, perhaps some more wine." Collins indicated to the midshipmen to top off the men's glasses. The captain found he liked the young lieutenant who never seemed to take sides and was always quick with a quip or remark to lighten the mood. He was glad to have someone on board with this ability because he sensed that Bromley's enmity towards Robertson was a powder keg ready to be ignited, probably at the worst possible time.

He was tired of this bickering. In fact, he felt tired of the burden of command. He had seen much in his long and distinguished career as a naval officer. He had started as a midshipmen aboard the HMS Agamemnon, one of the early steam-powered battleships—so early in fact, that it continued to use sails for propulsion. He had been part of the bombardment of Sevastopol and had not forgotten its horrors.

From there he took positions on many ships of various configurations until he rose to the rank of captain. Seeing the exciting possibilities of airships and the ability to sail not just over the seas but over land as well, Collins volunteered to join the nascent Royal Air Service and captained many of the early airships. When the HMA Daedalus was built, Collins was the most qualified captain in the Air Service and received the honor of captaining the Air Service's flagship.

A ship run by Captain Archibald Collins ran with the precision of a fine watch. Discipline and adherence to naval regulations and traditions were paramount. Crews around the Royal Navy and Air Services used the nickname "Iron Neck Collins" to describe his rigid attention to regulations and protocol. From most, this nickname was given in loving tribute. Although Collins expected the most out of his men, he treated those who responded well. And those who did not respond had a very difficult tour of duty until a transfer could be arranged.

But Collins was tired. The dark hair and beard of his youth had long since turned silver. Years of service on the sea and in the sky had etched deep wrinkles in his face. The fire in his fierce grey eyes did not burn with the same intensity of youth. Nearly forty years of sailing on sea and air was enough. He wished to see his wife and get to know the children, although now grown, who had not known their father except through letters from exotic, far away locations and precious few trips home. He knew in his heart that this would be his last voyage. He would ask for a desk job in the Admiralty, or retire outright.

Just then, the clatter of boots approaching quickly could be heard. "I believe that is our tardy engineer," said the captain. The boots slowed to a measured step shortly before a knock was heard on the bulkhead door.

Malcolm burst through the door, saying, "My apologies, Captain Collins, I was detained in Engineering. Please forgive my lateness."

"Anything serious?" asked the captain.

"There was a slight vibration in the main engine. One of the drive gears was a bit dodgy so I stopped to realign it before it could cause a bigger problem."

"And this had to be dealt with now?" asked the captain.

"Better now than after the engine stops," joked Malcolm. He caught the captain's stern gaze. "Um, no, sir, it didn't have to be done now. It probably could have waited until later. I apologize, Captain. I just don't like to wait for small problems to become big problems when you can nip them in the bud."

"Yes, Mr. Robertson. Small problems need to be dealt with early before they become large problems... like tardiness."

"Sorry, Captain. It won't happen again."

A flicker of an amused smile crossed Captain Collin's face. "Of course it will, Mr. Robertson. Your dedication to ship is admirable, if somewhat misplaced at times. You must remember, Mr. Robertson, a machine is a tool. A tool only does what a man directs it to do. This ship is also a tool—a tool for His Majesty's will. We serve His Majesty, not the tool."

"Yes, sir," Malcolm said quietly.

"Very well. Mr. Robertson, please sit down. Midshipman Brown, fill Mr. Robertson's glass and tell Chef that we are ready for dinner."

As midshipmen hustled about with the food and quietly served the officers, Malcolm was silent. He tried to be on time, but he just hadn't liked the sound of the vibration. And the captain's rebuke stung. He was in danger of becoming like that gear—something that needed to be replaced to keep the ship running as a whole.

As the soup was served, Malcolm always dreaded this part; which of the damnable utensils was he supposed to use? He could never remember whether the utensils were used from inside out or outside in. He was thankful that his wine glass had been filled so he knew which was for wine and which was for water. He decided to put off the decision of which spoon to use by drinking some wine. As he raised his glass, he saw Bromley watching him with a bemused look; he knew Malcolm was stalling and Bromley was waiting to make sure Malcolm's social inadequacy was made obviously apparent.

Just then, a sputtering cough came up from Lieutenant Saxon seated across from Malcolm. As Malcolm shifted his gaze to the lieutenant to see if he was alright, he had the sense that the lieutenant had pointed to the correct spoon as he raised his napkin to his mouth to cover his cough. "Here's a word of advice," he said when he recovered his breath. "Don't attempt to breathe the wine... it's much better to drink it instead."

The crew laughed quietly. Malcolm looked at the lieutenant, nodding ever so slightly. He kept an eye on Bromley who was ready to pounce. Malcolm's hand descended toward the wrong spoon, but at the last minute he moved to grasp his soupspoon. Bromley took a breath, about to say something, when he noticed Malcolm holding the correct spoon. Malcolm smiled and looked inquisitively at Bromley as if waiting for him to say something. Bromley glowered and returned to his meal.

The soup, Chef's infamous pea soup, was better than usual. Malcolm was pleasantly surprised when he was able to pick up the spoon from the bowl without bringing the bowl with it. Malcolm had heard the riggers say that they used Chef's pea soup to patch holes in the airship's skin and he never wondered at it. Despite its adhesive properties, Malcolm did have to admit that the soup was very good. Conversation came to a stop as all of the men concentrated on their meals.

The soup gave way to roast duck, potatoes, peas with mint, cheeses, and finished in a lemon pudding for dessert that was very delicate and flaky, much to everyone's surprise. All during the meal, Bromley and Malcolm exchanged looks—Bromley hoping to catch Malcolm in a faux pas, and Malcolm returning an inquisitive look that further infuriated Bromley. On those occasions where Malcolm's certainty of dining etiquette wavered, he shot a furtive look at Lieutenant Saxon who would take the opportunity to extravagantly praise Chef's culinary skills and with a gesture, point to the correct implement.

The midshipmen hustled the dishes away and brought out the port. Malcolm thought it a hideous replacement for a dram of whisky, but kept that thought strictly to himself. When the midshipmen left the room, Captain Collins drew himself out of his chair and addressed the officers.

"Gentlemen, these orders come directly from the First Lord of the Admiralty McKenna himself. We are to fly at best speed to St. Petersburg. Once there, we will take on a number of passengers and await further instruction."

"St. Petersburg? What are we doing in St. Petersburg? And since when have we become a passenger service?" asked Bromley.

"The orders say nothing of this, except that this is a mission of the utmost importance and secrecy is a must. Only those of us here must know our destination until we are within sight of St. Petersburg. Is that understood?"

The officers agreed.

Lieutenant Saxon ventured, "Is it to be some sort of cultural exchange? It was widely reported that the tsar and the king talked frequently at King Edward's funeral. Perhaps, this is some gesture of goodwill between our two nations."

"Perhaps," agreed Captain Collins, "but that is merely conjecture. And I insist that you all keep such conjecture to yourselves until such time as the Admiralty provides further orders."

"The Admiralty, like our Lord, moves in mysterious ways," offered Doctor Jenkins.

This brought a chuckle to all. "Indeed it does. And sometimes I think not even the Lord knows what the Admiralty is up to. Be that as it may, I need all of you to make sure your men are ready for any situation. Commander Bromley, you will be in charge of the navigators. Our orders are to take us over the North Sea, across Norway and Sweden, across the Baltic, entering Russia near St. Petersburg. The course is explicitly laid out in the orders. Under no circumstances is the Daedalus to fly over or near Germany. Got that Bromley?"

"Yes, sir."

"Lt. Commander Robertson, we'll need all and more that you can coax out of our engines. Since we're taking the long way to get there, we need best available speed and then some. Please use your magic to coax every bit of power out them."

"Aye, Captain," Malcolm replied.

"Lt. Saxon, I want you to keep the gunnery crews on high alert. Run fire control drills steadily. I'm not expecting any trouble, but I'm concerned about what's left unsaid in our orders and I'd rather not be caught unawares."

"Yes sir," replied Lt. Saxon.

Captain Collins continued to give orders to the other officers, leaving Dr. Jenkins to last.

"Well, Doctor, I have nothing specific for you other than to hope to God we don't need your services. I believe that's it. We all have our jobs to do, so I believe we should all retire for the evening."

As the officers filed out of the officer's mess one by one, Doctor Jenkins hung back. "Captain, may I have a word with you in private?"

"By all means, Doctor. Care for another port?"

"Don't mind if I do," Jenkins said. He didn't want to bring this up, but with what appeared to be such an urgent mission, he thought it best to get it out in the open. When the last officer had filed out, Jenkins closed the door, took the proffered port and sat in a chair facing the captain. "Captain, I have some concerns."

"Damn it, Edward. Call me Archie. None of that formal 'Captain Collins' claptrap. We've been friends for too long to stick to protocol." The captain passed the doctor another glass filled with port.

"Archie, that's why I want to talk to you." He paused, taking a sip of port and gathering his thoughts before he continued. "What do you think of Bromley?"

"Very good executive officer. Does what he's told, keeps the crew disciplined. Might be a bit too ambitious for his own good," he added, remember the near debacle of Constantinople. His ambition nearly cost the Empire the aid of the Ottomans. "Why do you ask?"

"I'm concerned about his attitude. Particularly his attitude to our chief engineer."

"What do you mean, Edward?"

"He takes every opportunity he can to make Robertson look like less of an officer to anyone who will listen. You heard his little dissertation before the meal. That kind of talk is dangerous."

"Well, Bromley does have a point. It is a bit preposterous that someone like that could be an officer, and third in the chain of command."

Jenkins looked at Collins with shock. "You really think that? You don't think someone who used only his God-given brains and talents to forge a position for himself is worthy of his commission? Is that what you think of me? Do you remember, Archie, when I first served with you? Do I merit that level of contempt?"

Collins reached over and put his hand on Jenkins' shoulder. "God, Edward, no that's not what I meant. I just meant... I don't know. Maybe I'm getting too old for this." He sighed heavily before continuing. "Do you remember what it was like to serve on the old ships, before steam ran everything? You could tell by the feel of the wind how fast you were going and with a sexton, always know where you're going. Officers were sailors first and foremost. Now, we have officers that know nothing about sailing or even flying. I guess I miss the old days when you had to be a sailor to be a captain."

"For crying out loud, Archie, you're remembering a past that never was. Do you remember that idiot captain we had when we sailed to India? What was his name?"

"Barclay."

"Right, Captain Owen Barclay. What a right git he was. I'll never forget when Commander Ferrence actually talked him ashore for a snipe hunt and Barclay led the hunting team himself."

Both men chuckled at the memory. Collins sighed. "I think I'm too old for this, Edward. This piloting is a young man's game. I think my time is past. Between you and me, this will be my last mission as captain of the Daedalus. I intend to retire when this mission is complete."

"I'll miss you, old friend," Jenkins said soberly. "Have you thought of who will take over for you?"

"Bromley, of course. Why?"

"I'm not sure he really is the right man for the job."

"What do you mean?"

"Does he know how to do anything other than give orders? Have you ever seen him actually perform any duties?"

"He's the first officer. He doesn't have to do the work, he's there to direct it."

"Aye, but look at Robertson. He has a full team of men and yet he almost always comes to mess with grease under his fingernails. His hands are those of a sailor—hard, calloused, scarred. Bromley's hands, I'm sure, are lily-white and soft. You were just lamenting missing men who knew something about being a sailor. I think what you meant is you missed men who knew hard work was part of an officer's life. Robertson wouldn't have any of his men do anything he himself wouldn't do. I don't think the same can be said of Bromley."

"Why have you soured so much on Bromley?" inquired Captain Collins.

"He's a nice enough fellow, I suppose. But he is ambitious and impatient—a dangerous combination in someone responsible for the lives of everyone on this ship. And dare I say, a bit of a bully. I think he thinks his name can shield him from much."

"Alright, I'll take your words under advisement. When did you take such a shine to our Scot?"

"I think it was the whole Constantinople affair. He could have made things even worse for Bromley if he wanted. When the time came to testify, he downplayed the damage that

Bromley had wrought and even tried to downplay his role. That's when I realized that he was a remarkable man."

"Thank you Edward. Your counsel, as always, is most welcome. But as I have to make first rounds in the morning, I must retire for the night."

"Good night, Archie," Jenkins said as he left the officer's mess.

Archibald Collins stopped for a minute and stared at the place where Malcolm Robertson had sat at dinner. Was he truly that bad a judge of character? Had the years finally made him senile? He would watch both Bromley and Robertson with a much closer eye in the days to come, he thought to himself as he shut the door to the officer's mess and retired to his quarters.

Chapter 3

Before turning in for the night, Malcolm stopped by the engine room and relayed the captain's orders that they should make best speed for the duration of the voyage. Satisfied that all was in order, Malcolm left orders for someone to get him if anything out of the ordinary happened and returned to his quarters.

Malcolm removed his dress uniform, carefully hanging it in his closet. He had learned long ago that taking a few minutes now would save him many minutes later. There was nothing that the other officers detested more than wrinkles in a dress uniform.

Collapsing on his bunk, Malcolm sighed in relief that the evening was over. He hated those dinners with a passion; with Bromley poised like a snake to point out and gloat over every faux pas. Bromley had been inclined to be like that even before Constantinople. After evenings like this, mused Malcolm, why did I ever bother to become an officer?

The answer came to him immediately: to become an engineer. Malcolm kept his promise to his granda and finished school with top marks in all his subjects with the exception of composition; he always hated the tedium of writing the essays and themes. But he finished his Leaving Certificate Examination with flying colors and was accepted to the University of Glasgow to study engineering.

In his second year of university, Malcolm's father was grievously injured at the shipyards. He was welding a large plate to the hull of a ship when the plate slipped and fell, crushing his whole left side. Malcolm left immediately for home. His father's injuries were severe. His legs and arms were broken in several places. Operations were needed to pin the bones together. Soon, all of Malcolm's tuition money had been used to pay for his father's medical bills. The Robertson's still had Kate's income as a maid and the rent from the greengrocer downstairs, but there was no longer any money for Malcolm's education. With his engineering degree incomplete, he might hope to be an apprentice draftsman, but nothing else.

Malcolm stayed with his parents for several months to help care for his father, missing not only the end of the current term, but the term after as well. As the days turned to weeks, Malcolm realized that his ability to return to university grew slimmer with each passing day and each medical bill.

Finally, one night after dinner, Malcolm informed his parent's that he was withdrawing from college to find a job at the shipyards.

"No son of mine is going to work in those bloody shipyards!" thundered George.

"Your da's right, Malcolm," his mother added. "Look what happened to him. I couldn't bear to see something like this or worse happen to you!"

"It takes money to go to university," Malcolm replied angrily. "Where's that going to come from?"

"I doona know Malcolm," his father replied, softening his tone a bit. "We'll think of something. We can sell the house, I can find other work."

"Where are you going to find work, Da?" You can't do much with your left arm and it's all you can do to walk to the privy. And selling the house won't help. At least you have income from the greengrocer downstairs."

"We'll think of something. I don't want you doing something hasty," George said.

"This isn't a hasty decision; I've been thinking about this for months. I think that maybe because I've had college classes, I might not have to work in yards. I could be a draftsman's apprentice, maybe even become a draftsman someday."

"Malcolm, no, I can't let you do that. I promised my da that I'd make sure you were an engineer, designing and building things of your own. I don't want to see you wasting your talent simply copying over someone else's designs."

"But, Da, I can't leave you and mum without anything so that I can go to university!" Malcolm protested.

"You will go to university, Malcolm Francis Robertson!!" his father thundered. "I promised my da and meself that you wouldn't work in those bloody shipyards!"

Malcolm said nothing. Knowing his father was too upset to continue, Malcolm dropped the subject and left the room. The next morning, he arose before dawn and took the early train to Glasgow. He wore his only suit, hoping that he might be able to find work as a draftsman's assistant. On the train, he pulled out a gold pocket watch, the one his granda had given him on the night he died. Malcolm had, with great difficulty, fixed the watch on his own, taking the movements apart piece by piece and carefully reassembling it until it finally kept time. But Malcolm had to wind the thing incessantly or it would start losing time almost immediately. As he wound the stem, he couldn't help but think back to that night and his promise to go to college. How could he fulfill the promise without pushing his parents to the poor house? They might be able to live on the rent for the store and his mother's meager wages as a housekeeper, but there was no way they could afford university.

Malcolm decided to try first at the university to see if there was some way he could continue. His hard luck story brought sympathy from school officials, but little else. Dejected, he started toward the shipyards when he saw a naval ship sailing up the Clyde to the shipyards, likely for repair or refitting. It was a huge ironclad battleship and appeared to be underway solely on steam power as no sails were furled. Malcolm stopped and watched as it neared, making out the name: HMS Bellerophon. He stared in wonder as the ship continued on to the shipyards and disappeared amongst the forest of masts and cranes.

Suddenly, Malcolm remembered a guest lecture in his last semester. A representative of Her Majesty's Navy had appeared to the startled class of would-be engineers, explaining that openings were now available for engineers in Her Majesty's Navy and the newly formed Her Majesty's Air Service. The officer explained that with additional training at both Keyham College in naval and aero engineering and an additional two years at the Royal Naval College at Greenwich, they would become assistant engineers—commissioned officers at the rank of sub-lieutenant.

Malcolm returned to the university, trying to find someone who knew of the officer who had visited his class. Finally he had a name, Commander Hugh Oakleigh. He was head of the recruitment center near the shipyards. Malcolm went to the shipyards, but instead of begging for a draftsman's apprentice position, he met with Commander Oakleigh and discussed a future in the Royal Navy or even the new Air Service. Malcolm relayed the tale of how he had left school because of his father's injuries in the shipyard and how he no longer had the finances to attend school. He also wanted to make sure his parents would be able to live in their home and support themselves, and perhaps even find an operation that could help his father. Commander Oakleigh was impressed with Malcolm's marks and was also impressed by Malcolm's sense of duty to his parents. He saw in Malcolm someone who believed in duty and doing the right thing. Those were qualities that the Royal Navy needed and he was anxious to bring Malcolm into the service. Oakleigh explained that to be accepted he would need a sponsor. As Malcolm was about to say that he had no sponsor, Oakleigh said, "Don't worry Malcolm. I will sponsor you." He looked at Malcolm appraisingly. "Although we've only just met, I can tell that you are honest, earnest, and loyal. You are the type of man we need in the Royal Navy." Oakleigh was ready for Malcolm to sign the enlistment contract, but Malcolm balked.

"I must talk this over with my parents; this affects them as much as me".

"I understand," said Oakleigh. "I will hear from you soon I hope?"

"If all goes well, you will see me tomorrow, pen in hand."

Malcolm returned home. After dinner told his parents about the meeting with Commander Oakleigh and the opportunity to continue his education while eventually being able to help his parents. At first they were reticent, but soon realized that Malcolm's arguments were sound; it allowed him to continue his education, it would get him out of shipyards, and it would give him a chance to know more of the world than Kilmacolm and Glasgow. They were concerned about him being in armed combat, and told him as much.

In the end, George looked at his son and asked "Malcolm, is this really what you want to do, laddie?"

Malcolm was about to say that it was the best he could do to keep his promise to Granda when he caught himself. "Do I really want to do this?" he asked himself. And the answer that came back surprised him.

"Yes, Da, I do. I know that it's the best way for me to keep my promise to you and Granda, but it's something more than that. I think I want to do something valuable and what's more valuable than using your talents for the good of your country?"

Tears welled in George's eyes. "That's all I wanted to hear from you, Malcolm. That you really want to do this. Because a sailor's life is hard and can be very lonely. I just wanted to know that this was your heart's wish."

"It is, Da," Malcolm replied.

"Then you have my blessing. Not that you bloody well needed it. You'd have done whatever you wanted to do anyway."

"But your blessing means a great deal to me, Da. Thank you."

"I think your granda would be proud. But most of all, I'm proud of you."

The next day, George met Commander Oakleigh to sign his enlistment contract and soon he was whisked away for two more years of engineering training and then two years of naval college. George and Kate Robertson scrimped and saved and were able to attend Malcolm's commissioning; George himself pinning on Malcolm's new rank of sub-lieutenant, assistant engineer.

Malcolm served on a couple of naval vessels before applying to the Air Service. He returned to Keyham College for refresher courses in aerodynamics, aero propulsion, flight control, and piloting. While at Keyham, Malcolm decided to complete the command course so that he might be able to captain an airship someday. He had no strong desire to captain an airship, but felt that it might increase his chances for promotion so that he might actually design airships rather than keeping them running.

That young idealistic engineer had no idea what a struggle it would be to gain the respect of the other officers. Many came from families with long traditions of military service. In all his assignments, Malcolm had always felt like a square peg in a round hole when it came to the other officers. His run in with Commander Bromley during the Constantinople incident made him feel like even more of an outsider. Malcolm sighed; it had been going on for so long that tossing and turning over it tonight wouldn't help. He turned the lights off in his cabin and grabbed a few hours of shuteye.

The next few days were routine as the Daedalus crossed the North Sea, continuing over Norway and Sweden before making for the Baltic. The weather, which could be treacherous over the North Sea, held and the Daedalus' trip was uneventful. When Malcolm turned in for the night after their third day of travel, the Daedalus was ready to begin the final push across the Baltic Sea.

When Malcolm woke, light was just filtering in. He grabbed his day uniform—in his case, a set of grease-covered overalls, a heavy tight fitting shirt and equally tight pants. No loose clothing in the engine room. Malcolm had seen first-hand what could happen if an engine grabbed a loose piece of clothing or hair and it was a sight Malcolm never wanted to see again.

Malcolm stalked to the mess and grabbed a ship's biscuit and a mug of tea. As he sat eating the dry hard biscuit, he heard several of the crew mention that the Daedalus had made excellent speed overnight and they were already over the Baltic. Malcolm couldn't help but smile to himself, proud of the efficiency he wrung from the ship's engines. Grabbing another mug of tea, he went aft to the engine room. As Malcolm approached, he could immediately hear that something was wrong. He pushed open the door and said, "What the bloody hell is going on? Why didn't someone get me?"

Blank faces looked up at him, "Commander, everything is fine," one of the engineering mates offered.

"You can't hear that rumbling under the cycle of the engine?" Malcolm demanded.

The engineering mates stopped to listen. Slowly, the realization crept over their faces. The sound had started gradually and hearing the constant hum of the engines, it was easy to lose track of the sound.

"Alright, first thing we need to do is to shut down the engines and see what's happening. I better call the bridge." Malcolm picked up the handset and punched the button to connect to the bridge.

"Bridge. Duty Officer Kelsey."

"Kelsey, this is Engineer Robertson. I need to speak to the commander of the watch."

"That would be Commander Bromley, sir."

Bloody hell, just my bloody luck, thought Malcolm. "Put him on," he sighed.

"Aye, sir." There were sounds of muffled conversation as the young lieutenant meekly asked for the commander to take the call.

"What is it, Robertson? We have important work to do here and don't have time for your complaints."

"Sorry to be an inconvenience, sir," Malcolm said, a little more pointedly than he meant. "There's something wrong with the engines, sir. I need to take them offline so I can figure out what's happening."

"What do you mean, there's a problem? We're running at full speed, there's no problem."

"Look, I know what I'm talking about. If we continue to run all three engines without doing anything about it, we won't have engines at all."

"I'm not convinced that there's really a problem. I think you're just doing this for some misbegotten attempt at attention."

"Bromley, you should know me better than that. I don't ask for attention and praise, I just do my job to the best of my ability. And those abilities tell me that we will have serious problems if we don't do something about the engines soon."

"Why should I take your word for it? Why hasn't Frye reported any of this? I believe he's in charge of the night shift."

"Remember what happened the last time you didn't believe me, *sir*," Malcolm added with special emphasis on the title.

The line crackled with static, as there was no response. Malcolm was sure he could feel the anger emanating though the receiver.

"Very well. But take only one engine offline at a time. That way we'll still be able to make good time. If that's aright with you," Bromley added venomously.

"That will work. We'll start with the main engine. The other two engines should be able to help us maintain speed."

"Anything else, Engineer?" he added in a mocking tone.

"No, sir. I'll report when all engines are back on line and running at full capacity, sir."

"You do that, Robertson," Bromley said. Malcolm heard the receiver slam heavily before the connection was broken.

"All right, laddies. Let's get this main engine off line and take a look and see what the trouble is." Within minutes, Malcolm and his capable crew had the main engine torn apart and he didn't like what he saw.

"Ach, the whole damn thing is gummed up. Look at how the fuel lines are all clogged and there's some kind of residue in the firing chambers. It's a bloody mess. It looks like some sort of carbonization." Malcolm pulled off his gloves and scraped at some of the carbonization with a fingernail until some of it flaked off. He examined it closely and sniffed at it. It had an odd smell almost sweet, like...

"Sugar! Someone has put bloody sugar in the fuel! Mr. Chapham, come with me, you and I are going to check the fuel supply. The rest of you, clean the engine up as best you can and get ready to fire her back up on my orders."

Malcolm and Chapham left the engine room and went to Fuel Storage. "Chapham, turn off the fuel pump; I'm going to check the fuel." Malcolm went to the large primary fuel tank. He carefully opened a spigot on the side and allowed a few drops to fall on his fingers. As he brought them to his nose, he could immediately smell a sweet note that definitely should not be in the fuel. Malcolm repeated the operation on the secondary fuel tank. This time, no sweetness could be detected. Malcolm put a drop of the fuel on his tongue. It tasted like fuel.

Malcolm went to the manual override switch. Malcolm had built a switch to allow the fuel pump to automatically switch to the secondary tank when a special float he had designed reached a predefined level. Now, he was thankful that he had had the foresight to leave a manual override option in place. Malcolm turned the switch and ordered Chapham to restart the fuel pump. The pump whirled to life and fuel from the secondary tank was flowing through the lines.

By the time Malcolm and Chapham returned to the engine room, the crew had the engine put back together and ready to go. "Walters, bleed out the fuel line for about 5 seconds and then we'll try a restart."

The crew bled the fuel line and initiated the engine startup. At first, the engine started hesitantly and sputtered as some of the last of the contaminated fuel made its way through the engine. The engine soon recovered and within seconds was purring at its usual low hum and Malcolm was satisfied.

"Good job, laddies. Now we have to repeat that on the port and starboard engines. I want you to take the engines down, clean the bloody hell out of them and bleed the fuel lines for a few seconds. We have a tank full of contaminated fuel that's gummed up our engines." Malcolm reached down and held up the can of fuel bled from the engines.

"Chapham, go find Mr. Frye. I want to talk to him. He's usually in the mess after his shift."

"Yes, sir." As he opened the bulkhead to leave the engine room, he nearly bowled over a surprised Lt. Saxon who seemed about to knock on the door. Chapham excused himself for nearly knocking over the senior officer and darted down the hall towards the mess hall.

"Ah, Lt. Commander Robertson. The captain asked that you come to the bridge immediately."

"Why?" Malcolm asked, still looking at the fuel can.

"I'm not sure. He said it was important."

Probably that dust up with Bromley, Malcolm thought. That bastard really seemed to have it in for him. But right now, Malcolm needed to get to the bottom of the mysterious contaminant.

"Alright, I'll be there soon. I have a wee bit of a crisis here to handle."

"He did say it was urgent," added Lieutenant Saxon.

"I said I'll be there as soon as I can. I will tell the captain that you delivered the message and it will be my head in the noose, not yours, Lieutenant," Malcolm said, pointedly emphasizing the officer's junior rank.

"Yes, sir," Saxon said hesitantly and turned to leave, nearly bumping into a surprised Lieutenant Frye. "Excuse me," Saxon sputtered at Frye and hurried down the hallway.

"What's his problem?" asked Frye.

"I don't know. Probably thinks he's going to be in trouble with the captain for my tardiness. Never mind that. Did you supervise the refueling before liftoff?"

"You know I did. It's right there in the log, sir. Why, is something wrong?"

"You could say that," Malcolm said. "Did the fuel smell funny to you yesterday?"

"No. It smelled like fuel. What are you getting at, sir?"

"We just bled off fuel from the primary tank. Smell this."

Frye sniffed the fuel. "Smells like fuel to... hold on, do I smell something sweet?"

Malcolm nodded. "Aye, laddie. It seems someone dumped sugar in the primary fuel tank. I would bet that Chef is missing a 50 pound bag of sugar from the pantry."

"So what do we do?"

"We cleaned the main engine and I've switched us over to the secondary tank which doesn't seem to be fouled. I've got the crews tearing down port and starboard engines and once they're set, we'll be good to go. I know you just got off of your watch Matthew, but do you mind keeping an eye on things here while I go to talk with the captain?"

"Any idea what he wants?" Frye asked.

"I had a slight, very slight, dust up with Bromley this morning about the engines. Hopefully this," he said, indicating the fuel can, "will change his mind."

Frye laughed, "You really do know how to make friends."

"Aye, why do ye think they put me in the engine room?" Malcolm laughed. "I should be back shortly." Malcolm turned and left the engine room with the fuel can in hand.

Malcolm climbed the stairs going up to the main level and proceeded down the main hall.

Suddenly, there was an ear-shattering blast and the whole ship lurched up suddenly. Malcolm, unable to keep his feet, was pitched onto his back and cracked his head on the metal walkway. Shite! What the bloody hell is going on, Malcolm thought as he struggled to pull himself up. The front of the airship seemed to be tilted up at a thirty-degree angle and Malcolm felt like he was climbing a wall. The fuel can clattered down the walkway after spilling its contents everywhere.

Malcolm got to his feet and used the walls and the doors to pull his way forward. There were sounds of frantic activity all around him, but oddly, no emergency klaxon. That was not a good sign.

Malcolm was about twenty feet from the bulkhead to the bridge. Desperately, he hauled himself from doorway to doorway, trying not to lose his footing so that he would slide back down the hall. After minutes of effort, he braced himself against the bulkhead leading to the bridge and opened the door.

Malcolm stared incredulously out the door where he only saw sky and ocean where the bridge should have been.

Chapter 4

Malcolm stared at the open sky. The bridge was gone! The bridge crew was gone. Malcolm struggled to organize his thoughts. Think. The command crew is likely gone. No Captain, no Bromley. Who's next in command?

Oh, shite, he thought, it's me. I'm in charge. Bloody hell, what do I do? Malcolm forced himself to focus. Alright, we have a problem. With no bridge, we've lost weight; that's why the nose is pointing up. We need to gain control of the flaps so that we can readjust to the correct altitude. And flight control... is somewhere over the Baltic. No auxiliary control room. Is there a place to tap in to the controls? No... wait...

Malcolm suddenly remembered. One of his first assignments on the Daedalus was to replace the typical levers used to control pitch and direction with a ship's wheel. Captain Collins insisted he was not captaining a ship without a wheel, so Malcolm fabricated controls to allow the wheel to replicate both the direction and pitch controls. And he had connected them right...there. He looked down the hall ten feet and found the section of decking.

If he could get to the engine room he could probably grab enough hardware, including the original levers that he held onto for some reason.

Crewmen started to appear in the hall on all fours to stop from sliding back in order to find out what was going and get orders from the bridge. Malcolm yelled to a crewman, "You, there, go to the engine room. Get Mr. Frye and tell him to bring a standard repair kit, a welding torch, and the spare control levers. He'll know what I mean. Move it, on the double."

The startled crewman, not used to taking orders from the engineer, hesitated for just a second and then hurried down the hall, aided by the downward slope of the hall.

Alright, he thought. That's settled until Frye gets back. What's next? Communication. Communication usually comes from the bridge and is relayed to the radio room where it's distributed to the ship. The radio room was amidships. Malcolm shut the door to the bridge and started to careen down the sloping hallway when he met Lieutenant Saxon climbing towards the bridge.

"What's going on?" asked Saxon. "I've been trying to reach the bridge ever since that explosion. I can't reach anyone."

"That's because the explosion was the bridge. It's gone, the whole thing is gone."

"Well, that's terribly inconvenient. We have another problem."

"Besides the fact that we have no control and no bridge crew?"

"Yes, immediately after the explosion, two zeppelins dropped out of cloud cover some five miles out in flanking position. When I couldn't reach the bridge, I decided to come here and report to the captain personally."

"That appears to be me at this point. I'm assuming that Bromley was on the bridge when you reported to the captain that you had relayed his message?"

"Yes."

"That leaves me as acting captain. Congratulations, you're now second in command."

"But..."

"No buts now, Saxon. I need you to go to the radio room. Ask the operator for a spare handset and some wiring tools. I'm going to wire up the bridge line right there," he said, pointing to space on the wall near the point he connected the wheel to the control lines.

"What good will that do?" asked Saxon.

"I'm going to throw together makeshift flight controls there. It's going to be our bridge. And we need to restore communications to the rest of the ship. Let the men know what's going on."

"But..."

"Saxon, we don't have time. Go to the radio room. I have an engineering crew coming in minutes. And we have to know what those zeppelins are doing. It seems awfully coincidental that they should appear minutes after we're in distress. Now get going.... Now!"

The authority in Malcolm's voice startled Saxon. "Yes, sir," he said and headed down toward the radio room. Malcolm followed, stopping at the junction point where he had connected the wheel to the flight controls. He struggled and with great effort was able to pull the decking up to access the lines. All control, electrical, and radio lines ran along a two-foot-wide trough that lay below the decking of the main hallway. The decking came up in five-foot sections so cables could be accessed for maintenance.

Malcolm located the gearbox he had fabricated to allow the turning of the wheel to direct the rudder and the forward and backward motion of the wheel as the lift control. Malcolm reached down, happy that he still had his tool belt strapped on after his work on the engines, and pulled out a screwdriver to open the gearbox.

Shortly, Frey came with a small cadre of engineering crew and the equipment.

"What's happened, sir?" Frye asked.

"You've been promoted to chief engineer, Mr. Frye."

"You're having a joke on me, Mr. Robertson. You're the chief engineer."

"Not anymore. We've lost the bridge and the bridge crew. I'm acting captain now."

"Shite," said Frye in amazement.

"Thanks for the vote of confidence, Mr. Frye," Malcolm joked.

"No, it's not that; it's just... shite."

"I know. Shite about covers it all. But now, I need you to focus. Remember how we disconnected the control levers and repurposed the gearbox for the wheel? We've got to reverse that process right here," he said, pointing to the open gearbox. "Can you do that?"

"I think so. Why aren't you doing it?"

"I've got to restore communications and try to get some order back to this ship. Ah, and here's what I need." Saxon arrived with a spare headset with wires hanging out of the end.

"Here it is. And while I was there, a message came over on the telegraph."

"Who from?" Robertson replied quizzically.

"The Germans. The message reads: 'British Airship. We will aid your stricken ship. We will board and escort you to Germany for repairs. Prepare to be boarded. Please respond.'"

"Have the Germans taken any action?" Malcolm asked as he took the handset from Saxon. Malcolm again opened the door to what had been the bridge, noted what was left of the cable and followed it back to the hallway. He shut the door and started to pull the cable from the hole where Frye and his men were working.

"No, they're waiting for the captain's response," Saxon added, slightly amused.

"How did the captain respond?" Malcolm asked as he was stripping the communication wires with his teeth and twisting them together with the corresponding wires on the handset.

"Bloody hell," Malcolm gritted through his teeth. Someone was calling the bridge and voltage, needed to ring the bridge phone, was now coursing through his mouth and it hurt.

"You haven't responded yet," Saxon prompted.

"What? Oh, shite. That's me isn't it? Alright, no response right now. Let's see if we can get control of this ship first."

"Do you intend to let them board and help us?" Saxon asked.

35

"I find it a wee bit suspect that these two guardian angels show up to help us in our hour of darkest need. And remember our orders from the Admiralty; we were to avoid the German mainland at all cost. Whatever it is we're doing, it appears that the Admiralty doesn't want the Germans to know."

"What should I do?" Saxon asked.

"For now, I want you to have your crews prepare all guns. I'm hoping it doesn't come to blows, but better safe than sorry."

"How will I know your orders?" Saxon asked.

"If I remembered my radiophony courses, you should hear right about now." After a quick wail of distortion, Malcolm's voice echoed through the ship.

"Attention crew of the HMS Daedalus. This is Lieutenant Commander Malcolm Robertson. There has been an explosion that has destroyed the bridge and its crew. As ranking officer, I hereby take command of the HMS Daedalus. We are currently working to restore flight control. In addition, two possibly hostile zeppelins are approaching us. All hands to battle stations and await my orders. Thank you, that is all."

Malcolm went to hang up the handset, and realized there was no place to hang it and no way to disconnect the circuit. That would tie up communications across the whole ship. Malcolm ordered one of the crewman down the hall to the radio room and instructed him to tell the radio operator that he would have to manually close and open the circuit to the makeshift bridge for the time being. Malcolm stationed additional crewmen down the hall who could relay signals to the radio operator if Malcolm needed to reach a particular station or if someone needed to contact him.

"Mr. Frye, how are the flight controls coming?"

"I think we're set, sir," Frye replied. "Do you want to try them?"

"Yes, level us out.... no, belay that order," Malcolm said. An idea was germinating in his mind. "Are you sure the controls are set?"

"I think so."

"Damn it man, yes or no. The fate of our ship depends on it!!" Malcolm bellowed.

"Um, yes," Frye stammered. And then, gathering his confidence, "Yes, I'm sure."

"Good. I want you to go back to the engine room. I need you to foul the mixture to the engines enough so that they give off smoke, but I'll need full power on a moment's notice. Also, at the same time I ask for full engines, I want you to drop the emergency ballast."

"Drop the ballast? Are you mad? With the bridge gone, we'll shoot up faster than a firework!"

"That's exactly what I'm counting on! Mr. Frye, you have your orders, hop to it."

"Yes, sir!" Frye said as he turned to leave.

"Mr. Frye," Malcolm said, more gently. "A chief engineer has to be absolutely confident in his work. You're getting that lesson much more quickly than I did. Good work on the controls."

"Thank you, sir. That means a great deal, coming from you." Frye turned and worked his way back to the engine room.

Malcolm signaled to the relay team that he wished to speak to the gunnery officer. The message went down the line to the radio and moments later the message came back that Lt. Saxon was on the line.

"Lt. Saxon, what are the positions of our angels of mercy?"

"Coming up fast on either side of us."

"This is what I want you to do. When they pull up beside us, sight a target 10 feet over the top of the airships and prepare to fire."

"You want us to fire over their ships?" Saxon questioned somewhat incredulously.

"Aye, I don't want to start a war, I just want to scare them."

"They'll likely return fire, you realize."

"I'm counting on it," said Malcolm a little mischievously.

"Are you going to let me in on this little plan of yours?" asked Saxon.

"Absolutely, not. That way if the whole thing goes to hell in a hand basket, you're not implicated and can command whatever is left of the ship."

"That's terribly comforting," Saxon said sarcastically.

"I'm going to have the operator close the line. When the ships pull up beside us, contact me. We'll have to time this just right."

"Will do."

Malcolm signaled to the crewman to disconnect the line. Again, the message travelled up and back from the radio room. Malcolm ordered a crewman to get some paper and a pencil. Malcolm scribbled a message on the paper with orders to relay the message to the German ships on his order and immediately after transmission, open the radio for ship-wide communication.

Now, all Malcolm could do was wait for the Germans to move into position. He hoped that this daft idea of his would get them out of trouble. He hated the thought of gambling everyone's live on this one desperate plan, but his only other alternative was to admit defeat and allow the Germans to take them in disgrace to Germany.

Minutes went by as Malcolm tortured himself with the myriad ways his plan could go awry. Then, he received the signal to pick up the handset. "The Germans are in position. They have us in their sights on either side of us."

"Good, I'm going to go to ship-wide now so we can coordinate this." Malcolm signaled to his relay crew. The message went down the line and thirty seconds later, the message came back that the following message was sent to the two German airships:

"German Airships. We would sooner die than to accept help from boffing cack like you."

Malcolm doubted that the German commanders would completely understand the very Scottish curse, but he was pretty sure that they'd get the intent.

Malcolm waited. After what seemed like an eternity, the radio operator cut in. "Captain, I'm receiving a reply. Prepare to be boarded."

Malcolm smiled "Very good. Patch me through to the whole ship."

Malcolm went to the flight controls, hoping that Mr. Frye was indeed correct in his assessment. Malcolm took a deep breath. "All hands, this is the captain. Prepare for immediate ballast release on my command. Lt. Saxon, fire all guns. Mr. Frye, release emergency ballast and go to full engines now. Everyone hang on!!!" Malcolm pulled the altitude level straight back and pulled the rudder hard to starboard.

First were the muffled explosions of the many guns of the HMA Daedalus firing in perfect unison. Suddenly, the nose pulled up sharply and then veered to the right. The ship shuddered as it nearly turned upside down. Crewmen slid down the hall as the violence of the maneuver knocked their feet out from under them and then they started to tumble down the port wall of the hall that was now the floor.

Malcolm struggled to keep his balance and stay at the flight controls. The door to the bridge suddenly flew open and Malcolm saw that the top of one of German zeppelins was only 10 feet below the Daedalus. And then he heard it. A massive set of explosions coming from everywhere. The Daedalus continued to climb and turn. As it did, Malcolm began to gradually bring the rudder back from full starboard. Within twenty seconds, the floor was once again the floor. Malcolm picked up the phone. "Commander Saxon, you'll have to be my eyes. Report."

"Bloody hell, Robertson, what did you do? I have men and guns everywhere!" yelled Saxon.

"Report. What's going on with the Germans?"

"I... I don't believe it. I'm seeing extensive gunfire damage to the carriages of both zeppelins. One looks like its losing buoyancy. I don't understand. We missed them. On purpose."

"Aye. My point was to provoke them and fire at them, but not hit them. That might make the angered captains fire back, at which point, thanks to the clever work of Mr. Frye, we were no longer in their sights so they fired at each other."

"That was bloody brilliant Robertson! Dangerous, but bloody brilliant," said Lt. Saxon.

"Thank you. Lt. Saxon. When you have your men squared away, meet me in the captain's office. We'll use that as a temporary bridge to converse. Appoint someone to be gunnery officer in your stead. I'll ask the crew chiefs to join us so we can figure out our next steps."

"Very good, sir."

"And Saxon, one more thing."

"Yes sir?"

"See if you can find a navigator. I have no idea of where we are or which way we're going other than away from the zeppelins."

Saxon unsuccessfully tried to stifle a laugh. "Yes, sir."

Chapter 5

Malcolm thought the hardest part of taking command was over once he got them out of the immediate trouble of the zeppelins. He was wrong. Malcolm stayed at the makeshift helm until a navigator reported. Unfortunately, most of the detailed maps were on the bridge and were likely ashes floating on the Baltic. The young navigator struggled to ascertain their position without a compass. Finally, one of the older crewman said he could find their position if he had a sextant. Malcolm remembered that the captain had one on display in his office. Within minutes, the crewman determined their approximate position on a much less detailed map found in the captain's office. Malcolm offered to make the crewman a navigator on the spot, but the crewman quickly turned down the offer and left the room.

Soon the chiefs of the crew were assembled in the captain's office: Mr. Frye represented Engineering; the young Sub-lieutenant Hensley who was the sole navigator now; Mr. Fletcher, Chief Signal Boatswain in charge of the radio room and shipboard communications; Dr. Jenkins, Surgeon; and Lieutenant Saxon, second in command.

Malcolm heard their reports in due order. First, Mr. Frye made an account of the damage to the Daedalus. Until they could land, they would not be able to do much about the bridge area. Mr. Frye's damage control team had routed what wires were left out of the remains of the bridge and replaced the door with a wooden wall and a window so that the navigator could see where he was going without freezing from the outside air. With the aid of Mr. Fletcher, Frye was able to wire a more practical handset that would allow Malcolm to address individual stations or ship-wide without having to work through the radio room.

"And, I have an idea that might allow us to use the contaminated fuel," Frye added at the end of his report.

"Contaminated fuel?" asked Saxon.

"Yes, sorry. In all of the excitement, it seemed like the least of our problems." Malcolm relayed what had happened in engineering prior the explosion. "If it hadn't been for the fact that I was busy bringing the engines on line, I might have been on the bridge." The thought sent a shiver up his spine. "Mr. Frye, what's your idea for the contaminated fuel?"

"Between losing the bridge and our emergency ballast, we're running exceptionally light. I think we can repurpose the fractional distillers that produce the helium to filter out the sugar."

"Excellent idea, Mr. Frye. Make it so," Malcolm said, feeling a little disappointed that he hadn't thought of it himself. Of course, he had other issues to contend with, so he might forgive himself this time.

The chief signal bosun reported that the Admiralty received the coded message Malcolm had sent apprising them of their situation and asking for additional orders. The reply instructed them to continue at best speed to St. Petersburg. The Daedalus would be repaired there before the Admiralty sent further orders. All of the men frowned, not knowing the nature of their real mission and knowing that the Germans seemed to be intent on preventing that selfsame mission.

Sub-lieutenant Hensley, now promoted to full lieutenant, was the only navigator left on the ship. He presented Malcolm with a list of the midshipmen who had shown the most aptitude for navigation, recommending Midshipmen Bennet for night navigator.

"Very good. Thank you, Mr. Hensley. Please inform Sub-lieutenant Bennet of his promotion."

Dr. Jenkins's reported only minor injuries from Malcolm's aeronautic maneuvers, but warned the captain that for the crew's sake, he ought to warn them before he tried something like that again.

"And I will be visiting each of the newly-promoted officers," he added, looking at Hensley, Frye, Saxon, and Malcolm in turn, "for your physicals."

"But we all had physicals before we left Kingsnorth," Malcolm replied.

"Aye, that would be for your old positions. I have no records that the current captain, commander, chief engineer, and lieutenant in charge of navigation have had their physicals. Regulations, you know."

"And where would we be without regulations," bemused Saxon. Everyone laughed and for a moment, the tension from what had been unsaid eased from the room.

Malcolm swallowed, "And now for the casualty report. We lost Captain Archibald Collins, Commander Arthur Bromley, Lieutenants Andrew Clairborne and Hugh Beauchamps, Midshipmen Michael Morrisey, Paul Castleton, and Leslie Hopkins, Signal Boatswain Arnold Tibbets, and Airman Guiles Shephard. Let us pause for a moment in remembrance of our lost companions."

All bowed their heads and were silent for several seconds. Malcolm looked up and broke the silence. "Thank you. We all have a great deal of work to do so let's get to it."

As the chiefs filed out of the office, Dr. Jenkins hung back for a moment. "When do you plan to hold the service, Captain?"

"Service? What? Oh." Malcolm hadn't thought of that. "I suppose when we get to St. Petersburg, once its official."

"Captain, permission to speak candidly, sir."

"Granted," Malcolm said, not liking the direction of this conversation.

"The men are hurting sir. They're happy to be alive and everyone is counting his blessing he hadn't been on the bridge, but at the same time, they think it could have been them. They need the time to say goodbye and know that the sacrifice that was made will be honored."

"You're right, I hadn't thought of that. But I don't have the foggiest idea of how to do it."

"I believe there's a standard ceremony in one of the captain's books. Do you mind if I look?" he asked, indicating the shelf of books behind Malcolm.

"Please, be my guest," Malcolm said, moving out from behind the desk.

Dr. Jenkins rummaged through the bookshelf, finally finding one well-worn book. "Ah, yes, the captain's ceremonies.... Let's see, marriages... no we don't need that... ah, here it is, funerals." Dr. Jenkins pointed to the section and handled the book to Malcolm.

"Ach, I'm a horrible speaker," Malcolm said, shaking his head as he looked at the service. "All of the officers will be scoffing at my accent and snickering at me behind me back."

"I really doubt that, Captain. I think every man on this ship knows if it hadn't been for you and your quick thinking, we'd likely be in a German prison."

"I don't know what to say; I never met half of these people. Being in the engine room limits your view."

"Aye, and on a ship this big, most captains don't know all of their crew. But good captains do. Go and talk to the men. Don't always eat at the officer's mess. Every once in a while, go to the enlisted mess. Get to know the men. Heaven knows I tried to get Archie, Captain Collins, to do it, but he was stuck in his old ways of thinking. That officers were officers and enlisted were enlisted. But you know, we're all just men trying to accomplish something. Lord knows, rank isn't always a measure of talent... present company excepted."

"Do you think it will help?"

"It certainly can't hurt. I think the best thing for a new captain is to know his crew."

"Thank you, Doctor. I'll take it under advisement."

"Please do. And Captain?"

"Yes?"

"I know you'll be fine," Dr. Jenkins said as he left the office.

Chapter 6

Malcolm scheduled the service for four bells, the next day. Since there were no bodies and no need of caskets, nine flags bearing the Union Jack were found and sewn to make a packet that was filled with weights. Malcolm asked anyone in the crew who knew the deceased to add something personal of the deceased to the flag. At four bells, the crew assembled in the bomb bay in the bowels of the ship. All were decked out in full dress uniforms. The nine flags were laid out over the bomb bay doors.

"I am the resurrection and the life..." began Malcolm. He led the crew through the expected prayers and responses. Malcolm departed from the prescribed text, stopping to let the crew share remembrances of each of the deceased. Some were funny and some not, but all were heartfelt. Commander Saxon came forward with a remembrance of Commander Bromley so that Malcolm was spared having to say something nice about him, and Dr. Jenkins gave a touching narrative of the captain, showing a side that the men had not known.

When all were finished, Malcolm continued, "In the sure and certain hope of resurrection to eternal life through our Lord Jesus Christ, we commend to Almighty God our shipmates Captain Archibald Collins, Commander Arthur Bromley, Lieutenants Andrew Clairborne and Hugh Beauchamps, Midshipmen Michael Morrisey, Paul Castleton, and Leslie Hopkins, Signal Boatswain Arnold Tibbets, and Airman Guiles Shephard and we commit their spirits to the air. While their bodies have returned to earth, ashes to ashes, dust to dust, may their spirits continue to soar the airs and find their way to your heavenly kingdom."

Malcolm nodded, and the bomb bay doors were opened. The flags fell and immediately were pulled away by the wind and flew into the air. When the bomb bay doors were shut, the ships guns fired twenty one times in salute. Finally, one of the young midshipmen played a very shaky version of Taps. After a moment of silence, Malcolm dismissed the assembly.

Malcolm returned to his quarters to change from his dress uniform. He was glad that that was over. He still had the unenviable job of writing letters to the next of kin. Fortunately, records of next of kin were kept with the purser who was not on the bridge. Malcolm was astonished to find that Boatswain Tibbets and Airman Shephard had no next of kin to notify. The thought mortified him. As horrible as he felt about the prospect of his parents receiving such a letter, he thought about what it would be like for no one in the world to care about your passing. Once his parent's passed on, would that be his fate? Who would his next of kin be in that case?

Malcolm opened a drawer of his dresser and pulled out a very old and dented metal flask. It was the very same flask from which he had his first taste of whisky. He looked at the flask, remembering his final time with his grandfather and took a careful swig. He had long since learned how to drink his whisky properly. As he stoppered the flask, he thought about when his father had given him the flask. Malcolm had been home on leave after just completing engineering college. He had a week before he had to report to Greenwich for naval college. The night before he left, his father took him aside.

"Son, I don't have much to give you, but I wanted to give ya something to tell ya how proud we are of ya."

"Da, you don't need to give me anything."

"Yes, I do. Now if you'd let me finish. The night your granda died, I heard every word. I was outside waiting and I heard you choking on your first whisky. It was all I could do to stop from laughing. But I heard how proud he was of you that night. And how proud he was of me, although he never said it to me face. But your mum and I want ya to have this—something to remember your family and who you are."

George Robertson handed his son a package wrapped in brown paper. Malcolm quickly unwrapped it to find his grandfather's flask. "Your mother wanted me to fill it with some sort of fancy brandy, but I knew you'd want whisky."

"I'm touched, Da. Thank you."

Malcolm raised the flask in a toast. "To family," he said, and drank another swallow.

The next days were chaotic. Without the bridge, the aerodynamic characteristics of the Daedalus changed so that the crew had a hard time maneuvering the great airship. It was nearly impossible to make best speed. And although Malcolm had passed flight school, he was not the best pilot. Sure, he could quote all of the aerodynamic principles at work and probably even calculate some of the equations in his head, but controlling the ship was a different matter.

And there were the myriad of day-to-day tasks in running a ship. Reports to review, orders to sign, inspections to conduct. It seemed the line to the captain's office had no end. It became so much that Malcolm excused himself, saying he had to check on something in the engine room and put Commander Saxon in charge.

Malcolm was only too glad to go to the engine room. The metal, the smell of grease, and sweat were a balm to his shattered nerves.

"Captain, what can I do for you?" asked Mr. Frye.

"Nothing in particular. Just wanted to see how things are going here," Malcolm asked.

"Fine, sir. While Damage Control was building our temporary bridge, I had the lads here strip the engines down to clean up the mess from the contaminated fuel. If we had to, I could run the engines at peak speed, just give the word."

"Excellent, Mr. Frye, although I think if I gave that order now, the ship itself might protest too much."

"I'm not so sure. I went out with the riggers this morning, checking the cabin section for any stress damage."

"You went out there?" Malcolm asked. It was a professional hazard as chief engineer, but Malcolm had never gone out willingly and was often sick upon return.

"Aye, I went for a dangle, as the riggers like to say. The cabin is secured to the ship and there seems to be no other structural damage. Also, sir, we've made the modifications to the fractional distillation system and have started to run the contaminated fuel through it. In another few days, the fuel should be good enough to use."

"Well, Mr. Frye," Malcolm said hesitantly, "it seems you have the situation well in hand."

"Aye sir, I learned from the best," Mr. Frye said.

Malcolm begrudgingly turned to leave. "Keep up the good work, Commander," he said, and left.

Malcolm was more dejected than he had been before coming to the engine room. He felt like he was in limbo—that there was no place for him on the ship. He didn't belong in the captain's office and it was clear that he didn't belong in the engine room. He wandered around the ship, watching the men at work, each having a specific task and executing it dutifully. Every man on the ship knew his task and what was expected of him, save Malcolm. He had no idea what to do.

Malcolm had always been a problem solver. It had held him in good stead at school and as chief engineer. Malcolm could quickly size up any given situation, figure out the possible scenarios, settle on the most likely choice and execute it quickly. When Malcolm solved a problem, his focus was intense and he acted decisively.

Once the immediate problems of what to do with a ship with no controls and two hostile airships surrounding them had been solved, Malcolm now had no idea how to solve the problem of being captain. Every decision he made, he second-guessed. He would rely on Saxon or one of the other officers to validate the decision or even make it for him. Aimlessly, Malcolm drifted to the mess hall and got a mug of tea. He sat in the mess, watching the men and letting the tea turn cold before he even drank a sip. Doctor Jenkins observed him in the mess hall and frowned. Tonight would have to be the captain's physical. Without a doubt, Jenkins thought.

Malcolm took his meal and retired to his cabin. In the uproar of the last few days, he hadn't had a chance to move into the captain's cabin. Saxon had wasted no time in moving into Bromley's cabin, but to Malcolm it just felt wrong. He supposed that maybe if he stayed in his cabin, things would go back to the way they had been.

Malcolm sat at the small desk of his cabin, reading more reports that had been brought for him. Malcolm picked at his meal, as he dutifully read each report. He had no idea what he should do with the information, but read them because that was what a captain did; at least that's what he thought a captain ought to do.

There was a knock at the door. Malcolm looked up, wondering who would want him in at this time of the evening or if some new calamity had occurred. Encouraged that there might be a problem he could solve, he sat up and said, "Come in."

Malcolm did not expect Dr. Jenkins to arrive with his black doctor's bag, a stethoscope hanging around his neck. "Sorry to bother you, sir, but I'm here for your physical."

Malcolm sagged, "Is this really necessary?"

"I'm afraid so, sir. Regulations, you know. I have to establish that you're fit for duty."

"Bloody hell, man, you already did that at Kingsnorth," grumbled Malcolm.

"As I said earlier, that was when you were chief engineer. I have to establish that you're fit for duty as the captain."

"Very well, let's get this over with," Malcolm grumbled. "What will it be first?"

"Take off your shirt," Dr. Jenkins said as he put the stethoscope into his ears.

As the doctor placed the apparently ice cold stethoscope on Malcolm's back, he flinched and quipped, "You couldn't warm that thing up first?"

"No, I couldn't. Now, keep quiet and let me do my job. Take several deep breaths. I'll tell you when to stop." Malcolm took four deep breaths and the doctor said, "I've heard enough, you can get dressed."

Malcolm start to put his shirt back on when the doctor said, "I'm afraid I'll have to mark you unfit for duty. It's your heart."

Malcolm froze for a second. "What? My heart? What's the problem?"

Dr. Jenkins said, "It's not in your work. A ship can't have a captain whose heart isn't in his job."

"What the bloody hell is this about? Are you having fun at my expense?"

"I'm afraid not, Captain. I've been watching you today; you're a balloon lost in the wind, blowing wherever the wind takes you. And you need to be a captain, setting a course and holding to it. Fortunately, I think there's hope for you. The prescription is first, a stern lecture. The second is this," he said as he pulled first a bottle out of the bag followed by two honest to goodness glasses. Jenkins handed the bottle to Malcolm.

"Auchentoshan single malt whisky? How did you get this?" Malcolm asked in astonishment. Auchentoshan was the closest distillery to his home and, not incidentally, his favorite whisky. "Did you know that I came from a village not far from where this was made?"

"Really?" the doctor replied in amazement. "I didn't know. I actually won this off an officer back at Kingsnorth, going on two years now. I never had the right opportunity to open it. But in this case," he said, appraising Malcolm, "I think it's a medical necessity. Go ahead, pour. But you should know, I'm going to deliver some harsh medicine with this. Think of this as honey to smooth its going down."

"I'd listen to a sermon from the Devil himself if it meant I could have some of this," Malcolm said as he poured two fingers for each of them.

"Cheers," Malcolm said, raising his glass.

"To absent friends," Dr. Jenkins replied.

"Aye, absent friends," Malcolm replied less enthusiastically.

They each took a swallow, Malcolm savoring the flavor and the warmth of the whisky. After a few moments, Dr. Jenkins said, "Permission to speak candidly sir."

"I don't suppose I have a choice in the matter, do I?"

"No sir, you don't."

"I didn't think so. Permission granted," Malcolm said, taking another drink and enjoying the warmth of the whisky.

"I was serious when I said that your heart isn't in this job. I watched you today. You were aimless, and if you'll forgive the analogy, rudderless. The captain of the ship sets the tone for the ship. If he is aimless and drifting, the crew will be drifting and aimless."

"That's all well and good, but I have no bloody idea what the hell I'm supposed to be doing! I'm an engineer; it's what I know. I don't know the first thing about being a captain."

"I wouldn't say that. You knew enough to get this crew out of a very sticky situation. I think I can speak for the crew when I say I'm very happy to not be spending time in Germany right now."

"That was different; there was a problem to solve. That's what I do, solve problems."

"What do you think a captain does? The orders he receives are solving a problem for the Admiralty. When officers come to him with reports, they are either telling the captain that they've solved a problem or looking for additional resources to solve a problem—resources they can't acquire on their own," Jenkins offered.

"But engineering problems, I know how to solve. I know the equations and principles involved. This..." Malcolm said, indicating the whole ship, "is more than I know."

"Then, learn, Captain. You have to learn what principles govern people, what motivates them. It's the same as engineering, just a little more... imprecise."

"That's easy for you. You deal with people all the time."

"True. But I had to learn that. Do you know how I started in medicine?" asked Jenkins.

Malcolm shook his head. "I started out as a veterinarian in the Army, tending to the horses. I was in Crimea and saw the bloody aftermath from that fool Cardigan. It became clear that the horses were lost, so I helped out with the men. I mean, I was a doctor and men are just another type of animal. After that tour, I left for medical school and became a doctor. I enlisted this time in the Navy, thinking that the duties on ship would be better. That's when I met Archie, I mean Captain Collins."

"You and he were good friends," Malcolm acknowledged softly.

"Yes, we were. We were together for several adventures," he stopped to chuckle. "Some of them actually happened in battle. But in that time, we both learned about men, what drives them and what motivates them. As a captain, you need to know when to push the men and when to step back and get out of their way. For all his faults and quirks, the one thing Archie was good at was letting competent men do their jobs. Did he ever tell you how to carry out his orders?"

"No, not once," replied Malcolm.

"That's because he knew there was nothing he could tell you that you didn't already know. But, I'm sure you saw how he told Lieutenant Clairborne exactly what to do and how to do it. That's because he knew that Clairborne needed more experience and frankly, discipline. A captain is like an engineer—he has to have a toolbox with a tool for every occasion. What's that expression, when all you have is a hammer..."

"Every problem is a nail," Malcolm said. He thought about this. Jenkins may be on to something.

"But the only way to do that is to get to know people, the same way you have gotten to know the ship. I'm told that you can tell if there's something wrong with the ship just by listening."

"Yes, but, it's not hard. The signs are there, you just have to look."

"That's what it's like with people too," Jenkins added. "Because I've been doing this for years, I can tell when a man comes to sick bay if he's really sick, hung over, or looking to get out of work. It's about watching and listening, knowing what to look for."

"How do I do it?" Malcolm asked.

"By watching and listening. It's an imperfect science, but keep it up long enough, you'll have plenty of empirical evidence to support your theories. I'd say start with Saxon. What do you know about your second in command?"

"Hardly anything."

"Invite him to dine with you, then," the doctor said. "Break bread with him, drink with him, and take his measure. It's important for the two of you to trust one another." The doctor looked down at his drink. "Listen to me, wise old fool giving advice to a much younger man."

"No, really, I do appreciate it," Malcolm said in earnest.

"Thank you, you're too kind. I should go before I have too much of this," he said, indicating his glass. He drained what little was left and packed the glass back in his bag. Malcolm handed him his empty glass and started to hand the bottle over when the doctor pushed the bottle back at Malcolm and said, "No, you keep it. I know you'll appreciate it far more than I ever could."

"Thank you, doctor," Malcolm said, meaning both the whisky and the advice.

"I think you have the makings of a great captain in you, Malcolm. I told Archie as much before he died. Prove me right son." He put a hand on Malcolm's shoulder for a brief moment, picked up his black bag, and left the cabin.

Chapter 7

The next day, Malcolm followed the doctor's prescription. As he listened to the morning reports, he tried to figure out what problem needed to be solved or was being solved by the report. It worked. It was much easier for Malcolm to grasp the contents and know what to do with them, even if it was to file the information for future reference.

He toured the ship, this time not in an aimless daze, but with purpose. He again returned to the enlisted mess where he grabbed a mug of tea and sat down with a small group of off duty crewmen. The crewmen were nervous; the captain coming to sit with them could not be a good thing. After a minute of extremely polite conversations, the crewmen suddenly remembered duties or errands that they had to perform and scurried away.

Perhaps the direct approach wasn't the best, Malcolm mused. Instead, he opted to watch the crew's interaction and try to judge each man's mood. He wasn't sure if he was right or not, but the exercise helped.

When the doctor had told him last night that he had thought Malcolm was unfit for duty, Malcolm was hurt. That instant made him realize that he really did want to be captain, and a good captain at that. Malcolm returned to his office and asked a crewman to have his personal affects moved to the captain's cabin. He went to the engine room and personally told Mr. Frye that he should move to the chief engineer's cabin and his effects had been moved out.

Malcolm returned to the makeshift bridge. Commander Saxon had the watch and was making sure that they were on course and moving at best speed.

"Good afternoon, sir. We should be seeing the Russian coast by daybreak and arrive in St. Petersburg by early morning," reported Saxon.

"Excellent. Commander Saxon, would you care to join me for dinner tonight in the officer's mess? Nothing formal, I just want to go over a number of things with you."

The Reluctant Captain

"Very good, sir. I look forward to it. What time?" asked Saxon.

"Four bells," replied Malcolm.

"Very good, sir."

Malcolm said his farewells, confident all was well on their sorry excuse for a bridge, and went to the chef to make preparations for dinner. Malcolm returned to the captain's office—his office, he had to keep reminding himself.

As he sat in the chair, he surveyed the room in detail for the first time and saw the souvenirs of a man's life. On the desk were pictures of Captain Collins—first as a young man with his equally young bride, moving forward several years to a man with his wife and four children, moving forward several years to a picture taken somewhat recently, a grandfatherly captain sat with his now matronly wife surrounded by their adult children and several grandchildren. Grandchildren who will never get to know their grandfather, Malcolm thought.

But the markers of Captain Collins' life were not just the pictures on the desk. On the bookshelf were several ship models, probably ships on which Captain Collins served. The oriental carpet on the floor was probably found on a trip to India. There was a native mask from somewhere in Africa, and even a small flag of the Confederate States of America, a prize that must have been gathered as a blockade-runner during the Civil War in the Colonies. On the wall, he saw the empty spot where the sextant had been. Malcolm walked to the large globe next to the desk; as he turned the globe, he saw x's over several of the cities. As he stopped to examine them, he realized that they must represent a city that the captain had visited. He noticed with interest that St. Petersburg was unmarked. And now would stay so forever.

Malcolm returned his attention to the reports on his desk and began writing the letters to the next of kin. He had put this task off; how could he tell them that their loved one died in a freak accident? Or was it an accident? Malcolm had not taken the time until now to examine the string of events. First, the contaminated fuel. It's very likely that had Malcolm not heard something off with the engines, they might have failed not long after the bridge explosion. The bridge explosion had completely disabled the ability to steer the airship. And with the command crew killed, there would be no one to step up and take command of the ship. Whoever took over would likely have no choice but to take the German aid. The loss of the bridge, while taking some of the technology of the Daedalus, would not significantly hamper someone who wanted to take the Daedalus apart for its secrets.

There was a saboteur and collaborator on board, Malcolm realized with a start. And with the frayed relations between German and the Empire, something like this could touch off a powder keg that might consume all of Europe. Malcolm hoped that his actions over the Baltic had no repercussions. He was counting on the fact that it wouldn't look good for the Germans that a disabled British airship had effectively stopped two German zeppelins without laying a shot on the Germans. There had been no word from the Admiralty, so he assumed there were no further repercussions. The thought of a collaborator on board disturbed Malcolm greatly.

Malcolm filed this thought away for further reference and realized that it was nearly time for his dinner with Commander Saxon. He retired to the captain's quarters—his quarters. He was immediately struck by how few personal affects he owned. Malcolm refreshed himself, took the bottle of Auchentoshan with him and went to the officer's mess.

At exactly four bells, Commander Charles Saxon strode into the officer's mess. The midshipman led him to the seat and poured two tall glasses of a brown ale. "Please, sit," motioned Malcolm, already at the table. Intrigued, Saxon took his seat, already noting that this was not a typical dinner at the officer's mess.

"This is Tennants. It's brewed not far from where I grew up," Malcolm said, pointing to the glasses. "I thought tonight, you and I should get to know one another a little better. Up until now, we haven't had much of an opportunity to talk, what with our duties and all. But I thought we ought to become better acquainted. To that end, the meal tonight is the type of meal that I prefer. And it will be much less formal than Captain Collins' dinners. Cheers," he said raising his beer glass and taking a long draught.

"Cheers," replied Saxon in a somewhat bemused tone of voice. He did have to admit that he rather enjoyed the beer, but he had little experience with beer against which to judge it.

Malcolm indicated to the midshipmen that they should bring in the food. The midshipmen brought the plates and uncovered them with a flourish. Saxon was surprised to see what looked like a very thick stew with vegetables and meat sitting underneath a mound of mashed potatoes.

Malcolm picked up his fork and indicated that Saxon should eat. Saxon looked and noted there was only one dinner fork.

Saxon hesitantly prodded the food with his fork. "Forgive my ignorance, but what exactly is this?"

Malcolm paused to finish a bite. "Shepard's pie. Although it might technically be cottage pie since there's no lamb. Actually, I'm not sure what the meat is, but for now I'll pretend its beef."

"You make it sound so... appetizing," Saxon said drolly.

"It's better than it looks. And the potatoes are particularly good. I'll give Chef one thing—he knows how to cook potatoes."

Saxon wrinkled his nose, took a forkful of the food and hesitantly ate it. Surprisingly, it was quite tasty. Simple, but tasty. "You're right, this is good," he said as he started to eat in earnest.

Malcolm smiled, "Thank you. This is one of my favorite dishes." Silence fell as the two continued to eat. Malcolm ate his meal with great relish and Saxon had to admit that he found the meal quite satisfying. When dinner was finished and the dishes cleared, Malcolm brought out the Auchentoshan and two glasses. He poured a finger for both of them.

"Whisky is my preferred after dinner drink. I never could stand the port that Captain Collins liked to drink."

Saxon was at least familiar with whisky. He sipped slowly, savoring the flavor. "This is quite excellent."

"Thank you. This is made at a distillery not far from my hometown."

"Where is that?" inquired Saxon.

"Kilmacolm. It's a small village not too far from Glasgow. Many people live there and commute to Glasgow by train. My father did that. He worked in the shipyards, until..."

"Until?"

"There was an accident; he was a welder and a large sheet of metal fell on him, crushing his left side. He survived, but it's difficult for him to get around and do anything. After his accident, I left university and enlisted in the Navy. What about your family?"

"Not much to say really. It's an old family, but I am from a poorer branch. While I was growing up, we stayed with various relatives, at least for as long as they could stand us. I have lived many places throughout England and Scotland, but I can't call any one place home. When I came of age, I was given a choice of making a career in business or the military. The thought of being stuck behind a dreary desk counting coppers everyday was enough to drive me to madness. I opted for the military and the Navy, in particular. Since I have no permanent home, the travel of the Navy appealed to me."

Silence fell between the two as they regarded their whisky. Malcolm looked up. "I never had the chance to thank you for helping me out with Bromley at the captain's dinner. Thank you."

"You're welcome."

"I'm curious, why did you do it?" asked Malcolm.

"Growing up as the 'poor' relation, I have been the butt of many jokes from my so-called betters. I hate to see that happen to anyone. And besides, Bromley was a pompous twit and I rather enjoyed watching him turn every shade of red when you did nothing wrong that night."

"It was rather amusing. It's a good thing the doctor was there; I thought Bromley might become apoplectic," Malcolm said, laughing. "Did you know him very well?"

"I can't say that I did. I believe that he was the son of some landed gentry. Had a House in the Midlands I believe. He knew that I came from similar stock, so he left me alone. But he certainly liked to show his superiority to those of humbler starts, like yourself and the doctor."

"The doctor? Really?"

"Oh, yes. I heard tell from one of the older officers that there was a historic row between the two of them such that the captain had to intervene. He told Bromley in no uncertain terms that he was not to insult the doctor and if he did, he'd be transferred to a watch post in the Orkney Islands. The way I heard tell, the captain was not kidding." Saxon stopped for a moment and asked, "Do you play chess?"

"I have, but I don't think I've touched a board since university," Malcolm said.

"Good, that will make you easy to beat," quipped Saxon. "You bring this exquisite whisky, I'll get my board and I'll meet you in your office."

"Very well." Within five minutes, Saxon had returned, the game board was set up, glasses were refilled, and the battle was joined. Malcolm, as white, started immediately with a bold strategy, freeing his queen and harrying many of Saxon's positions. Saxon, for his part, dodged most of Malcolm's forays and in counter, led a couple of feints that siphoned off pieces from Malcolm's defenses. Soon, through crafty maneuvering, Saxon had Malcolm pinned down and it looked like Malcolm was finished. Malcolm could see the end coming when suddenly he came up with a plan. If he could lure Saxon into taking his queen, he might be able to reverse the tables on Saxon and use his configuration to pin his king.

Malcolm began the trap with reckless attacks with first a knight and then a bishop. Saxon fell for the bait and moved into position to take them. Malcolm brought his queen forward and boldly put her next to Saxon's king. At this point, although Saxon could not reach the queen with his other pieces, his king could. He guessed that Saxon couldn't resist the prize and his guess was correct. Saxon hesitantly reached for the queen, trying to make sure that he was in no danger. What he hadn't seen was Malcolm's rook hidden in back that had a straight path to end the game.

When Saxon removed his fingers from the king, Malcolm took his rook the length of the board. "Check and mate, I believe," he said finishing the last of his whisky. Saxon stared at the board for a few seconds and realized Malcolm was correct. "Congratulations," he said as he raised his glass in salute. Saxon stood and began to pick up the pieces. "Thank you for a most illuminating game of chess sir. I should go as I have early watch tomorrow, sir."

"Please, call me Malcolm," Malcolm said.

"Only if you call me Charles."

"Very well. Thank you, Charles."

"Thank you, Malcolm," Saxon said offering his hand.

The two men shook hands and Commander Charles Saxon left the captain's office. Malcolm smiled as he poured another finger of whisky. Yes, it had been a most illuminating night.

Chapter 8

The Daedalus reached the coast of Russia that morning. Once land was sighted, Malcolm went to the radio room to radio for additional information. The response was: "Welcome Daedalus. Report to The Khodynka Aerodrome, coordinates 55.7883 N, 37.5333 E."

"That was bloody useful," Malcolm muttered as he took the orders back with him to the makeshift bridge. Handing the navigator on duty the coordinates, he met with Saxon and discussed the day's duties. They agreed that they should arrive in St. Petersburg looking like the best representatives of His Majesty's Air Service. Using the ship's radio, Malcolm informed the crew that there would be ongoing inspections that morning and all were to be in dress uniforms for the approach to Khodynka.

Malcolm and Saxon decided to split the inspections so they could cover more ground; Malcolm suggested that he inspect the gunnery stations while Saxon would inspect the engine room. For the rest of the day, the ship was a beehive of activity, and crewmen could be seen working feverishly or running from one point to another. After much spit and polish, both Malcolm and Saxon thought that the Daedalus was ready. Late that afternoon, the Daedalus gradually descended to dock with the mooring tower of the aerodrome.

When the Daedalus settled, the crew lowered the gangplank and the escort started out. Malcolm and Saxon, in their dress uniforms complete with white gloves, looked at each other nervously.

"Do you know any Russian?" asked Malcolm.

"None that won't get us shot on the spot for propositioning someone," replied Saxon.

"Alright, then, I better do the talking. After you, Commander."

Saxon followed the escort, with Malcolm bringing up the rear. As he concentrated on marching and keeping his bearing erect, he vainly tried to recall the protocol of landing in another country. Although he had landed in several foreign countries in his Air Service term, he had mostly spent his time in the engine room.

Malcolm marched to the receiving delegation, appraising the group. First was a man in a Russian military uniform, most likely the base commander; a decidedly British looking man in a morning coat and bowler, likely a diplomat from the British Embassy; and finally, the most beautiful woman Malcolm had ever seen. She was medium height, her auburn hair almost glowed in the afternoon light and her bright green eyes seemed to be lit within from fire. Malcolm arrived in front of the line and gave his sharpest salute, swallowing hard. The Russian in uniform returned the salute and immediately started speaking. Within seconds, the woman translated, "I am Grand Duke Alexander Mikhailovich, Commander of the Imperial Russian Air Service. Welcome to our country." When she finished her translation, he tipped his head slightly.

Malcolm bowed to the grand duke. "I am Malcolm Robertson, Captain of His Majesty's Airship Daedalus and as a representative of His Majesty King George V, I am honored to be your guest."

"Well done, young sir," said the British diplomat. "I'm George Buchanan, His Majesty's Ambassador to the Court of Tsar Nicholas II." Malcolm shook the ambassador's hand. "And this is Special Envoy Joan de St. Leger."

Malcolm took her proffered hand and kissed it gently, remembering his gentlemanly manners. Her fiery green eyes locked on his and he thought for just a moment, the corner of her mouth turned upward as if in a smile.

"This is Commander Charles Saxon," Malcolm said, remembering at last to introduce him to the delegation. At the mention of the name, he thought he saw a flicker of recognition from the ambassador, but it passed so quickly that Malcolm was not sure if he had imagined it. He exchanged greetings with the grand duke and the ambassador and likewise kissed the proffered hand from the special envoy in a much more charming manner than Malcolm.

"Very good. The grand duke has graciously set up barracks for you and your men here at the airfield. The Daedalus will be moved to Hanger A shortly so work can begin on reconstruction of the bridge. I can't imagine how you made it this far."

"It was a wee dodgy at first, but we were able to keep her together," Malcolm said. He immediately regretted the words as they passed his lips. They made him sound like the bumpkin. This time, Malcolm was sure he saw a smile on the young woman's lips.

"With the help of the grand duke's staff, I've drawn up the lodging assignments. Please relay these to your crew and arrange for your personal effects to be brought to your quarters. Your presence is required at the British Embassy for discussions about your mission," Joan said passing copies of the lodging assignments to both Malcolm and Saxon. Her voice, although husky, had a very cultured accent.

Malcolm and Saxon looked at each other and then Malcolm said, "Yes, thank you. We'll see to the disposition of the crew. We'll be back shortly. Grand Duke, Ambassador, Miss de St. Leger," Malcolm said bowing to each in turn before leaving to return to the crew. When Saxon was level with him again, he murmured in a low voice, "I don't like the sounds of that. The meeting at the embassy."

"They can't hang us for treason, because we finished the mission. The worse that could happen is a court-martial for dereliction of duty or gross incompetence and life in the brig," Saxon said sarcastically.

"You're a ray of sunshine, you are," laughed Malcolm.

"I try to look for the worse possible outcome," offered Saxon. "That way, I'm seldom disappointed."

Malcolm and Saxon reviewed the lodging assignments, briefed the other officers on what would happen, and assigned crewmen to bring their affects to their new quarters. Malcolm drew Mr. Frye aside for a quiet conversation. "I want you to keep an eye on the reconstruction on the bridge if I'm unavailable."

"Why? Aren't you staying here?" asked Frye.

"Perhaps not. Commander Saxon and I are to leave shortly to go to the British Embassy. I don't know how long I'll be there. In the meantime, I want you to take charge of the crew and offer any assistance you can in the repair. There should be a copy of the blueprints with all of my modifications."

"In the engine room," Frye finished. "I've seen you pull those blueprints out so many times, I see it in my sleep."

"Yes..." Malcolm said, caught off guard. "One thing. If I'm not back when they rebuild the flight controls, make sure they put a ship's wheel back, just like Captain Collins had."

"I thought you hated that thing and it was, and I quote, 'A bloody waste of manpower and engineering to rig that primitive control to a state of the art airship.'"

"Aye, that's true," said Malcolm. "But because we had that primitive control, we were able to connect in the flight controls somewhere else. I like having that bit of redundancy. Just make sure they don't run off with the levers."

"Aye, aye, sir," Frye replied, now understanding the captain. "Consider it done."

"Good man. Good luck," he said, offering Frye his hand.

"And to you, too," Frye said, shaking the hand and then throwing a quick salute.

Malcolm returned the salute and strode over to Saxon. "Ready to face the firing squad?" Malcolm asked.

"I told you, they can only try us for gross dereliction of duty or incompetence. That's only punishable by prison."

"Ever the eternal optimist, eh?" smiled Malcolm. He sighed and said, "Let's get this over with" as he and Saxon walked back to the waiting delegation.

Chapter 9

Malcolm, Saxon, and the delegation were ushered into a Rolls-Royce Silver Ghost. It was already running when the party reached the waiting vehicle and, to Malcolm's surprise, the engine noise was very soft.

Before Malcolm got in, he stopped and admired the beauty of the machine. The silver paint and chrome shone with brilliance and he lovingly touched the metal of the door. He could see the superb workmanship that had gone into this machine and he was mesmerized.

"You'd think he's never seen a car before," quipped Miss St. de Leger.

"This isn't a car. It's a work of art," Malcolm said, slightly awestruck.

"It is the grand duke's prized possession. We're very fortunate to be riding in it. Very few people get the opportunity," offered the ambassador.

"I can see why," Malcolm said as he settled in next to the young woman. "Please thank the grand duke for allowing us to ride in this work of art."

"Thank you," said the grand duke in heavily accented English, who was sitting in the driver's seat. No one but the grand duke drove his car. Malcolm was startled to note that the grand duke spoke English. "It is good to meet a man who sees the beauty of this machine," the grand duke said with a sparkle in his eyes. "Are we all here? Very well, let's go." The grand duke pulled his driving goggles down to cover his eyes and put the car in gear.

Soon they were blurring through the streets of St. Petersburg as the Rolls Royce roared to life. The grand duke was a very good driver, adeptly maneuvering the large car through the narrow streets of St. Petersburg. Malcolm tried to take in the quickly dissolving scenes, but the car was going too fast.

After several minutes, the car slowed, pulling up before a building surrounded by a stone wall about five feet high. In the center of the wall was a large stone arch. As the car approached, the guards opened the wrought iron gates. Malcolm at first thought they would not make the turn into the arch, but the grand duke expertly timed the application of the brake with his turn. Even so, Malcolm was thrown into Miss de St. Leger. Blushing, he murmured a quick apology. She smiled quickly at him and then her face returned to her businesslike mask.

The delegation disembarked, save for the grand duke. Malcolm again bowed to the grand duke and thanked him profusely for the ride. The grand duke nodded, put the car in gear, and sped out of the embassy compound. Now that his duty was complete and he had his car out, he would drive for many more hours.

The party entered the ornate building. Once inside, the ambassador led the party directly to his office. Butlers soon entered carrying snifters of brandy on silver trays, which were promptly offered to the guests. Malcolm dutifully took his brandy. He did not have much use for the stuff; it tasted like engine fuel to him, but without even that much flavor. Still, he figured he could use a stiff drink and this would certainly do.

"I'm sorry this has been so secretive," began the ambassador. "His Majesty's government considers the success of your mission imperative and given the... troubles you have encountered, we want to go to great lengths to ensure secrecy."

"And why exactly are we here?" asked Malcolm, getting straight to the point. "I don't see anyone from the Admiralty, so it cannot be a court-martial."

"Oh, good heavens, no," laughed the ambassador. "Please, let me set your mind at ease. Hold on a minute. Ah, yes," he said as he produced a piece of paper. "This is a telegram from the Admiralty. 'Brevet promotions granted to Malcolm Robertson to captain. Stop. Charles Saxon to commander. Stop. Robertson awarded Air Service Cross for saving ship and all hands. Stop. Award to be presented upon return to London. Stop.'"

The Reluctant Captain

The ambassador put the telegram side. "No, gentleman. The Admiralty is very pleased with your bit of quick thinking, Captain Robertson. It was vital that the Daedalus make it here to St. Petersburg to continue its mission."

"Which is?" asked Malcolm.

"What I am going to tell you will sound farfetched, but I assure you that the matter is deadly serious. Please sit," the ambassador said, indicating the chairs in front of his desk. When Malcolm and Saxon were seated, the ambassador began. "I suppose there's no good way to begin, but to just dive in. Have either of you gentleman read H.G. Wells' 'War of the Worlds'?"

Malcolm was puzzled. "You mean the book about a Martian invasion? What does that have to do with our mission?"

"Possibly, much more than you realize. What if I told you that events unfolded very much like they were detailed in the book and that a Martian ship did in fact land on British soil?"

"I'd be wondering if you drank something even stronger than this brandy," exploded Malcolm. Martians? Could the ambassador possibly be serious?

Seeing Malcolm's disbelief, the ambassador smiled. "It does seem far-fetched, does it not? Perhaps this will change your mind." The ambassador handed Malcolm a folder. As Malcolm opened it, his eyes were immediately drawn to a photograph of machine of a type that Malcolm had never seen. He was amazed even further when he found photographs of a·creature not of this world. It had a glistening skin, dark eyes not protected by a brow, a rounded head and tentacles around its mouth. In place of arms were two long tentacles, not unlike those of an octopus. The creature lay on a table marked out with ruler markings. If the photograph could be believed, the creature stood over seven feet tall. When the shock had worn off, Malcolm handed the folder to Saxon.

"Almost exactly as detailed in Mr. Wells' book, vehicles from the planet Mars crashed in Horsell Common in 1894. Attempts for peaceable contact were met with instant destruction. The military and civilian population could do little or nothing to stop them. Fortunately for the Empire, germs defeated the

Martians. Their Martian bodies had no immunity to Earth germs and as a result, they succumbed to common Earth illnesses. Before cooler heads could prevail, the Martians and their ships were destroyed. The only evidence that they were here are the photographs you hold in your hand."

"And H.G. Wells' book? Why was it printed?" asked Malcolm.

"To discredit anyone who was there," offered Saxon. "If they offered details, it would sound uncannily like Mr. Wells' novel and they could be dismissed as crackpots."

"Very good, Mr. Saxon. You are correct. Those who tried to come forward were quickly discredited because their account matched the book so closely. Which brings us to your mission."

"On June 30, 1908, something fell from the sky and exploded near Tunguska in Siberia. Descriptions of the explosion indicated that a metallic cylinder of fire fell from the sky and there was an earth-shattering explosion that shook the ground as if it was an earthquake. The concussive force toppled trees over thirty miles away from where it is presumed to have gone down."

The ambassador continued, "The tsar mentioned this in passing to His Majesty at King Edward's funeral, who happened to relay it to the First Lord of the Admiralty. He remembered the file on Horsell Common and wondered if whatever happened in Tunguska had some relation to Horsell Common. The First Lord has been working with the grand duke to prepare an expedition to Tunguska to find the source of the explosion. If the source is extraterrestrial and there are any survivors, it is hoped you can make peaceful contact. Failing that, you are to return anything you find to London. The Admiralty hopes that the severe cold of the Siberian winter will have helped to preserve any organic remains and the extreme remoteness of the territory will have prevented people from tampering with the site.

"Captain Robertson and Commander Saxon, you are to take a group of Russian and British scientists to Tunguska. Once work there is completed, you will make a brief stop at an aerodrome near Moscow for refueling and you will proceed back to London.

"I must impress upon you both the secrecy and urgency of this mission. It seems that the Kaiser also has heard of this event at Tunguska. It is possible that he knows about the incident at Horsell Common and has likewise pieced together a possible connection. If there is any alien technology to be recovered, the nations who owns that will have an advantage over the rest of the world."

"Who are the experts that we will be taking to the site?" asked Malcolm.

"Ernest Rutherford, a physicist and chemist of great note; Nikolai Kolstov, a Russian expert in biology and zoology; and Nikolay Yegorovich Zhukovsky, an engineer and expert in the new science of aerodynamics. He is personally overseeing the reconstruction of the Daedalus. In addition, a Mr. Davenport from His Majesty's government will act as an observer and Miss St. de Leger will accompany you as translator and cultural liaison."

Malcolm's eyes moved to the young woman who caught his gaze. Malcolm, embarrassed, turned back to the ambassador. "Do you really think we'll have any problems from the Germans?"

"It is entirely possible. The Germans are allies of the Ottoman Empire. It might be conceivable that they might try to sneak a convoy in through the south. It is isolated country and it would be possible to avoid people. I wouldn't put anything past the Germans. Any more questions? If you'll excuse me, there are many arrangements that must be made."

The ambassador rose and offered his hand to Malcolm, "Thank you, Captain Robertson for all you've done so far. I'm afraid His Majesty must ask even more of you and your crew."

"Thank you, sir," Malcolm said, returning the handshake.

"And you, Commander Saxon. Thank you," the ambassador said, shaking Saxon's hand. Malcolm noticed a look of apparent recognition by the ambassador, but it quickly left. "Miss St. de Leger, will you escort our officers back to the airfield?"

Malcolm, Saxon, and Joan left the ambassador to his work and waited until a carriage could be brought to return them to the airfield. In the much slower moving carriage, Malcolm was able to see the sights of the capital city. They passed cathedrals with traditional spires, cathedrals with the tower topped with gold domes, palaces, and, as they drew near to the water toward the port, a cathedral with towers that were topped with what looked like colored onion bulbs.

When the carriage returned to the aerodrome. Malcolm turned to say farewell to Miss de St. Leger, but was surprised when she went to disembark. Malcolm quickly held her hand and helped her out of the carriage. She smiled and said "Thank you," and turned to the driver and spoke something in Russian. The driver immediately took off. "You're not returning to the embassy?" asked Malcolm, somewhat surprised.

"No, I'm to remain at your disposal to facilitate communications between you and the Russian crew.

"Russian crew?"

"Oh yes. The Russians have insisted that they have some of their men onboard. Not that they don't trust us, but they don't trust us."

"Where in the bloody hell am I supposed to house all these people? The Daedalus is an airship, not a bloody luxury hotel." As soon as the curses rolled off of his tongue, he regretted them. "Sorry, Miss de St. Leger. I apologize for my rude behavior for cursing so extravagantly before you."

"Please, Captain, your apology is unnecessary. I have known a few sailors in my time—some of whose curses could peel wallpaper. That was nothing. In order not to overcrowd the ship, the same number of men will be left here. I believe that it will be called a cultural exchange."

"Will they at least speak English? I'm fresh out of crew that speak Russian."

"I believe that the crew does speak basic English."

"I hope that they will be useful. Come, let's find my ship."

Joan stopped a Russian airman and asked where the Daedalus had been taken. He pointed to one of the gigantic

The Reluctant Captain

hangars across the airfield. Joan returned to Malcolm. "Shall we go?" she asked. Putting her arm through his, she motioned to the hangar.

Malcolm's head was abuzz. He suddenly found it very hard to think straight. He quickly shook it off and very formally took her arm and escorted her to the hangar. As they started, he shot a look at her. She was beautiful. Her auburn hair was a mass of ringlets. Although it was pulled back, a few stray curls fell around her face. Her face was porcelain white, in contrast to her dark eyebrows that arched gracefully over those fiery green eyes.

Malcolm quickly snatched his attention away before he might be caught staring at her. Malcolm decided he ought to say something. "I see you speak Russian. How many languages do you speak?"

Joan, looking up at Malcolm, "I'm fluent in English and Russian, as well as German, French, Italian and I can read Ancient Greek and Latin."

"That's amazing!" he said, in awe of her ability. He had tried to master some basic German for reading technical papers and it was a struggle for him to master even the rudiments.

"Not as amazing as you might think. I've been surrounded by many languages since I was little. My grandmother was Russian, my father English, and I grew up in Switzerland where French, German, and Italian are all spoken. In fact, the only languages I've had to *learn* were Latin and Ancient Greek, but even that wasn't difficult, because knowing French and Italian, I immediately saw its connection to Latin, and Russian uses nearly the same alphabet as Ancient Greek, so in that sense I didn't have to learn a new alphabet. And, if I may say somewhat immodestly, I have a knack for picking up a language. Do you speak any other languages?"

"Not really. I can read some German because I try to keep up on some of the latest technical papers, but it takes me far too long." As they approached the hangar, Malcolm indicated signs. "I'll definitely need your expertise in deciphering that," he said, pointing to a sign over the hangar. "I can't make sense of that, what with its backwards N's and R's and other strange characters."

She laughed, "You have to remember that the Russian alphabet is based on Ancient Greek, not Latin. Do you know any Greek letters?"

"Some. Greek letters are often used in science for expressing equations."

"They sort of fit in the Russian alphabet. But that kind of mental decoding is difficult and too slow. The best way is to just learn the alphabet, like you did as a child."

Malcolm laughed, "I think that ship left the port a long time ago. It was all I could do to understand the German alphabet. Look, we're here." They had, indeed arrived at a colossal hangar. They were in front of a door guarded by two Russian airmen wearing crewmen uniforms, not unlike Malcolm's crew—blue jackets and trousers with a scarf, tied in front almost half a foot down from the soldier's neck, and the brimless blue cap. Without the Russian letters and insignia, he could almost be mistaken for a British soldier.

Joan said something to the two guards in Russian. Both soldiers jumped to attention and saluted Malcolm. After Malcolm returned the salute, one of the guards said, "Welcome, Captain Robertson," in moderately good English.

"You speak English?"

"Da... I mean yes, sir," he said.

"Whom do I talk to about the repairs to the ship?" Malcolm asked.

"Professor Zhukovsky is personally overseeing them. You will not be able to miss him. He will be the one bellowing orders and shouting at everyone," replied the airman.

"Ah, thank you, airman," said Malcolm cautiously. He turned a questioning eyebrow to Joan, but she merely shrugged. "Let's see what they're doing to my ship." As Malcolm stepped towards the door, the other airman quickly ran and opened the door for Malcolm and Joan.

Malcolm nodded his thanks and when they were passed, he murmured to Joan, "I could get used to this kind of respect."

"As a lady who is constantly having doors opened for her, I can say that it's overrated."

As they stepped into the hangar, even Malcolm, who had been in more than his fair share of hangars, was amazed at the colossal size of the hangar. The hangar itself continued nearly another 100 feet above the Daedalus, the ceiling held aloft by steel girders arching gracefully from one side to another. These girders held a number of very strong spotlights. A series of girders also ran the length of the hanger and seemed to hold a number of cranes and pulleys, apparently used to move heavy equipment or supplies. The ship was in the front quarter of the hangar. Spotlights shone on every inch of the topside of the ship, making the silver skin glow. Portable lights were brought along the side to illuminate the underside of the ship.

For the first time, Malcolm was able to truly assess the damage to the Daedalus. It looked like the shot must have hit the front of the bridge. To Malcolm's surprise, there were actually some pieces of the bridge still attached to the carriage of the ship. He could only imagine that the sudden destruction of the front of the ship must have created a small vacuum and sucked everyone out of the bridge to fall to their deaths in the ocean, if the explosion hadn't killed them first. In his mind, he could see the bridge the moment before. Captain Collins conversing with Commander Bromley, the navigator plotting the course—everyone attending to his duties. And the next, a blinding explosion with those nearest obliterated instantly, the sudden shock wave drawing everyone out.

A thought crept in Malcolm's brain. If the Daedalus had been shot at, the explosion would have blown into the cabin. There would be debris scattered inwards and people, although injured, would have been thrown back against the wall, not out the front. And when the Daedalus lifted suddenly from loss of weight, anyone left would be thrown back against the door.

That means the explosion came from within the Daedalus. Could it have been a mechanical failure? Not on my ship, was his first thought. But what systems ran through the front of the bridge? Electrical to some gauges, lighting and radio, heating, ventilation, and physical systems for the flight control. Nothing there that would be explosively combustible, even if some sort of chain reaction had occurred.

A loud, booming voice jerked Malcolm out of his thoughts. He followed the sound to a large man, whose stern face was framed by white hair above a high forehead and a large full beard and mustache. If he wasn't red faced from screaming at some poor crewman, he might look like Father Christmas.

Malcolm approached the man, putting on his polite face. "Hello, you must be Professor Zhukovsky. I'm Malcolm Robertson, Captain of His Majesty's Airship Daedalus," he said, offering his hand.

The professor looked at him disdainfully. "You must be very brave or very stupid to pilot such a death trap," he said in heavily accented English.

Malcolm's temper flared. No one insulted his ship. "Well, I assure you, Professor, that the ship was perfectly fine when we left England."

"Then you must be incompetent to bring it back here in such condition," sneered Zhukovsky.

"Incompetent? I'll have you know I rebuilt flight control and escaped two German zeppelins." Malcolm was about to blow. He could feel the heat rising in this face and he began to curl his hands into a fist.

"That horrible mess amidships? A monkey could do a better job."

"A monkey? Listen, you overbearing, know-it-all windbag. I've had about enough of your arrogant, overbearing attitude. I don't care if you're the father of aerodynamics or the Lord himself; no one talks that way about my ship or my engineering ability. If it weren't for engineers like me, your stupid theories would be absolutely useless. As the old adage goes, those who can do; those who can't, teach." Malcolm's face was now inches away from Zhukovsky's face.

Silence fell for several seconds as the two men glared at each other. Without warning, Zhukovsky broke into a grin and started laughing. With both hands he clapped Malcolm on the shoulders. "I like you. You are a man who says what he thinks. Come, let me show you something." Zhukovsky started toward the damaged cabin.

In utter confusion, Malcolm turned to Joan. "What the bloody hell just happened?"

"I don't know. I thought for a minute you were going to hit him and start an international incident. I couldn't think of anything to say to diffuse the situation."

"I thought I was going to hit him. Come on, we should see what he wants to show us."

"And Malcolm, this time try to keep your temper!" Joan urged.

"No promises," Malcolm said. They moved to where Zhukovsky was standing. He pointed to where the cabin ended.

"Look here," Zhukovsky pointed, "and here. Note how the wood seems torn. It means whatever destroyed the bridge came from inside the bridge."

"I thought the same thing when I saw the Daedalus from the outside," Malcolm said. "If we had been shot, we would see indications of shrapnel or splinters of wood."

"Exactly!" said Zhukovsky beaming as if a student had answered the question correctly. "Which means..."

"The explosion came from within the bridge," the two men said simultaneously. Zhukovsky looked at Malcolm. "You are a quick young man, almost as quick as I am. I see that you are an honest man who speaks his mind. I wanted to know whom I was dealing with before I showed you this. You know what this means, da?"

Malcolm nodded grimly and said, "Yes."

Joan looked confused. "What? What does it mean?"

Malcolm turned to her. "There's nothing in the bridge that could have caused the explosion. That means whatever caused the explosion was brought to the bridge. In other words, there's a saboteur aboard the Daedalus!"

Chapter 10

Zhukovsky and Malcolm began discussing the repairs over the blueprints of the Daedalus. Joan watched them and noted that although they were speaking English, she had no idea what they were saying. Several times, their discussion became heated over some point of engineering. She did almost have to intercede when the discussions came to the flight controls. Zhukovsky insisted that a modern airship should have modern controls instead of a ridiculous ship's wheel. Malcolm countered that if his predecessor had not forced him to put in a ship's wheel, they might not even be having this discussion. Zhukovsky then understood that what Malcolm wanted was not the wheel itself, but the redundancy that might be available. Zhukovsky smiled and said, "I like the way you think. I will give you your ship's wheel and I will give you a way to reconnect flight control levers and bypass the wheel from amidships." Soon, the men were back to discussing the myriad of details that had to be resolved to begin reconstruction of the bridge.

Joan stared at the gigantic ship that seemed almost a toy in this cavernous hangar. The repair crew had removed the makeshift windshield and she could see down the long main corridor of the cabin. A series of wires, pipes, and metal rods jutted out from under what would have been the floor of the cabin. She could see that the flooring was actually a series of metal plates with a series of metal honeycombs underneath. She watched with interest as repairmen took a strange tool that looked like a handle with two rubber ends on it, slapped it on the metal plating, and easily pulled up a section of the flooring.

It was amazing to her just how these ships were able to hold so much and travel so far. She had ridden in a zeppelin once and had been amazed that although it never felt that you were moving quickly, it was much faster than the same trip by train. The trip had a peaceful feel to it so she had imagined it was always like that. It never occurred to her that there would be explosions, frantic maneuvers, and even death on such a ship.

She returned to Malcolm and Zhukovsky who seemed to be finishing up. Zhukovsky was preparing to retire for the day. Blueprints were sticking out of a beaten brown valise and he had a load of notes and other papers held under one arm. He offered his hand to Malcolm. "Good night, my young friend. We will talk tomorrow afternoon. I have morning lecture."

"Thank you, Professor," he said, shaking the proffered hand.

"And maybe I bring back a real man's drink and we toast to the Daedalus," he chuckled.

"Oh, you mean whisky?" Malcolm said smiling.

"No, Vodka."

"You bring the vodka, I'll bring the whisky and we'll see which one is the real man's drink," said Malcolm.

"And I'll have to bring a wheelbarrow to collect the two of you when you both pass out," Joan quipped.

"I like her too," said Zhukovsky. "She is fiery!"

"Igrat' s ognem, i vy mozhete obzhech'sya starik!" she said. Malcolm looked at her, confused. She whispered, "Play with fire and you might get burned old man!"

"And she speaks Russian! Would you marry me?" he said. "Of course, I'd have to ask my wife first." He burst out in a deep laugh.

Zhukovsky kissed Joan on the cheek and was off with his bundle of papers. Joan turned to Malcolm and said, "That went much better than it started."

"Aye, he's an odd, old man. But in a strange way reminded me of my granda." He reached into his pocket and pulled out his pocket watch. "Bloody hell! Is it really that late? Perhaps you could direct us to the mess hall so we can get some food." Joan took the lead and guided them out of the hanger and across the base to the mess hall and barracks. As they reached the food line, it looked like they were beginning to break down mess. They were able to get some sort of meat, potatoes, cabbage, some sort of cold, thick, dark green soup and black rolls. The soups rather made Malcolm think of congealed engine grease. Dutifully, he took his food and found a place to sit. He stood, waiting for Joan, and pulled the chair out for her and had her seated before sitting himself.

"Before you ask what it is, try the okroshka, the soup. I know it looks hideous, but it is very good. Usually," she qualified, the reputation of military food preceding itself. Malcolm looked at the green slop hesitantly, took a spoonful, hesitated a second more, and put it in his mouth.

It had a distinctive sour taste, which wasn't unpleasant, mixed with cabbage and spices. "This isn't as bad as it looks," Malcolm said. He ate the rest of the soup, more out of hunger than a desire for the strange soup. "What did you call the soup?" Malcolm asked.

"Okroshka," she replied. "Do you like it?"

"Like may be too strong a word," he said. "Don't get me wrong, I can eat it, but I won't be going out of my way to order it." Malcolm looked doubtfully at the black roll, but bit into it. "This is actually quite good," he said, using the roll to sop up the remains of the soup. Malcolm had learned that it was eat what you were given in the Air Service or go hungry.

"It's rye bread. It's considered an uncouth and peasant bred in Europe."

"Must be that's why I like it," smiled Malcolm.

"Beg pardon?" asked Joan, confused.

"My grandfather was a blacksmith and tinker. My father worked in the Glasgow shipyards constructing ships. My grandfather wanted me to go to college. When he passed on, he had directed my father to sell the shop and use the proceeds for my education. That worked until my father was hurt in an accident at the shipyards and unable to work. I joined the Royal Navt so I could finish my engineering schooling. What about you and your family?"

"I come from a little less humble conditions. My grandmother was Wilhelmine Bayer, the mistress of Aleksandr II, Tsar of Russia. My mother was their child. She married my father, Richard Fleming St. Leger, a member of a privileged family. I grew up in Switzerland where I learned I had a gift for languages. I begged my father and he sent me to Zurich where I studied languages. A friend of my father, Mr. Holmes, took interest in my skills in language and offered me a chance to work for the British Home Office. I accepted and have since traveled around all of Europe, using my linguistic skills for the Empire."

Malcolm stared. Here he was, grandson of a blacksmith and son of a ship builder, having dinner, albeit a very simple one, with near royalty—someone who had travelled around the courts of Europe. Sometimes the world seemed a very strange place, Malcolm thought. Malcolm, realizing that Joan had stopped speaking and that he was staring, turned his attention to the rest of his meal. The rest of the meal was much more like the food Malcolm recognized from both home and the Air Service—meat, potatoes, and a vegetable. "This must seem very boring to someone like you who must eat at royal courts and what not."

"Frankly, I never cared for much of the 'refined' food. In my travels, I have made it a point to try to eat what the locals eat and by that, I mean the people who do the work and toil. I find that if you understand the food of the country, you understand its character. That's a big aid when dealing with other cultures."

"So, what would you learn from... this," Malcolm asked as he indicated his meal.

"The bread is simple and filling. They use everything wisely. Did you know that the main ingredient in your soup, kvass, is made from fermenting the very same bread you had with your meal? The foods they use—cabbage, pickled cucumbers, and root vegetables—are foods that keep for a long time during the long winter. They are tough, resourceful, patient, and resilient."

"That's fascinating! I never thought how food and culture were so intertwined. I wonder what you would say about haggis."

Joan laughed, "Like the Russians, the Scots, too, make the most out of whatever resources they have. I also think it is part of the Scots' perverse nature to love that which most people would disdain."

Malcolm laughed, "I think you're right." Malcolm could not help finding himself entranced with this woman. She was intelligent, fierce, and funny. Not to mention, very beautiful. He found himself again staring at her. He quickly said, "Well, Miss de St. Leger, I suppose I should escort you to your quarters. It wouldn't do for you to be walking unescorted around a base full of seamen." Suddenly, realizing how that sounded, he tried to recover, "I mean, I, well, I mean..."

Joan laughed as crimson embarrassment completely enveloped Malcolm's cheeks. "Thank you for your concern, gallant captain. I'm sure you can keep me safe from all of the seamen," she said, putting a special emphasis on the last word to make him blush even more.

"Come," she said, standing up and offering her arm for the escort. "And please, call me Joan when we're together like this. I do so hate formal titles between friends. Forgive me for being forward, but I do find you fascinating, Captain Malcolm Robertson."

Malcolm was dumbstruck. This beautiful, intelligent, scion of nobility found him fascinating? Malcolm chuckled to himself, wishing old Bromley could see him now. And then he felt bad for thinking ill of the dead. He said to her, "Thank you, Joan. I find you fascinating as well. Come, let us see about getting you to bed."

And at once, his face flushed red and he started to stammer.

Chapter 11

Malcolm managed to escort Joan to her quarters with no further faux pas. He returned to his quarters and realized that he was now exhausted from the day's activities. Had it really only been one day? In one day, he had met an archduke, received a commendation, seen the capital of a major European city, and met the most fascinating woman he had ever encountered. He almost blushed again, thinking about his poor choices of words, but she had taken it in stride. He was now tired and soon succumbed to sleep.

The next morning, he was up at dawn and about to go to the mess for a cup of tea when he saw Saxon dressed in athletic training clothes. "What are you up to, Commander?" Malcolm asked inquisitively.

"I was looking for some exercise. I was horribly afraid I might have to run or something. Do you fence, Captain?"

"Not much. I passed my required sword work for the Naval Academy, but I was never good."

"Well, you're lucky because I'm very good. And instruction will give me a workout. Go get changed and we'll have a fencing lesson."

Malcolm thought for a minute. "I think that's a capital idea, Commander. I'll be back in just a bit." Malcolm left and returned minutes later in similar athletic training clothes. Saxon opened a case containing two weapons—sabers, if Malcolm remembered the distinction correctly.

Saxon tossed him a fencing mask and jacket. "I chose the saber because it is the most nautical weapon we use in fencing. Alright, let's see what you remember from fencing class. En garde," he said, pulling his mask over his face and assuming guard position.

Malcolm likewise moved into guard position. He waited a heartbeat and then drove at Saxon, starting by feinting low, and then two swings high. He never connected, but soon felt the poke of Saxon's sword in his chest.

"I've seen worse," quipped Saxon, "but in his defense, he was blind."

"Ah, surely I wasn't that bad."

Saxon sighed. "Where to begin? Your grip, stance, footwork, and swings were all horrible."

"It has been a few years since I fenced."

"And it shows. We need to do some serious work with you. Let's start with the basics."

Saxon spent the next two hours pushing Malcolm through all of the mindless drills that reminded him exactly why he didn't fence anymore. First, it was reshaping his grip, and then countless minutes holding the blade straight out and perfectly still. And then it was long minutes of assuming the positions as Saxon barked them out: "Prime! Seconde! Tierce! Quarte! Quinte! Sixte!" Saxon corrected his posture in every position.

Finally, Saxon had had enough of torturing Malcolm and let him go shower and change so they could get breakfast. When the two men met again, Malcolm was moving notably slower. "I think I pulled something."

"Very likely. But you'll get used to it and soon it won't bother you."

"Bloody hell, you mean to do this every day?"

Saxon smiled. "I intend to. You told me about yourself at dinner; I'm trying to do the same. Although not rich, I was trained in fencing at an early age and it's one of my favorite pastimes. It keeps both the mind and body quick."

"You have a very funny idea of fun pastimes," muttered Malcolm.

"Says the man whose idea of a good night is reading technical journals," said Saxon, raising an eyebrow.

"Well, that's... touché, you've got me there," laughed Malcolm. "Come, let's see what delicacies our Russian friends are serving us. Did you have any of that soup last night?"

"The green stuff? No, I rather thought that was something you used in the engine room to lubricate the engines," he said disdainfully.

"It wasn't that bad," said Malcolm.

"You ate it? You truly are a brave man, Captain."

Today, the mess appeared to be serving a thick porridge called kasha. Saxon remarked, "Perhaps this was meant as an adhesive for the repair of the cabin and they delivered it to the wrong place," and instead settled for a few slices of toasted black bread, which he ate but did not seem to enjoy. Malcolm, on the other hand, enjoyed the kasha. Although it had many different grains, it reminded him very much of the oatmeal his ma would make when he was young. Malcolm knew that this stuff would stick in your stomach and keep you full for quite a while.

After mess, Malcolm sought out Mr. Frye, who true to his word, was at the hangar watching the repair work beginning on the Daedalus. Malcolm related his encounter with Zhukovsky the previous day and told Mr. Frye that under no uncertain terms should he back down from something he knew was right when talking with Zhukovsky. Malcolm said, "He likes to test people. He figures that if you're confident enough to challenge him, then you might know what you're doing. Then, you have to prove it." Frye looked uncomfortable at this and Malcolm said, "Don't worry, I intend to be here as much as possible, I just don't know what the ambassador or the Admiralty have in mind for me now."

After the same baptism of fire that Malcolm received when meeting Zhukovsky, Frye soon found his place and his voice in the afternoon meetings with Zhukovsky as they discussed first the repair of the Daedalus and then Zhukovsky's passion, aerodynamics. Malcolm had to admit that Zhukovsky was the pioneer in this field and although his research and theories were more suitable for heavier-than-air vehicles, Malcolm could easily see applications to make the Daedalus more maneuverable. Malcolm, Frye and Zhukovsky were soon discussing potential modifications to the Daedalus' rear airfoil and rudder to take advantage of Zhukovsky's work. Sometimes, the discussions were heated and passionate, but always respectful and, now that they understood one another, without the threat of physical violence. And all the while, Joan sat nearby watching men behaving like schoolboys planning a prank.

Soon, the days began to follow a certain rhythm. Early morning fencing with Commander Saxon followed by breakfast with Joan. Some days, Saxon joined them, other days he did not. Malcolm spent the rest of the morning seeing his men, making sure they were kept adequately busy and out of trouble. In the afternoon, Malcolm, Frye, and Zhukovsky argued and oversaw the rebuild of the cabin. When Zhukovsky left for the day, Malcolm escorted Joan to dinner where they talked, sometimes for hours, learning more and more about each other.

Through the course of their conversations, Malcolm suspected that Joan's skills and role in this mission were more than just that of a translator. From things she said and left unsaid, he had a feeling that she could take care of herself, had a quick mind, and could think her way out of many a dangerous situation. Malcolm's suspicions were confirmed one morning when to his surprise, Joan came to one of Malcolm's fencing lessons with Saxon. As with every lesson, it began with tedious drills consisting of Saxon calling out positions and Malcolm responding. Joan sat with a book, periodically looking up from her reading to watch the training. Malcolm's form was much better now and Saxon rarely needed to correct it or his footwork. Midway through the session, Saxon would join Malcolm. Saxon would call out the position he would use to attack Malcolm and it was Malcolm's job to pick the correct defensive position. Malcolm had become much better at this and the tempo for the drill had become steadily more rapid. The session would end with a small match, best two out of three. Many times, the match ended quickly after two rounds, or sometimes, if Saxon wanted the exercise, he would draw it out, casually blocking Malcolm's attempts until he bored of it, and would attack Malcolm.

That morning, the two rounds were over quickly. Malcolm, panting from the exertion of the day's practice said, "You're too good for me. I don't think I'll ever beat you."

"Oh, I wouldn't say that," said Joan, looking up from a book she brought to keep her company. "He's certainly an adequate swordsmen, but I've seen better."

"Miss de St. Leger, I'll have you know I've been trained by some of the finest swordsmen in all of Europe," Saxon said, somewhat disdainfully.

"Well, if I were you, I would seek my money back. I'm sure I could beat you."

"You?" he laughed. "A woman? Beat me? That's preposterous!"

"Care to put your talent to the test?" asked a bemused Joan.

"I usually don't make it a point to humiliate a lady, but if you insist, I must oblige," said Saxon haughtily.

"Very well, challenge accepted. Captain, if I may borrow your jacket and mask."

"They're very sweaty. Are you sure you want them?"

"That's fine. I won't need them for long," Joan said confidently.

Joan put the fencing jacket over her dress, removed her hat, and placed the fencing mask into position. She swung the saber around to get the feel of the weapon and when she was satisfied, she held the sword up in salute and move to en garde.

Saxon did the same. But before he could begin, Joan looked down and said, "Oh, dear, I seem to have torn my dress already."

Saxon pulled off his helmet and walked toward her "Are you sure? I heard..." and stopped midpoint in the sentence when he felt the tip of Joan's saber at his chest, directly over his heart.

"See?" she said looking at Malcolm. "I win."

"That was hardly fair and hardly..."

"Fights are seldom fair. And when dealing with real swords, you don't win by points. You win by surviving. Here's a lesson for you, Malcolm. Form and technique are important because they help you to master the weapon so you know how it works. But the best weapon in surviving a fight is your mind."

Saxon said nothing. He waited for her to remove his equipment. When she did, he snatched it from her, hastily packed them away and said perfunctory, "Good day." When he had left, Joan said, "Oh dear, our Mr. Saxon appears to be a rather sore loser."

Malcolm looked at her again, this time seeing a very dangerous woman. "Well, it wasn't a fair fight."

"That was rather the point of my lesson," she said. "Fair fights are for fools. Most people aren't as honorable as you or Saxon. I can tell, you are one who plays by the rules, does the right thing. But remember, in a fight there is no honor. Just death or victory."

"What would a young lady like you know about fights to the death?" asked Malcolm tentatively.

She smiled disarmingly. "Why, what are you talking about, Captain?" she said, batting her eyes. "I'm just a translator."

"I see," he said. He could tell he would get no more from her, but this woman was intriguing, without a doubt. "Come, let's get some breakfast," he said, offering his arm.

She grew deadly serious for a moment. "Remember what I said Malcolm, your best weapon is your mind," she said. Then, she smiled and took his arm.

Chapter 12

The weeks sped by quickly and soon the Daedalus was made whole, with a few improvements courtesy of the combined brains of Zhukovsky, Malcolm, and Frye. Malcolm was itching to try out the new improvements. He notified the ambassador that the ship was ready and he was going to take it out for a test flight. The reply baffled him. Under no circumstances was the Daedalus to leave the hangar until it was ready to leave for Tunguska.

Confused, Malcolm, accompanied by Joan and Saxon, took a coach to the embassy to gather more information about the order. Malcolm sat between the two. Joan, for her part, was trying to be warm and gracious. Saxon, on the other hand, still wanted nothing to do with her. It was a very long and silent ride.

When they arrived, the ambassador kept them waiting for over an hour and when he finally let them in to see him, he did not look pleased to see him. "What do you need? I'm very busy and don't have time for a social call."

"We're not here for a social call. We came because these orders make no sense. The repair crews worked around the clock so that the Daedalus is fixed and we can't take her out?"

"There have been... complications. It seems that the Germans have indeed figured out our little scheme. An attempt was made on Ernest Rutherford's life as he prepared to leave Stockholm for St. Petersburg. Mr. Davenport, who accompanied him, was killed. As a result, we are keeping security high. The Admiralty decided that we should keep the Daedalus under wraps until the expedition is ready. Mr. Holmes himself will accompany Professor Rutherford." At the mention of the name, he noticed Joan visibly start.

"Until Mr. Holmes and Professor Rutherford arrive in St. Petersburg, we need you and the crew of the Daedalus to keep a low profile. Stay at the aerodrome. The Admiralty has listed the Daedalus as missing in action and is orchestrating a hunt in the Baltic near your last known location."

"But, we're not missing!" scoffed Malcolm.

"You know that, I know that, the Admiralty knows that, but the Germans do not. They know you bloodied their noses, but they also know that the Daedalus had sustained major damage. The Admiralty hopes that the story of your disappearance will shake the Germans off your trail and allow us to get the expedition off in near secrecy.

"When Mr. Holmes and Professor Rutherford arrive, we'll send for you. But, I must ask, until then, please do not leave the aerodrome. I'm sorry that I cannot offer you more. Please excuse me; I have a number of other duties to attend to. Good day, gentlemen, Ms. de St. Leger," the ambassador said as he picked up a portfolio and hurried out of his office.

Malcolm was not pleased by this news. All he could think of was his mum and da who might think him lost. But, he had to concede, missing was better than dead. There was still a glimmer of hope the ship or survivors might be found. He also hoped that he would have the opportunity to offer the men liberty, but now that was clearly out of the question. They would have to remain at the base. Malcolm would have to find something for them to do.

The three returned back to the aerodrome in near silence. Only short, polite conversations broke the rhythm of the click clop of the horses pulling the carriage. Suddenly, the carriage came to a stop some distance away from the aerodrome. Malcolm shot a quizzical look to Saxon and Malcolm turned toward the door to see why they had stopped. Suddenly the door burst open and a man dressed in black, his face covered in black fabric save for his eyes, entered the carriage. He had a small revolver in his hand and pointed it immediately at Joan. From his seat, Malcolm dove immediately under the aim of the attacker and tackled him while pushing the man's arm up into the air as he struggled to reach the attackers gun. He managed to reach it and stuck his finger behind the trigger. The attacker tried to pull the trigger back, but instead crushed Malcolm's finger. Malcolm was sure he heard something snap and suddenly felt white-hot pain emanating from his hand.

Malcolm had the attacker down, but they still continued to wrestle for control of the revolver. As long as Malcolm's broken finger remained where it was, there was no chance that the gun could go off. Malcolm, on top, was able to pin the man down

The Reluctant Captain

with weight and had the leverage to keep the man from firing the gun.

Suddenly, Malcolm felt a white-hot stab of pain in his right side. He looked down and saw a knife stuck into his side, blood already beginning to gush out of the wound. The attacker had managed to draw a knife while Malcolm was focused on the revolver. Sensing Malcolm's distraction, he used the opportunity to throw Malcolm off him, pushing the dagger in for more affect. Malcolm howled in pain and watched as the attacker sat up, turned to Joan, and raised his revolver. There was a flash and a deafening sound as the shot rang out in the enclosed cabin of the coach. To Malcolm's amazement, the attacker fell back in a lump, a single perfect bullet hole in the center of his head. When he looked up, he saw that Joan was holding a very small one or possibly two shot revolver. It must have been hidden and all she needed was a second to retrieve it and for Malcolm to get out of the way so she had a clear shot.

Malcolm started to get up, but found his legs made of lead and he couldn't raise himself. "You alright?" he asked Joan. It was getting hard for him to concentrate between the pain of the finger that had been broken in the trigger and the pain in his side. Absently, he put his hand over the wound in his side, trying to staunch the flow of blood.

"Me? What about you, you idiot!!" she half-screamed, half-sobbed as she dropped to her knees to attend to him. "Saxon, signal the driver to get moving and take us back to the base as fast as possible." She pulled a handkerchief from her purse and pressed it against the wound. Saxon obediently rose, opened the door a crack and called to the coach driver to hurry at all possible speed to the aerodrome. Whatever obstruction had caused the coach to stop had apparently cleared. The coach lurched into motion, throwing everybody against the back of his or her seats.

"Nothing a little whisky won't fix," Malcolm said as his eyes slid closed.

Joan slapped Malcolm hard across the face. "Oww!! What was that for?" he mumbled.

"I'm trying to keep you alive, you silly man. What were you thinking tackling him like that?"

"I was thinking I didn't want to see that pretty face of yours with a bullet hole," he said. He suddenly felt very giddy, like he wanted to laugh.

"Obviously you weren't thinking, tackling him like that," she said.

"Shows what you know," he said. "I stuck my finger behind the trigger so he couldn't fire. See?" Lifting up the hand with the broken finger, he tried to focus on it. He wasn't sure, but he really didn't think it was supposed to bend that way. It would be funny, if everything didn't hurt.

"I think he's going into shock. Quick, get my wrap and cover him," she ordered Saxon.

"That's nice. It is so cold in here. Is it winter?" he said groggily as he was covered in the wrap.

"No, Malcolm. Now, don't close your eyes on me. Stay with me."

"Damn it, driver. Can you get this thing to move any faster?" Saxon yelled out the coach to the driver. Saxon could see that they were approaching the airfield. "We're nearly there. Hold on, Malcolm," he said, his voice filled with concern.

When the coach was within twenty yards of the gates to the airfield, Saxon jumped out of the coach and yelled to the guards to get the gates open immediately. The guards were startled at first, but soon complied. The coach barely had to slow down as it flew past the gates. Joan said to Malcolm, "I've got to talk to the driver. You stay awake while I'm gone."

"Alright," he said dreamily. As he lay there, the pain seemed to ease. He suddenly felt warm and very drowsy. He really wanted to sleep. But he'd promised Joan that he would stay awake. Maybe if I just close my eyes for a second, he thought.

Slap! Everything came back into sharp focus, as did the pain in his side, his hand, and now his cheek. "I told you to stay awake. I had to tell the coach driver how to get to the hospital. I leave you for a minute and here you are napping."

"Ow, that slap hurt. Who taught you how to fight? The Marquis of Queensbury?" he asked.

"You pull through this, you courageous idiot, and I'll tell you."

"It's a deal," he said.

The coach lurched to a halt, making Malcolm wince as it jostled him and the knife still protruding out of his side. Joan was afraid to remove it because it was doing a decent job of plugging the hole it made and she was afraid he might bleed out if she removed it. She jumped out of the coach and called for the guards to get orderlies as the captain was hurt and needed immediate assistance. Within twenty seconds, two large orderlies came out with a stretcher and tried to gently lift Malcolm onto the stretcher. He cried out in pain but soon relaxed. The orderlies immediately carried Malcolm into the building. Joan started to follow, but was barred by the guards. She tried to explain who she was and that she was needed to translate, but the guards would not let her in as she was a woman and not a soldier. "All that blood, it is no place for a woman," said one of the guards.

"Too much blood! Look at me, you stupid bastard! I'm covered in blood! And I was the one who put the hole in the head of the attacker. Now let me in!"

"Nyet," he said. "Not until we have orders."

Joan was mad and wanted to take her revolver out and shoot the stupid guard right there, but that wouldn't get her in to see Malcolm. She stood there shaking with fear and impotent rage. Seconds later, Saxon reached her at a sprint. "How is he?" he asked, trying to catch his breath. After getting the guards to open the gate, he ran at a full sprint to reach the hospital.

"They took him in and they won't let me in."

Saxon tried, also unsuccessfully, to gain admittance but was met with equal resistance. "Wait, I know. Do you know where Doctor Jenkins's quarters are located? He could get us in!"

"Yes! Of course!" said Joan. "Follow me!" She grabbed Saxon's hand and they ran to the officer's barracks. Fortunately, when they arrived, they found Dr. Jenkins in his quarters, reading. When they relayed what happened to Malcolm, he immediately grabbed his medical bag and followed them back to the infirmary.

When they approach the guards this time, they recognized Dr. Jenkins, but would not allow Joan and Saxon to come in until the doctor said, "Damn it men. I need these two to donate blood for Captain Robertson. Do you want his death on your hands because he couldn't get the blood he needed from the only two known donors?"

The guards hesitated for a second and then stepped out of the way. Soon the three were in the infirmary. Joan stopped an orderly and inquired about what had become of Captain Robertson. The orderly told them that he had been taken immediately to surgery. Joan told the orderly that Dr. Jenkins was the ship's surgeon on the Daedalus and would like to assist in the surgery. The orderly took the doctor off to prepare to enter surgery. When the orderly returned, he found Joan and Saxon a place to sit and wait.

Joan and Saxon slumped into the chairs and leaned against one another. Joan, now that the immediate crisis was over, let her guard down. Now, the dam of pent up emotion burst and the tears came in sobs. All she could say was, "That stupid man!" She repeated it as if a mantra as the tears flooded out of her.

Quietly, Saxon put an arm around her and pulled her close so that her head rested on his chest and let her cry. "It'll be fine. Doctor Jenkins is the best doctor in the fleet. He's in good hands." He didn't really know Jenkins' competence as a doctor, but assumed that if he was serving on the Air Service's flagship, he had to be at least competent.

"Really?" Joan sniffled. Her eyes were red from crying and her nose now started to take on a reddish color.

"Really," he said, laying his hand comfortingly on her head. "Nothing to do but wait," he said comfortingly.

"Nothing to do but wait," she whispered.

Chapter 13

Time seemed to drag on as Joan and Saxon waited for news of Malcolm. After an agonizing hour of waiting, hoping for the best and imagining the worst, Dr. Jenkins found them waiting. As soon as they saw him, Joan and Saxon jumped up and hurried to the doctor. "How is he? Is he..." said Joan.

"He's alright," interrupted the doctor. "He's stable. He lost a great deal of blood, but we stopped the bleeding and miraculously, no vital organs were punctured. He's a very lucky man. Assuming there's no infection, he should make a full recovery."

Joan slumped in visible relief. "Thank God! Thank you, doctor."

"There's really no reason to thank me. The base surgeon was the one who did all the work. He had experience with bayonet wounds, which isn't all that different. What in blue blazes happened?"

Saxon related how on their way back, the coach was stopped, the gunman boarded, and the struggle ended with the death of the mysterious assailant. "The gunman," said Joan. "We never searched the body for any clues."

"I think I heard them say a body was brought to the morgue, but my Russian is very rusty," said the doctor.

"You speak Russian?" asked Joan, surprised.

"A little. Picked some up when I served in the Crimea. Mostly curse words and medical jargon."

"Do you know where the morgue is?" asked Saxon.

"No, but we should be able to find it easily enough," said the doctor.

"When can I... we see Malcolm?" asked Joan.

"I'd let him rest overnight. He'll have to recover from the ether and the surgery. I suspect that he will be out until sometime tomorrow morning," the doctor said as he led them down the hall. He stopped an orderly and asked for directions to the morgue. The trio hurried through the hall to the morgue.

The body lay on a stretcher waiting for its autopsy, although the hole in the center of his skull from Joan's shot was the obvious cause of death. The mask had been removed from the man's face. He was in his early twenties, with blonde hair cropped close in what might have been a military haircut a couple of months ago. He was medium height and medium build—in most ways, nondescript. Joan and Saxon searched the body, finding numerous hidden knives and a single shot revolver in his boot, some coins and money, and little else. Joan looked next at the man's hands and noticed a ring on his right hand. When she examined it closer, she realized that it was a signet ring bearing a black cross, eerily similar to those on German airships.

"This man was a member of the Teutonic Knights," she said.

"The what?" asked Doctor Jenkins.

"The Teutonic Knights. An order that goes back to the Crusades. They have all but died out, except in Austria. The order is headed by one of the Hapsburgs."

"So that means Austria is in on this too?" asked Saxon.

"Apparently," replied Joan.

"So, we are being watched," said Saxon. "How could they know we were going to the embassy and how did they know where to ambush us?"

"Excellent questions," Joan replied, "and ones to which I don't have any answers."

Believing there was nothing further to be gained in examining the body and little or nothing they could do for Malcolm, the three were at a loss. Finally, Saxon suggested that they return to the Daedalus and inform the crew. They drifted back to the hangar. Again, the booming voice of Zhukovsky could be heard. When he saw Joan, he smiled and said, "Where is our lazy Scottish engineer? Lying in bed, eh?"

Joan quickly told the story of the attack, deliberately leaving out that she was the apparent target. Zhukovsky's face darkened. "This is not good. Why would someone attack Malcolm?"

Saxon looked at Joan and realized for the first time who had been the real target of the attack. "Malcolm wasn't..."

"...The type to take something like that sitting down," Joan cut in, glaring at Saxon and willing him to keep quiet.

"No, he wouldn't. Headstrong, that boy is. Come. Sit. I have vodka."

Saxon realized why she had cut him off and relented, for the time being. "I know I for one could use a drink after today," Joan said. Joan introduced Commander Saxon and Dr. Jenkins to Zhukovsky and they exchanged pleasantries. The four of them went to the desk where Zhukovsky kept his blue prints. From one of the drawers, he pulled a bottle of vodka and four shot glasses. They looked at him with surprise that he was prepared for so many people.

"What?" he asked. "Malcolm said he would make me drink that horrid whisky. I was going to give him, Mr. Frye, and our young lady vodka!" He poured four shots. "To Malcolm," he said holding his glass in salute.

"To Malcolm," they murmured. Saxon was soon sputtering, unprepared for the straight vodka. He had tried to sip it instead of throwing it back. Both the doctor and Joan knew how to drink their vodka—the doctor from his time spent abroad, and Joan from her family. Zhukovsky poured another round and this time, the three showed Saxon the trick to throwing back the vodka. Another toast to Malcolm, and the four of them tossed back the shots.

Before Zhukovsky could pour another round, Saxon begged off, saying he still had to inform the crew and thought it might be a good idea if he were more or less sober. He also realized that his clothes, like Joan's, were covered in dried blood and thought it an excellent idea if they changed. The doctor, Joan, and Saxon returned to the barracks to wash up and change. Saxon left word that the crew of the Daedalus should report at four bells to the hangar in front of the airship.

The Reluctant Captain

Saxon, feeling refreshed after taking a quick shower and putting on clean clothes, took a deep breath and addressed the assembled crew. "Crew. I have difficult news. Captain Malcolm Robertson was gravely injured in a fight as an unknown assailant attacked the coach carrying the captain, Ms. de St. Leger and myself back from the embassy." A murmur rose up from the crew. "The Captain is stable and resting and should be back to himself in the next few days. In his absence, I will be in command.

"Our current orders are to stay at the base and keep a low profile. As a result, no member of the crew, officer or enlisted, will be allowed to leave the base. Likewise, the Daedalus will remain hidden in its hangar until such time as we have new orders.

"I know this comes as a disappointment that no liberty passes will be issued, but I hope that you can appreciate the seriousness of our situation, especially given the attack on our captain. As ranking officer, everyone's safety is my first priority. There are obviously people that mean to do us harm and it's our responsibility to one another to make sure that does not happen. Thank you. Dismissed."

Saxon walked over to Joan who had been standing some distance away from the assembly. "Do you have a moment, Miss de St. Leger?"

"Yes. What is it, Commander?"

"Who are you really? And why was the attacker after you?" he asked.

Joan had known this was coming, ever since she had cut him off while talking to Zhukovsky. "This isn't the right time or place to discuss that, Commander," she said, using her eyes to indicate the large number of crewmen still milling about the hangar.

"Fine. Where do you suggest then?" he asked.

"Perhaps you'd escort me to the hospital so that we can check on Captain Robertson? We can talk on the way there."

"Very well," he said, offering his arm.

They left the hangar and when there was no one in sight, Joan began. "You think that the attack today was meant for me?"

"I'm certain of it. The attacker pointed his gun directly at you."

"It is known that I am your translator. Perhaps he meant to disrupt your mission."

"Perhaps," he said, skeptically. "But that doesn't explain the derringer and your expert shot."

"I am a woman, but I know that the world is a dangerous place. I keep it for self-defense."

"So you say," said Saxon, still unconvinced. "I haven't forgotten your little display during our fencing lessons. You know something of sword play and fighting as well."

"My father was in the military. He made sure that I knew how to defend myself."

"And that's your story?"

"Indeed."

"Very well. I believe we are here."

They arrived at the hospital and were let in this time, having received orders that they should be allowed to visit Captain Robertson. They arrived to find Malcolm still asleep. He was still pale, but he no longer had the deathly pale pallor he had had when they arrived there and his breathing was regular and strong.

They were able to find the doctor who told them that Malcolm's condition was unchanged. He had not developed a fever, which was a good sign that there was no infection. He seemed well on his way to recovery. He believed that Malcolm should awaken sometime tomorrow morning.

They bade the doctor farewell as Saxon escorted Joan to her quarters. They were silent on the trip back to the barracks. As they arrived at the door to her quarters Joan turned and said,

"Thank you for accompanying me, Commander Saxon. After today's events, it's nice to have a strong arm to rely on to keep me safe."

"It's my duty as both an officer and a gentleman," said Saxon. "Good night Miss. de St. Leger."

"Good night, Commander Saxon," she said, as she entered her quarters.

As he walked away, Charles Saxon thought, "The day she needs my protection to keep her safe will be the day pigs fly."

Chapter 14

The next morning, Malcolm awoke and it felt like a train had run over him. It seemed every muscle hurt, but worse was the throbbing pain in his left hand and the burning pain on his side. As his eyes open, he found Joan sitting in a chair next to him holding his hand in her gloved hands.

For a moment, in his disorientation, he thought she was in his quarters and here he was barely dressed. He started to sit up, but the pain in his side was intense. As he tried to pull the bed covers further around him, he saw a splint and cast around his left index finger. He fell back to the bed and realized that he wasn't in his quarters. "I'm in a hospital, aren't I?" he asked.

"You're damned lucky you're not in the morgue. That was a damn stupid thing you did. Do they not teach you self-defense in the Air Service?"

Malcolm looked bewildered. Hadn't he risked his life to save hers? He thought that there might be a better reward for his gallantry than a lecture. "Yes, well, I did manage to stop him from shooting you, didn't I?" he said, indicating his splinted finger.

"Yes, only so he could stab you. And I should remind you, I was the one who shot him and saved your life."

"Well... yes, I suppose that's true... but..."

"No buts, Malcolm. Look, I am very grateful for your attempt to save my life, but I'm afraid I'm going to have to tell you a hard truth. You are not a fighter. It's not in your temperament. You're competent, but you would never prevail against trained assassins physically. You're too old and you don't have the training."

"So, I'm bloody useless, then," he said with a note of hostility.

"Absolutely not. You're not using your greatest weapon. Your mind. You have a way of looking at a problem and seeing a solution that is not obvious to anyone else. Your escape from the Germans was exactly what I'm talking about. Few would think to act more crippled than you were, provoke the Germans into attacking and then, with the tricks of engineering and aerodynamics, escape the German attack. Do you see what I mean Malcolm? You were outgunned and out-positioned, but you managed to singlehandedly defeat two German airships."

"Well, I didn't do all that by myself. I had a little help."

"True, but the idea was all yours. Look, Malcolm, all I'm asking is that you think before you react. Like you did with the Germans."

"So I should have let him shoot you while I thought of something?" he said.

"Well, something other than throwing yourself at him in front of his gun. But I will give you credit for thinking of putting your finger behind the trigger so he couldn't fire."

"So, Miss Tactician, please tell me what I should have done."

"For starters, distraction would have been appropriate. Failing that, you should try to immediately disable him instead of going for the gun. An unconscious man can't fire a gun. And what you also failed to notice is that I had already drawn my derringer and was about to shoot when you tackled him. You're very lucky I didn't shoot you."

"That would have been embarrassing. Being shot by the person I thought I was rescuing," he said, with a hint of smile.

Joan laughed, "I imagine it would be."

Malcolm looked at her and said evenly, "You're not just a diplomat. You work for the Secret Service Bureau, don't you?"

"What? That's preposterous! I'm a woman. Espionage is a man's work."

"And as my granda would say, 'Pull the other one, it has bells on it!' I have had dealings with them before. Prior to becoming chief engineer, I had a stint as radio officer. We had one on our ship. Always sending special, apparently nonsensical messages. Since all we had was a wireless telegraph, he was forced to use one of the radio officers to key his messages. I knew."

"And then there are the signs," he said. "You are aristocratic, move in circles most people can never reach, you speak almost every language on the continent, and you know how to use a saber and a gun. As a beautiful woman, you can dazzle men with your beauty and get them to say almost anything. And, I saw you react when the ambassador said that Mr. Holmes would be coming here. A certain M. Holmes was the person to which the Secret Service member sent his telegraphs."

"Is my cover blown so quickly?" she said, astonished. "I think I managed to allay Saxon's doubts, but he didn't see the other signs. Not only are you very smart, you're very observant."

"So, now, is this the part where you have to kill me because I know?" he asked.

She smiled. "Sadly, yes," she said as she suddenly produced a derringer.

Malcolm thought at first she was kidding, but her eyes showed no hint of humor. He remembered he had a glass of water next to his bed. He quickly grabbed the glass, threw the water in her eyes and pulled an empty bedpan from under the bed and swung it at her head as his other hand reached for the gun.

The bedpan connected and sent her sprawling, as Malcolm was able to wrench the gun out of her hand. He now had the gun pointed at her with the bedpan clenched in his other hand, ready to use it as a shield. Two orderlies came rushing at the sound. He used his gun to wave them away and they wisely complied. His side was on fire and his hand throbbed, but he had her.

"So what should I do with you, Miss de St. Leger? I can't very well shoot you, but I can't very well have you trying to kill me every time my back is turned. Tut," he said as she started to move. "I would move very slowly and carefully if I were you. If I report you to the ambassador, I'm only going to end up with someone else that I don't know. I prefer to keep my enemies in the open where I can see them."

"Malcolm, I'm not your enemy here. We're on the same side."

"Then explain to me how you killing me is in my self-interest?"

"My orders are to eliminate anyone who could compromise the mission. I was hoping it wouldn't come to this."

"And how is my knowing your identity going to compromise the mission?"

"It might not, but I don't like to take chances. You were suddenly elevated to captain...." she said.

"You think I *wanted* to become captain? Are you out of your bloody mind woman? I'm an engineer, that's all I wanted to be. I was happy where I was. I don't want to be the one responsible for all the lives on that ship; I don't want to be the one who has to make life or death decisions. And the only thing I've gotten since becoming captain is more work that I don't understand how to do and a bloody attempt on my life! DO YA THINK I WOULD CHOOSE THAT ON PURPOSE?!" he yelled. That got the attention of the orderlies who came over. Malcolm put his hand up and indicated that all was well.

"Someone had a clear motive to eliminate the bridge crew and command structure."

"For your information, I was supposed to be on the bridge. I was summoned to the bridge moments before the explosion, but I was in the middle of fixing the engines and I was delayed. If I had been there, the top three officers of the ship would have been killed."

"Interesting, anyone who can back up your story?"

"Everyone in the engine room at the time that Commander Saxon delivered the message."

"Commander Saxon, you say. And who would have been next in line had you been on the bridge?"

"Commander Saxon.... you're not saying that he's responsible."

"He has a motive. Whether it's the motive is left to be seen."

"So where does that leave us?" he asked.

"A very good question. You seem to be holding all the cards, as they say," she said, indicating the gun.

"True. I propose a truce. I won't kill you now, you promise not to kill me until either the mission is over or I betray you. Fair enough?"

She regarded him. "Fair enough. May I have my derringer back?"

"Only if you promise to keep hold of it," he said as he handed the derringer to her.

She quickly put the derringer out of sight. She touched her head gingerly, "I do believe that was the first time I have been hit by a bedpan."

"Thank your stars that it was empty!"

Chapter 15

Malcolm continued to convalesce and Commander Saxon took charge of the men. He asked for, and received, the twenty Russians who would be joining them on the journey to Tunguska. He had the men continue their duties and shifts aboard the Daedalus, and no day was complete with at least one inspection and drill.

Each day, Malcolm gained strength and could walk a little farther. But he felt useless. Saxon seemed to be doing a masterful job with the crew and Mr. Frye had the engines purring. After a week, he was able to tour the new bridge of the Daedalus and see the results of the work.

The work was amazing and, at first glance, one wouldn't know that the bridge had been changed. Upon closer inspection, it was obvious that Malcolm, Zhukovsky, and Frye had made some changes. Captain Collins had liked brass finishing because it looked nautical. Malcolm had suggested, and the others agreed, that they should attempt to replace any brass with aluminum where appropriate. Aluminum was much lighter and usually had sufficient strength for most tasks, especially trim.

Malcolm, Zhukovsky, and Frye had taken the opportunity to reorganize the bridge according to function and not looks. Malcolm's ship wheel sat at the center of the front of the bridge. Compass, air speed, level, and altitude gauges were on a panel to the left of the wheel in shared space where the navigator could monitor course and speed for plotting course headings. Next to the navigator's position, extending backward was a new chart table where the trio built a frame of clear glass that would fit over the charts. The navigator could then use a wax pencil to mark course without marking the original map. To the right of the wheel was the engine speed control. On the panel in front were gauges for each of the engines including revolutions and temperature; also included was generator output and helium levels. There was a position here where an engineering officer—or captain, thought Malcolm—could keep track of the ship's status. Continuing along the right wall was a radio station that could, like the main radio station, patch messages through to any section of the ship. Part of the radio station included a new ship's bell for signaling the time and the official ship's clock. Malcolm and Frye had tinkered with parts of an old analog computator and managed to automate the job of signaling the bells via the radio to every location on the ship.

Malcolm walked to the wheel and held it in his hands. It was a big wooden wheel with spokes on the outside. He pushed gently against the wheel and could feel that flaps were lifting. Pleased, he put his hand on the speed control lever and imagined putting it to full speed ahead. And when he looked, he was dismayed. The speed control was a jumble of strange and backward appearing letters. Bloody hell, he thought. The whole thing is in Russian. And with that, he looked more closely at all of the gauges. They, too, were in Russian. For the numeric gauges, it wasn't as much of an issue, but for the compass, it was a challenge. Gone were the familiar north, south, east, and west, replaced by the confusing C, a figure that looked like a fish, a B, and something that looked like a 3. Malcolm made a mental to note to have Joan provide translations for these gauges and for the speed control lever.

Satisfied that the ship would be ready to take off when given the word, Malcolm returned to his office. He sat at the captain's desk and found it devoid of anything. Commander Saxon had taken the reports while Malcolm was recuperating, and there was no captaining to do or engineering work to discuss. Malcolm sat at the desk, trying to figure out what to do next when there was a knock on the door. "Come in," said Malcolm, trying to look busy with captain's business.

Doctor Jenkins opened the door. "I hope I'm not interrupting anything, but I saw you come aboard and I thought I'd check on you."

"I'm fine, doctor. I am cleared to be out and about."

"That's not what I meant. A man has his first brush with death, it tends to have an effect."

"That? I'm fine, I guess. I feel a bit like Captain Duff—useless. Saxon seems to have the crew in good shape and Frye has the ship in excellent shape. I feel completely useless. The one thing I know how to do is no longer my responsibility and the thing I'm supposed to do, I have no idea how to begin."

The Reluctant Captain

"You can do it, Malcolm. The crew likes you. They don't know you as captain yet, but they realize that the only reason they are here and not in some prison in Germany is because of you. There was genuine concern when Saxon announced you had been attacked. If the rumors are correct, Saxon had to intervene to stop a number of them from going AWOL to go find the people who attacked you."

Malcolm smiled. That was good to know, but he had no idea what he had done to engender such loyalty. The smile quickly faded. "Doctor, I am at an utter loss. I find that everything I know is useless and everything I thought about the way things would be is bloody wrong. Even people aren't all they appear." He thought of Joan but immediately stopped talking, in fear he might give more away.

"It's natural," said the doctor. "You've had a brush with death and all of a sudden, you see your life in a new light. You begin second guessing yourself and re-examining your choices. That's valuable, to a point. But when all you're doing is gazing at your navel, it's time to buck up and do your job."

"But..." started Malcolm.

"No buts, Captain. You are a captain in the British Air Service. You have a duty to His Majesty and to the men under your command. Here's my prescription: get stinking drunk tonight and feel bad for yourself. Tomorrow morning, when you feel like hell, kick yourself in the ass and take command of this ship again." Dr. Jenkins turned to leave. "If you need help with either part of the prescription, come see me." As he closed the door, he turned to say, "Although personally, I'd rather help you with the first half."

Malcolm decided to comply immediately with the doctor's prescription. He made his way to his quarters—the captain's quarters. Although Malcolm had his effects moved here, it still firmly reflected the previous owner. It was dark, with the wood stained a deep mahogany. Brass was used in any conceivable place that metal should be found. The lighting fixtures, the radio handset, and the picture frames all were brass. The fabrics used to cover upholstery were deep burgundy, maroon, and gold. Malcolm felt like the room had a dignified and solemn tone, two words he knew would never describe him.

For the first time, Malcolm sat down at the small writing table the captain kept in his quarters. He opened the one drawer of the desk and found, among sheets of stationary and fountain pens, an envelope addressed to "The next captain of the HMS Daedalus."

Malcolm opened the letter and started to read, startled by the fact that it was written on the night before the explosion that took the captain's life. It read:

"To the next captain of the HMS Daedalus,

I write this letter as helpful advice to next captain of the HMS Daedalus. I have decided to retire upon completion of this mission. Before I do, I want to leave some parting words and advice for the next captain.

Being a captain is a very lonely job. You must, to some extent, remain aloof from your crew so as not to encourage favorites. In the end, your decisions affect the lives and well-being of every person on this ship. You will need to find someone who can listen to you and provide you the truths you don't want to hear. For me, that man was Dr. Edward Jenkins. He's wise and a good judge of people. And, God help him, cantankerous enough to give you the truth unvarnished. My advice is to listen to him, or find someone else just like him.

The Daedalus has a first-class crew and is capable of nearly running itself. Although it seems like you will need to do nothing to keep the ship running, ignore this temptation. In many ways, the captain is the rudder of the ship. It can move, it can rise and fall, but without a rudder, it will get nowhere. And with the rudder, a light hand is needed. You will face hard resistance if you force the crew to your will; better to make them think it's their idea.

Although a light hand is needed in directing the crew, discipline is important. Demand the very best from your men. And knowing the crew of the Daedalus, they will comply. Drills and inspections seem stupid and bureaucratic. The repetition of drill will make the crew react by instinct when fear might otherwise overpower them. Inspection makes sure that the ship itself is ready for anything that may be required. And the Lord himself knows how much I hate doing them, but they are critical to a well-functioning ship.

In all likelihood, this letter is addressed to Arthur Bromley who I will have recommended for promotion when I retire. To Arthur, I address the following to you: You are an excellent officer and it's been my pleasure to have you as my executive officer. But for you to succeed as a captain, you must do one thing—you must start treating Lt. Commander Malcolm Robertson with the respect he deserves.

I know you look down on his peasant manners and Scottish upbringing. But Malcolm represents the future of the Air Service. There are few of us officers from the important families and perhaps that is for the best. We have both seen for ourselves what can occur when people with titles buy commissions and then lead the men into disaster. When I was younger, I thought breeding was the determination of a man's worth. But in my life in the service, I have seen highborn men become cowards while men of so-called low birth perform acts of heroism and valor worthy of an epic poem. It's taken nearly a lifetime for me to see that what matters is not a man's social standing or if he knows what utensil to use in a formal dinner, but what's in his heart.

You would do well to listen to Robertson, Arthur. He is unconventional, yes, but he sees everything as a problem that can be solved and he has a mind that can usually solve it. Whether anyone else knows it or not, he has single-handedly saved this ship on more than one occasion by using that unconventional thinking to repair a critical system, provide us with just enough power to escape, or return control to the bridge at the critical moment. I've probably done him a grave disservice by not recognizing his contributions more openly, but I did not want to contend with the backlash I would receive from you.

Whether we like it or not, Arthur, Malcolm is the future of the Air Service. We will need bright young men to take our places someday, and they will have to come from somewhere. People like Malcolm who have worked their way up from nothing will no longer be the exception, but the rule. I suggest that you re-evaluate your feelings towards Robertson and find a way to work together.

In the end, whoever is captain of the Daedalus will need to be his own captain and he can disregard my advice. But I only ask that you consider the advice from someone who has spent his life in the service.

Being captain may be the hardest job in the Air Service, but it has its own rewards as you bring your airship back from a mission with all hands and you know you've done your duty for king and country to the best of your ability. The feeling is indescribable.

Good luck and Godspeed to the captain of the Daedalus!

Yours,

Edward Collins"

Malcolm put the letter down and was astonished. He had never known how the captain had viewed him or that the captain even had an opinion on the feud that Bromley had with Malcolm. He went to the cabinet where he had stored the Auchentoshan and poured himself a glass of the whisky. He settled into the chair with his whisky and re-read the words of Captain Collins.

As he read, he could see how truly lonely Captain Collins was and he now understood Dr. Jenkins more than he did before. Malcolm had never understood the captain's mania for drills and inspections, but he now saw it as his way to make sure his men were prepared. Malcolm was pleased to know that Captain Collins hated performing inspections and drills as much as Malcolm did.

The thought that the captain was the rudder on a ship where everyone knew his duty intrigued Malcolm. He knew he had to keep that in mind, especially when he despaired that everything seemed to be happening without him. Malcolm thought about having the doctor join him, but decided against it. Tonight it would be him, Captain Collins, and the Auchentoshan.

Chapter 16

The next morning, Malcolm rose and decided to follow the advice from the letter immediately. He went to the mess and was happy to find beans, tomatoes, and eggs on the menu. After he got a mug of black tea, he took his tray and sat at a table where several crewmembers sat. He chatted with the crew, many saying that they were glad he was up and around. As he sat, he tried to listen to what they weren't saying—that they were sick of the waiting. They either wanted to be out on leave or on the mission, whatever that was. He thanked them for their well wishes and when he was finished, went to Commander Saxon's quarters where he found the commander hard at work in scheduling the day's activities.

"Good morning, Commander. Why don't you bring that to the captain's office and we can go over today's activities?"

"Captain", said Saxon, standing at attention, "I didn't realize that you had been released to return to duty."

"At ease, Commander. I've released myself. I've been sitting around far too long watching everyone else do all of the work. Let's go over the schedule you've worked up for the day and then notify senior officers that we'll have a staff meeting at the end of first watch. I'll expect reports on our current status and readiness to leave when we receive liftoff orders. Speaking of which, has there been any news on our departure date while I've been out of things?"

"None yet. Although I do believe that Miss de St. Leger returned to the embassy yesterday with an armed escort, so I believe something is in the works."

Malcolm nodded. "Very well, if she happens to return before our staff meeting, please send her to my office. When you're set, bring the schedule and your report of what has happened since I was injured."

"Very good, Captain."

"Thank you, Commander," Malcolm said as he left the commander's quarters. He felt a little more like a captain and the rudder on the ship, but he tried to ignore the nagging voice in the back of his head that told him he couldn't pull this off.

Some time later, Commander Saxon entered Malcolm's office. Malcolm listened carefully to Saxon's report and asked a few questions for clarification. When Saxon finished, Malcolm said, "Thank you, Commander. Excellent work."

"Thank you, sir. I thought that giving the men something to do would keep their minds off of being stuck here and your attack. Some of the men were quite... agitated."

"Very good thinking, Commander. I intended on building on what you started."

"Building on what I started? I don't understand, "said Saxon.

"I want to continue the drills and inspections, but also create new drills. For instance, I want Frye and his men to be able to establish auxiliary flight controls quickly; I don't intend for a repeat of our adventure with the Germans. I want to keep up the inspections so that whoever bombed the bridge does not get a second chance to do it."

"I'm... surprised, Captain. I know you haven't been captain for very long, but that never seemed to be something you were interested in doing."

"You're right, Commander. Let's say I have had a change of heart. Almost dying from a stab wound has a miraculous way of changing your thinking. And I received some excellent advice recently."

"Very good, sir."

"Let's go pay a surprise visit to the engine room. I daresay I think I know where we can find a few things out of regulations."

The two officers arrived in the engine room. At first the crew did not react, as accustomed as they were to seeing him in the engine room. Malcolm raised his voice. "Is this the way you react when the commanding officer comes to the engine room? ATTENTION!" Although confused, the crew quickly snapped to attention. Mr. Frye, who had been working on an engine part, looked up and said, "Hello, Captain. Give me a second, I just need to..."

"I said 'Attention' Mr. Frye. That is an order, not a request at your convenience!" Malcolm yelled. His vehemence surprised even himself.

Frye dropped the wrench he was holding and jumped to attention. The clatter of the wrench on the metal flooring seemed like an explosion. Malcolm and Saxon proceeded to inspect the engine room from top to bottom. The engine room seemed to be the model of organization and efficiency, until Malcolm walked to a space behind the main engine housing that contained a closet. Malcolm, knowing what would happen, opened the closet and quickly stepped out of the way. As the door opened, an avalanche of parts and metal flowed out of the closet and across the floor of the engine room. "What is this, Mr. Frye?" he asked, indicating the pile of metal parts lying on the floor.

"As the captain is well aware, that's spare parts closet A," Mr. Frye said with teeth clenched. He didn't understand what Malcolm was doing. He had seen Malcolm cover any multitude of sins by throwing things in the closet so that they could pass inspection. Why was he persecuting him?

"And don't regulations require the parts to be stored in a manner where they are easily identified and available?" he said.

"Yes, sir," Frye said through gritted teeth.

"Very good. I expect this to be shipshape by the next time I visit. And Mr. Frye, please report to my office in another hour. Return to your duties, gentleman."

After they left the engine room, Commander Saxon remarked, "You knew what was in that closet, didn't you?"

"Of course. I put it there myself."

"But why the engine room?" asked Saxon.

"I'm setting a precedent. No area receives special preference, even the engine room. I want to put a little fear into the men. I need them to be prepared for anything. I don't like the way this mission has gone so far and I want to make sure everyone is as prepared as they can be. And if it means being called a heartless bastard by the crew, I can live with it."

"Shall we have a surprise inspection of the gunnery section? I may know which closets also hide a few skeletons."

"An excellent idea, Commander. Lead on." Malcolm and Saxon repeated the surprise inspection in artillery, this time with Commander Saxon pointing out non-regulation items camouflaged from view if someone wasn't a gunnery officer. Malcolm likewise ordered the gunnery crew to get things shipshape and ordered Gunnery Officer Brown to his office immediately after Frye.

After the inspections, Malcolm returned to his office to review Saxon's reports. He could tell there was buzzing around the ship. Everyone was hustling around looking very busy. Malcolm had guessed right. News of the inspections in the engine room and gunnery had spread rapidly through the crew. They knew that Malcolm meant business and things were going to be strictly Air Service again. Soon, there was a knock on the door and Mr. Frye came into the room and saluted sharply. Malcolm returned the salute and promptly said, "At ease, Mr. Frye. Please sit."

Frye looked ready to speak and Malcolm held his hand up. "No, let me speak first Mr. Frye. I'm sure you think it's horribly unfair that I pulled a surprise inspection in the middle of your maintenance work and then opened our hidden junk closet, where I myself used to hide things I didn't want found during inspection."

"Yes, sir."

"And you would be right, it was unfair. But, I want to be clear about one thing Mr. Frye. This is not about you or the quality of your work. What this is is a signal to the crew; a signal that things will no longer be lax and no department is exempt."

"I don't understand," said Mr. Frye.

"With all of the time we've spent here, we've become lax. Mr. Saxon started bringing the discipline back by having the crew work as if we were underway. I want the crew to know that we have to be nearly perfect. The reason I opened the closet is I realized that if we needed a part suddenly, you and I are probably the only two people on the ship who know where it might be and what it looks like when we find it. I think that that might not be good enough anymore. And regulations, God help us, insist on everything having a place where it's clearly marked. I don't want you to get disheartened Mr. Frye, you are doing a fine job. Other than the fact that our whole bridge is in Russian, the repairs and improvements you carried out with Zhukovsky are first rate. And you have my thanks. What I want from you for now is to put on a brave face about the inspection and just make sure everything, and I do mean everything, is shipshape when I conduct another surprise inspection in, shall we say, three days?"

"Yes, sir," Frye said, somewhat relieved.

"You're dismissed, Mr. Frye," Malcolm said.

"Just one question sir, if I may sir?" asked Frye.

"Yes?" asked Malcolm.

"Why the sudden change for discipline and order? You were never like that in the engine room." asked Frye hesitantly, afraid he'd overstepped his boundaries.

"A couple of reasons. I've recently been reminded that things are seldom what they seem. And I've been reflecting on what happened over the Baltic and realized that we were very lucky—lucky that I had accidentally built a bypass for flight control, lucky that I knew how to fix it and knew where the parts were to fix it. If you remember, I had been summoned to the bridge and delayed going there. I could have been on the bridge when the explosion occurred and where would the Daedalus be?

"That's why I want people to share knowledge and make sure everything, and I do mean everything, is labeled within an inch of its life. I intend to run drills until you can perform the skills in your sleep. For the simple reason that you might very well have to perform them under stress or when you're extremely tired.

"I won't lie to you Mr. Frye. This mission seems easy and straightforward, but I have a feeling in my gut telling me this will not go well. I want to make sure that we're ready for anything that might come out way."

"Thank you, sir," Mr. Frye said as he turned to leave. He saluted smartly, and this time Malcolm thought he discerned a more respectful manner in the salute. Malcolm returned the salute and as Mr. Frye shut the door, he just hoped he was doing the right thing.

Chapter 17

Malcolm had a very similar conversation with a very nervous Gunnery Officer Brown, who Malcolm thought would either vomit or just pass out. After Malcolm repeatedly assured the young lieutenant that he would not be court-martialed or even reprimanded, the young officer finally seemed to relax to the point where he could understand Malcolm.

An hour after the lieutenant left, there was a knock at the door. "Enter," replied Malcolm, still looking at his reports.

Joan de St. Leger entered. "You know I could have come in and shot you while you're staring at the report."

"Not before I shot you with the gun that is even now pointing at you from under this desk. I think its trajectory might be excruciatingly painful were it to impact," he said nonchalantly.

"Very good. You are a fast learner. A little too fast," she remarked, rubbing her cheek where Malcolm had hit her with his bedpan.

Satisfied she wasn't going to kill him, he returned the gun to its holster under the desk and stood. After his tussle with Joan in the infirmary, he had attached a holster to the underside of his desk and had taken to putting his service revolver there when he was in the office. He had learned the lesson of never knowing who was after him. "Please, have a seat," he said.

She crossed to the seat and Malcolm watched her in spite of himself. Her auburn hair was mostly tucked under a rust-colored hat that matched her jacket and skirt. He could see the petticoat move under the skirt. He held the seat for her as she sat. He could smell her perfume and the fresh smell of soap. He shook his head to try to clear it and returned to his seat.

"What may I do for you, Miss de St. Leger?" he asked.

"Please, just call me Joan. I don't want you to hold a grudge just because I tried to kill you. Besides, you struck me, a woman, with a bedpan."

"Something I'm not altogether proud of, Joan."

"Men," she muttered. "Try to kill them just once and they act like babies."

"Excuse me?"

"Nothing, just making a note to myself."

"To what do I owe this visit?" he asked.

"I've been asked to inform you that the members of the expedition will be arriving tomorrow and that we are scheduled to liftoff at 1900 hours."

"In the dark? You do know that nighttime takeoffs are more difficult than day time?" he said, raising an eyebrow.

"Yes, but the Admiralty feels that leaving under the cover of darkness might allow us to escape unnoticed. It's also to be a dark take off. No lights of any kind."

"Has the Admiralty lost their bloody minds?" he asked. "Do you know what you're asking?"

"If you don't believe me," she said, reaching into her bag. Malcolm's hand went under his desk to the handle of his revolver. She smiled, slightly amused, and pulled out a sheath of papers and placed them on his desk.

Malcolm's hand returned from under the desk and he was perusing the papers. "What's all this?" he asked.

"Orders for the mission, crew and cargo manifest, and storage requirements for the object's retrieval and return."

Malcolm scanned the papers. As he looked at the cargo manifest and the requirement that they keep nearly two tons available for retrieval of the object, he realized that Mr. Frye was going to have a great deal of fun with the ballast calculations for the trip. Looking at the cargo manifest, Malcolm found drills and other mining equipment. Add to that a myriad of scientific equipment, some of which Malcolm recognized, and others that were beyond him. His eyes lit on one item: "1 zoological catalog, insects (live)." He looked up in disbelief.

"Yes?" she asked bemused.

"A live bug collection? Why in the bloody hell do we need one of those on board?" he asked.

"Professor Kolstov is a biologist, geneticist, and zoologist. Based on the sketchy information available from the landing at Horsell Common, it was conjectured that the aliens might be similar to insects. As a result, the professor insists he have his catalog for comparison. It was also conjectured that they may share some characteristics with cephalopods, but we can't very well bring live octopi on board, so those will remain preserved in formaldehyde."

"Obviously," Malcolm said sarcastically. He returned to the papers. "Anything else I should know before I make preparations."

"Yes. It is vitally important that all of the scientists are assigned very similar cabins. They are highly competitive; any perceived advantage to one will be taken as slights by the others. They are men of tremendous intelligence, and unfortunately, also tremendous egos. Each thinks he alone holds the secret to scientific truth, although Rutherford is probably the worst of all."

Malcolm was disappointed. He had hoped to have some time to discuss some of Rutherford's theories with him. He had tried to keep current with the physics of the time and he found Rutherford's advances in the nature of matter fascinating. "Are there any special accommodation needs for your Mr. Holmes?" he asked.

She started to shake her head and said, "Yes, it would be best if he had a cabin as far away from other people as possible and preferably some place quiet."

"Needs somewhere quiet to spin his webs?" he asked mockingly.

"Yes, but the real reason is he's not comfortable around other people. He prefers to gather his information from reports and analyze it without dealing with people. He finds them... messy."

"Alright," he said uncertainly. "And you, do you require any special accommodations?"

"All I ask is that I have a room near yours so I can be at your disposal."

"Don't you mean so you can slip in and kill me?" he asked.

"I've been instructed that airship captains seem to be in short supply at the moment and you're all we have."

"Thank you for your vote of confidence," he replied acerbically.

"And besides," she said with smiling eyes, "I can keep better track of you that way."

"You still suspect I have something to do with the sabotage of the Daedalus?"

"I didn't say that," she said smiling. Those fiery emerald eyes were staring right at him and he suddenly found his throat was very dry. He coughed—trying to regain his composure—shuffled the papers, and rose.

"I should probably begin preparations for liftoff. Are you going back to the embassy today? Do you need an escort back?"

She rose. "Yes, I'm returning to the embassy and no, I can find my way out." She walked to the door, stopping before leaving. "Malcolm, I do regret attempting to kill you. I hope we can let bygones be bygones. I do look forward to working closely with you," she said. Maybe it was Malcolm's imagination, but he swore he heard an emphasis on the word closely.

"Yes, well, we'll see," he muttered, somewhat flustered.

She smiled, blew him a kiss, and left the flummoxed captain as the sheaf of papers he had in his hand fell out one by one.

Chapter 18

Malcolm convened a meeting of senior staff to ensure preparations were made for liftoff the following evening. Supplies had already started to arrive. In addition to all of the mission equipment and scientific apparatus, several crates carried fresh meats, eggs, and many delicacies not normally available on a military airship. God forbid the scientists should be fed what the military men had to eat, Malcolm thought. The cargo worked itself out fairly easily since the quartermaster was an old hand at stocking the ship. Mr. Frye found himself in a maelstrom of activity as he tried to ensure that everything brought aboard was weighed prior to finding its final destination as it was critical in determining ballast requirements. He helped Mr. Frye double check all of the numbers—he with his trusty slide rule, Mr. Frye with the aid of the analog computator.

Malcolm always hated computators. It seemed to him that it took too long to program the punch cards necessary to operate them when he could just find the answer on a slide rule. Very rarely, he needed the level of precision available from the analog computator. He received high marks in his required analog computation class, but not for his excellence in programming the machines. When his first assignment was due, a series of trajectory tables, Malcolm performed the work on his slide rule and manually wrote the tables. When he handed in the assignment, his instructor asked, "Where are you punch cards, Cadet?"

"Didn't need them, sir. Since this is analog computation, I used my slide rule."

"The purpose of the class is to demonstrate proficiency in analog computation. That means demonstrating proficiency in the use of the analog computators."

"I don't trust them, sir. I'd much rather do the work with this," he said, indicating his slide rule. "Gears can't think and machines break down. I'd rather do my thinking for myself."

"I see. I'll tell you what. If, by the end of the semester, you can prove to me that the slide rule can solve a problem better than the analog computator, I will give you the highest marks available in the class."

"It's a deal."

For the rest of the term, Malcolm continued to turn in all of his assignments calculated via slide rule, but spent every spare moment learning more about the analog computator used to run student assignments. He found blueprints to the design of the machine and poured over them for hours. He watched as cards were processed and he watched how the mechanism moved to turn the gears, which in turn turned other gears that represented registers, adders, multipliers, subtractors, and dividers. He soon submitted his own jobs, watching carefully for the performance of the machine. He begged for extra cards and bought as many as he could with what little pocket money he had. The night before his last class, Malcolm brought a deck of punch cards to the student computation desk for processing. He watched with anticipation as his deck was fed into the hopper for processing.

Within seconds of processing Malcolm's deck, the analog computator began to vibrate and shake. A few seconds later, the shaking became more violent. Gears began to misalign and the whole machine screeched to a grinding halt as misaligned gears began to pop out of the machine. Malcolm slunk away and proceeded to build a duplicate of the calculations he had performed and wrote out the same answers to the problem using his slide rule.

The next day in class, Malcolm waited until the end of class and handed the instructor a deck of punch cards and his calculations. "Here, sir. Here's my proof that the slide rule is more reliable than the analog computator. Perhaps you heard about the trouble with the computator last night? It happened while processing a duplicate of this deck."

"Really?" said the instructor. "I will double check your work. See me tomorrow and I will let you know if this is true or if you will have to repeat my class next term."

"Very good, sir," Malcolm said, confident of his success.

Intrigued by the cocky young cadet, he fed Malcolm's deck into the faculty computator. Within a minute, it too suffered the same fate as the student computator. The next day when Malcolm returned, the instructor shook his head and handed Malcolm a perfect grade in the class and had given him an academic commendation for original thinking.

The dean of analog computing, however, was not as amused or impressed with Malcolm's work. He gave Malcolm a demerit and mandated that in order for his grade to be accepted, he would spend the next term assisting in the rebuild of both computators and devise a way to thwart future attempts at destroying the college's computators.

Malcolm made history as the first cadet to receive a commendation and demerit from the same coursework. Legends of Malcolm's handiwork had since been handed down to future cadets who had all tried and so far failed to recreate Malcolm's algorithm. He had promised the dean of academic computing that he would not divulge his algorithm to anyone and in fact, it was a condition of his graduation.

Frye had done good work and Malcolm found no faults in his analysis, even if he did have to rely on the ship's computator. Frye probably had to nearly rebuild it because Malcolm never used it in his whole time as chief engineer and it sat neglected. Intricate machines like the computator required a great deal of care; Malcolm had let it sit idle. It was surprising the thing could actually turn. Still, the scientists would surely make use of it, but he still preferred his trusty slide rule.

While ballast calculations were easy, the logistics of trying to house the guests were not. The cabins on board were limited to officers, which meant that some officers had to be displaced. Malcolm gave this unenviable job to Commander Saxon, who seemed to actually shine at this. With a little work and convincing, he managed to convert storage areas into makeshift cabins for some of the sub-lieutenants and allow the guests the use of the cabins. Saxon located a cabin for Mr. Holmes by turning a storage area into a room in the aft end of the ship. It was near the engine room and the vibrations from the engine could be felt, but it was not near other people and with Saxon's work, might actually be a comfortable room. For a brief moment, Malcolm considered making it his room, but he remembered Captain Collins' words to "be the rudder" and decided it was merely wishful thinking. Saxon was even able to find a cabin for Joan, halfway between his and Malcolm's cabin. His logic was that she would be available for translation for whoever needed her. The idea rankled Malcolm, but he had no idea why. It certainly made sense and was perfectly logical, but it bothered him nevertheless.

Together, Malcolm and Saxon worked with Chef to prepare a dinner for the honored guests in the officer's mess after liftoff. Saxon had a good idea of the kind of meal that could be created with what they had on board, Chef's ability, and their guests' palates. Malcolm informed the senior staff that they would appear in full dress and the only excuse for not attending was death.

By the end of the day, everything seemed ready for the liftoff. Malcolm had personally inspected the quarters that seemed more than adequate for the scientists, and the current cargo and supplies had been loaded. The only thing left for tomorrow was the scientists, any last minute gear, and the pre-flight checklist. He asked Mr. Frye to certify the engines at his earliest convenience. Malcolm knew from his own experience that something was bound to come up tomorrow and crossing any item off the pre-flight checklist would be helpful.

When Malcolm returned to his office at the end of the day, he realized that he actually felt content. Today, he understood what needed to be done. He had problems to solve and he had the skills to do it. And those that he didn't have the skills to do, he delegated. He was beginning to think that he had a hang of this captain thing.

And then he thought about the nighttime liftoff. With no lights, the Daedalus would have to fly out of the hangar, while making sure that she didn't rise and clip the ceiling of the hangar or the top of the door on the way out. From there, the night takeoff wasn't difficult per se, there just tended to be changes in the wind patterns right after sunset and it could make a smooth liftoff difficult if one didn't read the winds correctly.

Malcolm knew that he was a mediocre pilot at best; it had never been something he cared about because he had wanted to be in the engine room. Now he had to guide the ship. Be the rudder. And suddenly the enormity of the task overwhelmed him. He tried to find something to do—some problem with logistics that he could fix—but the crew seemed to have everything in hand. The crew was ready and anxious to sail.

Malcolm slept little that night. What little sleep he did have was filled with recurring dreams of crashing the Daedalus into the ceiling of the hangar or into the hangar doors, or a myriad of other ways he could mess up the takeoff. When it was time to wake, Malcolm felt like he had hardly slept. His first order of business was finding an extra strong cup of tea.

Midmorning, Joan arrived to help coordinate the arrival of the expedition team and the rest of their gear. Knowing Joan would be arriving, Malcolm prominently wore his service revolver; when she saw it, she smiled. "Why, for me?" she asked, indicating the revolver. "Why, you shouldn't have."

The rest of the day was a blur as crewmen came in with reports on liftoff readiness. Frye was frantically trying to keep up with the ballast calculations as more personnel and equipment arrived. Malcolm ordered a crewman to bring a table and chair and set it up in the hangar as a makeshift office so he could read the preflight reports, supervise cargo, and greet each dignitary as they arrived.

Zhukovsky was the first of the dignitaries to arrive. Malcolm greeted him warmly, thanked him again for his magnificent work on the reconstruction of the bridge, and invited him to join him on the bridge for the liftoff. Zhukovsky was delighted by the invitation and even more delighted when Joan escorted him to his quarters. Next came Professor Nikolai Koltsov, a middle-aged man with thick white hair and an enormous mustache that hung like a curtain over his mouth, hiding it from view. He reminded Malcolm of a walrus. Professor Koltsov spoke no English, so Joan acted as interpreter as Malcolm welcomed him aboard. He looked at Malcolm, muttered something in Russian, and started inside, not waiting for Joan to show him where he was going.

Later in the afternoon, Ernest Rutherford arrived with Mr. Holmes. Holmes was a tall, heavyset man whose hair was long, but receding. He wore a rumpled suit and looked very ill at ease in the hangar. Although it was not warm in the hangar, he seemed to be mopping his forehead frequently with his handkerchief. Malcolm offered a hand, saying, "Welcome aboard the Daedalus, Mr. Holmes. It is a pleasure to meet you."

Holmes looked at the extended hand and said, "Yes," and likewise strode into the Daedalus, Joan racing to keep up. Malcolm turned to Ernest Rutherford and said, "Professor Rutherford, it is indeed a great pleasure to meet you. I've read much of your research and am fascinated by your work in radioactivity." Rutherford was the embodiment of an Edwardian gentleman. His hair and mustache were neatly trimmed and his suit impeccably tailored. Although Malcolm knew he was originally from New Zealand, he had the manner and bearing of an English gentleman.

"You, an airship captain, reading about radioactivity?" Rutherford inquired.

"My promotion to captain is recent. I've been a ship's engineer for nearly ten years," Malcolm replied.

"Oh," Rutherford replied with a note of condescension. "Yes, thank you. Will you show me to my quarters?"

Malcolm looked around for Joan, but she was obviously still busy with Mr. Holmes. "Yes, certainly."

"Here are my bags," he said, handing Malcolm a small bag while indicating two suitcases and a steamer trunk. "Well, don't just stand there, let's get moving man!" he ordered as he briskly strolled towards the gangplank.

Malcolm stood there dumfounded for a moment. While he didn't hold a great deal to the trappings of military honor and prestige, he was a captain and most certainly not a porter. He called to a passing crewman and ordered him to bring the luggage to Rutherford's quarters. When that was set, he hurried to catch up with Rutherford. Malcolm led Rutherford to his quarters and showed him inside. Rutherford surveyed the room and said, "No, this simply won't do. I require larger quarters."

Malcolm's anger started to flare, but he took a deep breath before replying, "I'm sorry sir, but we are a bit cramped for space and this is the best we can do."

Rutherford turned to him and said, "Then find someone who can. I need room to think, to analyze, and to ponder.

This," he said, gesturing to the room, "is little better than a shoebox."

Malcolm again swallowed his anger and said, "I apologize again, Professor, but as I said, this is the best that can be arranged."

"I am a Nobel laureate and I will not be stuck in this hovel of a room!"

"And I'm the captain of this airship!" Malcolm growled. "This is my ship and if I say these are your quarters, these are your quarters."

"I will not be talked to..."

"And I wouldn't push my luck if I were you. I can have you assigned to a storage closet right next to the engine room that will make this 'shoebox' look like the Taj Mahal." He paused. "Do I make myself clear?"

Rutherford looked at him and could see that Malcolm was not going to back down. "Very well, but I will report this when I return."

"You do that, sir," Malcolm snarled. As he left, he took a deep breath and said, "I'll be hosting a dinner tonight for the members of the expedition and my senior staff. I do hope you'll be able to attend." And if I'm lucky, you'll choke on the meal, Malcolm thought. He started out the door and saw Joan approach. "Miss de St. Leger. This is Professor Ernest Rutherford. Professor, Special Envoy Miss Joan de St. Leger. Miss de St. Leger, perhaps you can help settle the professor into his quarters. Ah, here comes his baggage."

Malcolm left the room, but managed to hear Rutherford say, "He has a bit of a temper."

Joan replied, "It's probably the stress of preparing for liftoff. A captain's job is a demanding one."

Malcolm had barely stepped off the gangplank when Frye came up to him. "Captain, we have a problem."

"That, Mr. Frye, would be the understatement of the new century," he said dryly. "What is it?"

"We're nearly two thousand pounds over capacity," he said.

"Are you sure? Let me see," he said. He pulled his slide rule out and quickly rechecked Frye's numbers. "Bloody hell, what do we have loaded on board?"

"Well, for starters, Professor Rutherford insisted that he drive his car aboard."

"A car? There's a bloody car onboard? Where?"

"Just inside the main cargo hold; it was the only place I could find to put it."

"For starters, we can get that bloody thing off the airship. Where in the bloody hell does he think he's going? For a ride in the country? We're going to bloody Siberia! There's nothing around for miles!"

"He said no one was to touch it."

"Don't worry, Mr. Frye, I'm already on his good side. I'll take personal responsibility for removing it. Anything else?"

"Mr. Holmes brought in a rather large crate that was very heavy. He had it brought directly to his quarters."

"I suppose I'll have to see what that's about," said Malcolm. "Anything else we can get rid of?"

"I'm not sure. I think if we get the car off, I should be able to find a few other things that can be left behind."

"Good job, Mr. Frye. I'll go find Mr. Holmes and sort that mess out."

Malcolm went back up the gangplank, trying to recall where Mr. Holmes had been settled. He remembered and headed aft. It was not a part of the ship that most people liked. It was above the engine room and tended to be noisy. It had been quarters early on, but the crew complained enough that it soon became storage. Malcolm took the aft stairs up to the level of

Mr. Holmes' cabin. Malcolm could not understand why anyone would willingly settle here. He knocked and after receiving no response, pounded on the door to be heard over the background purring of the engine room. The door opened a crack and Mr. Holmes' eyes could be seen through the crack, "What do you want?" he demanded sharply.

"It's Captain Robertson. I wanted to make sure you're settled and to talk to you about your cargo. The ship is a little overweight and I was just wondering if there might be something we can leave behind."

Mr. Holmes paused for a moment in thought, and then nodded to himself. "Before I let you in, I must tell you that what you will see is classified and if you breathe a word of what you see here, you will not breathe again."

Taken aback that the man would threaten him on his own ship, Malcolm said, "Of course."

Malcolm entered the room and thought he was in the wrong part of the airship. He recognized something that looked like a radio receiver, but it had numerous wires tied between it and an analog computator. In front of the computator was a typewriter. It took Malcolm a few seconds to realize that the radio received transmissions, and the computator translated them to words and pressed the various keys on the typewriter to print the message. As Malcolm looked closer, he realized that there was a switch that also allowed transmission as well as receipt of messages.

"That's..." Malcolm started.

"A vision of the future, Captain Robertson; although I suspect that given your background, you would have little use for such devices. You prefer your slide rule as I understand it."

"Yes," he said, still staring at the apparatus. The engineering of this device was truly impressive; Malcolm doubted that he could have designed this, even if he desired. "This is the future, you say?"

"Oh, yes," said Mr. Holmes. "We have several of these machines in London; this is merely a portable version. It is limited, but it will serve its function. We believe that the

Germans have several of these and have already begun to build a version small enough and light enough to serve on their zeppelins."

"What do you use it for?" Malcolm asked.

"That, I'm afraid, remains highly classified."

"I know, if you tell me, you have to kill me," Malcolm joked.

"Yes, I would," he said seriously.

"Do none of you Secret Service types have a sense of humor at all?" asked Malcolm.

"When it comes to protecting the Empire, no."

"Very well. I can see that we won't be leaving anything behind. Is there anything you need, Mr. Holmes?"

"Just to let be left alone so that I can work."

"I see. I also wish to personally extend my invitation to a dinner with the other members of the expedition in the officer's mess this evening after liftoff."

"I'm afraid I won't be able to attend. I'll send Miss de St. Leger in my stead."

"I'm afraid I must insist," said Malcolm. "I would like the expedition to get to know each other so that we might work more effectively together."

"I don't wish to work more effectively with them," replied Holmes.

I know that you mean, thought Malcolm, immediately thinking of Rutherford. "Be that as it may, I'm afraid I must insist. Captain's orders."

"And if I don't comply, I'll have to walk the plank?" asked Holmes.

"No, we don't have a plank. But the drop from the bomb bay doors is a very effective alternative."

Holmes raised an eyebrow. "Ah, then it seems I have no choice in the matter."

"No. I'm sorry, you don't."

"Very well, I will join you."

"Thank you, Mr. Holmes," Malcolm said. "If there's nothing else I'll leave you to... this," he said, gesturing to the equipment.

Malcolm turned to leave, but stopped when Holmes said, "You are a most intriguing person, Captain Robertson. Miss de St. Leger was right about you."

"Thank you, sir," he said, somewhat confused. Then Malcolm left the cabin and headed back to the gangplank to supervise the pre-liftoff activities. He was still a distance away when he could hear yelling and screaming, something about "What have you done with my car?" Malcolm sighed; it meant another run in with Rutherford. He was beginning to give serious thought to letting Saxon deal with the dignitaries. This was becoming too much.

As Malcolm approached, he could see a red-faced Rutherford screaming at Mr. Frye, spittle coming from his mouth. "By whose authority did you remove my car?"

"By mine," Malcolm said loudly so he could get their attention. "Mr. Frye, I believe you have more important duties than to be yelled at for following my orders. I'll take over here."

"Yes, sir," said Mr. Frye, relieved to be going anywhere else but here.

"What gives you the authority to remove my vehicle without my permission?" yelled Rutherford.

"His Majesty. I am captain of this airship and that gives me the right to do what's best for the airship and the mission. And since we would not be able to lift off because the ship was overweight by almost the same amount as this car, which I might add would be nearly useless, it was a fairly easy decision."

"That is preposterous. I am a Noble laureate, not some common soldier that you can bully."

"Then, bloody hell, act like a Noble laureate instead of a spoiled child having a tantrum. For Christ's sake, show some dignity."

Rutherford looked apoplectic, his face turning beet-red and he lunged at Malcolm. Malcolm had realized that it might come to this, and used a standard military combat response to side step Rutherford, grab his arm, and quickly pull it behind his back while bringing his other arm across his throat. If this were a real threat, he could tighten that arm to cut off Rutherford's air, rendering him unconscious. But that's not what Malcolm had in mind.

"Professor Rutherford," he whispered, "do you know what the penalty is for attacking an officer? If this was war, it would be death."

"What? You can't?" sputtered Rutherford, fear appearing his voice.

"Oh, I could. But I won't," he said. "Crewmen, please escort our guest here to the brig where he can have a chance to simmer down and think about where he would like to spend the rest of this mission. If I chose to press charges, I would be obliged to keep you in the brig until such time as we were to reach a British base where court-martial procedures could be brought against you."

"But I'm a civilian, not a soldier. The court-martial has no power over me," he said more arrogantly.

"That would be true if we had just met on the street. But the article for striking a superior officer or offering any violence against him also applies to civilians under the command of the commissioned officer."

Rutherford was crestfallen, realizing he had lunged at the captain in a room full of witness, probably very eager to testify against him.

"Please escort Professor Rutherford to the brig. He's to remain there until such time as I order his release."

Two crewmen grabbed Rutherford and escorted him out of the cargo bay. A quiet hush fell over the cargo bay and activity around the cargo bay came to a halt. All eyes were on Malcolm. "Do you all have something to do?" barked Malcolm, and the crew immediately leapt back to work.

Malcolm knew now that this was going to be a very long mission.

Chapter 19

After dealing with Rutherford, the rest of the preparations went off without a hitch. Word of Malcolm's encounter with Rutherford had travelled through the ship quickly. The crewmen seemed to be smiling more at Malcolm when they encountered him, a few even murmuring, "Good work, sir". Rutherford had placed Malcolm in a horrible position; first, he was bullying one of the crewmen, then he exacerbated it by trying to bully Malcolm and, finally, actually attacking him. Malcolm had been careful not to throw the first punch; he knew his career would have been over. He also knew that he couldn't use too much force for the same reason. Instead, he had remained calm, avoided a fight, and reminded the headstrong scientist whose ship it really was. That display had gained him a measure of respect from the men who knew that people wouldn't be allowed to bully the crew and the captain himself would not tolerate insubordination.

When Joan had heard, she bustled over to him from inside the ship. "Captain Robertson, are you out of your mind? Holding a Noble laureate in the brig?"

"Miss de St. Leger, the good professor lunged at me and is accused of attacking a commanding officer. Until I decide if I wish to press charges, he will remain in the brig." He saw the look of anger and defiance in her eyes. "Perhaps I need to make room for you as well?" he asked.

She exhaled and sputtered, uttering sounds indicating equal parts disgust, anger, and impatience. She stamped back into the airship and Malcolm didn't think he would see her for the rest of the day.

As the time approached, Malcolm left the crew to final flight preparations and went to the brig. It was really a couple of closets that had bars and locks across the way. They had been used in the past for storing valuable cargo that needed to be secured. There was a bunk and a very small commode and little room for anything else.

He found Rutherford lying on the bunk. "Professor Rutherford, do you have a minute to talk?"

"Oh, I don't know, let me check my busy calendar," he said bitterly. He lay on the bunk staring up at the ceiling.

"Alright, then I'll do the talking, you do the listening. First and foremost, I am the captain. I make the decisions for this airship; I am not your servant, bellhop, or yes-man. I have responsibility for the success of our mission and the responsibility to return every soul aboard home safely. I take that responsibility seriously. In order for me to uphold that responsibility, there can be no question about who is in charge. I cannot allow threats to go unchallenged because it weakens my authority. And it may become necessary for the crew to respond without a second of hesitation."

"I bear you no ill will, Professor Rutherford," Malcolm continued. "I have nothing but respect for your tremendous intellect and your accomplishments. I'm just disappointed that you don't seem to be grateful."

"You know, Captain, it's been a very long time since anyone said 'No' to me," he said.

"I can imagine," said Malcolm sarcastically.

"Do you know that I came from humble beginnings? My father and mother travelled from Scotland to settle a ranch in New Zealand. I grew up on that ranch, but was fortunate enough to get a scholarship to go to university. You probably wouldn't understand. You officers come from a different strata than the son of a New Zealand sheep rancher."

"Don't be so sure," Malcolm said and related his tale of how he found himself captain.

Upon hearing this, Rutherford softened. "All this time, I thought I had to act like an upper-class gentleman because I was worried that you would look down on me."

"On the contrary, Professor, I hold you in even higher regard. I respect a man who rises to great accomplishments through his own talent and hard work. Now, what do you say we leave the spoiled upper-class gentleman in the brig, and why doesn't the rancher's son who made good come out?"

Rutherford looked up. "Yes, I think we can leave that cad behind."

Malcolm ordered the crewman watching the brig to unlock the door. "Come on, let's get you cleaned up," Malcolm offered. "I'd like you to be my guest to watch the liftoff from the bridge."

"I... I would like that very much, Captain."

"Very good, Professor."

Rutherford offered his hand. "Please, call me Ernest."

"Very well, Ernest," Malcolm said, shaking Rutherford's hand. "You can call me Malcolm."

Ernest clapped Malcolm on the shoulder. "Very good, Malcolm. Now how do I get to my quarters?"

"I'll take you there," said Malcolm. On the way, Rutherford started to tell Malcolm stories from his university days and the trouble he used to get into with his rugby teammates. Ernest and Malcolm were laughing at one of Rutherford's anecdotes when Joan came upon them, a look of shock on her face when she saw them laughing and talking. She followed the two men until they came to Rutherford's quarters. "I'll send Miss de St. Leger to bring you to the bridge for the liftoff."

As Rutherford closed the door to his quarters, Malcolm turned to Joan, very much proud of himself. "Yes?"

Joan's mouth bobbed open and shut like a fish for a few seconds as she started to say something, changed her mind, and started to say something else. Finally, she said, "Did I miss something? The last time I saw the two of you, he was in a murderous rage and you were threatening to leave him in the brig until we got back to London."

"We came to an understanding," Malcolm said.

"And this understanding didn't come from, say, a blow to his head?"

The Reluctant Captain

"No," said Malcolm. "I just told him how it was going to be and he accepted that. We found out that we really shared similar backgrounds. From there it was easy."

"Well," she said, "congratulations. I thought I would be defusing the situation between the two of you for the rest of the mission."

"It may still come to that, but I don't think so."

"Well, good job," she said. Malcolm noticed that the situation had put her off her guard and for once, she was at a loss for words. Malcolm liked having the upper hand on her for a change.

"Thank you. Do you need anything else?" asked Malcolm.

"Ah, no, thank you," she replied.

"If you'll excuse me, I need to get the bridge to prepare for the liftoff. I trust that you'll bring Professors Rutherford and Zhukovsky to the bridge for the liftoff."

"Yes, of course," she said, watching the resourceful Malcolm leaving. She thought to herself, this is a man not to underestimate.

Malcolm seemed to have dealt with the immediate crises. He found Commander Saxon who had likewise been dealing with the Russian crewmen assigned to the Daedalus and had been working the new crewmen into the duty rosters. Together, the two officers did a quick tour of the ship to make sure everything was set for liftoff. They started with the bridge and methodically made their way through every station on the ship: radio room, mess, quartermasters, gunnery, sick bay, and ending in the engine room. This time, Malcolm made a point of checking the fuel. As he looked through Mr. Frye's preflight certification, he found a note that Frye had both fuel tanks tested.

Malcolm and Saxon returned to the bridge and continued to prepare for the liftoff. Now that it was becoming real, Malcolm felt the butterflies in his stomach turn to bats. There were no other problems to distract him from what he had to do. It was a tradition that the captain pilot the ship out of dock and set its course for its destination; the advent of the airship hadn't changed that tradition.

Malcolm and Saxon kept busy reviewing the navigation charts with the navigator so that they were certain of their heading and course. Like all officers, Malcolm had learned the basics of navigation and knew about plotting elliptical courses to compensate for the curvature of the earth, but that was the limit of his knowledge. He was comfortable with his navigator's skill, but he wanted to know for his own knowledge. He also spent time talking to the flight control officer who typically had control of the wheel while the captain or first officer wasn't available. The flight control officer showed Malcolm that the current weather conditions were calm, which made Malcolm feel better about piloting the Daedalus.

Malcolm could see the sun beginning to set through the hangar doors and knew it would only be a scant hour before he would have to maneuver the Daedalus through the hangar with no lights and set course to begin their mission in earnest. Malcolm's stomach was more uneasy at the thought of piloting the Daedalus. At one point, he even felt a little lightheaded, but he could not show his discomfort to anyone. He had to be the rudder. Rudders aren't allowed to fly free; they have to be true and steady to guide a ship.

After what felt like an interminable wait, Malcolm saw that it was dark outside the hangar. He noticed that Zhukovsky and Rutherford were on the bridge, accompanied by Joan. Joan looked very distracting in a green dress with a tight-fitting jacket. Malcolm realized that he probably needed to make some sort of speech and that he had no idea what to say. He moved to the radio station and asked the radio officer to patch him through the ship.

"Honored guests and crew of the HMA Daedalus. We are about to embark on a mission into the unknown. We are heading deep into an unforgiving land. This mission will require the very best of all of us and I expect every crewman to rise to the challenge. To everyone, I say good luck and god speed!"

Malcolm radioed for the hangar to kill the lights; the hangar was pitch black, save for the slight light that could be seen through the open hangar doors. Malcolm eased the speed control ever so slightly forward and the Daedalus eased forward. Malcolm read the altimeter, but at this height it was no use. He judged, based on the angle that they faced the hangar door, that he was perhaps twenty feet up. He held the wheel steady and let the Daedalus creep to the open door. Minutes seemed to go by as the Daedalus crept closer. Malcolm could see the hangar door growing as they approached it. Malcolm could begin to make out the ground outside of the hangar. Malcolm decided to nudge the Daedalus just a bit up because he felt like he hadn't kept altitude level as they approached the door. Malcolm was relieved to realize that he had lined the Daedalus up perfectly. He gave the engines just a little more power and soon they were out of the hangar. Malcolm slowly nosed the airship up and began to gradually apply power. He could have opened it up when they had cleared the hangar, but there were many passengers who might not have airship experience, and he didn't want to give them a bad experience, at least not until he had no choice.

"Masterful job, Robertson," boomed Zhukovsky, "although I could have done it better." There was a chuckle in his voice.

"Well, I could have done it even better if all of my gauges and instrumentation weren't in bloody Russian," he retorted.

"That's what I mean; I read Russian, you don't," he said clapping Malcolm on the back.

The Daedalus continued to climb. Using the compass and the coordinates from the navigator, Malcolm slowly steered the Daedalus on its course to Novosibirsk. When he was satisfied with both the altitude of the ship and its distance from St. Petersburg, he ordered the running lights turned on and after a few minutes, locked the wheel in place. That was an ingenious little addition that he and Frye had come up with. Malcolm thought that officers had better things to do than to keep hold of the wheel. So, the two of them had added a brake to prevent the wheel from being pulled forward or backward and a bar that would run through the ship's wheel to prevent it from turning. The whole thing could release instantly by simply pressing the release lever with your foot; although, it was a good idea to have your hands on the wheel because it did tend to send the wheel spinning.

Malcolm radioed the crew that they were underway and they were headed for Novosibirsk. Malcolm suggested to the guests that they follow Joan to the officer's mess where drinks would be waiting for them. He would join them shortly after making sure things were in order on the bridge. Before he left, Rutherford came over to Malcolm and shook his hand. "Thank you, Malcolm. That was magnificent. I've never seen or imagined what it takes to pilot an airship. It was most educational."

"I'm very glad, Ernest. Please join the others; I'll be there shortly."

"Yes, of course," he said.

Saxon came over to Malcolm, "Did you hit him on the head or something? I thought I'd have to referee for the two of you the whole trip."

"And why does everyone think I won him over by hitting him on the head and not my charming personality?" Malcolm tried to say with a straight face, rather unsuccessfully. "We had another dust-up and I threw him in the brig for an hour or two. We had a discussion and it went rather well."

"You are a surprising man, Captain," said Saxon.

"Thank you, Commander. Now, let's view the duty cycle and join our guests."

Malcolm and Saxon quickly reviewed the duty cycle and, when they found all was in order, left the control of the ship to the Flight Control Officer, Mr. Carston. Together, the two officers strode toward the officer's mess. When he reached the door, Malcolm took a deep breath, opened the door, and entered the officer's mess.

The guests were talking with one another. Zhukovsky was explaining his theories of aerodynamics and Rutherford seemed to be interested in the discussion. Joan was talking to Kolstov and she seemed to actually have the grumpy looking Russian smiling, but it was difficult to tell as his mustache obscured his mouth. Malcolm wondered how he was able to eat with that thing. Saxon took a glass of wine from one of the midshipmen and sauntered toward the discussion with

Zhukovsky and Rutherford. Malcolm looked around and eventually found Mr. Holmes observing quietly from a corner of the room. Malcolm himself took a glass of wine and meandered through the room, talking to the groups until he found himself with Mr. Holmes.

"Not much of a conversationalist, Mr. Holmes?" Malcolm asked.

"I am capable of being quite the conversationalist, Captain, if I chose to. But I choose not to for two important reasons."

"And they are?" prompted Malcolm.

"First, one learns very little from talking, but one can learn volumes from listening and observing. And secondly, I don't like people."

"That seems odd for someone in your line of work," Malcolm said.

"Not really. My job has me analyze situations and people; I cannot help but be disappointed in my fellow man. When given the chance to do the right thing, very few do."

"That's a rather cynical view," Malcolm said.

"I prefer to think it's a more realistic view."

"I assume that you've been observing our guests. What are you impressions?" asked Malcolm.

"You are very direct, aren't you?" mused Holmes.

"I find it takes too much time tiptoeing around things. I like to get straight to the matter."

"I see," said Holmes. "My observations: Rutherford was interested in talking to Zhukovsky at first, but now is bored and would like to talk to Miss de St. Leger instead, but can't think of a way to do so without being rude. Your first officer doesn't seem to care much for Zhukovsky, but seems to be hanging on Rutherford's every word. He seems to sense Rutherford's upper class bearing, although you and I both know differently.

"Miss de St. Leger is flawlessly enchanting and encouraging Kolstov to talk about his work; she has no interest in it, other than to figure out what she can about the man. He has, I believe, a less than gentlemanly interest in our Miss de St. Leger. She knows this and is both encouraging and frustrating him simultaneously.

"And meanwhile, I'm having a conversation with a man who doesn't really want to be here at all. He would rather be in his quarters, reading I guess, rather than entertaining all of us. I, too, would rather be elsewhere, but was forced to take part in this only because the man with whom I'm conversing threatened to drop me out the bomb bay doors."

"Threatened is a harsh word. I merely indicated that that was the airship equivalent of 'walk the plank'; you made your own judgment."

Holmes stopped for minute, his face deep in the thought for a second before he answered, "Yes, you're right."

Malcolm stared. "You have a photographic memory?"

Holmes said, "No, I have what is called ticker tape synesthesia. It means whenever I hear a conversation, I see it as a string of words. Coupling that with an excellent memory, I can recall with near perfection what was said in any conversation I have heard."

"That's fascinating. How fortunate you are, given your line of work."

"One would think so, but it is a bit of a curse. I cannot walk down the street because I see so many words flying about that it becomes hard to function. On a crowded vessel such as this, it can be very difficult. That's why I'm much obliged for providing me quarters well away from the crew."

"You're welcome. I wish I had known; I wouldn't have pressed so for you to join us."

"No," Holmes said. "You were right. I must get to know these people; in a relatively small environment like this, I can manage." Holmes regarded Malcolm for a moment. "You are a most interesting man, Captain Robertson. Perhaps you would do me the honor of conversing with me in my cabin, when your duties permit."

Intrigued, Malcolm agreed. Before he could add any more, a midshipman came in to announce that dinner was ready and led the guests to their seats. Before Malcolm sat at the head of the table, he held his glass up in a toast. "To my honored guests and crew of the Daedalus: may we have untroubled air, safe passage, success on our mission, and a safe return home. Cheers!"

"Cheers!"

The meal, Commander Saxon's idea, was a combination of English and Russian foods. Chef managed to make a passable version of the okroshka soup that Malcolm ate in the Russian mess hall. He also made a salad out of greens and pickled beets that seemed to please both the English and Russian guests. The main course was roast beef, done in the traditional English style. Instead of Yorkshire pudding, Chef had provided rolled pancakes called blinis in their place. For dessert, Chef prepared a traditional treacle pudding and brought out both regular and sour cream for the dessert. Malcolm made a note to himself that he must stop by and complement Chef on his work because this dinner turned out to be popular with all of the guests.

During dinner, there had been a modicum of conversation, mostly about the food. Once dessert was finished, Rutherford seemed eager to start the conversation. "Malcolm—I mean, Captain—do you know why we have been brought together?"

"You mean, you don't know?" asked Malcolm, taken aback.

"I certainly don't know. I was asked by Mr. Holmes to lend my considerable technical skills to an expedition deep in Russia. I was told it would have something to do with radioactivity, which is my area of expertise. I was given a companion, a Mr. Davenport, who was shot when I reached Stockholm. I fled to the British embassy. Eventually, Mr. Holmes arrived and we were taken, by a destroyer no less, to St. Petersburg. I have no idea why I'm here."

"Me, either," boomed Zhukovsky. "First, the Defense Ministry ordered me to rebuild this ship. Then, they tell me I am to go along as an observer."

Kolstov interrupted in Russian, Joan translating as he went. "I, too, was ordered by Defense Ministry to accompany as an observer. I was told to bring along my zoological catalog as well. But I don't understand why I would be needed."

Malcolm looked at Mr. Holmes, who spoke up. "Some of you may know that a tremendous explosion occurred near Tunguska on June 30, 1908. The few eyewitness reports describe something falling from the sky and the sky erupting in fire."

"If this is a meteor or some other extraterrestrial object, you are here Professor Rutherford to analyze the meteor to ascertain its radioactivity and makeup. Professor Zhukovsky is here to reconstruct its trajectory, and Professor Kolstov is here to analyze the impact it may have on the local flora and fauna."

"And your role is..." asked Rutherford curiously.

"I'm with the Home Office and I am His Majesty's representative in these proceedings."

"What is so important to summon all of us together?" asked Zhukovsky.

"Although I'm not privy to exactly what went on, it seems that the tsar talked with our King George about the event. Both governments are interested in seeing what we can discover in Tunguska."

"Then why all the secrecy? Why was Davenport killed?" asked Rutherford.

"And why was the Daedalus barely able to fly when she landed?" add Zhukovsky.

"I won't lie to you; Germany strongly wishes to prevent us from completing this mission. It is the Home Office's belief that they seek to cause a split of the alliance between our great nations. The death of Mr. Davenport and the attack on the Daedalus seem to validate that theory."

"But what possible interest could they have in Tunguska?" asked Rutherford.

"From all indications, the destruction wrought by this event was considerable. If this is indeed an object that fell from space, imagine what kind of damage could be wrought if the Germans were able to replicate this using some sort of artillery."

Kolstov tapped Joan's arm and said something to her in Russian. "Is that why we are here? To do that before the Germans?" Joan translated.

"No, that is not the intent of the mission. Our intent is simply to understand what happened. Any findings will be shared jointly with both governments."

Malcolm decided that this might be a good place to bring things to a close, before more discussion could discern the real purpose of their mission. "We have a long journey ahead of us, ladies and gentleman. I trust that everyone here will do his or her part to make this expedition a success. I must regretfully retire for the evening as I have a very early watch in the morning. I drew straws with Commander Saxon and I rather believe he cheated." This brought a chuckle from the room. "Please continue to enjoy the port and coffee. Miss de St. Leger or Commander Saxon are available to escort you to your quarters should you need assistance. Good night."

As Malcolm left, Mr. Holmes followed him. "Captain, perhaps you could show me back to my room? I too, have much to do in the morning." Together, they left the officer's mess and Malcolm led the way to Mr. Holmes' quarters. He couldn't help himself, but he kept finding himself keeping one eye on Mr. Holmes. When they reached Mr. Holmes' quarters, Mr. Holmes turned and said, "Captain, may I have a word with you?"

"Now? Mr. Holmes, this really isn't a good time. It's been a very long day and I have a very early shift in the morning."

"I'm afraid I really must insist," he said and indicated his hand that held a small derringer that seemingly materialized out of nowhere.

"Well, I guess I must comply," said Malcolm ruing the fact he had elected to not wear his service revolver with his dress uniform. Malcolm felt the derringer dig into his back and he entered the room.

Mr. Holmes followed in and shut door, all the while keeping Malcolm covered with his gun. He moved to a device that looked like a radio and turned it on. "There," he said. "Now we can speak where we won't be heard. It's a device of my own construction. It creates vibrations that are complimentary to any sound waves and, in effect, cancels them out."

"Clever," Malcolm remarked. "But what, pray tell, is so important that you must bring me here at gunpoint?"

"Captain Robertson, we both know that the so-called attack on the Daedalus was an act of sabotage. I brought you here to tell you that the saboteur is still on board and is planning something new."

Chapter 20

Malcolm was caught off guard for a moment. "How do you know this?"

"I have eyes and ears everywhere," he said, indicating his equipment. "Today, while I was setting my equipment up, I caught a fragment of a radio conversation that said, 'Cast in place.' I thought little of it until we talked about the need for secrecy."

"Aren't I a suspect? Your little diplomat tried to kill me on my sick bed because she thought I might be a traitor," said Malcolm.

"Well, yes, we did consider you, but you have been shadowed all day by either Miss de St. Leger or one of our other operatives..."

"You have spies on my bloody ship?" shouted Malcolm.

"We have, as you say, spies on every bloody ship, Captain. It's important for the Home Office to have eyes where action actually happens. Now, if you can sufficiently recover your wounded pride, we believe that you had no part in the sabotage of the Daedalus and we know for a fact that you did not send the message today. Since I didn't have my equipment completely calibrated at the time, I have no idea if the transmission occurred from the main ship's radio or a portable transmitter."

"My analysis leads me to believe that the saboteur intends to turn the Daedalus over to the Germans," Holmes continued. "If we do find what we think we'll find at Tunguska, the consequences of that failing into German hands are quite severe. My best guess is that the saboteur will let us proceed to the site, complete the recovery, take possession of the Daedalus and fly it to Germany. I could be wrong and he may try to take it earlier, but I think he's been instructed now to wait until we complete our mission and return everything to Germany."

Malcolm was stunned. Someone was actively trying to sell out the ship? And apparently would stop at nothing to let it happen. As Malcolm ran through Holmes' analysis, he could find no flaw. It would be exactly what he would have done. Lay low until the time was right to spring the trap. "So, what do I do about this?" asked Malcolm.

"Nothing at present. You seem to be a very capable man. Miss de St. Leger's analysis of your abilities is very complimentary. She seems to think that you could be as intelligent as I am, but I find that difficult to believe."

Before Malcolm could interject, Holmes continued, "I'm not sure how the spy will attempt to take the Daedalus. I believe that our spy's message—'Cast in place'—means that he has agents on the Daedalus. Do you have any new crewmen on board, Captain?"

"Only twenty or so Russian crewmen," said Malcolm. "Part of a 'cultural exchange.'"

"The exchange may be on the up and up, however no one knows any of these crewmen. It would be child's play to replace them with impostors."

"That's simple enough, we just arrest them all."

"And the Russians will think you are up to no good. They don't know that German agents have likely replaced their crewmen. I'm afraid we may have to let this play out and act accordingly."

"Act accordingly? What if they try to kill me? Or you?" asked Malcolm, more than a little uncomfortable with the direction of the conversation.

Holmes looked at him for a moment and said, "That's brilliant. I wish I had thought of that."

"Thought of what?" asked Malcolm, still confused.

"We let them kill you," Holmes replied.

"What the bloody hell is it with you Secret Service types where you want to kill me all the time? What the bloody hell have I done to deserve it?"

The Reluctant Captain

"No, no, you miss my meaning. If you could, Captain, could you fetch Doctor Jenkins? My stomach is suddenly very upset and I don't feel well."

"What? I don't understand." Malcolm saw the glare from Holmes and then just said, "Very well."

Malcolm dutifully went to Doctor Jenkins' quarters. He banged on the doctor's door until Jenkins came. "One of the guests needs medical attention," Malcolm said apologetically.

"Very well. You know, I became a ship's surgeon so I wouldn't have to make house calls in the middle of the night," he grumbled as he grabbed his bag. The two trekked back to Mr. Holmes' quarters. When the doctor entered, he started with a look of recognition. "Mycroft? What in the world are you doing here?"

"How are you, Edward?" he asked, shaking the other man's hand.

"Does everybody on this ship work for the Secret Service?" asked Malcolm.

"No, Mycroft and I know each other from university. I used to let him cheat off me in biology. You work for the Secret Service now?"

"Your memory is faulty, my dear Edward. It was you that cheated off of me. And yes, I work for the Secret Service. Which brings me to the medical attention I require. It's not for me, it's for Malcolm."

"I don't understand," replied Malcolm.

"You will in due time," replied Holmes.

Holmes outlined his plan to Malcolm and the doctor. Doctor Jenkins would fit Malcolm with a false tooth that would include a dose of curare. If Malcolm bit down hard on the tooth, it would crack and inject the curare directly into his gums and from there, into his bloodstream. The curare would act almost immediately to paralyze Malcolm, giving him the appearance of death without killing him. If used at the right time, it may allow a non-lethal injury to appear lethal. Neither the doctor or

Malcolm liked it very much, but Holmes' plan seemed like the best course of action. The doctor left and returned sometime later with a bottle. He soaked a cloth in the bottle's contents and told Malcolm to breathe through the cloth and count backwards from ten. Malcolm only got to six before he stopped counting.

Malcolm awoke the next morning in his quarters. He was groggy and his head hurt, but he was able to struggle to the mess for tea and a biscuit before finding his way to the bridge. He received the report from the night watch commander. They had made good time last night; the navigator estimated that they would arrive in Novosibirsk by noon the next day. From there, they would pick a more direct course to the site. Malcolm talked with the navigator, made a minor course correction, left the flight control officer in charge, and went to his office.

Malcolm thought about his conversation with Holmes last night. There was a traitor and possible saboteur on board who was very likely going to try to kill him. Malcolm found himself again wishing he were back in the engine room. People rarely tried to pull a gun on you in the engine room, and the strain of making arrangements for liftoff yesterday was an order of magnitude harder than work in the engine room. Malcolm picked up his list of reports and forced himself to find the energy to read them. As Malcolm started, Commander Saxon entered.

"Good morning, sir. I just wanted to make sure you were alright."

"Alright?" asked Malcolm. "I'm fine. Why the concern?"

"Rumor has it after escorting Mr. Holmes back to his room, you had to be carried back to your room sometime later."

"Ah, that." said Malcolm. "Mr. Holmes apparently had a very small collection of some rare single malt whiskies. He had heard that I was rather fond of them and well, let's just say that he doesn't have his collection anymore and I have a bloody awful headache."

"That seems... unlike you sir. You never struck me as one who would allow yourself to get into such a condition."

"Then you really don't know me well, Mr. Saxon. I have stories from my university days that would make you think it surprising I don't drink more. And after the day I had—*we* had—yesterday, getting rip-roaring drunk was just what I needed, even if I regret it this morning," Malcolm said, rubbing his temples.

"You will have to fill me in some time," Saxon said, smiling.

"Yes, but not now. The thought of that much alcohol is not helping. How are the Russian crewmembers working out?"

"Very good, sir. Their English is excellent and they are very responsive and obedient."

"Well, there's some good news for a change. Anything else I should know about?"

"It appears that Dr. Kolstov's terrarium containing Madagascar hissing cockroaches was broken and many of them escaped."

"Bloody hell. What is a Madagascar hissing cockroach?" Malcolm did not like the direction this conversation was taking.

"They look pretty much like regular cockroaches, but they're bigger. About two or three inches long."

"So, now I have bugs loose on the ship? That's just bloody awful."

"The worst part is that Kolstov is insisting that we captured them all alive. One of our men found one and stomped on it with his boot. I thought Kolstov was going to have a stroke."

"Tell the crew to catch them alive if they are able to, but dead is certainly a preferable choice to letting them run free. I don't need the little blighters getting into everything. They can make a real mess of things if we don't get hold of them. And, please make sure that the crew member who stepped on the bug gets an extra ration of ale tonight."

"Very good, sir."

"Anything else?" asked Malcolm.

"No sir, I think those are the emergencies du jour."

"Thank you, Commander."

Saxon turned and was halfway through the door when Malcolm said, "Wait. Do you mind if I ask you a personal question?"

"Go ahead, sir."

"Are you happy with your promotion?"

"Sir?" Saxon asked, clearly confused by the question.

"Do you like being commander? Do you like your duties?" Malcolm asked.

"At first, it was a little overwhelming, but, yes, I do like my duties. I like being in in the thick of the action and playing a vital part in making sure everything works. Why do you ask?"

"No reason. Just wanted to make sure that you were making the adjustment. Crew morale and all that."

"Thank you, sir. I'm fine and everything seems to be going well. Unless you have some complaints."

"No, none at all," said Malcolm.

"Very good, sir," Saxon said as he turned and left Malcolm's office.

Malcolm sat in his office, looking at the reports. Was he the only one who felt overwhelmed by the current circumstances? He never intended to become a captain. He resigned himself to the fact that he would only ever be a chief engineer a long time ago, and he had little doubt that he would have been promoted past lieutenant commander. In theory, there were higher-level engineering positions in the Admiralty, but those went to people with family names or political connections. Malcolm was at peace with that. If not happy, he was certainly content.

But now, he felt like a fish out of water, gasping. He apparently had a traitor looking to either destroy the ship, kill him, or both. He was a captain for a top-secret mission flying

The Reluctant Captain

out to the plains of Siberia, looking for something from another world. He had an airship full of men of great intellect with egos to match—and at least three spies from the Secret Service.

Malcolm stared at the reports on his desk. He abruptly got up and started for the door, intent on going to the engine room. No, that would be hiding, he thought. I need to break this down and find a single problem I can solve. If he stopped to look at the big picture, it was too overwhelming. He would handle one thing. He looked at the reports piled on his desk. Alright, he thought. I'll start with those. He sat down and dutifully read through each of the reports, noting orders that needed to be drawn up based on the reports or confirmation of courses of action.

He continued to work doggedly, handling each item and resolving it efficiently. When he was done, he realized that he felt much better and even if he had impossible tasks to deal with, he felt slightly more able to handle them. In talking with Holmes the previous night, they decided that Joan would be the best agent to work with Malcolm in discovering the traitor and what was truly meant by "Cast in place." Malcolm could only assume that meant that the traitor had the resources in place to do whatever it was he was going to do. Perhaps Joan would be able to help him discern the traitor's intent, if not their identity. He still wasn't pleased about being the bait for the traitor; Holmes felt very strongly that the traitor would attempt to kill Malcolm in an attempt to take control of the ship.

Malcolm left the captain's office and went directly to Joan's quarters. He knocked and waited for a response. A voice from within said, "Who is it?" Malcolm announced himself. The door opened a crack, until Joan could verify that it was the captain and opened the door. "Yes, Captain, what can I do for you?" she asked.

"I believe Mr. Holmes may have talked to you about my translation problem. Do you have time to work on that with me now? I also thought that I should give you a tour of the ship."

"Yes, I presently have no duties. And I would love a tour of the ship." She didn't have the heart to tell Malcolm that she had already been through the ship from stem to stern, including many places that had been locked and restricted until she put her lock-picking skills to good use.

Malcolm knew that she was likely lying about seeing the ship. He had noticed a few things out of place in both the captain's office and his personal quarters. He had assumed that it was Joan once he knew she worked for the Secret Service. He would allow her to continue to think that she had duped him. "Excellent. Shall we go?" he asked, offering her his elbow.

As she left her cabin, her beauty again struck Malcolm. Her auburn hair was now curled in ringlets, a pair of these framing her porcelain face. Her eyes were hidden by the small fedora that perfectly complimented her dress. Today, it was a white dress with navy blue stripes. She had a matching bag and white gloves; if they were outside, Malcolm was sure she would have a matching parasol as well.

Malcolm escorted her to the bridge to begin the tour. The bridge itself was still a little foreign to him so he had a hard time being an eloquent tour guide. They continued down the corridor, indicating his office. He noted the quarters of various officers, sick bay, the mess hall, and the officer's mess. They then worked their way down through the ship, all the way to the cargo level. They extensively toured the cargo hold and continued to the engine room that was also on the lowest level of the ship. Here, Malcolm could talk for hours about the engine room, but he quickly knew he was droning on and that Joan had lost interest for some time. He ended the tour with a visit to the fuel supply storage tanks.

"Oh, Captain, you take me to the most interesting places," she teased, her nose wrinkling from the smell of diesel.

"I brought you here because this is where our friend attempted to sabotage the engines."

"Well, I didn't believe it was for its idyllic beauty. Interesting. You said that he put something in the fuel supply. Sugar, wasn't it?"

"Yes."

"What effect would it have had on the engines if you hadn't noticed?"

"It would have fouled them up. We wouldn't be able to move until we cleaned the engines up and changed the fuel."

"So, no permanent damage would have been done to the engines?" Joan asked. Malcolm nodded. "And at same time, a bomb detonates that not only took out flight control, but also most of the command structure. What would be the end result?"

"The Daedalus would be dead in the air."

"At the same moment as two German zeppelins appear out of nowhere," she said. "If you had been eliminated with the bridge crew, what would the end result likely have been?"

"Whoever took over would likely be forced to accept the German offer and land in Germany."

"Where the Daedalus would likely have been dissected for its design secrets," she said. "I think the bomb and the sugar were attempts to turn the Daedalus over to the Germans. The only thing that prevented that was you. If you hadn't noticed the difference in the engines and been delayed while you fixed it, you would be dead and the Daedalus would be in German hands."

"We have a bigger problem now, though," Joan continued. "They likely now know the purpose of our mission. I agree with Mr. Holmes' analysis that our friend is under orders to do nothing until we recover whatever there is to find in Tunguska. Mr. Holmes believes that we are safe until we fly back. Somewhere on our return, our friend will strike. I don't think he'll attempt to disable the ship because we will be over Russian airspace for quite a while. I don't see the Germans provoking the Russians by violating that airspace. I likely think there will be an attempt to kill you or at the very least, discredit you so that someone else could take over."

"So what do we do until then?"

"Very little," Joan said. "We watch and wait. I'm afraid we have to wait for our friend to make the first move."

"That would be comforting if I weren't the one being used as bait. Who am I kidding, that's not comforting at all," Malcolm retorted.

"Just go about your duties as normal until we get to Tunguska. We'll come up with something then."

"Go about my duties as normal? And what would that be? I have no bloody idea what I'm doing so I can't even tell you what my normal duties are, and on top of that you want me to walk around with a bloody bullseye on my back? I—"

Malcolm was stopped mid-sentence when he suddenly found Joan's lips covering his mouth in a kiss. Malcolm was shocked. Joan grabbed him by the lapels of his uniform and dragged him close to her. His hands found her body and pulled her close as he started to respond to the kiss. After a few seconds, she pulled away, much to Malcolm's disappointment, and smiled at him. "You talk too much. I didn't want the crew to hear you. Let's get back to the well-travelled corridors or there may be talk."

"And you know what they say about loose lips," she added, walking away.

Chapter 21

Malcolm's head was still spinning from Joan's kiss later that evening when the Daedalus reached Novosibirsk and changed course for Tunguska. Malcolm sent invitations to the guests and the senior officers for a planning breakfast to organize the search for the cause of the explosion. Once that was complete, Malcolm returned to his cabin, but sleep seemed elusive. What if this whole thing was a wild goose chase? What if they really did discover something from out of this world? At this point, Malcolm wasn't sure which would be worse. Before he went to bed, he had reviewed the Air Service's standard protocol for search and rescue. That was the best guidance Malcolm could find in any of the Air Service regulations. In his mind, he imagined that the impact point of the explosion would probably be obvious, especially from the air. From that central point, he would probably establish a base camp. With the Daedalus, he'd initiate an aerial search in an ever-widening spiral. Any potential areas of investigation would be marked and a ground search would be initiated. And from there, who knew what would happen.

If the enormity of the task ahead wasn't enough, he still had to contend with the traitor on his ship who would likely strike sometime after they left. The return trip required them to refuel in Moscow before returning to Britain. Malcolm imagined that the traitor would strike before they got to Moscow and hoped that the Daedalus had enough fuel to carry them to somewhere in Germany. Who could the traitor be? If he had gone to the bridge, who would have taken command in his absence? Likely it would have been Saxon, but Malcolm supposed that Saxon had also been summoned to the bridge. If Saxon too had perished, there would have been any number of junior lieutenants who could have taken command. And in that confusion, there would have been no choice but to surrender. Whomever it was had planned to get all of the senior officers on board in one place and eliminate them. The more he thought about it, the more he realized that it really could have been anyone on board.

Failing to resolve that problem, he turned his thoughts to Joan. She had kissed him. He had never known a woman that was so forward. But was it, just as she said, to shut him up or had something else been involved in that kiss? He wanted to think so, but then quickly remembered that she had also tried to kill him. She was a maddening woman, but he couldn't deny that she was attractive and smart—a combination that he found seductive. But, he reminded himself, she was dangerous. He decided that although he wished otherwise, the kiss was just part of her continuing campaign to keep him off balance and that a lady like her would not have anything to do with a shipbuilder's son.

Malcolm reached some sort of peace as he realized that he had at least solved one problem and fell into a fitful sleep. When he dreamed, he dreamed of kissing Joan and Joan returning his kiss. When he awoke the next morning, he felt like he hadn't slept at all. He dressed and went to the mess for a mug of Chef's strong black tea that he always thought could be used to seal the airship's outer skin. But this morning, he needed to wake up and be at his best when dealing with the collection of egos at the meeting.

Malcolm went to the officer's mess and waited patiently for everyone to arrive. It was no surprise that the first people there were his staff. One by one, the members of the expedition made their way in; Malcolm was pleased to notice that Rutherford was one of the few guests on time. Joan arrived with Koltsov who was talking to her in animated Russian— probably about the escaped cockroaches. Miraculously, all the escaped cockroaches were found, however only two had survived to be caught. Zhukovsky and Holmes were the last to arrive.

Malcolm asked the midshipman serving the officer's mess to bring in the traditional full English breakfast: buttered toast, marmalade, bacon, sausages and dishes of fried and scrambled eggs. Rutherford and Malcolm's staff dug into the breakfast with gusto. Kolstov and Zhukovsky were a bit hesitant at first, but after tasting the bacon and sausage, they eagerly tackled the breakfast. Joan and her boss Mr. Holmes were rather restrained in their eating.

When the dishes were cleared, Malcolm had the navigator bring in the maps for the area and a glass covering so that he could annotate a map without ruining it. Malcolm drew a circle and pointed. "Based on the best information we have, we believe that the explosion occurred somewhere in this region. We will use the Daedalus to identify the epicenter of the explosion. I believe that it should be somewhat easy to do from the vantage point of the Daedalus. We will establish a base camp at the epicenter. Professor Rutherford, we'll need your skills before we can establish camp. I would like you to scan the area for radiation and make sure that the area is safe for our crew."

"Yes, of course," said Rutherford. "As soon as we finish, I'll get my equipment unpacked and working. Perhaps we might find something before we get there."

"Very good. Once the camp is established and the immediate area is searched, we will conduct a series of aerial searches in a spiral with an ever-increasing radius from the base camp. The Daedalus will mark areas of interest and we'll dispatch ground crews to search. Anything found will be brought back to the base camp where initial investigations can occur. Once we're sure whatever we have found is safe, we'll bring it back aboard the Daedalus. When we're satisfied that we've found whatever it is we're looking for, we will depart for Moscow."

"And how will we know when we have what we're looking for?" asked Zhukovsky.

"If it's some sort of extraterrestrial body like a meteorite, we should be able to find fragments. And if it's something else, I think we'll know."

"What about the rest of us?" asked Zhukovsky, indicating himself and Koltsov. "While I have enjoyed the voyage on your airship, I presume we are here to do something."

"Once we establish base camp, I intend to have you accompany us on the aerial search, Professor Zhukovsky. I was thinking that given an aerial vantage point, we might be able to reconstruct the path of the object that exploded. And I could use your help to plot a trajectory for anything that might have flown off of the explosion.

"Professor Koltsov, I'd like you to analyze the impact of the explosion and any effects on the local wildlife. That will be useful in identifying what's happened here." He waited for Joan to translate, and Koltsov looked at him and nodded his understanding.

"Any other questions?" asked Malcolm.

"What about him? What are his duties?" asked Zhukovsky, who pointed at Mr. Holmes.

"Mr. Holmes is..." Malcolm started.

"Capable of answering for himself," Holmes said testily. "I am His Majesty's representative, making sure that His Majesty's interests are represented, much as you are representing the interests of Tsar Nicholas."

Malcolm was shocked and he turned toward Zhukovsky. Malcolm looked at Zhukovsky, but the man looked nonplussed.

"I don't know what you're talking about!" boomed Zhukovsky.

Holmes laughed, "Come off it, Professor. I have known since you were assigned to assist in repairs of the Daedalus. Please do not insult our intelligences to assume that the tsar would not have his own representative to make sure nothing untoward happened. And you have been with the Daedalus since it limped into St. Petersburg."

Zhukovsky said nothing, but continued to glare at Holmes. Malcolm said, "I think this is an excellent time to adjourn. If everyone is set, I suggest that you start any preparations that you may need. Professor Rutherford, I realize that my engineering crew has limited experience in radiation science, but if you need any assistance, please don't hesitate to ask."

"Thank you, Captain. I believe I can manage," he said a little frostily. A second later, he softened and said, "Thank you for the offer, Captain. I will make use of them if I have a need."

"Very good." Malcolm addressed the rest. "I'll let you all know when we are in visual range of the explosion site. Thank you for attending." Malcolm watched everyone file out with the exception of Joan.

"You didn't give me any orders," Joan said as she rose from her seat.

"I assumed that Mr. Holmes already had given you orders."

"Nothing other than I'm to make myself available to serve at the captain's pleasure."

Malcolm's mouth suddenly went dry. Was he imagining that she had placed an emphasis on the words "captain's pleasure?" "Very good. At present, I don't really have anything that would make use of your talents. I'm off to read some terribly exciting reports from the overnight watch, then return to the bridge and watch for some sign of the explosion."

"That sounds fascinating. I've always wondered what an airship captain does. Do you mind if I tag along?"

"You can if you want, but you'll get to see the real truth of being an airship captain. It's not the gallant swashbuckling that everyone imagines, it's managing hundreds of details in order to keep things running. Still not dissuaded?" he asked. Joan shook her head. "Very well, don't say I didn't warn you." He offered her his elbow and escorted her to the captain's office. They entered the office and Malcolm left the door partially open so that the guards and anyone passing by would see the captain was clearly at his desk and that nothing untoward was going on in his office.

Malcolm started reading the overnight reports. Joan sat waiting for a moment to see if he truly intended to read the reports. After several long moments, it appeared that he was going to read the reports. Just then, she saw that he was looking at her, apparently trying to be undiscovered. Joan met his eyes and smiled. Malcolm suddenly choked, coughed, and returned to his work. Joan suppressed a small chuckle and continued to watch the captain. She did have to admit that he was a handsome man in a rugged sort of way. His features had a chiseled quality, but the effect was striking. The lighting in his office seemed to further emphasize this.

Suddenly, Joan felt uncomfortable. She realized she had been staring at Malcolm and now suddenly felt flush. I will not fall for him, she said to herself. I will not let myself go down that path again. It will only end in heartbreak, she reminded herself. She opened her bag, looking for something to distract her, and found her drawing journal and pencil case. It would give her something to do. She looked around the room and realized that Malcolm was the most interesting thing in the room to sketch.

She stared for a moment and then started roughing out the shape of his head. Periodically, she would lift her eyes to study his hair, the shape of his eyes, ears, and nose, and the contour of his jawline. Reducing his appearance into a series of details of lines and shapes helped Joan re-establish her emotional control. She was no longer flush and only focusing on the lines, shapes, and shadows.

Malcolm finished his last report and looked up at Joan, who appeared to be furiously scribbling in a journal. "What are you doing?" he asked and she nearly jumped out of her seat.

"I was just drawing you. Hold still. I'm almost done. Read something else," she said.

Malcolm picked up the mission briefing he had received from the embassy and re-read it. It wouldn't really hurt to refresh himself on the mission. This time, he did keep sneaking quick looks at Joan and saw her concentrating. When she concentrated, her nose would wrinkle in a very endearing way. Malcolm had the feeling that he best not say that to her, lest she threaten to kill him again.

Malcolm re-read the report, trying to pretend he was interested, but he found himself more interested in the woman sitting across from him. He shook his head and went back to the report when Joan finally said, "Done."

"May I see?" asked Malcolm.

"I'm not sure. It is a private drawing, but then again, you are the subject. If you promise not to make fun of it, you may look at it."

Joan handed the journal to Malcolm. What Malcolm saw amazed him. He saw a handsome man with rugged determination concentrating on a report. He had the dignity and the confidence that everyone thought every airship captain had.

"Not very good, is it? I had trouble with your nose. You have a very different nose."

"That was probably because it was broken in a fight at a pub when I was in university. This is amazing. Do I really look like that?"

"You do to me," she said softly.

Malcolm handed the journal back to her and said, "Thank you. That is the most amazing drawing I've ever seen." His hand touched hers as he handed her the diary and it was if he had grabbed on to a live electrical circuit. And like a real electrical circuit, his hand wanted to grasp the hand and hold it forever.

A knock on the door broke the moment. Malcolm moved his hand away quickly before the crewman would see, but Joan did not have a firm grip on the journal. It fell on the floor in front of the desk. Malcolm thought he saw other drawings as it fluttered down.

"Sir, we've spotted something and we thought you ought to see it for yourself."

"Thank you," Malcolm said. "I'll be on bridge momentarily."

The crewman left, but the spell was already broken. Joan had packed the diary away in her bag and was already rising. "Shall we go?"

Malcolm and Joan went to the bridge and moved to the area in front of the wheel. Below them, for as far as the eye could see, every tree from the forest had been knocked down. It was as if the trees had been bowling pins swept down from a giant's ball. Those that weren't knocked over were broken midpoint up the trunk. Each tree lay facing away from some point out of Malcolm's vision, like rays emanating from the sun.

"I think we're near our destination," Malcolm said.

Chapter 22

A hush fell over the crew as they gazed at the destruction. Malcolm took the helm, slowed the Daedalus to quarter speed and sailed the ship higher to get a better vantage point. Malcolm climbed as high as was possible without putting the Daedalus in the clouds. The explosion had destroyed the tops of the trees and blackened the remaining stumps. From the vantage point of the Daedalus, it looked like a giant black butterfly had landed on the ground. Malcolm conjectured that the epicenter would be near the body of the butterfly shape. He brought the Daedalus down, looking for a place to land. This was not as easy as Malcolm would have first thought. Trees a mile from the epicenter were still miraculously standing, but they had been blackened from what must have been intense heat and had no bows or branches left. They looked like black pins stuck in a pincushion of land.

Malcolm carefully brought the Daedalus down inside the center of the destruction area, which was devoid of any life. He followed Professor Rutherford to the cargo area where his equipment had already been uncrated and partially assembled. When the gangplank was lowered, Malcolm accompanied Rutherford outside with the equipment. It took Rutherford several minutes to re-assemble the pieces. Soon, his equipment was brought back to life and he was turning dials and reading instruments.

"Well," asked Malcolm, "is it safe?"

"I'm picking up trace levels of alpha, beta, and gamma radiation. They are higher than the concentrations naturally occurring, but they are not substantially higher than what would be expected in this area. Whatever caused this explosion left very little radioactivity in its wake."

"That is comforting," said Malcolm.

"I may need your assistance, Captain," Rutherford said sheepishly. "My equipment is at home in a laboratory and not necessarily suited to be out in the environment like this. Perhaps there's some way we can provide some kind of protection for it."

"I'd be happy to..." help you, Malcolm almost said. But he caught himself and remembered that he was the captain now and had other worries. "...to have Mr. Frye and his crew see what they can do to help you."

"I'd be in your debt," he said, nodding.

Malcolm ordered a crewman to fetch Mr. Frye and soon he and Rutherford were in discussion of modifications that would protect the equipment from wind, dust, and exposure. It was all Malcolm could do to tear himself away from this discussion, but he had other duties. He started with the establishment of a base camp with a portable radio transmitter and maps of the area. He even had the crew lug out an analog computator, although Malcolm still had his slide rule. They would use the base camp to coordinate aerial searches with the Daedalus, with results added to the maps. Before the crew raised the circus-sized tents of the base camp, Malcolm sent several samples of the surrounding soil to Rutherford for analysis. Malcolm wouldn't take any chances on losing information or evidence that might aid them in their search.

Once the construction of the base camp was well underway, Malcolm directed the crew to set up a second tent next to the base camp. This contained areas for all of the scientists to work, although the only person with any work to do at this point was Rutherford. He analyzed the soil samples for radiation, again finding traces of radiation, but nothing substantial. He then put his chemical knowledge to the task of analyzing the soil samples. Although he didn't have any training as a geologist, he did encounter small deposits of glass in the soil, indicating a rapid heating of the ground to very high temperatures so that the natural silica in the soil instantly became glass. That news did little to make Malcolm feel better.

When the base camp and science stations were up and running, Malcolm returned to the base camp and, together with Saxon, worked out assignments for search parties, base camp personnel, and the aerial reconnaissance crew that would be needed to adequately search the surrounding area. Malcolm insisted on taking the Daedalus with Zhukovsky. He felt that the two of them might have the best chance of estimating where an object might continue to fall from the sky; Saxon would man the base camp radio and coordinate the search parties with any information that Malcolm could provide from the sky. Malcolm intended to have Joan remain at the base camp and assist Koltsov with translation, but Joan would have no part of it. She pointed out that there were now a number of Russian crewmen fluent enough in both English and Russian to assist and Mr. Holmes expected her to be both an integral part of the search and watch out for Malcolm. Malcolm, knowing he was beaten, gave up and told Joan that she should report to the bridge in the morning.

That night, Malcolm ordered the crew to stay inside the Daedalus, but posted a number of guards in a perimeter around the airship. Although Malcolm thought there would be no trouble, he didn't want to take any chances. The night passed uneventfully. After grabbing breakfast and a mug of tea from the mess, Malcolm went to the base camp to review the arrangements for the day's searching. Search parties would conduct grid searches in the immediate area near the base camp; each group would search up and down the center of the grids that it was assigned and then repeat the pattern from left to right. Once each grid was searched, the group would report any findings to the base camp before being reassigned a new grid. The search groups were told to be on the lookout for anything out of the ordinary, even a rock that didn't seem to match others nearby. They would mark the location on their maps of anything that they found that couldn't be brought back for examination. A party would be assigned to analyze the find depending on the nature of what was found.

In the meantime, Malcolm would take the Daedalus in an ever-increasing spiral over the base camp and look for anything that could be seen from the air that might indicate the fate of whatever caused this explosion. Malcolm had a number of spotters with him on the bridge, including Professor Zhukovsky and Joan. All were issued binoculars and held various observation points around the bridge. Malcolm would try to observe when he wasn't busy piloting the ship.

When everything was set, Malcolm nudged the airship up. The Daedalus rose very quickly because of all the weight that had been offloaded to the base camp. He cursed himself for not reviewing the ballast calculations that Mr. Frye gave him this morning that factored in the lack of equipment and personnel on the ship. Malcolm started making a slow circle, following the compass from north, to east, south and west,

The Reluctant Captain

before starting to north again. Malcolm started his second pass around at a distance of about a mile due north of the base camp when Saxon contacted him on the radio.

"Captain, one of the teams brought back a hunk of metal of unknown origin. There seems to be some sort of writing on it, but much of it is obscured because the metal has been blackened."

"Where did they find it?" asked Malcolm.

"In grid 42," said Saxon.

"Do we know anything about the metal?" asked Malcolm.

"It seems to be as strong as steel, but is much lighter. Professor Rutherford is examining it now."

"Very good. For now, let's focus our search in the direction they found the metal."

"Already done, sir. I dispatched the next party to start searching in grid 47."

"Excellent, Mr. Saxon. I will consult with Professor Zhukovsky and we will try to lay out a projected course based on the location of the metal and the epicenter. I'll take the Daedalus in that direction. If we don't find anything else, we'll re-establish the existing plan."

Malcolm and Zhukovsky went to the navigator's desk. Malcolm pulled out the map and, on the glass that sat over the map, marked an X for the epicenter and then drew a circle to indicate the location where the metal was found. Malcolm quickly marked out two lines from the epicenter to each side of the grid and continued those for some distance on the map, leaving a large cone that might indicate the path of whatever dropped the metal. Malcolm drew a third line through the center of the cone and indicated to Zhukovsky that this should be their course. Zhukovsky studied the map and then nodded his agreement.

There was a sense of excitement on the bridge. Malcolm brought the map over to the wheel, holding the map with the hand that was on the wheel and trying to peer through his binoculars. Realizing that he couldn't do everything, he put down the binoculars and concentrated on piloting. Malcolm had to manage the navigation himself, as the navigator was one of the spotters. Malcolm kept looking up from the map to find the landmarks indicated on the map. Between trying to keep the altitude and the heading on the compass and trying to find his bearings on the map, Malcolm was floundering. He was not a natural flyer and found the task of trying to keep all of these variables balanced while trying to ascertain their location a herculean task. But Malcolm kept struggling and eventually found the Daedalus over the grid where the mysterious metal had been found.

"Look sharp, everyone. We're over the spot where they found the metal."

Malcolm slowed the Daedalus to a crawl, engaged his autopilot to lock the course and altitude, and went to the window with his binoculars. He surveyed the land and couldn't see anything that looked out of place to him—but then again, the whole scene seemed foreign. The desolation of the flattened forest made everything look like a logjam that he'd seen near Kilmacolm as a boy.

Minutes seemed like hours as silence fell over the bridge. Suddenly, Joan broke the silence. "Over there to the right... that way," she said while pointing. Malcolm swung his binoculars over and tried to find the point that she had indicated. It took him a few seconds when he caught the glint of sun off of metal. He focused in and found another piece of metal that seemed to be much longer than the sample they heard about from Saxon. Malcolm stopped the engine so the Daedalus was hovering over the site.

Malcolm radioed Saxon. "Commander, we've found another piece. This piece looks bigger than the piece that was brought in earlier. It's in..." Malcolm examined the map and located the grid where Joan had found the debris. "...Grid 58. We may need to load it on the Daedalus. We'll continue on course out to five miles. If we don't find anything, we'll come back and we'll try to bring it up with the winch. I'll keep you posted."

"Very good, sir. Nothing more on the sample that Rutherford is analyzing."

The Reluctant Captain

"Inform me if you hear anything. Over and out."

Malcolm marked the location on the map and took a few minutes to adjust his original heading, reorienting himself with map. He disengaged the autopilot and eased the Daedalus back into motion. Once Malcolm had the Daedalus moving in the right direction, he re-engaged the autopilot and went to the window. He peered out the window with his binoculars. Malcolm was confused; he looked at the map. Malcolm kept looking between his binoculars and the map. "Mr. Barrows, could you assist me for a moment?" Malcolm asked.

The young sub-lieutenant came over immediately.

"Yes, sir. What do you need?"

"I don't know. I thought that I was smart enough to read a map, but apparently I'm lost. Can you tell me where we are?" Malcolm asked sheepishly. Malcolm looked out in the distance and saw a lake some two to three miles ahead, but there was no lake on the map. Mr. Barrows was soon repeating Malcolm's actions—looking out through his binoculars, looking at the map, and repeated this action several more times before turning to Malcolm and saying, "I don't understand, sir. I can't find our location either."

"That's comforting only in that my navigation skills aren't suspect, but I can't say I'm comforted in not knowing where we are." Malcolm returned to the wheel, disengaged the autopilot, stopped the engines and left the controls in place. Malcolm went to the navigator's station. "What do we know, Mr. Barrows?"

Barrows looked at the dials available at the navigator's desk. "Based on our coordinates, I believe we are somewhere here," he said, drawing a circle on the map. "Based on our last course projection, I can't find any lake on this map. But, I did see this small hill here, and the small creek here. I believe we're right here, but I can't account for the lake. It's clearly not on the map, but it's also clearly right there in front of us."

"It seems that the map is missing the lake. When was the map made?" asked Malcolm.

"That's just it. It's only five years old. Lakes don't form in five years, sir."

"Normally, I would agree with you, Mr. Barrows, but I don't think this is a normal situation. What happens if something large, like a meteorite, strikes the ground?"

"It forms a crater, sir."

"Right. And what does a crater resemble? A bowl! Now if something crashed here, what would happen to any snow that accumulates in the crater come spring? It fills the bowl! I think we may have found something."

Malcolm went back to the wheel, disengaged the autopilot, and slowly pushed the engines to life. Malcolm steered the Daedalus straight to the lake. "What are you doing, Captain?" asked Joan. "I can't see anything when you fly this fast."

"I'm following a hunch. I think yon lake is not exactly a lake. I think that's where we're going to find our prize." Malcolm confidently steered the Daedalus, with one hand on the wheel and another on the speed control. The Daedalus flew quickly to the lake. As the Daedalus approached the lake, Malcolm slowed the engines to a near crawl and slowly circled the lake.

Malcolm realized that his theory may have more validity than he originally thought. A river entered and exited the lake on the west side. If the object had created the crater across the river's path, it would have filled that much quicker. And with snow from a Siberian winter, it was likely that the crater would have filled and then became an outlet for the river.

All eyes were focused on the lake. Malcolm circled the lake and still nothing had been discovered. Malcolm circled two, three, and four times and there was still no sight of anything. Malcolm didn't understand. It made sense; the mysterious lake that hadn't been on the map was the result of an impact. It had to be. Why hadn't they found anything?

Malcolm turned the Daedalus around for one more pass in the vain hope that they would find something. Malcolm was about to give up when Mr. Barrows piped up and said, "Sir, I think I've see something. There, about 48 degrees starboard."

Malcolm killed the engine and ran to the window to see. At first, he still didn't see anything and thought that it was a trick of the light. But then, the sun moved and deep within the water of the lake, he saw the glint of metal.

"Ahoy, there she be," he said.

Chapter 23

Malcolm maneuvered the Daedalus over the lake and over the place where they sighted the flash of metal. He left Sub-lieutenant Barrows with the helm and went down to the cargo bay. Malcolm had the crew let the winch out slowly to gauge how deep the lake was. Malcolm counted on the fact that the big hook at the end would eventually hit the bottom and likely topple over. Once its weight was no longer pulling down the cord, it would be possible to guess the depth of the lake. That would play a huge part in how the object could be retrieved from the lake. Malcolm guessed, based on the length of rope and their height, that the lake must be nearly 170 feet deep, give or take 10 feet.

This would have been a problem in normal circumstances, if it hadn't been for the fact that the Daedalus' previous mission had been to secure a wreck of a British warship off the northeastern coast of Scotland. A couple of diving suits had been left on board. The pressurizers, already used to pressurize the helium used to lift the ship, could easily send pressurized air to the diving suits. Malcolm thought that it would likewise be possible to modify the observation car and pressurize it so that it could be sent down to observe the object and act as a base for the divers.

Malcolm was convinced that there was nothing more to be gained here today and immediately set course back to base camp at full speed. He immediately radioed Commander Saxon and told him to call off the search party. He was certain that they had found the object of their mission. He talked with Zhukovsky about ways they might be able to raise the object or at least drag it up out of the lake. The Daedalus arrived quickly back to the base camp. By now it was late afternoon. Malcolm landed the Daedalus near the base camp and convened a meeting with his senior staff and members of the expedition to discuss the day's findings.

Rutherford started with analysis of the metal fragment found by the search team. Although his portable equipment couldn't conduct as thorough of a test as in a fully supplied laboratory, it appeared that the metal was actually an alloy of some kind. He was certain it contained nickel, aluminum, iron, titanium and one or more rare elements in small quantities he couldn't differentiate. The alloy could withstand a high heat and was very strong, but it was also lighter than a similar piece of steel. "While it's possible that someone could have made this, the knowledge needed to create this alloy doesn't exist. I like to think that I'm well-read on the leading developments in chemistry and I've never heard of this kind of alloy." Turning to Malcolm, he asked, "Do you have anything like this in military use?"

"Not that I've heard. I'm not privy to everything, but I've never heard of it. You could spend a long time just discovering the engineering properties of an alloy like that. It could be used in all sorts of applications here on an airship or a plane. It'd be perfect... Sorry, I'm an engineer. Old habits die hard," said Malcolm. He turned to Joan. "You don't suppose that Mr. Holmes would have any contacts who would know if such an alloy was in use? Mind you, we don't have to know how it's used, just if it exists."

"I will ask," she said, "but don't expect any answers."

"I don't, but I'm trying to rule out the obvious. Once you rule out the obvious, the solution, however outrageous, presents itself."

"Don't let Mr. Holmes let you hear say that. His brother says that all the time and it infuriates him to no end," said Joan, aghast.

"Hold on, that's a quote from Sherlock Holmes," said Malcolm with sudden realization. "You mean that Mr. Holmes is..."

"Yes, Mycroft Holmes. Brother of the detective Sherlock Holmes. Mycroft is not very happy with the way Arthur Conan Doyle portrays him in the books, although I believe them to be a pretty fair representation. What he really hates is that the books have made his brother even more arrogant and harder to manage."

"I'll keep that under advisement," said Malcolm. He proceeded to describe the flight, the discovery of the lake, and the object at the bottom. Malcolm spread out the map on the table. He drew a projected flight path for the object that he had worked out with Zhukovsky based on the epicenter of the explosion and the final destination of the object. Zhukovsky had conjectured that the explosion occurred some distance above the ground. Considering the force and the impact it made on the surrounding area, it too represented more energy than anything so far discovered.

"I'm planning to attempt to retrieve the object," Malcolm said. There was a murmur around the room. Malcolm waited for it to die down. "The first order of business will be to determine the nature of the object. To do that, we'll have to go down nearly 170 feet. Mr. Frye, I'd like you to start work immediately on making the observation car waterproof and able to withstand sufficient pressure."

"Observation car?" asked Rutherford. "What is that?"

"It's a small, well, vehicle is being awfully generous, where one or two people can sit and be connected to the Daedalus. We use it for navigation if the Daedalus is hiding in the clouds. It contains a radio and running lights so I think it would make the perfect submersible vessel, if Mr. Frye can keep her waterproof and airtight."

"Yes, sir. Consider it done," Mr. Frye said enthusiastically.

"Who is going to pilot that monstrosity?" asked Rutherford, clearly thinking this was not a good idea.

"I intend to pilot it. This is my cockamamie scheme and I don't want anyone else risking his or her life. Besides, if something does go wrong such as an equipment malfunction, I'm the best person other than Mr. Frye to deal with it. And Mr. Frye is needed here far more than I am."

"But, Captain," offered Saxon. "Regulations are clear that the captain is not to use the observation car in flight."

"Ah, but I won't be using it in flight, we'll be using it in the water. And I won't hear another word about it. I will be the one going down in the observation car."

"And I will be going with you." All eyes turned to Mr. Holmes who had, until now, refrained from talking in any of the meetings. "I am His Majesty's personal representative on this mission and as such, should be present."

The Reluctant Captain

"It will not be a very safe trip, Mr. Holmes. A million things could go wrong."

"A million things can go wrong on an airship, and yet here I have been traipsing across the Russian steppe in one." Mr. Holmes gave Malcolm a steely glance that said he would brook no further discussion on the matter.

"Alright, then. You're with me," said Malcolm. "After our reconnaissance mission, we'll figure out if recovery is an option and how best to achieve it. I think we should break down camp and re-establish our base camp near the lake. While Mr. Frye and company are busy retrofitting the observation car to make it a submersible, we can focus search teams along the flight path we outlined to see if we can find any other pieces of the object. If there are no further questions, Mr. Frye and I will make preparations for liftoff. Commander Saxon, please oversee breakdown of the camp. Thank you all. It's been a very exciting day and I can tell that we have much more to discover."

Malcolm went to the bridge and prepared for liftoff. Joan followed him. While he was busy checking flight status and gauges, she stared at him coldly. Finally, he looked up and said, "Yes, do you want something?"

"You can't go down in that contraption! It's too dangerous!" she fumed.

"Aye and that's exactly why I should go. I don't want my crew to do anything I wouldn't do."

"But you're too valuable to go!" she said angrily.

"Don't be so sure. Commander Saxon would probably make a much better captain than me. Mr. Frye is a capable ship's engineer. Everyone else is needed in his or her job. Quite honestly, I'm expendable. If something happens to me, the mission will continue. I can't say that about anyone else." Before she could say a word, he continued. "Besides, if something goes wrong down there, I'm one of two people with the wherewithal on this ship to do something about it."

"I know all that. That doesn't make a bit of difference. You can't go down there!" she ordered.

Malcolm was starting to get angry. "Hold on one minute, miss. I am the captain of the ship and no one gives me orders on my ship! If I say I'm going, that is the decision. Otherwise you can walk back to St. Petersburg!"

"OHHH!!" she vented, sounding like a teakettle that had been filled with too much water and was bubbling and sputtering all over the stove. "Men are so stupid!" she said and stormed off the bridge, even managing to slam the heavy bridge door.

"What the bloody hell was that about?" Malcolm said to no one in particular.

"Damned if I know, sir," piped up Mr. Barrows.

Malcolm rounded on Barrows. "Don't you have work that you should be doing... NOW?!"

Barrows quickly left to retrieve a map from the cabinet and leave the captain by himself. In fact, the whole bridge crew did their best to give him a wide berth for several minutes.

It took several more hours for the crew to repack the Daedalus and head off to the lake. Now that he knew where to look, Malcolm was able to quickly see the glint of metal. Whatever it was, it was clearly made of metal. This made Malcolm both excited and uneasy. If it was metal, that meant it had been constructed and was likely not of this world. Malcolm wasn't sure how he felt about that. It was one thing to think that there might be other life in the universe, but another to see it.

After circling the lake several times, Malcolm and Saxon agreed that the north shore looked like the best place to set down the Daedalus and to set up the base camp. Just west of the landing site was a rocky outcropping that stood above the plain and would give them a good view of the surrounding area. Malcolm and Saxon agreed that it was too late to set up a camp, but they both agreed that setting up a perimeter guard around the ship was a wise precaution.

Malcolm wandered down to the lake just before sundown to get an appreciation for what lay ahead of them. The lake was calm as there was no wind that night and it seemed to mirror the blue and tangerine of the sunset. Malcolm watched, but there were no ripples indicating fish coming to the surface to feed on the twilight insects. The lake seemed completely lifeless. Malcolm walked to the shore and knelt by the water. He put his hand in and removed it almost immediately. The water was barely above freezing. Anyone who spent any length of time in that water would surely die of hypothermia. Malcolm thought of the observation car and what really could go wrong and suddenly, he wasn't as eager to dive to the bottom of the lake.

Chapter 24

The next morning, the area around the Daedalus was a buzz of activity. Again, Commander Saxon led the work to create a functioning base camp. Malcolm worked with Mr. Frye and convinced Professor Zhukovsky to assist them in retrofitting the observation car for duty as a submersible. At first, Zhukovsky resisted. "I know little about fluid dynamics. I don't know how to make things float or sink. I know air flow."

"Aye, but air flow and turbulence are just like the same effects you see in water," persisted Malcolm. "Besides, we also have to account for pressure of the water on the observation car and..."

"Yes, I know, figure out the pressure within so she doesn't get crushed like an egg. I see what you're doing, Captain, and I must say it's working," Zhukovsky said with a grin. And then the three of them began in earnest to figure out how to accomplish their task. They had several problems to solve if this project were to be successful. First was the woeful inadequacy of the skeleton of the observation car itself. Structurally, there was no chance that the observation car could stand up to the water pressure at 170 feet. Malcolm calculated that the pressure on the bottom would be nearly five times what the observation car was meant to take. Malcolm had remembered from naval engineering history class that in addition to being strong, a submarine needed to be rounded as that would help disperse some of the pressure. In addition, it also needed to be somewhat flexible in order to deal with the intense pressure. The observation car was certainly rounded; it was shaped much like a bomb in order to give it an aerodynamic shape. Malcolm had the ship searched from stem to stern for additional sheet metal that could be used. After two days of scrounging, the trio was certain that they had enough metal to cover the observation car and even had an idea on how to resist the pressure at the depth.

The next issue the trio needed to address was how to waterproof the observation car. Although the Daedalus did carry a supply of tar for patching holes, it certainly didn't have enough to cover the observation car. Malcolm wracked his brain trying to figure out how they could waterproof the observation car, but didn't come to an answer until he was

The Reluctant Captain

making the rounds that night and heard a great deal of hissing from the sentry fire. The crew used the fallen wood around them to build the fire, but some of it was new and the resin from the pine trees rose to the surface when the wood was heated. The next day, Malcolm and Mr. Frye assembled a detail to collect as much fresh pinewood as possible. Over the next several days, while one engineering crew worked on assembling the new metal hull to the observation car, Malcolm and Mr. Frye worked to extract enough resin to cover the ship. It was a slow and painstaking process. The crew harvested too many logs to count from the fallen trees around the area. They heated the logs over a fire until all the pitch and tar started to bubble out of the wood. Malcolm and Frye took one of the pieces of metal destined for the observation car and turned it into a v-shaped trough that would lay under the log and catch and funnel the drippings to a large barrel.

After a week of non-stop work on the observation car, now christened the Nautilus after the infamous submarine of Jules Verne, it was ready for its first submersion test. They added an additional hose line to the ship and pumped air inside the little submersible. The crew hefted the submersible into the water and pushed it out until the water covered it. Malcolm ordered Mr. Frye to pump more air into the ship; everyone was disappointed moments later when a number of bubbles rose to the surface indicating that there were still leaks in the submarine.

As the crew continued to work on the Nautilus, those men not dragging logs in to make resin searched for more pieces of metal. The crew found a few additional fragments in the flight path that Malcolm and Zhukovsky had plotted. Professor Rutherford continued to analyze the metal from the fragments. Once done, he gave the fragments to Professor Zhukovsky who would be tasked with reassembling the object once it was raised from the lake.

Several more days passed as the Nautilus was filled with air, sent into the lake, and bubbles appeared. But each time, there were fewer and fewer bubbles. On the fifth attempt, no bubbles emerged from the makeshift submersible. Later that same day, the Nautilus was lowered to the bottom of the lake while filled with air and ballast so she would sink. When it was brought up, there seemed to be no leaks formed by the increased pressure. It looked like the Nautilus was ready to go.

As it was late in the day, Malcolm scheduled the first dive for early the next morning.

At dinner that night, Malcolm looked for Joan who was absent from the officer's mess where the guests ate. Apparently, she brought her meal to her cabin. Malcolm went to see her and knocked on her door several times. She either was not there or didn't want to be disturbed. He didn't want to leave bad feelings between the two of them, although he still wasn't sure what he had done. He knew that what he was going to attempt was dangerous, but he really was the best man for the job.

Malcolm returned to his cabin early, poured himself one finger of his whisky, and tried not to brood on the myriad of ways this mission could go wrong. He only hoped that if something did happen, it would be over quickly; he didn't relish the comparatively slow death of drowning. His dreams that night were of darkness, water, being trapped, and not being able to get out. He slept fitfully at best and long before dawn, he got up and went to the mess hall for a mug of strong tea. He stared into the mug, its darkness reminding him of the inky blackness that would envelope him once the Nautilus was submerged. Again not wanting to contemplate the mission ahead, he toured the ship, making sure all was in order in an effort to take his mind off of what was going to happen.

The morning ground along slowly, time seeming to almost stop. Malcolm felt the dread rise as each second ticked by. At long last, it was time. He went to the bridge to tell Commander Saxon to maneuver the Daedalus into position. He went to Mr. Holmes' cabin, but found that he was not there, apparently already down in the cargo bay where the Nautilus would be lowered into the lake.

Malcolm reached the cargo bay doors, took a deep breath, and entered the cargo bay, exuding a confidence that he didn't really have. He knew it was important for his crew to think that he was confident, that this was going to be easy, and that everything would be fine. That was the attitude he adopted as he strode confidently across the room. He could see Mr. Holmes fidgeting nervously, talking to Mr. Frye. Frye was triple-checking the compressor that he and the engineering crew had brought down to supply air to the ship. Next to that was a radio transmitter/receiver that Frye retrofitted to supply radio capability to the Nautilus.

"Well, Mr. Holmes, ready to go for a dip?" Malcolm asked jauntily, trying to sound confident.

"No, but I suppose it shouldn't be put off any longer," he said dryly.

"Mr. Frye, are we set?"

"Yes, Captain. I'll pump her full of air once you're inside and everything is sealed. I'm guessing it will be a pretty bumpy ride until you hit the water. Good luck, sirs."

"Thank you, Mr. Frye. See you shortly," he said.

Malcolm and Holmes walked to the Nautilus. It wasn't much more than two seats, although in front of one, a piece of plywood ran the width of the Nautilus with a few switches and a couple of levels attached. Upon seeing this, Malcolm looked quizzically at Frye. "What's all this?" he asked.

"Me and the boys thought you might need to see, so we attached some exterior lights that you can control from here," Frye said, pointing to one of the switches. "We also jury-rigged an electric motor and an old propeller to give you some mobility while you're down there. It's not much more than a trolling motor and we cobbled together some controls for rudder and flaps. It's not much, but it's better than dangling on the end of a chain with no control over where you go."

"Thank you, Mr. Frye. You and the boys never fail to surprise me."

"Just doing my job," Frye said with a smile.

"Well, Mr. Holmes, after you," Malcolm said, indicating the seat away from the controls.

"Um, yes," he said hesitantly. Holmes was a tall and large man and he found it difficult to fold himself into the small space in the observation car. When he was done, his knees were tucked up against his chest. Malcolm likewise would have had a problem fitting, but he had served on an airship long enough and taken more rides in the observation car than he ever desired. He knew exactly how to get into the chair and arrange oneself for the most comfort. Malcolm looked at the plywood that served as his control console. He found a handset wired to it and put it on. He picked up the microphone that was attached to the makeshift console.

"Nautilus to Daedalus, can you hear me?"

"Perfectly," said Commander Saxon from the bridge. "Are you ready to descend?"

"Nearly. Just completing preflight—I mean pre-dive—check."

"Very good, sir. We await your signal."

Malcolm completed his preflight check; there weren't a great deal of instruments to check, but it always made sense to make sure instruments were working properly and to know their locations. Malcolm found the switch for the motor, lights, and the rudimentary flight controls. He was giving them his usual preflight check when Holmes turned to him and said, "What do you have on your head?"

Malcolm looked up. "What? This? This is my flight hat and goggles for missions in the observation car." When he left for the cargo bay, he had put on the standard issue leather flight hat that covered his head to keep his head warm, goggles to deflect the wind, and leather gloves. He laughed, "It's standard uniform for observation car duty. Not much use underwater, is it?" he said. He took off the helmet, goggles, and gloves and returned to his preflight check.

"Mr. Frye, what's this red switch here?" he asked, pointing to a switch painted red that was set to the far left away from everything else.

"It kind of does the same thing as our emergency ballast release. It will basically push most of the air out of the Nautilus through the bottom, essentially pushing it straight up quickly. But it could get hard to breathe, so I recommend only doing that in case of dire emergency."

"Agreed. Is there anything that you didn't think of, Mr. Frye?"

"Oh, I had a few more tricks up my sleeve, but I ran out of time."

"When I get back, you'll have to fill me in."

"Yes, sir. Good luck, sir. Are you ready for me to seal the hatch?"

"Yes, Mr. Frye. Seal the hatch." He turned to Holmes. "Last chance to escape."

"I would take you up on it, but my orders are clear on the matter. I'm to be there at first contact."

"First contact?" asked Malcolm.

"Yes, first contact between us and the Martians. You don't really think this is anything other than a Martian ship, do you?"

"I had rather hoped it was an asteroid," Malcolm said. "The alternative is a wee bit unsettling."

"Which is why I am here. To make sure that any contact between our two races remains peaceful. His Majesty really doesn't want another Horsell Common on his hands."

"Are you ready?" Malcolm asked.

"As much as I will ever be," Holmes monotoned.

"Very well," Malcolm said. He turned the microphone on. "Nautilus to Daedalus. We're ready to descend."

"Very good, sir. Initiate descent."

The doors of the bomb bay opened and the Nautilus suddenly dropped outside the ship. Malcolm had expected that initial drop, having experienced it many times in the observation car, but Holmes had not and looked a bit worse for the experience. "Don't worry," he said to Holmes. "That should be the worst of it."

"How reassuring," Holmes drolled.

The descent was a little jerky as the weighted observation car descended through the air until it landed on the water. It broke the water's surface and soon the windshield showed nothing but inky blankness.

"Nautilus to Daedalus. We've broken the surface. Call out depth every ten feet."

"Understood." There was a long pause. "Ten feet." Another long pause. "Twenty feet." Malcolm flicked the switch for the outside lights and a small area approximately 10 feet ahead of the Nautilus was illuminated.

"That's better. At least we can see a little," Malcolm said.

The long descent continued. The winch crew in the cargo bay continued to call out depth in terms of the amount of rope being used to lower the Nautilus. It wasn't perfect, but it was the best they could do. The expedition had certainly not expected to have to do reconnaissance and recovery in deep water. As the Nautilus descended, Malcolm and Holmes heard the groans of the hull as the pressure of the water increased with the depth. They both looked at each other nervously for a moment and then turned back to look out the windshield.

When they reached approximately one hundred and twenty feet, Malcolm switched on the electric motor and set the flaps to keep their depth relatively constant. "Nautilus to Daedalus. I'm keeping her steady at 120. Please continue to give us additional line."

"Roger, Nautilus."

Malcolm pulled out a map of the lake he had drawn during one of the many reconnaissance trips, noting the point where the glint of metal was spotted and the point he designated as the point that the Nautilus would enter the lake. Malcolm estimated that he was between twenty and forty feet away from the object. Malcolm wasn't sure what direction the Nautilus had been facing when it entered the water, so he had to take a guess as to whether to turn right or left. Malcolm turned left, thinking that they had been lined up in the same direction as the Daedalus.

The Reluctant Captain

The little engines thrummed to life and strained to move the ship forward. The Nautilus moved slowly, almost barely noticeable. But the ship did pick up some measure of speed and continued forward slowly. There was still nothing ahead, until suddenly the windshield was filled with reflected light.

As Malcolm's eyes adjusted to the glare, his jaw dropped. There ahead of him appeared a curved metal surface. "Nautilus to Daedalus. We've found the object. We're beginning our reconnaissance."

"What is it, Nautilus?"

"Uncertain, Daedalus. We only have approximately 10 feet of visibility, so we can't make the whole shape out. We'll advise you when we know more. Nautilus out."

Malcolm swung the Nautilus around until he thought he was running the length of the object. The Nautilus followed the object up, as it seemed to ascend to the surface. Eventually, the cylinder ended. Malcolm swung the Nautilus around to look at the top of the cylinder. There was a large hole at the bottom of the cylinder.

"Are you seeing this, Mr. Holmes?" Malcolm asked.

"I am. What do you think that hole does?" he asked.

"I don't know. It looks like it's some kind of nozzle capable of directing some sort of gas or something. It might be some kind of propulsion."

"That is my analysis as well," Holmes said.

Malcolm directed the Nautilus back down the length of the cylinder. As they descended, they noted that the cylinder was more or less intact; there were a few places where pieces of metal seemed to be missing, but the ship was more or less whole. In some places, there were markings that looked like a mixture of pictures and script. Neither Malcolm nor Holmes could make it out, although Holmes did note that it had elements of the ancient cuneiform script.

As they travelled farther down the length of the cylinder, they could make out the end of the cylinder. It looked like it would become a cone, but much of it was buried in the dirt at the bottom of the lake. Then Malcolm saw something glint in the light and he saw what looked like a dark glass. He pointed it out to Holmes and piloted the Nautilus to the location. As he approached, he noticed what looked like a broken windshield, where shards of glass still stood in the frame. Malcolm gently maneuvered his ship so that he might peer into the ship.

He was not ready for what his lights displayed. Strapped in a chair before the windshield looked like a giant octopus, but with many more limbs. It appeared that several supported the creature in its seat while others looked like they were still wrapped around a number of controls. Although a large piece of glass was imbedded in its head, Malcolm still thought that the thing would start moving at any moment.

"Good God," Malcolm said. "It is true. There really are Martians and they've landed."

"Yes. We must keep this as absolutely quiet as possible. You must tell no one, unless I authorize it," Holmes said seriously.

"Do you really think this will be able to be kept quiet on an airship?"

"I think it can be managed. Let the crew gawk over the strange contraption we found, but do not under many circumstances let them know that it was piloted by creatures like this. Say it seems to be a probe of some kind."

Suddenly there was a sudden pinging sound, as if a bearing had been thrown against the wall, and then the sound of running water.

"What's that?" asked Holmes nervously.

"It's not good," said Malcolm.

Chapter 25

Malcolm turned around and his worst fears were realized. One of the rivets popped because of the pressure. There was now a small stream of water coming into the back of the Nautilus.

"Nautilus to Daedalus. Pull us up immediately. We're taking on water. Repeat. Pull us up immediately!"

"Aye, Captain."

Malcolm took the headset off and gave it to Holmes. "Here," he said as he thrust the headset at him. "This is the microphone. Press here to talk."

"Where are you going?" asked Holmes in alarm.

"I'm fixing the leak. Hopefully it will buy us enough time for the Nautilus to pull us up." Malcolm climbed over the seat to the small space behind his seat. He had feared that something like this might happen, so he grabbed the small can of tar he had placed aboard before their descent.

Malcolm quickly found the hole and first tried to fill the hole with a glob of tar. Every time he tried, the pressure would just push it back out. Malcolm looked around and found a discarded screw, left over from the retrofit. Malcolm examined it and realized that it had been stripped, but that didn't matter for now. Malcolm covered the head of the screw with the still hot tar. He was about to brace himself for the pain, when he remembered his leather flight gloves. He put them on and pushed the screw in place. As soon as it was there, he put another glob of tar to seal it from the inside. He slowly stepped away and the screw seemed to hold. It wouldn't have to hold too long as long as they kept climbing. The closer they got to the top, the less pressure there would be.

And then there was a sudden jolt and the observation car then started rocking from side to side. "What the bloody hell is going on?" asked Malcolm.

Holmes looked around, trying to find the microphone that he had been holding. He found it and asked, "What the bloody hell is going on?" He looked at Malcolm. "Just relaying your communication," he said.

"This is Frye. It looks like the motor has burned out on the winch. We won't be able to pull you up with the winch any farther."

Malcolm moved back to the pilot's chair and took the microphone and headset from Holmes. "This is the captain. Commander Saxon, begin to climb as prudently as possible. I think we'll be alright; my patch is holding." Suddenly, the same pinging sound happened again, followed by the sound of water. "Never mind, the patch is not holding. We need to get out of here fast. Do you have any idea how far down we are?"

"I reckon about 70 to 80 feet," Frye responded.

"Very good, Commander Saxon. Tell me when you've gained twenty feet more altitude."

"Very well, Captain, but the ship is not responding to the drag of the Nautilus in the water. I'm struggling to get her aloft."

"Keep trying," Malcolm said. "Anything you can give me will help."

There was another ping and the sound of more water rushing. It was what he feared; a single leak would exert more pressure on the hull, causing more pressure, causing more leaks until the whole thing cascaded out of control. Water was beginning to collect quickly in the compartment. Malcolm could feel the cold water beginning to swirl around his feet.

"How are we coming with that lift?" asked Malcolm.

"About five feet sir. Should I drop the emergency ballast?" asked Saxon.

"No, not yet. Just keep trying to get us up," Malcolm said. "Mr. Frye, any idea how much lift we can expect to get from blowing the air?"

"I don't know sir. I need to get the computator to run the equation."

"Never mind," Malcolm said, pulling out his slide rule. He estimated the volume of air in the ship, the force that the air would have when escaping, the mass of the ship, and the effect that the water would have on the ship. It was at best an educated guess for all of this, but Malcolm manipulated the slide rule, getting answers to his calculations. He guessed low and figured that at best, it might lift them sixty feet.

This was a gamble. If he blew the air in the cabin and they weren't high enough, they would have no air and nothing to pressurize the cabin. They would be crumpled like a piece of paper. But if they were close enough, it might bring them to the surface. Malcolm grabbed the controls and angled the Nautilus as far up as he could and had the little engine working as hard as possible. The nose of the Nautilus began to rise and Malcolm thought he felt a little less tension in the line.

As he did, he felt the water recede from his feet and he heard it slosh back to the rear of the compartment. Good, he thought, that would help keep the nose up. But no sooner had he finished the thought than there was the sound of sparks and with dread, Malcolm realized that the water had shorted out the electric motor. Malcolm had no way to steer the tiny ship.

"That wasn't good, was it?" asked Holmes.

"No. The engine shorted out. I have no way to help the Daedalus pull us up," Malcolm said grimly.

"Oh, is that all?" Holmes asked, adopting an attitude of indifference. "Do you have any ideas on how to get us out of this predicament? His Majesty would be very upset if his personal representative would die while under your protection."

"Funny, I think if that happens, I won't have to worry much about His Majesty's displeasure," Malcolm said.

Suddenly, the ship jerked up again, the play in the towing line suddenly gone. When it did, water splashed up and the interior lights momentarily went off, leaving the cabin in utter darkness. "Bloody hell," Malcolm muttered. The water that continued to fill the compartment had caused a momentary short when it hit one of the lights. Fortunately, it hadn't burned the light out, but Malcolm knew they faced a bigger problem.

The electricity for the car was being fed directly from the generators on the Daedalus. If the lines carrying the electricity within the cabin became submerged, the water would conduct the electricity all through the cabin.

Malcolm grabbed the radio. "How are we coming on gaining altitude?"

"We've gained about 15 feet, sir," Saxon replied. "That last tug upset things up here, but no real damage."

"Give me as much as altitude as you can. We're running out of options down here."

"Will do, sir."

Malcolm heard another ping and even more water started to rush into the cabin. The nose of the ship began to slowly lift to a vertical position as the water continued to collect in the tail section. Malcolm turned and kept an eye on the rising water, while one hand went to the emergency switch that Frye had pointed out earlier. "Mr. Holmes, I'm going to blow the air just before the water hits the electrical systems. On my mark, take as big a breath of air as you can manage."

Malcolm watched in alarm as the water began to pour into the compartment at a furious rate. Suddenly, he realized to his horror that he hadn't accounted for the weight of the water inside the cabin. He realized with a shudder that there would not be enough force to push the Nautilus to the surface when he forced the air out of the cabin. Unless...

Malcolm grabbed the radio. "Commander Saxon, prepare to release the emergency ballast on my mark."

"Aye sir," came the reply on the radio.

"What do you have in mind?" asked Holmes.

"We won't have enough force to push us to the surface by forcing our air out of the cabin," he said. "But I think if I can time it with the release of the Daedalus' ballast, we might be able to get to the surface. We'll use the momentum from the Daedalus to get us moving up and use the force of the air to keep climbing. We need to move quickly. Are you ready?"

The Reluctant Captain

"As ready as I'll ever be," he said.

"Daedalus, release emergency ballast!" Malcolm yelled into the microphone. There was a two second delay and suddenly, the Nautilus was tugged up. Malcolm could feel the movement through the water. Malcolm turned around to see that the water was getting dangerously close to the electrical mains. Even if he wasn't electrocuted, if they shorted out, he wouldn't be able to push the air out of the cabin.

Malcolm turned back to watch the forward progress of the ship. Malcolm could feel that it was beginning to slow. "Take a deep breathe now!" he ordered. He waited one more second and flipped the emergency switch. Almost simultaneously, the lights went out, indicating that the electrical system had shorted out. The cabin was pitch black now as all electricity to the ship was nonexistent. Just as Malcolm was ready to resign himself to drowning or suffocation, he felt himself pushed back into his seat as the Nautilus kept moving. Seconds ticked by as the Nautilus kept moving and pushing him back against his seat. Ahead of him, through the windshield, it began to get lighter and lighter until sunlight flooded the cabin, blinding them. Malcolm felt his stomach rise and fall as the Nautilus leapt into the air like a mechanical dolphin and splashed on the surface of the lake.

A little lightheaded from lack of air, Malcolm had the presence of mind to find the explosive release that would blow the canopy of the Nautilus off of the body. The air rushed in and Malcolm savored its cool freshness. In a few minutes, the Daedalus was able to pull the car out of the water, fly it over the shore, and drop it near the base camp.

Once the Nautilus came to rest, Malcolm first helped Mr. Holmes out of his harness and then released himself. When he stepped onto dry land, a cheer broke out from the crew of the base camp who had been huddled around the radio, desperate for news.

Malcolm waved to the crew to acknowledge the cheers, when he saw a figure racing toward him. Before he could turn his attention to the racing form, he felt a powerful slap across his face that stunned him momentarily. He heard Joan's voice say, "You arrogant, egotistical bastard! I told you not to go down in that death trap!"

Malcolm opened his mouth to speak, but found that his mouth was covered by Joan's who had grabbed him and was kissing him passionately. Again he heard the cheers of the crew, but this time he did not acknowledge them, instead enjoying this moment.

Chapter 26

Malcolm reluctantly pulled himself away from Joan. "We'll talk tonight," he said, squeezing her hand. "I have to be captain again."

"We'll see if I decide that I'm still talking to you," she said with a mix of humor and seriousness that Malcolm found worrying. She may very well stop talking to him after this and the thought of that bothered him.

Malcolm trudged up to the base camp to relay orders when Doctor Jenkins stopped him. The doctor insisted that both Malcolm and Mr. Holmes submit themselves to medical examination before he would allow Malcolm to resume his duties as captain. Sighing, Malcolm knew there was no point in arguing and reluctantly followed the doctor to the ship.

To Malcolm's annoyance, the doctor insisted on examining Holmes first. Malcolm was seething, knowing he should be doing countless other things, but he was stuck there while the doctor took his good sweet time examining Holmes, who wasn't even a member of the crew. Finally, the doctor summoned him to the examination room. He started to unbutton his uniform when he saw he was not alone in the room; in fact, the small room was nearly filled. Doctor Jenkins, Joan, Mr. Holmes, and Mr. Frye were all there looking at him expectantly.

"Are you all here to tell me, I told you so? With the exception of Mr. Frye, I believe you all warned me against this endeavor," he said.

"No, Malcolm," said Joan, disregarding any pretext of propriety. "We came here to warn you. Again."

"Warn me about what?" asked Malcolm. He was suddenly very confused.

"It appears our saboteur has struck again," said Mr. Holmes. "It is possible that I was the target of this attempt, but I rather think that given all that has occurred, you might have been the real target."

"Sabotage? What sabotage?" asked Malcolm.

"The winch, Captain," said Mr. Frye. "As soon as it froze up, I started trying to tear it down to fix it. When I did, I found the gears had been broken. The winch could let out all of the rope it wanted, but it just couldn't wind it back up."

"Does anyone else know about this?" Malcolm asked.

"No. Doctor Jenkins was with me, watching the expedition from the cargo hold. He saw the broken gears firsthand. It was his idea to fetch Miss de St. Leger and then he told me to wait in the sick bay until you arrived."

"I find it curious that so many attempts would be made on your life," mused Holmes.

"Curious is not the word I would use," Malcolm said sarcastically.

"That's not what I meant," Holmes replied coldly. "What would happen if you were to die?"

"Commander Saxon would take command, and I assume that either Mr. Frye or Mr. Hensley, the navigator, would be in line for second in command."

"Let's examine that train of thought for just a moment," Holmes said. "If Saxon were to pick Mr. Frye as second in command, who would be chief engineer?"

"I don't know," said Mr. Frye. "Most of the boys are pretty green, nearly as green as I was when I started under the captain."

"So, in one stroke, the saboteur could effectively rid the ship of any technical capability. Interesting," Holmes mused.

"But to what end?" asked Malcolm.

"I'm not sure. It is an interesting line of thought that may bear some fruit. Why indeed would one want an airship without engineers?"

The Reluctant Captain

"It would limit her ability to come out of a fight on top," Malcolm said. "Also, it would make it difficult for anyone else to correct anything done to the ship."

"Why go to all the trouble to sabotage the winch?" Malcolm asked.

"Because it needs to look accidental," said Joan. "Whether you know it not, you have the respect of your men. They know it was you that got them out of the mess with the German zeppelins and they know you're the one to get them out of any other tight spots. I daresay that your little expedition today further cemented the notion that you're someone who will spit in death's eye when the time comes."

"Suppose all of this is true," Malcolm said. "Although personally, I don't buy it. Who's after me and why? Is Saxon a suspect?"

"Of course Saxon's a suspect. But then again, so is everybody not in this room. Miss de St. Leger, you've been observing him. What is your report?"

"I'm uncertain, sir. I haven't observed him doing anything out of the ordinary. The crew likes him, but I don't think they bear him any great love or malice. He's rather an unknown entity to them. Although he's very charming, he's able to talk for a very long time and say absolutely nothing—not in the way a pompous politician might, but as in someone who doesn't want to show himself to anyone. I can't tell if he's hiding something or not, because he never lets anyone get near him." Malcolm wondered when she had time to compile all of this information.

"Then he is as much a suspect as anyone else at this point. The intriguing question is what does Saxon have to gain besides becoming captain?"

"I can say that being captain is not a prize worthy of killing someone over," said Malcolm.

"No, I don't suppose it would be," said Holmes. "For now, we'll continue on as usual. Be vigilant. Take no unnecessary chances. That most certainly includes you, Captain," he said pointedly. "No more submarine expeditions."

"I think my last trip rather cured me of that particular interest," Malcolm said. "Am I cleared for duty, Doctor?"

"Of course you are. It was only a pretext to get you here," said Doctor Jenkins.

"Of course, I'm always the last one to know." Malcolm said. "Mr. Holmes, perhaps we can have a brief discussion on the next steps for the current mission."

"Agreed," said Holmes. The two conferred on their course of action and within the hour, a select group consisting of Holmes, Joan, Saxon, Zhukovsky, Koltsov, Rutherford, Dr. Jenkins, and Mr. Frye was assembled in the captain's office.

"Thank you for coming on such short notice," Malcolm said. "As His Majesty's representative, I'm going to turn this meeting over to Mr. Holmes. Before I do, let me admonish you that what we discuss here is considered top secret by both of our governments and what is said here cannot leave this room. Mr. Holmes."

"Thank you, Captain," Homes said. "As Captain Robertson said, this matter is a top secret matter of the highest security to both of our governments. Despite the melodrama of our return to the surface, our mission below was successful. Captain Robertson and I were able to identify the object that caused the explosion and created this lake. It is in fact a vessel from another world carrying at least one alien."

This brought a flurry of discussion from the participants. Mr. Holmes raised his voice and continued. "We saw a metal cylindrical object nearly 100 feet long with a conical head that is buried in the bottom of the lake. The conical section had a window that was broken, probably by the impact, and through that we were able to observe a pilot of alien nature." Holmes went on to describe the tentacled being in as much detail as they had been able to gather. Koltsov started muttering excitedly, seemingly to himself.

"We need to retrieve this object. After discussing the matter with Captain Robertson, we believe that we should be able to

The Reluctant Captain

bring the ship aboard the Daedalus, refuel at an airfield near Moscow, and continue to England. The issue at hand is how best to retrieve the object and take it with us without alerting the crew to the nature of the object."

"How do you intend to get it out of there?" asked Rutherford. "It seems as if the submersible would not be useful for this endeavor."

"You're correct, Professor. I also don't believe that the winch would be powerful enough to lift the object on its own. I have a thought, that I've sketched out here," Malcolm said, as he pulled out a piece of paper on which he had sketched the object and a series of balloons tied to the object.

"This is the plan. First, we need someone with underwater welding experience to take one of the dive suits and weld several brackets so that we can tie balloons to the object. The balloons would be filled by our helium production gradually. Eventually, the lift should be enough to bring the whole thing up, assuming the ship is still structurally sound. I saw nothing that indicated that this was not the case."

"I'll do it, sir," said Frye. "I've had dive and underwater welding experience."

"Thank you, Mr. Frye. I was counting on you. Professor Rutherford, can you assist Mr. Frye in determining how best to weld something onto the metal alloy that makes up the object?"

"I believe I can, though I know very little about the welding process," Rutherford said.

"Mr. Frye can help from that side. What we need is your knowledge of chemistry to help determine the best method for welding the brackets to the object. Mr. Frye, after welding the brackets in place, it will be up to you to attach the balloons. Once you return to the surface, we'll inflate the balloons and give an assist with the winch. Once we get it to the surface, we might be able to figure out its approximate weight and adjust ballast accordingly."

"The next step will be to secure the interior of the object. Commander Saxon and I will take care of that duty. Before you object," Malcolm said, forestalling any disagreement, "we cannot leave this to other crewmen due to the need for secrecy."

"Actually," Mr. Holmes interrupted, "this would be an excellent opportunity for Miss de St. Leger. His Majesty's interests must be preserved and I don't think we can risk our two senior officers in such as scouting mission."

Malcolm was about to object on the grounds that Joan was a woman and couldn't possibly have the combat skills necessary. But the look she had on her face told him he best keep that opinion to himself.

"Professor Koltsov," Malcolm continued, "once we get that ship secure, I will need you to analyze the remains of the creature we saw. Dr. Jenkins, I also want you to lend your medical expertise to the matter. There may have been some decomposition, but I'm hoping there's enough for you to tell us more about the alien." After Joan finished the translation, he nodded, saying "Da, da."

"Professor Zhukovsky, once the ship is secure, you and I," Malcolm hesitated to see if anyone had another objection, "will examine the ship to try to understand its technology and even what caused the crash. Once this is accomplished, we'll try to get the ship on board the Daedalus. I have an idea that may just allow us to get it through the bomb bay doors. When our preliminary analysis is completed, we will take off and head for London for debriefing by the Admiralty. Does anyone have any questions? Very good, we all have jobs to do, so let's get moving."

"Captain, I'm glad you survived that nasty business in the submersible," said Saxon who had lingered after everyone left. "Are you alright?"

"I'm fine, Commander. It was a bit touch-and-go there, but I'm fine. Thank you for asking."

"What should I be doing, Captain?" Saxon asked. "I feel rather useless at this stage."

"As do I," agreed Malcolm. "I'm afraid that we should leave this up to the experts at this point. For now, I'd like you to

The Reluctant Captain

personally oversee the security detail around the spaceship after we raise it. I'd also like you to think of ways we can keep the crew occupied so that when the spaceship does rise to the surface, we don't have many curious eyes peering down."

"Very good, sir. Perhaps some sort of drill might keep the crew's attention away from what's happening."

"Excellent idea, Saxon." Malcolm replied. "However, make sure you don't involve the engine room in the drill; we'll need their expertise and attention to pump helium down to the balloons."

"What will you be doing, sir?" asked Saxon.

"Right now, I'm going to find Rutherford and Mr. Frye. I believe that I can at least assist in the calculations for the needed lift to pull that spaceship out of the water."

"It really is a spaceship?" asked Saxon curiously.

"Aye, and with one ugly squid-faced alien in the pilot seat," said Malcolm.

"Remarkable," said Saxon.

"Aye, that it is." said Malcolm as the two officers rose and left the office. Malcolm continued to the engine room where he found Rutherford and Frye discussing the chemical composition of the metal. Malcolm let them bicker and when they stopped for a moment, he told them that he was here to lend a hand in figuring out how many balloons would be needed to lift the ship from the water. The two men barely acknowledged him and went back to work. So much for being captain, Malcolm thought. Malcolm grabbed some blueprint paper and started to sketch out the ship as best he could from memory, with estimates of the size of the ship. He pulled his slide rule from the holster that he always kept on his belt and soon began estimating the weight of the ship based on the density of the metal alloy that Rutherford had analyzed. Malcolm had to assume that the ship was flooded with water and that would also contribute to the weight that would need to be lifted. Malcolm soon realized that his original approach was not going to work; they would need far more balloons than they had to be able to lift the ship to the surface.

Malcolm stared at the ship's design. He knew that water had entered from the cabin, but had no idea if there were any other openings in the hull; he hadn't seen any on this reconnaissance trip. But the problem was the volume of water inside the ship. Malcolm thought they might be able to lift it if it had still been sealed, but the weight of the additional water was too much. Malcolm stared at the picture of the ship, in his mind applying forces at various places to figure out how be to make it rise. As he did so, he was absentmindedly playing with his mechanical pencil, flipping it between vertical and horizontal with his fingers. He stopped and looked at this hand. The pencil was the same shape as the ship. Then, an idea came to him. He left the engine room and returned several minutes later with a couple of small balloons filled with helium and a bowl of water. He took apart his mechanical pencil, set the inner workings aside, and dropped the pen into the water. He waited for the bubbles to subside as the water filled the inside of the mechanical pencil. First, he tied a balloon to the center of the pencil, all the while keeping the pencil submerged. The pencil rose somewhat in the bowl, but didn't break the surface. He then slid the line to the front of the pencil. This time, the front rose, but the bottom still rested on the bottom of the bowl. Finally, he slid the line to the end of the pencil. The rear stopped for a second and gradually continued to rise.

Malcolm suddenly realized that the engine room had become very quiet. He looked up to find all eyes fixed on him. "I just figured out how we're going to raise the object," he said triumphantly. "What did you think I was doing?"

"I wasn't really sure, sir," said Mr. Frye. "I'm still not sure what you're doing."

"Look," Malcolm said, indicating that Frye and Rutherford should join him. "I did some calculations and quickly realized that we were not going to have enough lift to bring the object to the surface. We needed another way and I needed to simulate what we needed to do. Behold, the lake," he said, indicating the bowl, "and the pencil is our object."

"Our biggest issue," Malcolm continued, "is that the object is filled with water, making it even heavier than it already is. Assume for the moment that there are still some pockets of air in the object and that the water was not able to completely fill the object. If we try to lift it up in the middle," he said as he slid the string to the middle of his pencil, "we can only lift a little. If we try to lift it by the nose, any air in the object will bubble out and it will fill with more water," he continued as he pulled the string to the front of the pencil. It lifted the nose only very slightly.

Malcolm removed the pen from the water and emptied the water. He again submerged the pen and waited for the bubbles to stop. "If we lift it from the end, here," Malcolm said, moving the string to the rear of the pencil, "the air will bubble to the end we're lifting and will give us an assist." He moved his hand from the pencil and, as before, it lifted slowly and then continued to lift. "I believe that with a number of balloons affixed to the stern of the object, we can get it mostly to the surface and then use the Daedalus to drag it to shore."

Rutherford stared at the blueprint and then the bowl of water. "How in the world did you come to this?" he said, staring in wonder at Malcolm.

"The same way I imagine that you extrapolate from postulation and observation. In this case, I happened to notice how much my mechanical pencil looked like the object. Thinking on the smaller scale let me take things I knew about buoyancy and apply them on the large scale. I just used the bowl to prove my hypothesis."

Rutherford shook his head in amazement. "When I started this trip, I had no time for engineers; I thought they were just untalented scientists who had neither the intellectual capacity nor character to pursue pure research. I've come to realize that what you do is just as intellectually demanding and hard as pure research."

"Thank you, Professor," said Malcolm.

"May I interrupt the mutual admiration society to get back to the problem at hand?" asked Mr. Frye. "We still have to figure out how we're going to be able to weld anything to this alloy."

The three continued to work until well after midnight before determining the right temperature to weld stainless steel to the alloy. Exhausted but exhilarated, the trio left for their respective quarters and fell asleep as soon as their heads hit the pillows.

Malcolm was up the next morning at dawn and ready to oversee the lifting of the spaceship from the lake. He double-checked his figures with Mr. Frye, Rutherford, and Zhukovsky to give the best possible estimate of what was needed to raise the spaceship. During the morning, the engineering crew fabricated the necessary brackets for the balloons. While Mr. Frye prepared for his part of the mission, Malcolm turned to the issue of the winch motor in the cargo bay. As he tore the motor down, he realized that the damage was not irreparable, but would have taken more time than he had in the Nautilus. He could clearly see where the gears had been sabotaged, allowing it to feed out but not pull up. Malcolm was determined that this would not happen again.

Malcolm spent the better part of the day getting the winch back into service and when he was finished, he felt a surge of happiness in his heart. He had ceased to be an engineer for what seemed like months and he missed it. He really did belong here, he thought. I'm going to ask to be allowed to return to my post as chief engineer when this is over. He turned to look at Mr. Frye, who was making sure that everything would be set for his dive tomorrow. What would happen to him if Malcolm became chief engineer? Matthew Frye had worked hard and deserved his chance to be chief engineer. And Malcolm had to admit, Frye was every bit as effective as chief engineer as he was. If not for his resourcefulness, Malcolm might be dead, having drowned in the Nautilus. Taking the chief engineer position away from Frye would be a poor way to repay him for saving his life. That's assuming I survive this mission, he thought to himself.

Malcolm re-assembled the select group prior to dinner to update everyone on the plans for the raising of the spaceship. Malcolm told the group about the updated plans for retrieval of the object; Zhukovsky boasted that he could have told them their original plan would never work and Malcolm was sorely tempted to argue with the curmudgeonly professor, but thought better of it. At first light in the morning, Mr. Frye would dive to the object and begin the welding work and attachment of the lift balloons. The group agreed that each system used in the retrieval operation would be double-checked—first by Frye, then by Malcolm just prior to the start to ensure that no further sabotage would occur. Mr. Saxon turned the retrieval operation into a rescue drill that would have everyone involved and too concerned about his duty to be distracted by what was being pulled from the bottom of the lake. At the base camp on the lake, Dr. Jenkins and Professor Koltsov set up a makeshift morgue, aided by translation assistance from Joan and a couple of the Russian crewmen. Once the Daedalus pulled the ship to land, Malcolm, Joan, Zhukovsky, and Frye would reposition the base camp tents over the nose of the ship to shield it from curious eyes. The next problem was draining as much water as possible from the spacecraft. Malcolm would oversee the use of pumps to empty the craft. He, along with Zhukovsky, would try to find another way into the ship besides through the windscreen.

Once the ship was drained of water, Miss de St. Leger would reconnoiter inside the craft and determine if there were any additional dangers. Once the inside was determined to be safe, additional teams would be allowed to enter to begin analysis. After initial analysis to determine if there were any dangers to bringing the craft aboard the Daedalus, the craft would be loaded aboard and they would depart. Malcolm bade all of them to eat and get a good night's sleep as it was going to be a very exciting and taxing day tomorrow. Doctor Jenkins made a motion to talk to Malcolm, but saw Joan march over to Malcolm with a grim look in her eye and decided his concerns about alien diseases could wait until the next day.

When they were alone, she said, "You didn't come to talk to me last night." Her tone was cold and Malcolm found himself immediately on the defensive.

"I'm sorry, Joan. I was working with Rutherford and Frye on trying to get this ship out of the water and I lost track of time. I am captain of this ship and I do have responsibilities."

"Do you have any responsibilities towards me?" she asked again coldly. Malcolm did not like the direction that this conversation was taking.

"Well, of course. You're a guest on my ship and a representative of His Majesty's government..."

"Is that all I am to you?" she said softly, tears coming to her eyes.

"What? No, I... I don't know..." he said. "You've tried to kill me, then tried to save my life. You kiss me and then walk away. What am I supposed to make of that?"

"For such a brilliant man, you are so stupid!" she yelled in frustration. "Against my better professional and emotional judgment, I've fallen in love with you, you stupid, pigheaded idiot!"

Malcolm felt like he'd been slapped in the face. "What?"

"There, I've said it," she said crying. "I hate myself for loving you, for caring for your well-being. Why do you think I was so against your trip on the Nautilus? I was afraid I would lose you and I nearly did! When things were going bad in the Nautilus, all I could do was sit there helplessly and listen. It was hell!" she shrieked.

"I'm sorry," he said, consolingly. "But, I had to do it. It was my duty."

"Duty?" she scoffed. "Do you think His Majesty gives one fig if you live or die? He only cares about power—the power this contraption will bestow on England. I think we'd be better off leaving the damn thing in the lake and flying back."

"So, why are you going inside that thing?" he asked. He was angered by her remarks for a reason he couldn't quite understand.

"Duty. Because it's the reason I'm here. I don't want to do it, but it's expected of me. I want to stay here with you where we're both safe."

"Then don't go! I think it's a mistake to send you in there because..."

"Because I'm a woman?" she interrupted. "You don't think I can take care of myself, do you? Because I'm a woman. You think you have to mollycoddle me and protect me from the big, bad world? I have news for you, Captain, I can drop you where you stand."

"But Joan," Malcolm started. Seemingly before the words left his mouth, she had dropped, swung her leg through his and swept them both out from under him. As he fell, she leapt from her crouch and was on top of him.

"Oww," Malcolm howled as the back of his head hit the floor. "I'm sorry, I can't tell. Are you telling me you love me or trying to kill me? I get so confused."

"Both, you idiot," she said, laughing. Her laughter faded and she stared at him for a time, her look becoming more serious. "All this time, you still haven't told me how you feel about me."

"You are the most infuriating, exasperating, stubborn woman..." Malcolm began. He could see her shoulders slump as he started. "...That I have ever had the misfortune of loving." He suddenly grabbed her and rolled over, pinning her to the floor. He kissed her softly at first, and slowly the passion of the kiss enflamed them both. When they broke off, Joan said, "You know, I can pin you just as easily."

"I know," Malcolm said, cutting off any further conversation with a kiss.

Chapter 27

The next morning, there was an air of nervous anticipation rippling everywhere throughout the ship. The crew knew that they would retrieve the long sought-after object and once recovered, would finally be able to begin the long trek home. Malcolm went first to Engineering to personally inspect the air compressor for Mr. Frye's air line as well as the lines used to fill the balloons with helium. Mr. Frye had the compressors working at full overnight to fill the Daedalus with as much helium as she could hold. In fact, the night crew had told Malcolm that they had a couple of moments when they thought that the Daedalus would become untethered. When Malcolm determined that everything was working to his satisfaction, he went to the cargo bay and inspected the winch very closely to make sure nothing had been done to tamper with the winch. A smaller winch that would be used to lower and raise Mr. Frye had also been mounted in the cargo bay and Malcolm inspected that as well. He received a message that Dr. Jenkins wished to talk with him, but in the preparations to make sure everything was ready, it slipped his mind.

Satisfied that he shouldn't receive any other nasty surprises, Malcolm waited in the cargo bay for Mr. Frye. Last night, they agreed that Saxon would command the bridge while Malcolm was in charge from a command post in the cargo bay. The command post consisted of a handheld phone receiver that would be hooked to a microphone in Frye's helmet and a microphone for communication with Saxon on the bridge. Soon, the sound of heavy stomping could be heard as Mr. Frye struggled over in the diving suit. The weight of both his diving boots and the diving belt around his waist made movement aboard the Daedalus a difficult proposition.

"If I had remembered how much bloody work it is to walk in this thing, I would have changed here," Frye muttered.

Malcolm smiled. "But you made it nonetheless. Are you ready?"

"I think so," Frye said. He began inventorying his suit and equipment. The canvas suit was attached to the corselet and everything seemed watertight. The welding gasses were then mounted on the rear of the corselet, becoming a backpack. The line leading to the welding torch was tied to his arm so that he could drop the torch, but not lose it. An igniter was fastened to his belt.

"Remember, Captain, you have to bring me up slowly or I might get the bends. It's a bit of a deep drive and the pressure change might do bad things to me."

"Is that the technical term? Bad things?" Malcolm asked with a laugh.

"I believe it is, sir," Frye said with a smile. Despite the outwardly calm demeanor, Malcolm could tell that Frye was nervous about the dive. He couldn't say that he blamed him. His own descent to the bottom had been scary enough and he at least had the shell of the Nautilus to protect him. Frye only had the suit.

Malcolm took a moment to go over the plan. "When you get to the bottom and signal us, we'll send the balloons down on the winch from the Daedalus," he began. "You can attach the balloons and give us the signal to begin filling. Lastly, you'll connect the hook from the Daedalus to the object."

"Check. Once I signal you that the line is attached, you should start bringing me up. I'd like to be back up here before that object shoots to the surface and I'm in its way."

When the equipment was ready, Malcolm checked that the air line was feeding air to the diving helmet. After the last nautical fiasco, he wasn't taking any chances. The round diving helmet was lowered onto the corselet and screwed into place. Malcolm heard the safety lock click, indicating that it would not come loose. Malcolm picked up the handset. "Can you hear me, Frye?"

"Loud and clear, sir."

Malcolm switched on the exterior electrical lights mounted around the view port of the helmet. "Ready?" asked Malcolm.

"Ready as I'll get, sir," Frye said and then jumped out of the bomb bay door. He fell only a few feet before the line holding him caught. Malcolm turned the winch on and gradually, Frye descended ten feet and broke the plane of the water. Malcolm slowly released the line from the winch to gradually drop Frye in the lake and to see if there were any bubbles indicating a leak in the suit or the seal of the helmet. Soon Frye was completely submerged. Malcolm waited a few seconds before calling Frye on the headset. "All set down there?" he asked. "No leaks?"

"None, sir. I'm nice and dry."

"Excellent. I'll let you descend more quickly now." Malcolm allowed the winch to pick up speed. After a minute or so, Frye spoke. "What a boring trip down. There aren't even any fish to watch," he said.

"I don't think there are any fish in the lake," Malcolm said. "The lake didn't exist before last year, remember?"

"I know, but I wish I had something to look at."

Several minutes went by before Frye spoke. "I've reached the bottom. Send down the balloons and the brackets. Once I have them, I'll make my way over to the tail section."

Several more minutes went by before Frye spoke again. "I'm at the tail. I'm beginning the welding." Now there was nothing to do but wait. Malcolm took the opportunity to monitor the air compressor sending air to Frye as well as the helium lines. An hour passed before Frye spoke again. "Brackets welded and hook attached. Bring me home, Daedalus."

"With pleasure, Mr. Frye," Malcolm said. Malcolm turned the winch on and began the painstakingly slow ascent necessary to prevent the nitrogen in Frye's blood from bubbling due to the change in pressure. The ascent continued with stops along the way for Frye to become used to the change in pressure. Eventually, Frye was raised back into the Daedalus with no mishap.

Malcolm began filling the balloons attached to the object. He decided to wait until Frye was back aboard so there was no chance that the object would suddenly rise to the surface with Frye in its path. Malcolm turned on the main winch and reeled in line to the object until it was taut. Several more minutes passed as the balloons below gradually filled with pressurized helium so that they could properly inflate. Eventually, the line on the main winch began to slacken. Malcolm activated the winch and ordered Saxon to drop the emergency ballast to give them lift. The Daedalus bucked up briefly as the ballast was released, but not much. From his vantage point, Malcolm could sense that they were very slowly climbing into the sky. Soon Malcolm could see water rippling and bubbling before first the balloons and then the tail of the ship came into view. The Daedalus began to rise more quickly and soon its ascent was pulling the ship out of the water faster than the winch. Once the cone cleared the surface of the water, Malcolm directed Saxon to navigate the Daedalus and its prize to the shore. Saxon carefully maneuvered the Daedalus to a suitable landing spot and lowered the Daedalus until the cone of the spaceship was touching the ground. Malcolm slowly released the line with the winch to lower the object to the ground. It landed with an audible thud.

Malcolm directed Saxon to release some of the helium from the ship so that it could once again land. When the lift on the Daedalus was such that it could no longer lift the object, Malcolm ordered the winch to pull the Daedalus down the rest of the way. By now, Frye was out of his diving suit and Joan suddenly appeared. He had to do a double take because he almost did not recognize her. Gone were petticoats, skirts and jackets and instead, she was in a form-fitting leather jacket and equally form-fitting trousers tucked into high leather boots. Around her waist was a belt with two holstered guns of a design that Malcolm had never seen before. They were much larger than his service revolver. They resembled revolvers, but were much bigger; the chambers were a good six inches long. The ammunition that must fit those chambers would likely stop an elephant, Malcolm thought. Malcolm thought they might only be used for short range, as they had virtually no barrel. They were stocky and serviceable, yet glinted of bronze and brass. They reminded him instantly of Joan, beautiful, elegant... and deadly.

In addition to the two guns, she also had a bandoleer full of knives and what looked like grenades. She was examining a small backpack, inventorying its contents. Malcolm saw a grappling hook and rope before she drew the bag close and hoisted it on her back. She looked at Malcolm and nodded that she was ready. Joan descended the rope ladder through the bomb bay door. Malcolm, Frye, and Zhukovsky followed— Malcolm carrying a portable phone set and wire, Zhukovsky carrying a tool box, and Frye carrying a gas powered sump pump and a long length of rubber hose coiled around his shoulder.

They approached the spaceship. Malcolm thought it looked almost as eerie in daylight as it did in the depths of the lake. Malcolm could now see that the ship was in fact a grey, metallic color that did not match the color of any metal that Malcolm recognized. Malcolm noticed in a few places the same odd script that he'd seen while in the Nautilus, but the ship seemed to be mostly unadorned. They explored the whole area around the ship, looking for a place where Joan could enter. As they approached the cone of the ship, Malcolm noticed a rectangular seam that might indicate a door or hatch.

Satisfied that they found the best point of egress, Malcolm, Frye, Joan, and Zhukovsky broke down the base camp tent and reassembled it over the front half of the spaceship. With only four people to try to set up the large tent, it took them some time to raise the tent. Malcolm did not want to use any additional manpower to limit the access to the spaceship.

Malcolm and Zhukovsky immediately started examining the area near what they assumed must be a door. A visual inspection revealed nothing. Malcolm decided to start tapping the area, looking for some sort of panel that might open. After several minutes, Zhukovsky found a panel that opened at his touch. Inside was a handle with more of the script above it. Malcolm examined it for several moments and realized that it looked like the handle could also be rotated and seemed to have places where the end of the handle would connect. Malcolm reached down, pulled the handle toward him, rotated the handle ninety degrees, and gradually let the handle slip back. It connected with a click and there was a sudden whoosh as the rectangular door opened. The stench of decay and mildew rushed out of the ship. Joan started to move toward the hatch, but Malcolm stopped her. "Let Mr. Frye pump out as much water as he can; it will give some time for some fresh air to get in there."

"I thought for a minute you were going to stop me from going in at all," Joan said.

"With all your guns and equipment? I wouldn't have a chance," said Malcolm.

"No, you wouldn't," she said and smiled.

Mr. Frye set up the pump and tossed one end of coiled rubber hose into the spaceship. Frye started the pump and after a few seconds, water started to flow out of the ship. After another thirty minutes, the water slowed to a trickle. After an additional five minutes, Joan asked, "Do you think it's safe?"

"Aye, I think so," Malcolm said. "Are you sure that..." but stopped when he saw the look in her eye. "Let's get you wired up then so you can tell us what's happening." Malcolm opened the phone set and connected the wire to the terminals on the set. He then took the other end of the wire and connected it to her headset. "You'll have to let the wire out as you go, but we'll hear everything you say."

Malcolm picked up the handset on the phone and listened as Joan tested her headset. Satisfied that they would be able to communicate, Malcolm went over to her. "Be careful," he said. "Don't take any unnecessary risks. If anything happens, get out of there as fast as possible."

"I know. I'm smart enough to know the best way to survive a fight is not to have one at all," she said. "But these," she said, indicating her holstered weapons, "don't hurt my chances either."

"One more thing," Malcolm added. He handed her a contraption with a single light on a headband. The headband was connected to a support that connected to a shoulder brace. In the contraption was a large battery that powered the light. Malcolm switched on the light. "This will help you to see without tying up your hands with a flashlight or lantern."

"You think of everything," she said with a laugh.

"That's my job," he said.

Joan checked her equipment one last time, nodded to Malcolm and climbed into the door. Malcolm moved to the phone set and picked up the handset. "Can you hear me?"

"Yes," she replied. "Coming in loud and clear."

"Good," Malcolm said. He wanted nothing more but to go in there himself, but he was half afraid that Joan would shoot him if he did.

"I'm in a hall," she said. "It continues to my left and to my right, there is door. I'm going to try to open that first. There seems to be some sort of switch by the door. There are lights on it. It seems to have power. Is that possible?"

"I suppose," said Malcolm. "Not knowing how the ship is powered, I assume it's possible. Since this ship was designed to travel in the vacuum of space, I imagine that all of the circuits are well sealed, so they may not have shorted out when the ship filled with water. "

"I'm going to press the button on this panel that seems to open the door," she said.

"Be careful," Malcolm said.

Malcolm heard another whoosh and then Joan screamed. "What is it?" he said, rising. He was ready to run in there after her.

"It's alright. I was just startled. I've found the remains of one of the pilots and it's in pretty bad shape. Its head seems to resemble a squid; it's a mass of tentacles. There are lights flashing on the control board in front of me."

"Don't touch anything until we can figure out what everything does," Malcolm warned.

"Don't worry, I'm not touching anything on that control board; it's covered with decomposing alien. The stench is horrible here," Joan added. "I'm going back out to explore the rest of the ship."

"Be careful," Malcolm said.

"I will," Joan said, exasperation coming through in her voice. "I'm in the main corridor. It seems to go another 30 feet. The walls are flat, so that means there's something between the corridor and the exterior. Wait, I think I found another door and panel. It looks identical to the panel in the cone. I'm going to open it."

Again, Malcolm heard the whoosh of the door through Joan's headset. "There's a small room, not very deep. There's a cylinder in the room. I'm going to examine it." There was silence for a few seconds when Malcolm heard Joan take a sharp inhalation.

"What is it? Are you alright?" he asked.

"Yes, I'm fine. There's another alien inside the cylinder. There are more of the strange markings and many blinking lights. I almost get the feeling that this cylinder is keeping the alien alive, but in some kind of sleep. Like Sleeping Beauty."

"But I imagine it'll take more than a kiss to wake him up," Malcolm muttered.

"Well, don't look at me," Joan said. Joan continued her reconnaissance of the ship. She found three other cylinders, two of which contained sleeping aliens. She found what she thought might be a closet or storage area that was filled with a number of odd-looking pistols. They were shaped like a pistol in that they had a handle, a chamber, and a barrel, but were oddly shaped and filled with many curves. There seemed to be no ammunition for them or any way to load them. She continued on until she found what she assumed was the engine room. It was vast. There seemed to be some sort of central furnace or reactor that throbbed with a low, steady light. Malcolm realized that this must be the source of the power for the rest of the ship. What he would give to be in there examining the ship, but there would be time for that later. When Joan was satisfied that the ship was secure, she exited the ship. "Well, that was rather anti-climactic, don't you think?" she said. She sounded disappointed as if she was hoping there would be trouble.

"I'm just glad that one thing went according to plan," Malcolm said, although he was glad that no harm had befallen Joan. "Mr. Frye, please inform Doctor Jenkins and Professor Koltsov that we're ready for them. Have them bring a gurney and something to cover the body."

"Very good, sir," Mr. Frye said and left for the Daedalus. Malcolm peered inside. "Do you think it would be acceptable for me to look around inside, now that you've secured the ship?" Malcolm asked.

"I suppose it would be. The risk seems to be low," she said.

"Good," Malcolm said and pulled the mounted light from Joan and put it on himself. He looked in awe at what was around him. He imagined that what he felt would be similar to an ancient Roman seeing an airship; he might think some of it possible, but he had no idea how it worked and it might just as well have been magic. Malcolm studied the switch at the door and pushed it several times, watching how the door worked.

"Are you going to keep playing with that switch?" Joan asked. "I would think you would be in the engine room trying to figure out what makes it tick."

"Aye, I should be," Malcolm said and immediately strode off toward the engine room. He had already seen the pilot and was in no hurry to view that monstrosity again. Malcolm strode down the hall and could see the blue light pulsing at its end. When he reached it and could clearly see the source, he was thunderstruck.

The large engine room, nearly two thirds of the ship, featured a large cylindrical device whose center was transparent and was the source of the blue, pulsating light. At the end of the cylinder facing Malcolm were hundreds of wires of all thicknesses connected to the top of the cylinder. At the back of the cylinder, five mammoth metal cones were connected to the cylinder.

"This device must provide both power to the ship," he said, indicating the wires at the top, "while also providing thrust for the ship," he added, indicating the cones. "I would love to know how that works. I bet Professor Rutherford would love to take that thing apart!"

"You should see the control room," she said.

"The bridge?" he corrected. "I'd love to!" Together, they returned to the front of the ship and entered the bridge. As Joan had described it, in front of Malcolm was some sort of control board, its function exactly similar to the one on the bridge of the Daedalus. But this was covered with lights, more of the strange script, and switches. In the tentacles of the dead pilot was a stick with a handle meant for grasping by a tentacle. Malcolm reached down, trying not to touch the tentacle, and gave the lever a push. To Malcolm's surprise, it responded smoothly in his hand. Malcolm assumed that the stick controlled both altitude and direction. Is there altitude in space, he wondered to himself. After several more minutes of following wires and switches around the bridge, Malcolm examined the cylinders holding the aliens. Although Malcolm had no medical knowledge, he had the sense that these cylinders were keeping the aliens in some kind of sleep state. For what purpose, he had no idea. Malcolm finally examined what must be weapons, being very careful not to point them at anything that might be important and keeping his finger away from the trigger. He had no idea what these could do, but if they worked like the so-called "heat rays" from H.G. Wells' book, he knew that he shouldn't do anything with them until they were studied in more detail.

Just then, he heard the approach of Doctor Jenkins and Professor Kolstov. Both were wearing diving suits, minus the weighted boots and belt. Jenkins stopped some distance away, opened the visor of his helmet and yelled, "You both were in the ship?"

"Yes, Miss de St Leger explored it and found that there was no danger. I just went in for a look around."

"Let me understand this. You both entered an alien spaceship from another world with a decomposing corpse inside and just spent several minutes inside there. Let me guess, did you touch anything, like something the dead alien may have handled?"

Sensing that he hadn't made a wise decision, Malcolm sheepishly said, "I may have."

"It's a wonder that you're both a captain and still alive at this point. Let me ask you, Captain, how did we defeat the aliens at Horsell Common?"

"We didn't," Malcolm said. "They died of the measles." And then Malcolm got it.

"What?" asked Joan.

"Now you've caught on, haven't you, Captain? Miss de St. Leger, the Martians died because they didn't have resistance to our germs and diseases and succumbed to something very common on Earth. Both of you have been in close contact with the atmosphere of the Martian ship and one of its dead crewmembers. You both very likely could be infected with some Martian pathogen."

"I'm sorry, Captain. I'm afraid I can't let either of you on the Daedalus. Until further notice, I am quarantining both of you in a tent some distance away from the Daedalus until we can determine if there are any ill effects from your contact with the Martian ship."

Chapter 28

Dr. Jenkins, true to his word, had had the crew set up a tent two hundred yards away from the Daedalus with two cots, a small table, and a lantern. Since Malcolm still had a ship to run, a portable handset was left in the tent. Meals were left fifty yards away and a crew member would call on the handset to tell them the food was there, only after everyone was nowhere in sight.

Dr. Jenkins returned with his modified diving suit to check on the patients. He gave Malcolm a note indicating that after he checked them, he would return to the ship and converse about his findings via handset because they would not be able to converse while he wore the helmet. The examination was rudimentary; temperature, pulse and blood pressure were taken, he felt for swelling of nodes in the throat, and he looked for signs of a rash. He left and sometime later, the phone rang and Malcolm answered immediately.

"Everything seems normal, Captain, for both you and Miss de St. Leger."

"Well, that's good. So we can come back?"

"No, I want to wait at least a week until we break the quarantine."

"A week?" yelled Malcolm. "I can't stay out here laying around for a week. I've got a ship to run."

"And you can run it from there. And don't yell at me. I'm not the one who went charging into an alien ship with complete disregard for my health or that of the crew."

"You could have warned me," said Malcolm.

"I tried last night and I sent one of the midshipmen to tell you I needed to see you; you never showed up. Frye told us that you had secured the ship and were ready to bring the aliens out. Before I could make preparations and get word to you, you had charged ahead."

"Oh," said Malcolm. "I'm sorry, Doctor. You're completely right. I should not have overlooked your message. That's your job to advise me and I totally ignored you. I'm sorry. It won't happen again."

"It better not," Doctor Jenkins said grumpily. But his voice soon warmed. "Both you and Miss de St. Leger seem to be feeling no ill effects so this is probably nothing."

"Thank you," said Malcolm. "How are things coming?"

"I'm completely out of my league here, as I think is Koltsov. My Russian is not very good, he doesn't speak any English and although one of the Russian crewmen is acting as a translator, it's hard for us to communicate. Although the alien has cephalopod traits, both Koltsov and I are certain that it isn't from this world."

"What do you mean by 'cephalopod traits'?" asked Malcolm.

"Like a squid or octopus. But unlike the cephalopods on Earth, which are a family of mollusks, these also have more humanoid traits like lungs, hearts, and other internal organs whose purpose I can't begin to fathom."

"Have you figured out the cause of death?"

"With the decomposed state of the body, it's very difficult to tell anything. I'm assuming that the large piece of glass in its head is the immediate cause of death, but even there I can't be sure. It's hard to know what it's supposed to look like. I've tried to use the other aliens in the tubes as reference."

"Excellent. We'll need to make certain the ship is safe to take aboard the Daedalus. Can you handle whatever we need to do to make that happen? The only caveat is we can't let the crew know what is in that ship if we can at all avoid it."

"We'll come up with something, Captain."

"Thank you, Doctor," said Malcolm. "Again, I am sorry for not getting back to you."

"You're the one paying the consequences," said the doctor. "But I have to say, if you're to be trapped with someone for a whole week, I think you're lucky to be trapped with a pretty young woman."

"Doctor," said Malcolm, more than slightly aghast, "I'm an officer and..."

"A gentleman. Yes, I know the traditions. All I'm saying is that if I were trapped with a lovely young woman like that, far away from prying eyes..."

"That's enough, Doctor. Thank you for the call," said Malcolm and he hung up the headset. He could feel his face turn bright red.

"What was that about?" asked Joan.

"Eh, nothing," Malcolm said nervously.

"Really?" Joan said, raising an eyebrow provocatively.

"Yes," Malcolm said with a little too much emphasis.

"Are you sure?" she purred as she moved slowly to the cot where he was sitting, her movement like honey oozing from a jar.

"What?" Malcolm said, as he watched her move slowly closer.

Joan was now standing in front, her belt and guns gone. "It's funny, because I could swear I heard him say how lucky you were to be trapped away from prying eyes with a pretty... young... woman," she said unbuttoning the front of her jacket—her very tight-fitting jacket.

Malcolm started to rise, "My, it seems rather warm in here. I think I need some air." He moved to try to go by her, but she stepped in his path.

"I don't think it's air you really want, is it?" she said, undoing one more button so Malcolm could see just the top of her cleavage.

"I... eh..." was all Malcolm could say before she had closed the distance and kissed Malcolm hard and insistently. He quickly surrendered to the kiss and soon returned it with equal insistence. Joan broke the kiss. "I think," she said, playful touching his nose with her finger, "we should follow doctor's orders and enjoy ourselves away from prying eyes... in a way that would never be possible for the honorable captain of the Daedalus, but might just be possible here."

Malcolm pulled Joan to him and kissed her with new insistence. His hands travelled over her body. After a moment, they found the buttons of her jacket and, with great speed and dexterity, the buttons were released. First her jacket, then her trousers fell, followed shortly by his uniform as they both moved to the cot, but not before Malcolm turned off the lantern.

Sometime later, they lay together under a scratchy wool blanket. Joan curled up next to Malcolm, her hands resting on his chest. Malcolm turned and looked at the brilliant green of her eyes that he could still see within the darkness of the tent. He stared at her for several minutes before she noticed him and said, "What?"

"Whatever did I do to deserve such a beautiful, courageous, and intelligent woman as you?" Malcolm said.

"You don't find that combination threatening?" she said.

"Absolutely! But I wouldn't have it any other way," he said. "But let me check. You're not planning on trying to kill me now, are you? Our usual rendezvous have traditionally started or ended with you trying to kill me and I just wanted to make sure I was ready."

Joan laughed and hugged herself tighter against him. "No, not today. I think we might be past the point."

"Good," Malcolm said. "Now I can save my strength for other pursuits."

"Such as?" she said arching an eyebrow.

Malcolm turned in bed to face her and kissed her passionately. He reached over and pulled her close to him until it felt like their bodies were one. She responded and once again, their bodies were one.

Malcolm had drifted off into a light sleep that was interrupted by the buzz of the phone. Joan made a groan of displeasure, but Malcolm sighed, "Duty calls." He picked up the handset and said, "Yes?"

"Captain, this is Commander Saxon. I trust all is well. I hadn't heard from you regarding orders and I thought I would make sure you're alright."

"Yes, I'm fine," Malcolm said. "Miss de St. Leger and I were comparing notes about our discoveries aboard the ship."

"Comparing notes?" she whispered. "Is that what we've been doing?" She started to curl up next to him and pull him back down to a laying position.

Malcolm playfully swatted her hands and started to get out of bed when he realized he was still naked. He sat back down— pulling the blanket over him— towards the end of the bed farthest from Joan.

"Very good, sir. What are our orders?" asked Saxon.

"Fill me in on what I've missed," said Malcolm.

Saxon told Malcolm that Doctor Jenkins and Professor Koltsov were continuing to examine the remains. They planned to flood the alien ship with a weak solution of carbolic acid to kill any alien germs left in the ship. Mr. Frye was working with Professor Rutherford to scale the reaction to the volume needed to cleanse the inside and outside of the ship. They would use the lake as a source of water for the reaction. Doctor Jenkins and Mr. Frye both agreed that weak carbolic acid would do little damage to the ship, but it would likely kill germs that had travelled with the ship.

"Once we have the ship decontaminated, we will need a means to get it aboard. I believe, sir, that you had an idea about that."

"Yes," Malcolm said. "Using the winch, we bring the nose cone of the ship into the Daedalus through the bomb bay doors at the bottom of the Daedalus. We then push the Daedalus against the ship so that it continues to slide further into the Daedalus until its weight will drop it inside and we can move it the rest of the way inside."

"My, that sounds, so... intriguing," purred Joan in a low voice. "Perhaps you can demonstrate that for me later," she said, fingers reaching for Malcolm.

Malcolm again playfully swatted her hands away and moved further down the bed. "If Mr. Frye has any questions about it, have him give me a call. I have nothing but time on my hands," he said, giving a look at Joan. She pouted in reply.

"Very good, sir. What about you?" Saxon asked.

"I believe that Doctor Jenkins intends to keep us here for five days. If we have no symptoms, he'll let us back aboard. For good measure, I suppose, we should be given fresh clothes when we return and we should burn everything here when we return to the ship. I believe that we still have the flamethrower I made for the Daedalus somewhere about the ship. Mr. Frye will be able to find it. What have you told the crew about my absence?"

"Doctor Jenkins came up with the ingenious story that you were both bitten by a wild animal that you thought might be rabid and you would be quarantined until that could be determined. It's worked to keep people away from the ship and his work."

"A wise man, that Doctor Jenkins," Malcolm said, looking at Joan and drinking in her beauty.

"Yes, sir. Anything else?" Saxon asked.

"No, I think that does it. Let me know if there is anything I can assist with from here."

"Yes, sir," Saxon said and Malcolm hung up the receiver.

"You, lassie, are a vixen and a tease," he said as he launched himself at her.

"Who, me?" she said with an innocent look on her face.

"So, you wanted a demonstration of how we'll get the cylinder inside the Daedalus?" he asked raising an eyebrow.

"That would be most... educational," she said, as she shifted beneath him.

"First, we lift the head inside the ship." A gasp escaped Joan's lips.

"Then," Malcolm said, rolling her over until she was on top of him, "the ship pushes against the cylinder until it's completely inside." A moan escaped Joan again.

"I think we might have to repeat that... several times," she said thickly, her voice full of passion.

"I thought as much," Malcolm said.

The remaining days of their quarantine were a blur. Malcolm had thought when things started that he might actually get some sleep. His days were filled with calls from the ship and visits from Doctor Jenkins. But his nights belonged to Joan and he got very little sleep.

Everything had gone like clockwork in his absence. Frye and Rutherford found the means to decontaminate the spaceship with carbolic acid. It turned out they were able to use the radiation from the ship itself to help produce the reaction. Once the ship was decontaminated, they repeated the procedure on the morgue. Soon, men in dive suits pulled down the makeshift morgue and it was brought over and draped against their tent. Apparently, Saxon intended to burn their tent right where it was and not tear it down.

On the fourth day, Malcolm watched as the Daedalus pulled the spaceship inside, the sight inspiring a re-enactment inside the tent minutes later. After Doctor Jenkins' visit before dinner, he called Malcolm on the headset.

"I think there's no reason to continue the quarantine past tomorrow. I've taken the liberty to have clean clothes delivered to you. You should change outside the tent so as not to contaminate anything, although at this point, I believe we should be safe. You can come back tonight if you wish or stay one more night, just to be prudent."

"I think staying one more night might be the prudent course. After all, one shouldn't go against doctor's orders," Malcolm said.

"Ah," said Doctor Jenkins, "I take it you have seen the wisdom in my advice."

"Yes," said Malcolm, smiling as he looked at Joan. "I've come to see the wisdom in your advice."

"That's good," said Doctor Jenkins. "We'll see you aboard the Daedalus tomorrow whenever you're ready."

"Thank you, Doctor," Malcolm said and hung up. Malcolm was dreading this evening. It was their last alone together—their last before the prying eyes of the crew or the myriad of responsibilities that would pull time away from both of them. Malcolm had so much to say to Joan, but didn't know how to begin.

"Joan, I…" he started and the handset rang again.

"Sir, we've delivered your food, and a set of clean clothes as Doctor Jenkins ordered."

"Thank you."

Malcolm left the tent and started the long march to the food. Next to the food was a parcel sealed in brown paper. Malcolm walked back to the tent and left the clothes outside behind the back of the tent. He went in through the front of the tent and said to Joan, "Dinner is served."

He set the tray on the table and they moved their cots to the table. Malcolm gave Joan her dinner first, poured her some water, and then uncovered his meal. Another unimaginative dinner from Chef—some kind of brown meat, green vegetable, and boiled potatoes all cooked to a nearly uniform mush. Malcolm took a bite of the meat and he thought it had a bitter taste. That was different, even by Chef's standards. He took a bite of his potatoes and again, there was that bitter taste. He tasted the vegetables and again, the bitter taste. He spit the vegetables out and took the tray away from Joan. "What?" she asked.

"The food—there's something wrong with it. A bitter taste, like medicine," Malcolm said, although he was beginning to have trouble speaking. The inside of the tent was beginning to spin and there was a darkness creeping into his vision.

"Drugged," Joan slurred and then fell over on her cot.

"Yesh," Malcolm responded before he too fell to his cot.

Some time later, Malcolm stirred. It felt hot in the tent, it was too bright, and why did he smell smoke? He opened his eyes. Gradually, his mind registered what was happening and he realized with horror that the tent was on fire.

Chapter 29

Malcolm rose and shook Joan. She murmured, but didn't stir. Malcolm found the water from their uneaten dinner yesterday and splashed the water on her face. She sputtered and stirred. "What did you do that for?" she said without opening her eyes. When she did, Malcolm knew she knew exactly what was happening. "Why is the tent on fire?"

"I told them to burn it when we were out of it. Apparently someone forgot the part where we were out of the tent," Malcolm said. He grabbed his belt and service revolver and found Joan's equipment. "Let's go. We'll go out the back where I left our clothes."

Malcolm took one of Joan's knives and cut a large slash down the back of the tent. This side of the tent had not yet caught fire, so they were able to easily exit. A few feet away from them lay the package with their clothes. Malcolm grabbed it and ripped it open, tossing Joan's clothes to her. He then undressed and quickly was in a clean, crisp uniform. He strapped on his service revolver. He glanced up and for an instant, saw that Joan was naked and quickly glanced away. She saw his reaction. "Really?" she asked incredulously.

"We've got to get to the Daedalus before she leaves!" Malcolm yelled to her. He looked up and saw she was in a very similar outfit to what she had been wearing when she entered the spaceship. He tossed her equipment to her, which she quickly strapped on, and they were both running to the Daedalus.

Two hundred yards away they could see that the Daedalus had already lifted off some fifty feet above the ground. Malcolm could tell that the spaceship was weighing it down because it did not seem to have much lift. It was slowly turning west from the site toward Moscow.

Together they ran as fast as they could. Fortunately, the engines of the Daedalus were being used to swing the great airship around and not propelling it forward. Much to Malcolm's surprise, they caught up to the Daedalus as it was still completing the turn. This told him that the ship aboard the Daedalus was taxing the ship's ability to fly. That at least

The Reluctant Captain

had helped them reached the Daedalus. Malcolm knew from past experience that no one would be looking out of the window; everyone would be focused on his job.

"I think we've missed our flight," Malcolm said.

"Nonsense," said Joan who pulled what looked like a grappling hook from her belt, placed it in a cylinder and loaded it into one of the odd-looking weapons she carried. She dropped a large round of cable on the ground in front of her, tying one end to the grappling hook. "Where should I aim?" she said and Malcolm realized what she needed. He scanned the cabin for a place where the grappling hook could catch, but far enough from the engines' propellers that they would not be dragged into them. He scanned the cabin and then found a support girder nearly halfway along the cabin. "There," he pointed, showing her exactly where to aim.

Joan placed her feet squarely on the ground, holding the gun with two hands. She took a deep, slow breath as she squinted at the target. She held the breath for two seconds and slowly released it as she pulled the trigger. There was a loud pop. Malcolm watched the grappling hook sail through the air and the line running out to follow the path of the hook. The grappling hook reached its mark and tangled in the girder. Joan grabbed the end of the rope and pulled it tight to make sure that it would hold. "Come on," she said. "Grab on, we'll have to climb!"

"Climb! Are you crazy? It must be nearly eighty feet!"

"Is that a problem?" she said, cocking an eyebrow.

"No," he said, not really meaning it.

They started to pull themselves up the rope. Joan shimmied up the rope quickly as if it were simple. Malcolm, however, was struggling. He'd never been adept at rope climbing, but had worked at it during the academy so he could pass the physical tests. He continued to work at it while chief engineer because he never knew when he might have to climb out on the rigging. But this was more than he had faced in a very long time. He hauled himself up five feet, ten feet, then fifteen feet and he could begin to feel his arms start to ache. By the time he reached 50 feet, his arms were on fire; by the time he reached a point where he could grab the cabin, they shook with the strain.

"Now what?" Joan yelled, barely audible over the wind and the sound of the engines.

"A little higher," Malcolm said. "There's an external door there," he said as he pointed, "that we use for when we need to inspect the balloon."

"You actually climb on the balloon, while the ship is moving?"

"Aye, we usually have safety harnesses though and are not dangling from the cabin," he said.

"You're crazy!" she yelled.

"Said the woman dangling from a rope on a balloon nearly a hundred feet from the ground," he replied.

"Touché," she said, and pulled herself up the rope.

They climbed to the door. Malcolm quickly found the panel used to open the door from the outside. With a start, he realized that it reminded him of the door release on the spaceship.

Malcolm opened the door and they both fell into the room. Malcolm lay there panting on the floor for several minutes before he pulled himself up and shut the door. He slumped back down next to Joan. "You alright?" he asked.

"I will be when I get my hands on whoever decided to try to cook us," she said.

"Wait," Malcolm said. "Whoever orchestrated this thinks we're dead. I think we should play along."

"You want us to kill ourselves?" she asked incredulously.

"No, of course not. But I think we should hide and let everyone think we're dead. Let them think it was a tragic accident. That will allow us the time to find out who is responsible and settle this once and for all."

The Reluctant Captain

"Agreed. So, now what?" she asked.

"Come on," he said, indicating a trapdoor in the ceiling. "I know every nook and cranny on this ship. I can keep us hidden." Malcolm pulled down the trapdoor that released a ladder so that they could climb. "Ladies first," he said.

Joan climbed and found herself on a platform at the bottom of a large rounded area. It was lighted from the side of the platform by electric lights that gave off a bluish light. A series of steel girders arced from below her feet to over her head, and disappeared on the other side. The girders were crisscrossed with steel cables. Joan could not see the ceiling from where she was, but she could see that it sloped down in front of here. To her left and right were what looked like giant bubbles of fabric tethered by steel cable. With recognition, Joan gasped, "We're inside the balloon!"

"Aye, Malcolm said, looking at his watch. "And unless we intend to be caught, we need to get out of here shortly. Maintenance crews do a visual sweep of the inside of the balloon once every hour. And we only have about five minutes." Malcolm moved ahead and led her to one end of the balloon. He found another door and shortly, they were inside an area filled with pipes. "We should be fairly safe here. This is used for access for the power distribution and water. Unless there really is a problem, no one should bother us."

"Malcolm, what just happened?" Joan asked.

"I think the person that has been trying to kill us thinks he's succeeded. I..." Malcolm was cut off by a voice over the intercom.

"Attention crew of the Daedalus. This is Commander Saxon. It is my unfortunate duty to inform you that there's been a horrible accident that has claimed the lives of Captain Malcolm Robertson and Miss Joan de St. Leger. Despite reports that both the Captain and Miss de St. Leger were aboard the Daedalus, they were both apparently still in the tents when I gave the order to burn the tent. By the time I learned otherwise, the tent was fully engulfed and it was too late to attempt a rescue. Given the urgency of our mission, I have chosen to continue our mission the way the captain would have wanted. We all feel the loss of Captain Robertson deeply and the Air Service has lost a great man. There will be a memorial service tonight at eight bells for the captain."

There was a slight pause before Saxon continued. "With a heavy heart, I take command of the Daedalus. I realize that I can only succeed Captain Robertson, and never replace him."

"That sanctimonious bastard," Malcolm muttered.

"I have relayed this news to the Admiralty and we have new orders which I'm not at liberty to discuss at present." Malcolm and Joan looked at each other, each with the same question on their mind: what new orders? "With heavy hearts, we continue our mission, but I know that Captain Robertson would want us to soldier on and stay true to our mission and our duty. Thank you."

"We need to find out what those orders are," said Malcolm. "I trust that Mr. Holmes would know of any new orders."

"Yes, he would have received a copy of the orders from the Admiralty."

"Then I think we should pay your boss a visit. I hope you don't have claustrophobia."

"What's that?" asked Joan.

"Fear of confined spaces." Malcolm replied.

"Why?" she said suspiciously.

"The only way we're going to get to Mr. Holmes' room unseen is to travel through the air ducts."

"How did I know you were going to say that?" she sighed.

Malcolm checked his pocket watch, nodded, took Joan's hand, and they travelled back into the balloon's interior. They went another twenty feet and entered another room, this one full of ductwork going in every direction.

"This is the main air exchanger for the ship. We take the outside air from there," he said, pointing to ducts that ran the width of the room, "and join the heater. The heater, with the aid of those fans," he said, pointing out several rectangular aluminum boxes, "push the heat out to the rest of the ship. We also use the ductwork to route power and other cables around the ship, so each duct is wide enough to accommodate a person. We frequently use these during maintenance to get around the ship. Now, if memory serves... ah, here's the duct we want." he said, walking over to one of the ducts. Malcolm twisted a handle and opened up a small door that allowed entry into the duct. Malcolm went to the tool rack near the heater and rummaged around until he found an electric torch. He climbed inside and said, "Come on, follow me," and disappeared inside the duct. Joan sighed and dutifully followed. She was happy to note that there was a latch on the inside of the door, so they would be able to get out.

They crawled on their stomachs, inching their way slowly towards Mr. Holmes' cabin at the rear of the ship. They didn't go far before Malcolm switched off the torch and they crept toward the light of a vent. Malcolm moved up and peered at the vent. He could see Holmes sitting at his desk, his face crestfallen and generally looking disheartened. One thing Malcolm noticed immediately was that there was no clacking from his computator. Malcolm frowned. This did not bode well. Malcolm called softly from the vent, "Mr. Holmes. Mr. Holmes, it's me, Captain Robertson."

Holmes sat straight up and looked around the room. He was puzzled at sound of the captain's voice. "Perhaps I'm growing as eccentric as my brother; I must be hearing things," he said out loud to himself. "And now I'm talking to myself."

"Mr. Holmes, it's me, Captain Robertson. In the air vent," Malcolm hissed, trying to keep his voice low.

"Air vent?" Holmes said. He looked around and caught sight of the vent near the ceiling of his room. Malcolm rattled the vent and he saw a look of recognition on Mr. Holmes' face. Silently, Holmes carried his chair to the wall, climbed on the chair, and looked into the vent at Malcolm. "Captain Robertson, I am entirely glad that the news of your demise has been greatly exaggerated. Is Miss de St. Leger safe?"

"Right here, sir," she said.

"Excellent! I have great need of both of you."

"What's happened?" asked Malcolm.

"Did you hear the announcement that Saxon made?" asked Holmes.

'Yes," Malcolm agreed.

"Rubbish. I was in storage bay and I watched a group of three soldiers with flamethrowers ignite the tent. When I returned to my room, I found that the vacuum tubes from my radio had mysteriously disappeared. When I went to report it to the captain, I found that my door was locked from the outside. After I picked it, I opened it only to find two armed guards who would not let me out. They said that they had strict orders for me to remain in my cabin at all costs to save me from any potential danger that could come from the object we are carrying. I tried to push past them, but," he said, rubbing his head, "they were rather insistent that I stay put. So that's what I've been doing ever since. And unless I'm mistaken, and I'm never mistaken, I think the two guards outside my room are Germans pretending to be Russian. I can hear their German accent in their horrible Russian accent."

The pieces were falling into place. The Russians who were sent to serve aboard the Daedalus never made it, replaced instead by German spies. That fit the enigmatic reference to "the cast in place" message that Holmes had intercepted.

"And I take it that you have not seen our new orders?" Malcolm asked.

"No, my equipment is mostly useless without the tubes."

"He's finally made his move, but what's the end game?" Malcolm said, thinking out loud.

"I've been puzzling that myself," Holmes said. "Given the supposition that the guards outside my door are German and the events you described over the North Sea, it appears our Mr. Saxon is eager to turn the Daedalus over to the Germans."

Malcolm thought about this and realized immediately how catastrophic that would be to the Empire. Without bragging, the Daedalus was the most advanced ship in the Royal Air Service. If the Germans were to take her apart, they could neutralize the

Empire's air superiority. Worse, with the alien technology already aboard the Daedalus, the Germans could leapfrog every nation on the planet and dominate the world.

"Let's say you're correct, Mr. Holmes. Where could he take the Daedalus?" asked Malcolm.

"I've been trying to work that out." Holmes got off the char, went over to the table and returned with a map. "According to our original orders, we had enough fuel to make it to here," he said, pointing to the location of the secret air base that was their original destination. "Given that he can't stop for fuel, it limits his options to where he could land. I think it likely that he plans to take the Daedalus to Königsberg in Prussia. It would be an excellent place to resupply before continuing on to our final destination, wherever that may be."

"That seems plausible. I think we should sit tight until we land in Königsberg and resupply the Daedalus. At that point, we should retake the ship and head back to..."

"That might be tricky," said Holmes. "We would have to navigate over Sweden, who may not be happy about our incursion in their airspace. That's the only course we have if we want to avoid Germany, which I think we all agree would be in our best interests. Hopefully by that point we can radio the Admiralty and find out where we should land."

"Agreed," said Malcolm.

"For now, it's important that the two of you continue to appear dead. The only chance we have to retake the ship will be if we have the element of surprise. How long before we reach Königsberg?" asked Holmes.

"Hold the map up closer so I can see it," Malcolm said. He reached down to his belt and found his trusty slide rule. Squinting through the vent, he guessed the distance based on the scale and figured that they wouldn't be able to make best time as they were heavily loaded, but they did likely have the prevailing winds at their back. "I figure five or six days."

"Very well. You'll need to make yourself scarce until then," said Holmes. "Come back here tomorrow and we'll lay out some sort of plan. In the meantime, I will try to find a means to remove the vent so that we can converse face to face."

"Very good. Tomorrow it is."

Malcolm started to move back and his feet kicked Joan. "Ouch!" she said. "What are you doing?"

"Sorry," he whispered. "I forgot you were there. I was trying to go back to the air handling room. This will be tricky; I've never done this backwards. You're going to have to go first. Just keep moving backwards and I'll tell you when to stop."

"Alright," she said. The trip that seemed to take minutes to get here, even crawling through the vents, seemed to take an hour in reverse. When Malcolm finally found the access door and they tumbled out on to the floor, they were both exhausted and relieved.

Lying on the floor, staring at the ceiling, Joan said, "There has got to be an easier way to get around!"

"We could climb outside," Malcolm offered.

"You're no help," said Joan, laughing.

After a pause, Malcolm asked, "Do you want to attend our memorial service?"

"It certainly would be a unique experience," Joan said. "Do we have to use the air vents to get there?"

"No, but we will have to travel down the service chute. From there, we have access to a ledge near the ceiling of the main hangar."

"Do you know every way to get around this ship undetected?" asked Joan.

"Pretty much," said Malcolm. "Chances are good I've had to fix something or install something in every location of the ship. And having memorized the blueprints doesn't hurt."

Malcolm decided that the air exchanger room was the best place for them to stay for the time being. It offered lots of ambient noise to disguise their conversations, and the array of ducts and pipes kept them shielded from view. After a few hours, Malcolm realized that they would soon need food. Fortunately, he knew how to access the ship's pantry from the ductwork. Malcolm left for nearly ten minutes and returned with a small jug of water and several ship's biscuits wrapped in cloth. "I was able to break into some of the long term rations and get these. The biscuits aren't particularly tasty, unless you like salt, but they will fill your stomach.... rather like eating a rock."

"Oh, you do know how to wine and dine a girl," Joan said in mock seriousness.

They both laughed and ate the biscuits in silence. Joan finished one and took a very long swallow from the jug of water. "It's a good thing you brought that water; I'm not sure if I would have been able to swallow that without it."

"I've eaten a few of these before. They are better than nothing," he said. "What a mess I've made of things," he said after a long pause.

"What? You can't be blamed for what Saxon is doing," she said.

"A captain is always responsible for the actions of his crew. If only I'd seen it sooner or confronted him..." he continued.

"And what purpose would that have served? He would have denied it or worse, found a way to kill you on the spot. There's nothing you could have done but let it play out. Now, at least we have an idea of his plans and we can thwart them."

"But now I've dragged you into this mess. If anything were to happen to you, I..."

"Don't worry about me, Malcolm. I can take care of myself. I won't let anything happen to me. I've been taking care of myself for a very long time." Malcolm thought he heard a touch of bitterness in her voice. He looked at her with concern.

She caught his look. "What?"

"I... I don't know. You sounded... hurt."

"You know nothing of my life, Malcolm," she said defensively and turned away from him.

"But I want to. After our time together, I thought..."

"Thought what? That now that we have been together, that you're going to take care of me? Marry me? I don't need you fawning over me and trying to make sure that I'm alright. I can take care of myself."

"That's not what I meant," Malcolm said bristling. "I just meant that I care about you... deeply. Maybe I'm even in love with you; I don't know. This is new to me."

"Well, it's not new to me. Malcolm, what we've had was good, but let's not make more out of it than it was."

"Why are you so determined to push me away?" he said, anger rising in his voice. "I just want to..."

"To know me better? To what end? So that you can decide to marry me?" she said angrily. "Malcolm, I'm a woman; that means that I'm supposed to behave a certain way, be demure, and let men take care of everything for me. Well, that's not me!" she said.

"What have I done that makes you so angry?" he said.

She looked at him and took a deep breath to collect her thoughts. "Let me tell you a story. My grandmother was the mistress of the Russian Emperor Alexander II. While he was alive, she had everything. When he was assassinated, my grandmother and mother were sent from their home and forced to take residence in Switzerland. She was dependent on the money that his son, Alexander III, sent to her. My mother grew up dependent on her ties to the family and used it to support our family. When that ran out, she had no recourse but to find a husband and she married strictly out of necessity. As a woman, and one of questionable parentage, there was no place for her in a world of men. My mother tried to love her husband, but she was miserable. I vowed at a very early age that I would never rely on anyone else to support me. I would find my own way in this man's world."

"My only assets are my beauty and my brains," she continued. "I used my father's connection to Great Britain to join the Foreign Service as a translator. Later, Mr. Holmes approached me about joining the Secret Service. I take care of myself and provide for myself. I am more than capable of taking care of anyone who might threaten me. I don't need a man to take care of me!"

"Even if that man... is in love with you?" asked Malcolm.

"Malcolm, don't get the wrong idea. I care about you—a great deal, in fact. But I have no need for a husband and I don't intend to abandon my career; I suspect that you feel the same way. Let's just enjoy our time together and not make more of it than it is."

"Very well, if that's what you wish," Malcolm said softly. He was not entirely sure if he was relieved or heartbroken over this turn of events.

"Very good," said Joan. The rest of the day passed quietly, both alone in their thoughts. After a long time, Malcolm consulted his pocket watch. "We should go if we want to catch our memorial service."

Chapter 30

They climbed back above the carriage into the balloon itself and followed its length to the aft end of the balloon where a trap door opened into a service chute that descended out of their sight. Malcolm secured an electric torch in his belt and allowed Joan to go first so that he could light her way. They slowly descended down a ladder built into the side of the chute. After climbing for several minutes, Malcolm whispered for Joan to stop and indicated a door just below her and to her left. Joan descended a few more steps and reached over to open the door slowly. She swung over and entered the doorway, disappearing from Malcolm's sight. Malcolm followed and closed the door behind him as quietly as possible.

They were on a platform overlooking the cargo bay. The girders that supported the roof obscured their view, but Malcolm could tell that they were out of sight and should not be detectable.

Malcolm looked down and saw that the crew had once again assembled in their dress uniforms before two Union Jack flags draped over the bomb bay doors. Commander Saxon stood, displaying the right amount of detachment and remorse. He began the prayers and responses for the burial service, just as Malcolm had for Captain Collins only months before. Had it only been months? thought Malcolm. It seemed like that had been a lifetime ago with the events that had happened since then.

When Saxon finished with the prescribed part of the service, he took a deep breath. "We're here to remember Captain Malcolm Robertson, captain of the Daedalus for too short a time, and Miss Joan de St. Leger who we only knew briefly." Joan barely was able to stifle a snort and Malcolm shot her a dirty look. She mouthed the words "I'm sorry" and continued to listen.

"I did not know Miss de St. Leger very well, but she was an exceptional woman. She killed the attacker who wounded Captain Robertson in St. Petersburg. She was intelligent—fluent in nearly half a dozen languages. She was gracious, courteous, and a credit to the Foreign Service. I'm sure I speak for Mr. Holmes when I say that she will be greatly missed."

The Reluctant Captain

Saxon paused for a moment. Malcolm looked at Joan, who had a grim look on her face. Malcolm shot her a quizzical look and she simply mouthed the word "Later." He nodded.

Saxon continued, "We are also here to remember Captain Malcolm Robertson. Mr. Frye has volunteered to give his remembrances." Frye moved to stand by Saxon and began to speak, his voice trembling.

"We're here to remember Malcolm Robertson, chief engineer and later captain of the Daedalus. And my friend." Malcolm felt his eyes moisten at the words. "I know that Captain Robertson wasn't always loved by the other officers of the Daedalus. They thought he was common, not of their station, and spent entirely too much time tinkering. But that was Malcolm; to him everything was a problem to be solved. But surprisingly, people were important to him. He took me under his wing when I was a cocky young lieutenant, just out of the academy, and had all of the answers. He listened patiently to my wild ideas and then would simply ask a few questions that made me realize my idea was not as well thought out as I had thought. Sometimes, he let me try out my wild ideas and then gave me a hand in picking up the pieces if it failed. He said, 'You can't truly know success until you have failed. If you don't fail at least once, you haven't learned.' I try to remember those words every day. I hope that someday I'll be half as good as he was as an engineer and a man. He was our captain for far too short a time and I'm sure that he would have been as successful at that as he was at engineering. I'm going to miss you, my friend." Frye tried to continue but couldn't find his voice and simply returned to his place.

Malcolm felt tears fill his eyes and Joan reached over and touched his hand. Malcolm squeezed it and turned his attention back to the ceremony.

"Thank you, Mr. Frye. I would like to add that I have had the honor of serving as Captain Robertson's second in command and I, too, have learned much from him. He was a man who loved simple pleasures and was more at home among the crew than he was with the officers. He had a brilliant mind and the Air Service has lost both a great engineer and captain. I know if he were here, he would want us to focus on our duty. I think the best memorial we can give him is to execute the rest of the mission to the best of our ability." This time, it was Malcolm who could barely contain a snort.

Saxon concluded the ceremony. The bomb bay doors were opened, the gun salute was given, and Taps was played. Gradually, the crew drifted out of the cargo room and everything was quiet. Malcolm and Joan slipped back up the service chute and returned to their hiding place. Malcolm started to sit down and stopped. He needed to see Matthew Frye. The pain he saw in his friend was too much for him to bear. "I'm going to see Matthew Frye," said Malcolm as he started to go back down to the balloon.

"Is that wise?" Joan asked.

"I don't know, but it's the right thing to do, that's all I know. He's in pain; I can't let him suffer like that."

"I just don't know if it's a good idea to let anyone know that you're alive."

"We may need his help; I have to chance it."

"I understand," Joan said. "Do you want me to come along?"

"No, I think it would be better if it were just me."

"Alright," she said. "Be careful."

"I will," Malcolm said and climbed up above the cabin.

It didn't take Malcolm long to get to the air exchanger and start shimmying his way towards Frye's quarters. Malcolm had used the air vent system to sneak aboard the Daedalus early in his assignment. He had been out late and couldn't be seen showing up for duty in his uniform from the night before. He had made this same journey up through the balloon to the air changer to his quarters so that he would be seen leaving his quarters and no one would be any the wiser.

He reached the vent that led to his room, but the room was dark. Malcolm guessed that Frye had gone back to Engineering to take his mind off of the service. Malcolm tried to wait patiently, but laying with his arms underneath him had made his arms go to sleep and he had trouble moving forward.

The Reluctant Captain

After a very long wait in which Malcolm thought he might be stuck, the door opened to the quarters and Frye turned on the light. Frye seemed to teeter a little unsteadily as he made his way to the bed and sat down. He put his face in his hands and Malcolm thought he could hear the sound of crying. "Matt," he hissed from the vent. "It's me, Malcolm."

Frye's head shot up and he looked around the room. Malcolm again hissed, "Matt. It's me. Malcolm. Go to the vent." Frye looked around again and unsteadily but slowly made his way to the vent. Malcolm saw that Frye had drawn his service revolver. Alcohol and firearms are never a good match, Malcolm though. "Matt, it's me Malcolm. I'm in the ductwork. There's just a clip that holds the vent in place." Frye looked at the vent again and cautiously moved closer. Eventually his eyes focused and he could see that someone was really in the duct.

"Malcolm, is that really you?" he said. He grabbed the chair and quickly unclipped the vent. He raised the cover and a smile filled his face. "Malcolm! You're alive! How in God's name?"

"I'll answer your questions in just a moment. Can you help me out of here? I think my arms have gone to sleep and I can't pull myself out."

"What? Oh, sure," said Frye. He grabbed Malcolm a little too hard and Malcolm slid half out of the duct and fell into Frye, causing both to fall to the ground with a crash. Malcolm landed on his shoulder, which would have felt worse if he had feeling in his arms. Frye hauled Malcolm to his feet and gave him a crushing hug. "I can't believe you're alive. How?"

"If you could let me go and not crush all of the life out of me, I could tell you," Malcolm managed to gasp.

Frye let him go and sat on his bed. Malcolm brought the chair over and sat down. Malcolm relayed details of the drugged food, waking with the tent on fire, escaping, climbing to the Daedalus, and their meeting with Holmes. "Thank you for the nice words at my memorial service."

"Thank you. I hope I never have to do that again anytime soon."

"Me either," said Malcolm. "What happened on the ship?"

"Saxon asked me to assemble two flame throwers for use this morning. A couple of those Russian soldiers came by this morning and picked them up. I didn't think anything of it; I was in the middle of getting the ship ready to take off. Which, with our additional cargo, is no easy feat. I'm surprised we can get any altitude with all of that weight. We have almost no ballast so if we start losing altitude, we're going to have to start throwing things out of the window. I digress," Frye said, seeing the impatient look on Malcolm's face. "A little while after we lifted off, we heard the message from Saxon. I can't believe that no one actually checked to make sure that you were on the ship before they burned the tent."

"Not unless someone wanted me dead," said Malcolm.

"Oh... that's right," said Frye. "Do you think Saxon is behind the attempts on your life?"

"Does he strike you as someone who would not confirm that we were on board before ordering the tent destroyed?" Malcolm asked.

"No, he doesn't," said Frye.

"And then there was the matter of our food. I'm sure it was drugged; we both feel asleep within minutes. I don't think the dose was correct. I'm sure that we were supposed to sleep through the attack on the tent."

"Are you sure it's Saxon?" asked Frye.

"Certain? No. But the evidence points to it. And I think he's lying about receiving new orders."

"But why does he want you dead?" asked Frye. "You weren't that bad as captain."

"Very funny," Malcolm said. "I think he was the saboteur that caused the explosion over the Baltic. I think he means to give the Daedalus to the Germans. It was bad enough when the Germans could have stripped the Daedalus down for her secrets, but can you imagine what would happen if they had our current cargo?"

"Shite," said Frye. "So, what do we do?"

"For now, nothing," Malcolm said. "I think he might try to get the Daedalus to Königsberg; it's a Prussian settlement not far from Russia. My guess is that he intends to resupply the ship, replace our crew with a German crew, and continue on to the Daedalus' real destination. We will need to be resupplied before we can make it home. We may as well let the Germans do it, considering all of the trouble they have given us."

"Until that time comes, and I think you'll be able to figure out when that is," Malcolm continued, "make yourself scarce. If possible, get yourself confined to quarters. The clip on that vent makes it easy to open from the outside and easy to close when you're in the vent. Join us in the air exchanger room. We're using that as our home base."

"Are you sure I can't come with you now?" said Frye.

"No, your disappearance would be too noticeable. We need the element of surprise."

"Very good, sir. Be careful," Frye said.

"I will. We'll be in touch." Malcolm climbed back into the air vent and Frye closed it behind him. A few minutes later, Malcolm returned to the air exchanger room. Joan was pacing. "What took you so long? I was almost ready to go looking for you!" she said sharply.

"Sorry, it took a while for Matt to get back to his quarters."

"How did he take your sudden resurrection?" she asked.

"Obviously, he was surprised, but we have him when we're ready to make our move... whatever that will be. Nothing to do now but wait."

Malcolm and Joan spent most of their time in the air exchanger room with brief forays into the ship. Very quickly, they realized that biological needs were going to be a major concern and neither was enthusiastic about using the equivalent of a chamber pot. Malcolm and Joan climbed through the air ducts to what had been her cabin. Malcolm took a small hand drill and a very small bit and methodically drilled the body off of the heads of the four screws that held the vent cover in place. He was able to keep the heads on the vent front so it would look to the casual observer like nothing had happened to the screws. When they arrived in the room, it had obviously been searched. Joan assured Malcolm that Mr. Holmes would have taken anything of an incriminating nature. While she was there, Joan took the opportunity to grab some clothes because she didn't relish the next few days stuck in her current clothes. She also opened her suitcase and opened a hidden compartment to gather extra ammunition. They left the mess as it was and returned back to their lair from the vent.

Malcolm wished that he could retrieve more clothes for himself, but he wasn't sure if Saxon had already moved into the captain's quarters. Malcolm was uncertain. His personal effects—the very few he had—were gone, presumably already boxed up and taken somewhere. But on the other hand, it didn't look like Saxon had moved in. The point was moot since it looked like Malcolm's clothes were gone.

Daily, they checked with Mr. Holmes. Malcolm used Mr. Holmes' observations of their speed and heading and Malcolm conjectured where the Daedalus might be. As Malcolm predicted, they were not running at full speed, although they were making good time with the prevailing winds at their back. Their current trajectory seemed to match Mr. Holmes' and Malcolm's analysis. They would land in Königsberg; they were already off course from their original heading or even Moscow. The three of them tried to analyze how Saxon would be able to get the crew to land in Germany and lie still while he took the Daedalus to some secret German laboratory. They agreed that the Russian impostors would be critical to the plan, but that's as far as they could figure.

They also took to following Saxon's movements as best as they could guess. They often followed the vents to the bridge where they could catch snippets of conversation. They observed the radio room, looking for abnormalities in the orders that were received. Fortunately, Malcolm could remember enough Morse code and the code in use aboard airships so that he had a decent idea of the nature of the messages. Nothing Malcolm heard gave him any clues as to what might be happening. They observed the captain's office in hopes of overhearing a staff meeting, but Saxon either chose to hold no meetings or they were held somewhere else. They

The Reluctant Captain

scurried through the ducts like mice scurrying thorough the walls of a house.

They continued this way for four days. Everything on the ship seemed to be running as normal. But on the morning of the fifth day, a day that Malcolm knew had brought them near their suspected destination, Malcolm knew the time had come. His confirmation came when he observed the bridge crew and realized that most of the bridge crew were the counterfeit Russian airmen.

Malcolm and Joan decided to return to the air exchanger room to wait for Mr. Frye. They were certain that he would show up. Late that evening, the trap door from the balloon opened and Mr. Frye descended. "Malcolm, I think it's happening. Saxon is making his move. He confined me to quarters and was going to make one of the Russians the chief engineer. I think he's going to do something to the engines."

"Not on my bloody ship, he isn't," said Malcolm. He turned to Joan. "Are you ready?"

"I'm ready, but I'm not quite sure what I'm supposed to be ready to do."

"We'll figure that out when we get to Engineering. We'll go back to the balloon and take one of the service chutes down," said Malcolm.

"Excellent idea, sir. Lead the way," Frye said.

Malcolm climbed the ladder. He barely got his hands off of the top of the ladder when hands shot from the darkness, covered his mouth, and hauled him up the ladder. Malcolm's arms were pinned behind him and he was gagged so he couldn't warn Joan, who was likewise grabbed and gagged. Finally, Frye came up and, to Malcolm's astonishment, was not touched. He was holding his service revolver pointed at Malcolm and said, "The captain would very much like to see you in Engineering, Malcolm."

Chapter 31

"Matt, what? I don't understand!" Malcolm said, struggling to pull away. "What are you doing?"

"I'm going to deal with you once and for all." Malcolm felt the barrel of a gun shoved into his back. "It would be a good idea not to provoke us," Frye said. "It would be a terrible shame for a shot to puncture the balloon and cause the ship to crash. Come along."

Malcolm's mind was in a state of utter shock. How could Matthew Frye be one of the saboteurs? But then pieces started to fall into place. Frye had been on duty when the engines were initially sabotaged; hell, he probably had done it himself. The sabotage of the winch holding the Nautilus. He probably had even worked out a way so that the Nautilus would fail structurally after it had reached its final depth. Frye had access and the knowledge to do all of it. But why?

"Why are you taking us through the balloon? Why don't you take us through the ship?"

"No, it will be safer this way. No need to tell the crew that the captain is alive. Especially when you'll be dead for real shortly."

"Why not kill us now and get it over with?" chided Malcolm.

"Because... I have some unfinished business," said Frye.

The airmen, who Malcolm guessed must be the German impostors, pushed Malcolm and Joan along until they reached the service chute once more. One guard climbed down to the engine room and kept his gun trained first on Malcolm, then on Joan. Frye followed after the rest of the guards had surrounded Malcolm and Joan.

Malcolm's mind was already thinking about escape, but his options were limited. Whatever he did, he would have to take Joan with him, which complicated the matter. This was not going to be easy. As they entered the engine room, Malcolm knew right away that something was wrong. The engine room was silent. It was usually a hive of activity—crewmen attending to the engines, monitoring the tachometers and the temperature gauges and manually releasing coolant undercut by the steady rumbling vibration of the engines. None of that was evident. Malcolm looked around and found the usual engine room crew tied up and gagged. The only crewmembers here were the impostor Russian crew.

Shortly, Commander Saxon walked into the engine room accompanied by another Russian impostor. "Mr. Frye, what was so important that you had to summon me from the bridge with an escort..." he trailed off upon seeing Malcolm. "Malcolm! Joan! Thank heavens you're alive!!! How? Oh, God! I'm so sorry! I had no idea that you were still in the tent. Mr. Frye assured me that you had come aboard when he sent the flamethrowers out. I thought I had..." Saxon stopped and turned to Frye "You!! It's been you the whole time. I'm going to kill you!" he said as he started to lunge for Frye.

"I wouldn't do that if I were you, Commander," Frye said. As he spoke, five guns, including Frye's, were pointed at Saxon. "Let's all calm down and I will tell you what is about to happen." Saxon's eyes were filled with anger, but he nodded and stayed still.

"Very good. This has turned out much better than I had anticipated. I have need for both of you to complete my plan."

"Which is?" asked Malcolm. He needed time. Time to think of something he could do.

"Isn't it obvious?" asked Frye. "My orders were to deliver the Daedalus to the German Empire. While that was the prize originally, my superiors are much more interested in what is in the cargo hold."

"The Martian ship?" asked Malcolm. He nonchalantly backed up and leaned against the casing for the main engine. Malcolm remembered that somewhere around here was a bolt that perpetually came loose. He had replaced it several times, but it seemed that the hole in the casing had become too worn and it always worked itself loose. He wasn't sure a bolt was going to be very useful, but it was better than nothing.

"Yes, and its technology. The Empire will soon have no equal and the world will tremble before Teutonic might."

"Yes, well, you don't have it yet, do you?" asked Malcolm. Joan looked at him and caught on instantly. She knew he was playing for time to devise a plan of escape. They had not yet disarmed her, thinking that with so many guns fixed on her, she wouldn't dare try to reach for a weapon. But, she too was assessing the situation.

"Soon, my friend, soon," he said.

"You're no friend of mine!" seethed Malcolm.

"What, and after all of the nice things I said about you at your memorial service? I'm hurt," Frye said in mock dismay.

"So, you said you have need for us? What possible need could you have for us?" Malcolm asked. He was going to need a distraction—a big one. Malcolm knew there was a steam pipe right above Frye. To Malcolm's great joy, he saw one of the large pipe wrenches about two steps away from him. If he had just a couple of seconds, he would have enough time to smash the pipe and flood the engine room with steam. It would give him and Joan enough time to escape.

"I suppose you have already deduced that we have landed at our site, Malcolm. What poor Commander Saxon doesn't know is that the order he was given for the rendezvous site is not in Russia, but is actually in Königsberg, Prussia."

"What? How?" asked Saxon, confused.

"My men have been your navigators. Given your limited knowledge of navigation, it was very easy for us to falsify our heading and trajectory so that you believed that we were headed for an isolated Russian island, when in fact we were headed to Königsberg the whole time. By now, the ship has been taken over by German soldiers and airmen and is being resupplied for its eventual destination."

"Which is?" asked Malcolm, who subtlety shifted an inch closer to the pipe wrench. Joan caught his glance. He looked toward Saxon and she, too, subtly shifted herself an inch closer to him.

"That's for me to know. Although there is no reason not to tell you as you will both be dead shortly."

"So, it's been you all along? How long have you been a German spy?" asked Malcolm.

"All my life," said Frye. "My family was selected for infiltration into your Empire; my real name is Matthias Frietag. I was trained to pass information since I first attended the academy. Although you wouldn't know it from my academy records, I am a crack shot and trained in multiple forms of unarmed combat. I believe I share those talents with Miss de St. Leger. It's been interesting observing you on this trip. My superiors look forward to interrogating you."

Joan looked at him appraisingly, wondering if she could take him in an unarmed fight. She decided, given the current odds, that would be something she would have to do later. "So, you're the spy we've been looking for all this time?" she said. "We knew that there was at least one of you in the Air Service for quite a while. We had not been able to track you down. You hid your tracks well."

"And I might just have gotten away with everything if it weren't for you, Malcolm. If you hadn't been so pig-headed and just gone to the bridge, everything would have been simple. Saxon would have had no choice but to surrender to the Germans and then all I would have had to do is let slip Mr. Saxon's ties to Germany and suspicion would have fallen on him."

"Ties to Germany? What is he talking about?" Malcolm said, looking at Saxon.

"My last name—Saxon—is Anglicized. It's really Saxe-Coburg. I am distantly related to Her Majesty Queen Victoria. My branch of the family had long ago abandoned its German holdings and came to England. As a result, we were the poor relations that stayed with others in our family. I changed my name when I entered the academy because I did not want to be targeted for either favoritism or accused of nepotism. I wanted to make my own career on my own terms." Malcolm could read the truth in Saxon's eyes.

"Charles, I'm sorry. I thought that you were the traitor and I humbly ask your forgiveness. It seems," Malcolm continued, "that we've both been played."

"Thank you, Malcolm. That means a great deal."

"Oh, how touching. I think I might vomit," said Frye. "If you two are done, I believe we have come to the end of our little drama. You both have one more part to play."

"Oh, what is that?" Malcolm asked.

"You, Malcolm, will kill Commander Saxon," Frye said.

"And why would I do that?" asked Malcolm.

"Because you are the German collaborator. You faked your death so that you could secretly commandeer the Daedalus and deliver it to the Germans. Saxon was in the way, so you killed him. After the Daedalus and its secrets are far away, I will break the rest of the airmen out of the prison and commandeer an airship to England. There, I will be a hero and given even more responsibility while you, Malcolm, will be left in a cell to die."

"So what makes you think I'll kill Commander Saxon?" Malcolm said.

"I don't know, let me think..." he said. He nodded to one of his men who immediately put a gun to Joan's head. "Of course, I don't actually trust you to do the job. You simply have to pass me your service revolver." He held out his hand. "Now!"

"Don't do it Malcolm," said Joan. "I'm not worth it."

An idea germinated in Malcolm's head. Malcolm gulped and lowered his head. As he slowly drew the gun from his holster, he made his hands visibly shake. As he turned the gun around to offer the handle to Frye, Malcolm used his palm to put the bolt in the end of the barrel. At that moment, Malcolm dropped the gun so it landed on the barrel, driving the bolt well into the gun. He picked up the gun, again with shaking hands, and presented it handle-first to Frye.

"You bastard, I hope you fry in hell for your crimes!" Malcolm hissed.

"Oh, how very clever, Malcolm. You have such a way with words," said Frye. "Any last words, Saxon?"

Saxon looked at the barrel of the gun and Malcolm thought he saw a glint of recognition. Saxon pulled himself up straight and said, "You will regret pulling the trigger". He looked at Malcolm and Malcolm knew that Saxon understood what he had done. Malcolm looked at Joan and could see an almost imperceptible nod.

"Very well. Goodbye, Commander Saxon," Frye said as he pulled the trigger. As Frye pulled the trigger, Saxon dropped to the ground. Joan stomped her sharp-heeled boot into the foot of her captor and Malcolm reached for the pipe wrench. The explosion boomed through the engine room, causing everyone to go deaf. No one could hear the screams of Frye as he tried to hold both his hand and his eye, blood flowing freely from both. For a split second, Malcolm thought he saw a sliver of metal protruding from Frye's eye. But Malcolm didn't wait that long. He took the pipe wrench and hit the pipe above Frye's head, dislodging the pipe. Malcolm had known for a long time there was a weak weld on that joint and had not had the chance to fix it. Apparently Frye never had time to fix it either, since he seemed too concerned with capturing the Daedalus.

Steam flooded the engine room. Malcolm reached down and grabbed Saxon by the collar, yanking him up. In the haze, he felt Joan grab his hand and he led the three of them to the service chute. They climbed quickly into the balloon section and, once up, used the pipe wrench to keep the trap door from opening by sliding it through the handle so it would be impossible to pull down from the engine room side.

"Thank you, Malcolm. You saved my life," Saxon said.

"There will be time for that later. Right now, I want my ship back," said Malcolm.

Chapter 32

They raced down the balloon section. "What now, Captain?" asked Saxon. Malcolm quickly considered his options. If the Germans had in fact boarded the ship, that meant either the crew was incapacitated or not even on board. Likely, the members of the expedition—like Rutherford, Koltsov, and Zhukovsky—had been moved to other quarters and Mr. Holmes was likely in a prison cell awaiting interrogation. Frye and his men would soon find another way to get to the balloon section, so further running wasn't necessarily the answer.

"Wait," Malcolm said, as he turned around and ran back nearly ten yards. "The access door we used to get in here. We'll use that to go outside."

"Outside! Are you mad?" asked Saxon.

"Never been outside?" asked Malcolm.

"Not since college, no," said Saxon.

"Consider this a refresher course," Malcolm said, opening the access door. Down the hall, he could hear someone attempting to open the jammed door. "Come on," he said, "we don't have much time before they find a way up here." Malcolm climbed out and grabbed the rigging, moving to the right. Joan came out next and Saxon followed, looking slightly green.

"This is easy," said Joan to Saxon. "We're not moving and we're only twenty feet from the ground. It's much harder when the ship is moving and you're much higher."

"I would imagine," said Saxon, trying not to look down.

Malcolm closed the access door behind them. Malcolm could see that they were moored in the courtyard of a castle. The main part of the castle itself was a short tower barely taller than the Daedalus. But the diameter of the tower was nearly the length of the Daedalus. Malcolm checked to see how the Germans had moored the Daedalus. Several mooring ropes led down and were tied off to iron rings in the ground. Clearly, other airships had landed here before. Malcolm smiled at his good fortune when he saw a mooring line tied from the central point of the front of the cabin below the bridge line on a diagonal slant to the tower. "There," Malcolm said, pointed to the line. "That's how we get down."

"That's all well and good," said Saxon, "but how do we get there? And how do we climb down that rope?"

"If Malcolm can get us there, I can get us across," said Joan.

Malcolm climbed the rigging to move ahead of the other two. They followed the edge of the gondola along the length of the balloon until they reached a set of rungs that went down to the ring holding the mooring rope. "The crew climbs down there to secure the rope once it's moored," Malcolm said, pointing to the rungs. "Joan, you said you can get us across?"

"Yes," she said. Holding herself with just one hand, she fished in her bag and produced three boomerangs.

"What are those?" asked Malcolm.

"Boomerangs," said Joan as she handed one each to Malcolm and Saxon. "An aboriginal weapon in Australia. But we're not going to use them as a weapon. Let me show you." Without hesitation, she climbed down the rungs. When she reached the bottom, she put the top of the v-shaped piece of wood on the line and, holding on to both sides, she pushed off from the Daedalus and slid down the rope all the way to the roof of the castle. When she reached the roof, she took her hand away from one side and dropped to land perfectly on the roof. She came back to the battlements and beckoned them over.

"I hope that's as easy as she made it look," said Saxon.

"Me too."

Saxon climbed gingerly down the rungs; clearly he was not accustomed to heights. He placed the boomerang over the rope, closed his eyes, and pushed off. He slid down the rope but didn't open his eyes in time to prevent himself from crashing into the higher wall of the castle. Malcolm followed, attempting to emulate Joan rather than Saxon. Malcolm landed hard on the roof, but managed not to hit the wall.

"I don't think I ever care to do that again," said Saxon.

"Now what?" asked Joan.

"We need to find the crew and the expedition members. We'll need to disable any guards we find as well as deal with the Germans already aboard the Daedalus. What do we have for weapons?" asked Malcolm.

"I have my service revolver," said Saxon.

"I'm fully armed. Frye never disarmed me before we escaped. Here, take one of my guns since you destroyed yours." Joan handed Malcolm one of the two oversized revolvers she had holstered. The heft of the gun was substantial.

"How do you carry two of these, let alone fire them both?" asked Malcolm.

"I've had a great deal of practice. So now what?"

"We should find the crew and our guests first. When we've found everyone, we'll need some sort of diversion." Malcolm looked around the courtyard and soon found his diversion. "There," he said, pointing to a large fuel tank some distance from the Daedalus. "If we can blow the fuel tank, it might draw out the Germans."

"Alright. Let's find the crew!" said Saxon.

They crept along the roof of the castle and found a trap door. Malcolm silently lifted the trap door, but before he could do anything else, Joan was through the hole and had dropped the guard at the bottom of the ladder by hitting him with her gun on her way down. He fell nearly silently to the floor, offering only a soft "Umph" as her weapon connected with his head. Malcolm and Saxon looked at each other for a second without a word and then Malcolm followed Joan down the ladder. He put both feet on either side of the rungs and slid down—a trick he perfected long ago aboard the Daedalus. "Showoffs," muttered Saxon as he shook his head and climbed down methodically.

They found themselves in a large, circular room with no windows and two doors on opposite sides of the room from each other. A wide, circular staircase descended down out of sight and was ringed with an ornate wrought iron railing. Joan listened at one door, then crossed to listen at the next. Satisfied there was no one there, she opened the door to reveal a hallway that curved around the outside the room in either direction. The hall was lit with electric lights, but there were a number of shadows between each bulb. Spaced every fifteen or twenty feet was another door on the opposite wall.

The trio crept into the hall. At each door, Joan listened, tried the handle to see if it was locked, and slowly opened the door. The first seven rooms they tried were unlocked and uninhabited. The next room was locked. Malcolm raised his gun to shoot the lock when Joan hissed, "Stop!! It will make too much noise. I can handle this." She pulled a lock pick from her belt. After a few seconds of work, she unlocked the door. "After you," she said. Malcolm raised the gun, opened the door, and held the gun in firing position.

"What is going on? I demand to know.... Don't shoot!" Malcolm recognized the voice as Rutherford's. "Captain, you're alive? What is going on? Why are we here? Who are those men?"

"All your questions will be answered in due time, Professor. Just not right now. We need to get you and the crew of the Daedalus out of here. Do you know if there is anyone else up here?"

"Yes. I believe that Professor Zhukovsky and Koltsov are in the next rooms. I haven't seen Mr. Holmes or any of the crew members."

"Very good," Malcolm said. "Come with us, Professor, but you must keep absolutely quiet. Our escape absolutely depends on stealth."

"Right," said Rutherford, starting to pack the steamer trunk that had been brought to his room. Malcolm stared at him until Rutherford looked up. "What? Oh, right. I have to leave the trunk."

"Very good, Professor. Follow us," said Malcolm.

In short order, all the members of the expedition were found, save Mr. Holmes. Malcolm decided to put off thinking about the room where the Germans would have taken Mr. Holmes. The crew slowly crept down the hallway, Joan several paces in the lead. Suddenly, her hand went up indicating everyone should stop. She crept quietly around the curve and, a few seconds later, they heard another muffled cry and the sound of a body falling to the ground. Joan returned with a rifle. "Can any of you shoot?" she asked the professors in English and Russian.

"I can," said Rutherford. "I grew up on a ranch. I think I still remember how." Rutherford checked the weapon and sighted down the barrel. "It's coming back to me," he said.

"Good," said Malcolm. They turned the corner and found the unconscious German soldier. Malcolm looked at the soldier and then at Saxon. They seemed nearly the same size. "Do you speak German?" he asked.

"No, of course not," Saxon said immediately. Then he stopped and remembered the conversation in the engine room when his secret came out. "Yes. Most of my relatives converse in German when they are alone and it's the only way to ever find out what's happening. Why do you ask?"

"Because I think you're about to impersonate a German." Malcolm checked the insignia on the German's uniform. "Private. Sorry for the demotion." Together, Malcolm and Saxon dragged the unconscious German into one of the unoccupied rooms and stripped him of his uniform. The arms of the jacket were a little short—as were the pants—but in the dark, it might work. They tied the German up with a bed sheet.

Joan found some water and splashed it on the soldier's face. After a bit, he came around. He drew a breath as if to yell, but Joan's hand shot to his mouth, covering it before the sound could escape. She brought her oversized revolver and placed it next to his temple. "Saxon, please come here; we need to find out where they are keeping the crew and Mr. Holmes."

Saxon came over in the soldier's uniform. The soldier realized that he was nearly naked in front of a woman and started to thrash around. Saxon said something in German and the soldier calmed down.

"What did you say to him?" asked Malcolm.

The Reluctant Captain

"I said that if he didn't cooperate, being unclothed in front of a woman would be the least of his problems—the biggest being a rather large hole in his head. What do you want to know?"

Joan replied, "We need to know the location of the crew of the Daedalus as well as Mr. Holmes."

Saxon nodded and started a conversation with the German. The soldier was young, barely out of his teens. Malcolm could see that he was scared, but could also see that a cocksure sense of right and wrong common in youth might be preventing him from seeing the danger of his situation accurately. A few times, Joan asked Saxon to remind him that he had a gun pointed to his head. The soldier seemed resilient to this and clamped his mouth shut.

Malcolm—realizing that the threat wasn't working—took his own gun, pushed Joan away from the soldier, screamed a nonsensical string of German expletives, and jammed the gun under the man's chin. Malcolm let all of the anger he felt toward Frye and his own lust for vengeance reflect on his face. Malcolm yelled to Saxon, "Tell him that I'm sick of dealing with German scum and will shoot him if he doesn't cooperate."

Saxon, taken aback by the captain's vehemence, repeated in German. The eyes of the young private went wide. The private stared into Malcolm's wild eyes and apparently saw his fate. The soldier was talking now, very quickly and insistently. The soldier looked pleadingly at Saxon when he was finished.

"He says that the crew is being held on the other floors of the castle. They were told not to hurt the crew in any way and treat them well. But he said they took one man to interrogation down in the cellar. He was a tall, middle-aged man. From the description, it sounds like Mr. Holmes."

Malcolm moved the gun from under the German's chin and relaxed his face. With a smile and a kindly look, he said, "Danke". The young German's jaw dropped at the change in Malcolm and Malcolm took advantage of it to gag the soldier with the pillowcase from the bed.

"Were you really going to shoot him, Captain?" asked Saxon as they prepared to leave.

"No. But I realized that he didn't consider Joan to be a threat. In his mind, she was a woman and he hasn't had the opportunity to realize just how dangerous she can really be. From what little I know of Germans, they seem to respect authority and power a great deal. So, I decided to use my rage against Frye to convince him I was unhinged and would kill him. Truthfully, I think I would have had a hard time shooting him in the foot, let alone killing him."

"Are you sure you aren't in the Secret Service?" asked Joan in amazement. "You read people very well—better than many people who do it as a career."

"Sorry to disappoint you," said Malcolm. "Let's get our crew and Mr. Holmes."

Joan still moved silently ahead of the group, with Saxon acting as a guard escorting the group. They returned to the central room and Joan crept silently down the stairs and returned to inform them that there was a guard at the next level. Joan crowded next to Malcolm, using him to hide. The group marched down the landing with Saxon prodding them along. The guard on the landing stopped them.

"What are you doing?" he asked Saxon in German.

"I'm taking these prisoners to interrogation," Saxon replied in German.

"Who are you? You don't look familiar to me," the guard said. Before he could say another word, Joan had noiselessly dropped him to the floor. She had used the distraction that Saxon had created to jump from her hiding place and onto the unsuspecting guard.

"At this rate, we should have enough weapons for the crew," quipped Saxon.

"We're going to need them," Joan said. She listened again at the door and when she was satisfied that she couldn't hear anything, she cautiously opened the door and slipped inside. After a few seconds, she opened the door and beckoned everyone to follow. She kept in the shadows ten feet ahead of the group. Once again, they came to a locked door. They used keys from the guards to open the door. This time, they found Lieutenants Hensley and Bennet and Chief Fletcher.

The cycle continued as they circled around the tower. The group stopped at every locked door and released the occupants. The few guards that had been stationed there were dispatched before they knew what hit them and the group now had accumulated half a dozen rifles. By the time most of the crew was released, they were on the second floor. Malcolm was sure that they would not be able to get the whole crew out of the tower, so Malcolm asked for volunteers who might want to climb across the line on the roof of the tower. The signal for them to move would be the explosion of the fuel tank. Several of the crew, mostly experienced men who regularly climbed the rigging, volunteered. To Malcolm's surprise, Lieutenant Bennet, formerly a midshipman, volunteered to lead the men.

On the second level, they encountered offices as well as holding cells. To Malcolm's astonishment, the radio room had been left unguarded. He and Chief Fletcher examined the German radio transmitter and receiver. It seemed that the Germans had attached the receiver and transmitter to a computator. Malcolm guessed its intent was to encode/decode messages. Malcolm remembered his conversation with Mr. Holmes and that the Germans had worked to link the computators. This seemed like a primitive way of achieving that. Malcolm looked at the computators and realized they were nearly identical to the models he had trained on in college. An idea began to percolate in his mind. He called Saxon over and together they went through the reports, papers, and books on the desk. After a minute of looking, Saxon found what Malcolm had been seeking: a maintenance book that seemed to be used to send updates of the coding algorithm, along with the sequence necessary to transmit to all stations. Malcolm's Morse code and German were both rusty, but with the help of Saxon translating and Chief Fletcher coding the transmission, Malcolm sent a new coding algorithm to every computator on the German network—the same algorithm perfected over a semester of work that would cause every computator to perform a series of operations that would wreck the machine.

At first, nothing seemed to happen as the message went out on the network. The maintenance routine on these computators sent the message forward to the next machine before trying to initiate the algorithm, so that the existing coding algorithm would not change before it was forwarded. Within thirty seconds of Chief Fletcher sending the algorithm, the computator started to buck and gears began grinding before the gears popped out of the computator and everything came to a halt.

"What did you do?" asked Saxon.

"With any luck, I think we just disabled the German network for transmitting coded messages. When we escape, it will slow down pursuit because I believe it will be very difficult to send a message now," said Malcolm. Frye had loved these things and now, Malcolm had once again brought them down. Maybe it wasn't honorable to get a little pleasure out of this, but he did anyway.

Joan snuck ahead down the stairs and came back to the radio room where the remaining men were collected. "We have a problem. The stairs open into a wide area. There will be no way to disguise our passage down the stairs. We're going to need some manner of distraction in order to get out of the tower. I don't know how we get to the cellar to find Mr. Holmes."

"Alright," said Malcolm, his brain churning. "Saxon, you're going to need to lead the crew out the front door and provide a distraction for Miss de St. Leger and me to sneak off to the basements. Take the crew and hide in the courtyard as near to the Daedalus as you can manage, but away from the fuel depot we intend to use to flush the Germans off of the Daedalus. If we don't join you in ten minutes, it will be up to you to lead everyone back aboard the Daedalus and get her out of here."

"Aye, sir. But how will we distract the Germans enough to get down the stairs?" asked Saxon.

"I'm not sure. I'm still working on that," Malcolm said.

Suddenly, there was a large boom and the sound of a great commotion. Malcolm could hear Frye shouting something in German, although he thought he'd caught his name. Joan and Malcolm looked at each other and nodded and Malcolm gave the order to move.

While all eyes were turned toward the departing Frye, Saxon and Fletcher ran into the center of the hall and started to spray bullets in the air all around the room, their intent to make everyone dive for cover so that the crew could run for the door. Their gambit worked. Everyone ran for a doorway or hit the ground. A few drew weapons and started to fire back before Saxon and Fletcher sent a rain of bullets in their direction. The crew sprinted for the door and Saxon and Fletcher followed behind, continuing to lay covering fire. They shut the door behind them. The Germans ran for the door, tugged it, and found it was barred in some way. Malcolm smiled. Saxon must have had the presence of mind to jam his rifle between the door handles, creating a makeshift bar. It wouldn't hold for long, but it would give the crew a chance to find a hiding place.

While all eyes were focused on the commotion caused by the crew, Malcolm and Joan slipped into an alcove where they remained while the firefight raged. When the Germans raced to the door to open it, Malcolm and Joan used the diversion to slip from alcove to alcove. "Any ideas where we should go?" whispered Malcolm.

"Other than down? No," whispered Joan. They surveyed the hall. A number of Germans had left the group trying to get the door open and had sped off in different directions. Some went upstairs, others went down a long corridor and another went into one of the rooms. As the soldier opened the door, he saw a glimpse of a railing. "There!" he pointed and Joan just caught a glimpse of the railing as the door shut. They made their way in the shadows as swiftly and silently as possible. The Germans were apparently still arguing among themselves and failed to notice the figures scurrying between the alcoves. Malcolm and Joan reached the door and slid inside silently.

The room was empty, save for a railing that led to a wide stone staircase that went straight down. There was a door in the room on the right. Malcolm locked this side door as Joan crept silently down the stairs to listen and to see what was ahead. Suddenly, she flew up the stairs, grabbed Malcolm and moved to the doorway. She opened the door and pulled the door in front of them to hide. Just then, Malcolm heard footsteps and talking as a group of soldiers came up the stairs. Malcolm held his breath, daring not to breathe for fear of make any noise that might be heard. The discussion was heated,

Malcolm could tell, but it was all in German. Malcolm could hear the steps leave, but one step stopped. For a second, Malcolm waited, afraid that whoever it was would close the door and discover them hiding. Malcolm heard an exclamation of confusion and a second later, he heard footsteps as the soldier closed the door on the way out without looking behind him.

Both Malcolm and Joan released their held breath simultaneously. Malcolm locked the door from his side and moved to the stairs. Again, Joan crept down a few steps to check their way. A few seconds later, Joan signaled that the way was clear and Malcolm crept slowly down the stairs to the cellar.

Chapter 33

The staircase opened into a lighted room with a single door opposite the stairs. Joan slipped silently to the door, stopping to listen for a moment before she opened it and peered down the hall. Malcolm heard sound down the hallway, but he couldn't make it out. He thought he heard some kind of buzzing broken up with long moments of silence.

They crept silently down the hallway and checked doors as they passed. Many of the rooms were cells, complete with a barred window in the door and a slot for food delivery. All were empty. As they crept down the hall, the periodic buzzing sound became louder. The door was locked. Joan continued down the hallway and stopped at another doorway. This one was not locked. Joan motioned Malcolm to join her and he crept up next to her. Silently, she indicated that she could hear people in the room. Malcolm nodded. She counted to three on her fingers and kicked the door open, Malcolm behind her.

The room was dimly lit and contained two inhabitants—a soldier and a man in a German naval uniform who seemed to be writing something. The man sat at the desk, but the soldier had been standing by the door. In front of the men was a wide window that looked into what appeared to be an operating theatre. Strapped to the table was Mycroft Holmes, wicked looking electrodes attached at various points on his body. A leather strap had been placed in his mouth and when Malcolm heard the buzzing sounds he could easily discern that they came from a large generator in the room. On a tray next to the table on which Holmes was strapped lay a number of wicked looking medical instruments whose function Malcolm was sure he didn't want to know. There were three other gowned people in the room, one overseeing Mycroft while another assisted and a third worked the generator.

Joan quickly moved in and dispatched the soldier. Malcolm moved in and had his gun pressed against the temple of the man writing before the man even realized that he was there. "Achtung! Sprechen sie Englisch?" Malcolm asked.

"Yes, yes, don't shoot!" the man said. Malcolm could see now he was a balding, middle-aged man with a round face and beady eyes whose excitement at the sight of torture couldn't be hidden by the bookish, wire-rimmed spectacles he wore. "Who are you? Why have you stopped my interrogation?"

"I am no one of consequence," said Malcolm. "Stop this interrogation immediately."

"Or?" said the man.

"I will blow your brains out," Malcolm said.

"I think not," the man said, crossing his arms. "You wouldn't do that to an unarmed man. You can only be the famed Captain Malcolm Robertson. And I know much about you from the reports of your friend, Matthew Frye. You seem to be a hard man to kill, Captain Robertson."

"And this lovely creature must be Joan de St. Leger. I have a file on you nearly an inch thick detailing all of your comings and goings. The descriptions in the reports don't do you justice.

"How rude of me! I know so much about you and I haven't introduced myself properly. I am Captain Ernst Toht of Imperial Naval Intelligence." He put out his hand to shake, but Malcolm would not take it. "No? Very well. I find this most interesting that you would risk your life for someone who would not do the same for you. If you were a liability to the mission, you would be discarded in a heartbeat. You, Miss de St. Leger—of all people—know that I am correct."

Joan looked at the man for a moment and without saying a word, took the soldier's rifle and shot the window twice. The window shattered immediately and everyone in the operating theatre jumped at the sound. Joan yelled something in German and soon the three men placed their hands above their heads. Joan covered them as she climbed through the broken window. Malcolm checked Toht for weapons and told him to join the others in the operating theatre.

Malcolm covered the Germans while Joan went immediately to the table. Quickly, she removed the electrodes. "Mycroft, are you all right?" she said, her voice wavering.

"Miss de St. Leger, there's no excuse to be informal," he said weakly. "I have felt much better, but I expect that I will survive this little rendezvous with Ernst."

"You know him?" Joan said, removing the straps from Mycroft and helping him to sit up.

"Oh, yes. We've played cat and mouse with each other for several years now. I must say that I rather do not like playing the role of the mouse when the cat likes to play with his food," he said. "I do seem to have misplaced my clothes. I'd rather you not see me like this, Miss de St. Leger. It breaks down the respect that you might have for me."

Despite herself, Joan laughed. "You are definitely fine, Mr. Holmes. Malcolm, do any of those men have clothes that will fit Mr. Holmes?" Malcolm surveyed the group and found that only Toht was nearly the same size as Mycroft.

"Time to disrobe, Toht. Your clothes are needed," said Malcolm.

Toht sighed. "Very well, if I must play a role in this charade. You do know that you have almost no chance of escaping, ja?" he said as he began to undress. Malcolm gave the discarded clothes to Holmes as fast as possible.

"Ernst, don't underestimate our captain," said Mycroft. "He has thwarted your plots for quite a while now. He is very ingenious and resourceful."

"I will remember that, Mycroft," Toht said. In minutes, Mycroft was dressed and Joan and Malcolm had covered their clothes with the gowns and masks. The room, although appearing to be sterile, was not an operating theatre. In addition to the generator there was a small laboratory table full of various chemicals with a number of syringes laying carefully on the table. On the far wall away from the mirror, there were three chains ending in manacles. Malcolm locked the three attendants in the manacles and gagged them so they could not shout.

"What do you intend to do about me? Do you think I will let you use me to escape?" sneered Toht.

"Not for one moment." Malcolm grabbed Toht and pushed him on the table. Malcolm had to put his gun down in order to wrestle Toht to the table, but with Joan's assistance he tied the thrashing Toht to the table like the German had done to Mycroft. They attached the electrodes to him. Interestingly, he did look like Mycroft. They placed the leather strap in his mouth and left the room.

When they were in the hall, Malcolm said, "Go ahead, I forgot my gun. I'll get it and join you at the bottom of the stairs." Joan helped Mycroft down the hall; clearly he was still weak from his encounter with Toht. Malcolm turned and re-entered the room, picking up his gun where he had set it down. He looked at Toht and said, "You're right. I'm not the kind of man who would shoot an unarmed man in cold blood." He walked nonchalantly over to the generator. "But I am a man who fervently believes in justice and getting your just rewards." Malcolm could feel the rage rising within him and his hand reached for the knife switch.

It would be so easy for him to flip that switch and give Toht a taste of his own medicine. His hand wavered for several seconds before he jerked it away. He walked over toward Toht. "The reason I didn't flip that switch is not because you don't deserve it. It is because I would become like you. And you are not worth that cost." Malcolm turned and jogged from the room.

Malcolm joined Joan and Holmes at the bottom of the stairs. Mr. Holmes seemed to be able to walk on his own accord. They climbed the stairs and Joan slipped to the door and opened it a crack to assess the situation. Things in the lobby were chaotic. Whatever Saxon had done to jam the door was giving the Germans fits. Half of them were trying to break the door open with a battering ram, with the other half trying to pull it open. "What now?" she whispered.

"The disguise is our best bet at this point. If we can find a room with an outside window, we could sneak out that way."

"I'll lead," said Mr. Holmes. "I think I know where we might find a room with a window."

The Reluctant Captain

"How?" asked Malcolm. He was certain that they had whisked Holmes directly to the dungeon and he wouldn't have seen much of the structure.

"I've been here before-once invited, and once not. And unless I am mistaken, I believe if we move three hallways to the right we will reach the commandant's office which contains a window."

"After you, Captain," Malcolm said, indicating his uniform.

"What? Oh, yes," said Holmes. He went to the door, stopped, took a deep breath, and opened the door. As he walked, there was a swagger in his step and he held himself more erect. Without looking back, he strolled confidently over to the commandant's office, knocked once, and strode in. Joan and Malcolm hurried after him to catch up. By the time they had arrived in the room, the commandant was already unconscious and slumped at his desk. Malcolm locked the door behind them and joined Joan and Holmes at the window. They were quickly able to unlock the window. Malcolm scanned outside; the window seemed to open to a private garden surrounded by a hedge.

The trio climbed onto the window ledge and dropped the five feet down to the ground. They crept along the wall and forced their way through the hedge wall. They continued to stay along the side of the tower, hiding in its shadow. Eventually, they found Saxon and the crew hiding behind a large row of crates that looked ready to be packed into the Daedalus. "You made it, sir!" Saxon said. "I'd almost given up hope."

"Is everyone ready to go? We need to get out of here before the Germans catch up with us," Malcolm asked. They were perhaps fifty yards from the cargo bay and main gangplank. This would be the best place to make their run for the ship. Malcolm turned to Joan and found her reloading her oversized revolver. Last time, she had loaded a grappling hook. This time the ammunition looked more like a small rocket. Malcolm raised an eyebrow.

"What?" she said. "You wanted a distraction. This will cause a big distraction!"

"That, my dear, may be the understatement of the year!" Malcolm said.

Malcolm, Joan, and Saxon, who would not be dissuaded, would provide cover fire only if necessary. The rest of the crew would take what guns they had and begin to retake the ship. "Commander, when we get aboard, I want you to take the bridge."

"But, you're the captain, sir. That's your place!" said Saxon.

"Usually, I'd agree with you. But I'm the only chief engineer we have right now and I have to get those engines going at full speed as soon as I can."

"Alright, sir," said Saxon. "But I expect you to come back to the bridge. That's your rightful place, sir."

"I will. You have my word," said Malcolm. "Is everyone ready?" Malcolm heard the group's quiet assent. "Miss de St. Leger, whenever you're ready."

Joan held the oversized revolver with two hands, steadying them on a crate. Closing one eye, she sighted down the length of the gun barrel, took a slow breath, and pulled the trigger as she exhaled. The gun fired with a loud bang that caused the ears of everyone in the vicinity to ring. A second later, there was a much louder explosion—one where they could feel the sound strike them. A giant fireball shot into the sky as the fuel storage went up. The explosion sent shrapnel and flames everywhere and soon, a nearby shed with a thatched roof caught on fire.

The sound brought many crewmen off the Daedalus, first in curiosity to find out what caused the noise, and then alarm as they ran to try to put the fire out. When the flow of men exiting the Daedalus seemed to slow, he waved the men to follow him. The crew got halfway to the Daedalus when one of the Germans spotted them and shouted. At nearly the same time, the doors of the tower burst open and another group of men, this time lead by Frye, came out of the tower and started running toward them as they opened fire.

Malcolm and Joan stopped, turned, and returned fire at the advancing Germans. "Saxon, get the men aboard now!" Malcolm yelled. Malcolm spotted a couple of crates nearby and he and Joan dove behind them to provide cover. They were still some fifteen feet away from the Daedalus when the two groups of Germans came together to form a line advancing steadily on them. It would be a matter time before they were shot.

Nearly simultaneously, Malcolm and Joan both ran out of ammunition. They looked at each other and both could see in each other's eyes. This was the end.

Chapter 34

Suddenly, there was another loud bang followed by several more and the line of Germans fell. Malcolm realized that the sound had come from the guns of the Daedalus. The Germans were in full disarray, caught between the burning fuel supply and the big guns of the Daedalus that rained destruction down everywhere. Large sections of the castle's wall collapsed, adding even more chaos to the situation. Malcolm could see Frye screaming to his men to attack, but no one was listening to him. Frye stopped and looked at Malcolm. His hand had been wrapped and his eye covered with a large gauze pad, soaked with fluid. He raised his gun directly at Malcolm and fired.

Joan tackled Malcolm and he fell to ground at the foot of the gangplank, the bullet whizzing over his head. Saxon came over to them and pulled them aboard the Daedalus as the gangplank was raised.

"I thought I told you to go the bridge," Malcolm said.

"You did, but I realized that you may need a little help and if I didn't get my chief engineer back, it wouldn't matter if I was on the bridge."

"Good point," said Malcolm. "Thank you. Now let's go."

"Bring some of the crew with you," Saxon said. "There are still a few Germans on board."

"Fine," said Malcolm. Malcolm grabbed Joan's hand and took a couple of men with him. They re-armed themselves and headed towards the engine room.

Saxon was right; before they reached the engine room, they came upon a trio of German airmen. Each party was surprised and both groups stood completely still before opening fire. Malcolm's group was faster and the German airmen lay wounded or dead. They encountered no more resistance until they reached the engine room. There, they found half a dozen Germans who, by now, had figured out that the English were retaking the ship. Three of them fired to provide cover as the other three started to open the engine casing with the hope of sabotaging the ship and preventing it from lifting off.

"Not on my ship!" Malcolm yelled as he took his gun and fired two shots above the three Germans. The Germans looked at Malcolm and laughed, thinking that Malcolm had missed them, when a large piece of air duct fell on them and pinned them underneath, unconscious. Without a thought, Malcolm turned and fired toward the other three, this time hitting the pipes just behind them. Soon, heated oil came squirting out of the holes and they were covered in hot oil. They screamed and jumped up, trying to get the oil off them and only succeeding in spreading it. The crew of the Daedalus quickly had them secured.

"Out of the frying pan and into the fire," said Malcolm.

"What?" said Joan.

"That oil that sprayed all over the Germans, we will need that for the engines."

"Oh," said Joan.

"But I think we can manage." Malcolm went to the toolbox and found one of the emergency repair kits. It was a half-circular piece of metal bent along the center while the whole underside was coated with rubber. With both hands, he pried the circle open and placed it over one of the holes. The metal immediately clamped itself to the pipe and the rubber sealed over the hole. The leak stopped immediately. Malcolm grabbed two more of the metal seals and put them over the other two holes that he had made.

Malcolm looked at the oil pressure gauge. It was a little lower than he would have liked it, but it was too late for that now. Malcolm began the procedure to start the main engine. Fortunately, the generator was still running and he would be able to use the electrical starter instead of starting up manually. Malcolm opened the choke and pressed the ignition. As Malcolm expected, the engine started on its first try. Although Frye was a saboteur and murderer, Malcolm knew that he would have kept the Daedalus at peak efficiency, if only to impress his superiors. Within minutes, all three engines were roaring.

"Engine room to the bridge. All engines are online."

"Understood," responded Saxon. "We're lifting off now. Some of the riggers have gone outside to cut the mooring lines free. As soon as I get the signal, we're going full throttle. When are you coming back to the bridge?"

"As soon as the engineering crew gets back here," said Malcolm. "If you could do anything to expedite that, it'd be appreciated." Malcolm had barely hung up the handset when Saxon's voice could be heard over the ship. "Engineering detail to the engine room immediately." Within a few minutes, the engineering detail arrived. Malcolm looked at the crew that was made up of one midshipmen who happened to be on his engineering assignment and a couple of older mechanics that knew their business. "Midshipman Preston, is it?"

"Yes, sir."

"Congratulations! You're now the chief engineer."

"But, sir, I don't know anything about..."

"Engines? No, I don't suppose you do. Trust your personnel and they won't steer you wrong. Most of the time," he added ruefully.

"Yes, sir," the midshipman said, saluting and snapping to attention.

Malcolm returned the salute perfunctorily and said, "Keep her in one piece lad. If you get over your head, I'll come back and help." He grabbed Joan's hand and they start up towards the bridge.

"Was that hard just now?" Joan asked. "Leaving the engine room when you really had a chance and good reason to stay there."

"Oddly, no. I know I belong on the bridge. The thing I love about engineering is solving problems. It's taken me a while to realize that's what I am best suited to do. And the captain is always solving problems. I think I like being captain and I'm not sure I can go back to just being chief engineer."

The Reluctant Captain

"Well, good, because I think we'll have plenty of problems to solve before we get out of this mess," Joan replied as she quickly squeezed his hand. She knew that he hated such public displays of affection, but she couldn't resist the admiration and respect she felt for him. If there was one man who she might let take care of her, it might very well be Malcolm Robertson. That thought scared her and she abruptly pulled her hand away as they hurried to the bridge.

They arrived and the bridge was in full swing. "Status, Commander Saxon."

"The mooring ropes have been cut. We believe all crew are aboard. I was just about to give the order to take us out."

"Make it so," Malcolm said. He didn't dare turn any lights on, as he didn't want to make a large target for the ground forces. So far, the barrage of gunfire had kept the German forces pinned down and prevented them from bringing any big guns to bear. Malcolm could tell that were not lifting very quickly and between the load of the spaceship and what Malcolm could only guess were numerous small leaks from gunfire, they were never going to gain any altitude or achieve any speed quickly. If there was any pursuit of any kind, Malcolm was sure they would not outrun it.

Malcolm grabbed the handset and addressed the ship. "This is Captain Robertson. As you may know by now, the news of my demise has been greatly exaggerated. Right now, I need everyone to find anything that is not a vital necessity and throw it overboard to lighten our load. As you know, we have very heavy cargo aboard and it's vital that we get it out of German territory and return to England. Scour the ship. We will likely have incoming hostiles, so keep a sharp eye out. Robertson, over and out."

Malcolm could hear the crew getting busy pulling anything that wasn't absolutely necessary. Later, he heard that Rutherford himself came and pitched off his own lab equipment to help. Each time something left the ship, Malcolm could feel it rise. They were slowly gaining altitude, but not fast enough. Malcolm sent a repair crew out to see what they could do about the holes in the balloon. Malcolm had the helium distillers working as hard as he dared to pump the ship as full of helium as he could. Malcolm was leery of running the engines at full speed ahead since he didn't have a very experienced crew in the engine room. They cleared the city and were now flying over the ocean. They had a long trip ahead of them if they were truly to escape the Germans' clutches.

Malcolm locked the wheel in place and went to the navigator's table. He needed to get to England, but the most direct route would take them very close to Germany. If he went northwest, he would cut could cut across nonaligned Sweden. They would not stop him from crossing, but neither would they come to his aid if the Germans chased after him. If he had been successful in disrupting the Germans' radio network, he would have a great advantage. He decided to change course, fly due north, and wait until he was in the northern part of Sweden before changing course and heading for Britain. He would come down from the north to the Shetland Islands. He knew there was a small air base where he could refuel the Daedalus and summon an escort. If he could make it there, he felt they would make it home.

Malcolm decided as well to keep radio silence. If he radioed his position or situation, there was a good chance that someone would be listening. He discussed his plan with Saxon and he agreed with Malcolm. At midnight, Malcolm sent Saxon to get some sleep so he could relieve Malcolm in the morning. In the middle of the night, Malcolm left the bridge to the navigator and went to check on the engine room. Young Mr. Preston had his uniform jacket off, sleeves rolled up, and face covered with grease, but together he and his crew were keeping the engines going. Malcolm knew that they would have limited use of full power, but he was confident that the engines were in attentive hands.

The rest of the night was uneventful. When Saxon relieved him in the morning, Malcolm impressed on Saxon the need to not push the engines for very long. Saxon agreed and nearly forcibly pushed the captain out of the bridge. Malcolm went back to his quarters. He was happy to note that Saxon had not moved in and he collapsed on the bed.

It seemed like seconds later when one of the crew woke him and told them that Commander Saxon needed him on the bridge. Malcolm blinked and grunted that he would come. Slowly, he sat up and tried to shake the sleep from his head. The light had moved in his cabin and he could tell it was sometime in the afternoon. He pulled himself up and went to the bridge after a quick stop at the mess for a mug of strong tea.

When Malcolm entered the bridge, Saxon beckoned him over immediately to the navigator's table. "Did you get us lost already?" Malcolm teased Saxon.

"No, I wish it were as simple as that," Saxon said. "Our aft lookouts spotted four airships due south. It looks as if we have company."

"Damn, my little stunt didn't stop the Germans from following us," said Malcolm.

"Not necessarily. I served in naval intelligence for a short time and I seem to recall that there was an aerodrome not far from Königsberg. It gave the Germans a way to threaten air travel into Russia. It's possible that Frye was able to scramble the airships and give pursuit."

"And Frye, knowing how I would act, set them on a course due north instead of trying to skirt Denmark. I imagine that they're coming up rather quickly."

"They seemed to at first. Now they seem to simply keeping pace."

"Because," Malcolm said, "like us, they don't want to start something over another sovereign country. My guess is that they'll try to catch us here", he said, pointing off the eastern coast of Norway, "when we're over open water and they won't cause an incident."

"But if they want what we have," said Saxon, "they can't very well shoot us down and expect to rescue it from the ocean's floor." He stopped and considered. "You don't think they'll try to board us?" said Saxon.

"Charles, I think that's exactly what they'll do. My guess is that they will maneuver ahead of us and go for high cloud cover. Since we're loaded and can only go so high and so fast, they'll simply wait until they are over us and they will drop soldiers on to the balloon, travel down the rat lines, and presto, the ship is theirs."

"And, if they are above us, we won't know when it happens and we'll have no way to fire at them. It's diabolical," said Saxon.

"Yes, we just need some way to change the playing field in our favor." Malcolm stopped and considered for a moment. "I think I may have an idea starting to form. Could you summon Professor Rutherford, Professor Zhukovsky, our new chief engineer Mr. Preston, Mr. Holmes and Ms. de St. Leger for a meeting in the captain's office at four bells?"

"Very good, sir," said Saxon and he went off to make the arrangements for the meeting.

Four bells arrived and everyone was seated in the captain's office when Malcolm finally entered. He had reviewed the Daedalus' blueprints and had matched them with a visual inspection of the ship.

"Thank you everyone for coming to this meeting. As with everything in this mission, we have another complication. We are currently being pursued by four German airships with the capability to overtake us. Usually, we would have the engine capacity to outfly them, but the addition of our cargo makes us much slower than usual and limits the altitude that we can reach. In analyzing the situation with Mr. Saxon, we both believe that the Germans will attempt to ambush us somewhere here," he said, indicating the western coast of Norway, "before we can make a run for Britain.

"In a gun fight, we would be able to give them a pitched battle. But we are in agreement that their mission will be to capture the Daedalus and its cargo. I'm sure they have no desire to try to fish it out of the ocean, especially as it gets closer to winter. Our conjecture is that they will fly above us and drop men to the top of our balloon. They would then descend down the lines and take the gondola.

"I've brought you all here to help me formulate an idea that came to me that might allow us to get out of this predicament." Malcolm then laid out the plan for one and all. When he finished, there was a single moment of silence and then everyone talked at once, each trying to have his or her say on the merits of the plan. Malcolm took each of their concerns one by one and was either able to address it or gave the person the task of addressing it. In the end, his plan had two main elements: a tactical element to which he assigned Saxon, Joan, and Mr. Holmes, and a technical element that he would work on with Professors Rutherford, Zhukovsky, and Mr. Preston. "We only have three to four days to complete our work before we likely encounter the Germans. Everyone is counting on the people in this room to get us home and I, for one, don't intend to let them down. Good luck everyone! Dismissed."

As the Daedalus flew north over the Baltic, the Daedalus was like a beehive, buzzing with activity. Malcolm spent most of his time in the cargo bay showing Mr. Preston the fine points of welding, while elsewhere, Professor Zhukovsky was leading crews to reinforce key struts and supports with any material available. Much of the useful metal had been jettisoned in fleeing Königsberg so they made do with anything they could find, resorting to using some of the fragments from the Martian craft that they had found. In addition to helping Mr. Preston, Malcolm worked with Rutherford on his task, helping him where he could but mostly just listening and hoping he understood half of what the professor said. Each night, they met to update each other on the status of their endeavors. By the end of the third night, they were crossing Norway and would reach the North Sea by the next morning. The group met quickly and realized that they had done all that they could; it was now out of their hands. Malcolm sent everyone to get a good night's sleep.

But sleep evaded Malcolm. He lay in his bed, his mind a tumble of all the things that could go wrong or right tomorrow. After nearly an hour of tossing and turning, he got up and walked the ship. He talked to everyone on duty. For many, this was the first time they had seen him since his miraculous return from the dead. He joked with the engine room crew, tried to lift the spirits of the lonely watchmen in the observation bubbles at either end of the ship, and went to the bridge where he studied the maps. At some point in the last two days, the zeppelins had dropped out of visual range of the Daedalus. Malcolm guessed that they were spaced strategically along the Norwegian coast and that they would be able to quickly converge once the Daedalus was over open sea. He went to the mess and drank some tea with some of the men who had come off of second shift. To his surprise, he saw Doctor Jenkins enter the mess. When the doctor sat down,

Malcolm excused himself from the crew and moved toward Doctor Jenkins. "Do you mind if I join you?" asked Malcolm.

"Not at all, please," said Jenkins. "Captain's pre-battle tour of the ship?"

"Something like that. Mostly, I couldn't sleep."

"Edward—Captain Collins—was like that. When he knew he was leading his men into battle, he had a devil of a time sleeping. My prescription to him, and to you, is a very large, very stiff drink; probably some of that whisky of yours would do the trick."

"I'll have to try it," Malcolm said. "So, why are you up?"

"Same reason," said Jenkins. "Battles mean wounded and casualties. I should be sleeping so I'm fresh tomorrow, but the thought of all the brave lads I won't be able to save tomorrow gnaws at me when I try to sleep. And before you say 'physician heal thyself', I am not going to drink if I have to operate tomorrow. And I most likely will have to do that."

The two men sat silently at the table, each lost in thoughts. Finally, Malcolm said in a whisper, "What if I am not up to this challenge? What if my decisions and plan doom the crew?"

"Malcolm, I can't promise that whatever you do will come out perfectly," said Doctor Jenkins. "But the crew believes in you. They figure anyone who can come back from the dead can handle a few German zeppelins."

"But, what if I can't?" he said.

"Will you do your best to protect the ship and its crew?"

"Absolutely!" said Malcolm, somewhat annoyed that the doctor would even ask this question.

"Then your men expect nothing more than that. You have led them through many scrapes in the short time you've been captain, and you've come out on top every time. That kind of streak is what gives the men confidence in you."

"But lucky streaks come to an end," said Malcolm. "What if mine comes to end tomorrow?"

"But what if it doesn't? Malcolm, it seems to me that successful men make their own luck. You have had the crew working non-stop for three days to prepare for whatever might happen. That is making your luck. I will hazard a guess that Frye is not as prepared for tomorrow as you are. He is arrogant. He thinks he has overwhelming numbers."

"He does," said Malcolm quietly.

"True, but I would wager he's not half as resourceful as you." Doctor Jenkins rose. "I should try to get some shut eye and you should too. We both have a big day tomorrow."

"Aye, you're right," said Malcolm. "Thank you."

"You're welcome," said Doctor Jenkins. He leaned in and whispered conspiratorially, "And if the whiskey can't relax you, spending time with a beautiful woman might just be what the doctor ordered."

Malcolm was about to scold the doctor when he realized that it might be exactly what he needed—to spend time alone with Joan. It might be the very last time. He left the mess hall and wandered the corridors until he found her cabin. He knocked softly, in case she was asleep.

A few seconds later, she said, "Who is it?" with a definite tone of annoyance.

"It's Malcolm. I thought that... I wanted to..." The words were as muddled as the thoughts in his head. He took a deep breath. "If it's not too forward of me, I would like to come in."

There was a pause and Malcolm heard the door unlock. Joan opened the door, dressed in a negligee covered with a gauzy silk robe. "Of course it's too forward," she said, "but come in anyway." She pulled him into the room and shut the door.

Chapter 35

Malcolm woke just before dawn, kissed Joan on the cheek, and made his way back to his quarters. He freshened up, went to the mess for a mug of tea, and went to the bridge. Dawn was nearly breaking and the sky was a mass of gray above them. It was usually like this over the North Sea, especially this time of year, and weather like this was expected. But it gave the element of surprise to the Germans. Malcolm suspected that one or maybe two of the zeppelins were below the cloud cover searching for the Daedalus while the other two would stay above the clouds, ready to deploy. All Malcolm could do was wait. He alternated between pacing and staring out at the sea.

First shift started in earnest and he knew everyone was at his or her appointed station. The waiting continued. Midmorning, Malcolm received a message from the radio room. Thanks to modifications that Mr. Holmes had made to their radio, they were able to enhance their signal reception and were picking up coded German transmissions. Also thanks to Mr. Holmes, they were able to decode the transmissions. One zeppelin would remain in cover and drop down immediately in front of the Daedalus; the other would drop behind the Daedalus. Besides creating a bigger impediment to the progress of the Daedalus, it would allow both ships to aim their full array of guns in a nasty broadside volley. The zeppelins were approximately five miles out and Malcolm anticipated that they would catch the Daedalus in twenty minutes.

That was all Malcolm needed to hear. He had the signal operator patch him through to the full ship. "Attention crew of the Daedalus. We are approximately twenty minutes away from meeting the Germans. The work of the last three days by all of you will determine what happens then. As captain, I have full faith that your talents and hard work will see us through this. I just want everyone to know that I'm proud to have served with all of you. Good luck and Godspeed to us all. Now, let's show the Germans what happens when you mess with the crew of HMA Daedalus!" A cheer went up among the bridge crew and Malcolm nodded in acknowledgement. "All hands, battle stations!" he said before hanging up.

The klaxon went off and was soon blaring in every part of the ship. Men hustled to their jobs. The riggers prepared to go outside to either repair any damage or hold off any boarders. The engine room was ready and Malcolm felt confident that he could have full power, if even for a short time. Saxon had the gunnery stations completely prepared. The ship was running at top efficiency. Malcolm just prayed that it would be enough.

The minutes slowly ticked by, each seeming longer than the last. Observers had been posted with handsets on all areas of the ship to radio the bridge at the first sight of German zeppelins. The silence in the bridge was only cut by the wail of the klaxon. Malcolm found himself scanning the skies, looking for any hint of an airship. There was nothing but the gray clouds and the blue ocean.

Fifteen minutes after the call to battle stations, the radio operator patched a message from the Germans to Malcolm.

"Captain Robertson. I bet you thought you'd never hear from me again, Malcolm," said a voice that Malcolm instantly knew belonged to Frye.

"I never was that lucky of a man. I figured you'd hang around longer than a case of the clap."

"Malcolm," Frey said in mock outrage, "such vulgarities. That's conduct unbecoming of an officer; I believe that's a punishable offense."

"Then why don't you come with me to Admiralty and report me? You tell them I hurt your delicate ears with my vulgarity and I'll tell them about your treason and sedition."

"As tempting as that offer is, I'm afraid I must decline," replied Frye smugly. "I trust you know why I radioed."

"It wasn't for the scintillating conversation?" quipped Malcolm.

"No," Frye said emphatically. "I'm asking you to save bloodshed on both our sides and simply surrender now. No one needs to get hurt. The crew of the Daedalus and your guests will not be harmed. I only want the ship and its contents."

"I take it that this generous offer does not apply to the captain of the Daedalus."

"You are correct, Malcolm. I have... special plans for you," said Frye.

"I bet you do. So what if I told you to stick you peaceful offer up your arse?"

"My, Malcolm, you are so diplomatic. Do you really think you can escape this?"

"Yes, I do. Because I've survived I don't know how many attempts by you to kill me. Did it ever occur to you that you're just incompetent?"

"You will not be so smug with me when you watch me murder every last member of your crew before I kill you," hissed Frye. "And you will watch me kill your precious Joan before I'm done with her."

"Oh, I think I touched a nerve. I imagine that your superiors aren't too happy with the number of times you've botched this job. How many times was it? The bomb, the Nautilus, and the flamethrowers. I'd give you credit for the stabbing attempt, but that was nearly successful so I know you had no part in that. Why have someone else do it when you can screw it up yourself?"

"Listen, you self-righteous..."

"Oh, spare me," said Malcolm. "You have to be the most incompetent operative the Germans have! You haven't done one thing right on this assignment." A crewmember ran to the bridge and gave Malcolm a message. When he finished reading the message, a grin came across his face.

"I will not be insulted by the likes of you," yelled Frye. "I should shoot you from the sky for your insolence."

"You won't, though. For one thing, you need what's in this ship to make things right with your bosses. And secondly, you're not competent enough to hit me."

"I would stop insulting me, if you don't wish a slow, painful death," said Frye.

"I'm afraid that won't be today, Frye," Malcolm said.

"And why is that?" asked Frye.

"Because of this," Malcolm said. He cut off the microphone and toggled the switch to the observation pods. "Fire at three two five mark twenty five, forty five!"

"Roger!" came the reply from Saxon.

A ray of bright, white light streaked in front of the Daedalus, traveling up to the clouds. A second later, a loud thump shook the Daedalus and the clouds became alight with fire.

"Bloody hell! What was that?" yelled Frye, not necessarily so that Malcolm could hear him. He must have distractedly talked with the bridge crew and forgotten his handset was still active. Malcolm could hear chaos on the bridge, but it didn't sound like the ship was in trouble.

Damn, Malcolm thought. I missed the bastard. He must be bouncing the radio signal among his other ships. Well, at least I have a one-in-three chance now. With Mr. Holmes' assistance, the radio chief had devised a way with multiple antennae to triangulate a radio transmission. Frye must have been transmitting to all of the ships so Malcolm was only getting the signal that bounced from the nearest ship. Saxon and Joan were stationed at either end of the ship in the observation pods, armed with one of the strange guns that shot a superheated ray. As Malcolm had expected, when that ray struck the hydrogen filled balloon of the zeppelin, it instantly went up in a ball of flames.

Malcolm watched as the gondola of the German zeppelin plunged by the Daedalus, fully engulfed in flames. The spindly remnants of the balloon superstructure were visible in a fiery outline, but the flames also consumed them. Malcolm shuddered to think of the number of lives lost, but this was clearly a battle for survival.

Malcolm toggled his handset back to Frye. "Are you still up there? Or did I get lucky?"

"I'm still here, you arrogant bastard. I will kill you personally. No more playing nice. Surrender this second and I will spare your crew. Otherwise I take your ship and kill your crew one by one."

"You have to catch me first, you incompetent dummkopf!" said Malcolm.

"Very well, this is on your head," said Frye.

"As the deaths of your crew will be on your head," said Malcolm.

Malcolm heard the line go dead. This was the moment. Malcolm waited five seconds and called the engine room. "Engine room, port and main engine at full, starboard engine full reverse!"

"Aye, sir!" came the reply. Malcolm spun the wheel of the Daedalus full to the right. The whole ship felt like it lurched to the right as the ship made a nearly right angle turn. Malcolm looked up to see the two German zeppelins descending in an attempt to block their path, but they were instead coming down parallel to the Daedalus. Mr. Preston had suggested the idea that the engines should be able to work independently so that the engines themselves could help turn the ship. Malcolm cursed himself for not thinking of that sooner. With Professor Zhukovsky's assistance and a little engineering know-how, it turned out to be relatively easy to create a mechanism where each engine could be operated independently or in tandem.

Malcolm knew that directly above them was the ship with the boarding party and that it too was descending so that the Germans could rappel to the balloon. Malcolm guessed that Frye would wait until the other two ships were on the same plane as the Daedalus. The next surprise would have to be executed perfectly.

"Gunnery officers, train all weapons on the German engines. Try not to hit the balloon, although if that happens, I'll shed few tears. And prepare to fire on my order."

The Reluctant Captain

Malcolm waited. The zeppelins were drifting down slowly; a controlled descent was a difficult maneuver to perform in an airship and it certainly was not one that could be made quickly. Malcolm counted the time in seconds, patiently waiting for the right moment. Malcolm felt his palms starting to sweat and his mouth was dry. Everything would likely come down to the next few seconds and he knew that his life and the lives of every soul aboard that Daedalus depended on him. He felt like he had a rock in his throat and he couldn't breathe.

"Just a little more..." Malcolm said to no one. He flipped on the handset. "Fire all guns! All hands, strap in!" Malcolm quickly wrapped his wrists into two pieces of cloth that were tied to the wheel. Malcolm waited two seconds after he had secured his wrists. "Professor Rutherford, fire the engine!"

"I don't know if this is going to work," he said. "We haven't had time to test it. It might blow us all to kingdom come!"

"I'd rather that than suffer the tender mercies of the Germans. Fire the damn engine!"

"Very well," said Rutherford.

"Everyone hold on!" Malcolm yelled into the handset.

For a brief second, nothing happened. Then, a horrendous roar blotted out all other sounds and Malcolm found his feet were no longer on the floor. If he hadn't been lashed to the wheel like a maritime captain in a storm, he would have sailed into the bridge wall. The German zeppelin blurred past his line of sight. Malcolm hoped the line was still open. "Joan, fire!"

The Daedalus hurtled forward at alarming speed; the speed gauges were useless. There was a sudden boom and the whole ship shuddered with it. The whole ship was shuddering and Malcolm thought he could hear supports groaning under the force. "Rutherford, disengage the engine!" The roaring stopped and the Daedalus still continued forward at a tremendous rate of speed. Malcolm's feet came back to the ground again and he was able to grab the headset. "Aft observation pod report!"

"The zeppelins are barely in visible range, Malcolm. We must be thirty or forty miles away from them. I can see smoke from the two zeppelins that attempted to box us in. I can't see the other zeppelin, Malcolm. I should see something, but I don't."

Malcolm felt a sinking feeling in the pit of his stomach. "Engine room, all engines full reverse."

"What are you doing, Captain?" asked the navigator. "Shouldn't we be putting distance between us and them?"

"Aye, but I have a sneaking suspicion..." Malcolm said.

Out of the view port of the bridge, a German zeppelin floated just ahead and above the Daedalus, held to the Daedalus by a steel cable.

Chapter 36

The German zeppelin was almost unrecognizable as an airship. The front superstructure of the balloon had been pushed back into the balloon, giving it an almost flat front. The frame of the gondola was twisted and was dangling precariously from the balloon. Worse, it seemed to slowly be losing altitude and if they did not get the ship untethered from the Daedalus, it would drag the Daedalus down as well.

"British Airship Daedalus, this is Captain Heinrich Mathy. We request immediate assistance. We have many wounded and we are losing altitude. We surrender unconditionally, please help us."

Malcolm heard Frye screaming in the background, "No! We must attack! We must capture them!" The German captain said something and background noise ceased.

"I'm sorry, sir. I had to deal with a… distraction. Please, I bear you no grudge. My men need assistance."

"Captain Mathy, this is Captain Malcolm Robertson of the HMA Daedalus. We will attempt to offer assistance. And please make sure that… the distraction is unarmed and bound."

"That will be my pleasure, Captain," said Mathy. The two captains got to work on the logistics. Riggers were sent topside to secure temporary mooring lines to the zeppelin and additional armed men were sent topside to supervise the German prisoners. The wounded were sent down in stretchers tied to lines. Once near the Daedalus, they were sent down the side to the infirmary window where the medical crew pulled them in and Doctor Jenkins got to work. As the two crafts moved closer, rope ladders were dropped from the zeppelin and unarmed German airmen descended the ladders. As soon as they were off the ladders, they raised their hands up in the air, eager to be off the dying zeppelin even if it meant surrender. The rescued Germans were herded into an auxiliary cargo hold where they would not be able to see the spaceship.

The evacuation of the German crew took several hours. The German zeppelin had dropped nearly 100 feet in that time and the Daedalus likewise descended to keep abreast of the ship. At long last, the final group descended from the zeppelin. The group contained a very large German soldier who had Frye slung over his shoulder as he descended, followed by the captain himself dressed in full dress uniform. A report from topside had warned Malcolm that the German captain was in dress uniform and was attempting to board the Daedalus armed with a sword. Malcolm immediately grasped the intent and ordered his men to let the captain onboard with the sword. Malcolm notified Saxon to get into his dress uniform and meet him in the auxiliary cargo hold, while he ran to his quarters and hastily donned his own dress uniform. This was the Air Service and there were traditions to be maintained.

Malcolm and Saxon arrived nearly simultaneously at the cargo hold and Malcolm was relieved to see that Joan was there, safe and sound. She'd even managed to put on a new dress and apply some makeup. It was all Malcolm could do to tear himself away from staring at her beauty to concentrate on the matter at hand. He pulled at the hem of his uniform jacket and said, "Shall we get this over with?"

The crew of the Daedalus surrounded the fifty or so German soldiers from the zeppelin. The cargo doors were open so it was breezy in the room. A rope was secured near the cargo bay door and tied to the German zeppelin. It was the last rope attached to the ship. The captains had agreed that the German zeppelin was a liability to both sides and that the best thing would be to cut it loose. Captain Mathy had suggested that Malcolm do it as part of the surrender ceremony.

Captain Mathy stood at rigid attention when he saw Malcolm enter the room and the rest of the German crew followed his example. Malcolm marched solemnly to the center of the room. Captain Mathy marched forward and addressed Malcolm. "On behalf of the crew of the L13, please accept our complete and unconditional surrender." He drew his sword and in a deft motion placed it in both hands and presented it to Malcolm.

Malcolm took the sword in both hands. "On behalf of the crew of the HMS Daedalus and His Majesty King George V, I accept your surrender. You will be treated as prisoners of war in full accordance of the Hague Conventions."

The Reluctant Captain

Suddenly, there was a commotion and Frye lunged out away from his guard, who now lay unconscious on the floor. Frye grabbed the sword out of Malcolm's hands and held it up, threatening Malcolm. Malcolm quickly drew his own sword and entered a guard stance. Suddenly the training with Saxon would come in very handy.

Saxon started to draw his own sword. "No," Malcolm ordered. "This is between him and me. Come on, Frye; see if you can do it right this time. How many more must die for your incompetence?"

"Only you," growled Frye. He lunged at Malcolm, but Malcolm was able to easily bat away the attack. Malcolm had thought that Frye would be a much better swordsman than him. And then he realized that unless Frye was very good at deception, Frye was right-handed and that hand was covered in a bandage. Frye was holding the sword in his left hand. That made it a much more equal fight.

"Really? That's the best you can do? You must really not want to kill me very much," Malcolm continued. Malcolm knew that if he kept insulting Frye, he would goad him into doing something stupid. And that's when Malcolm would deal with him. "I guess that's obvious since you haven't managed to do it yet!"

"WILL... YOU.... SHUT... UP!!" screamed Frye, his face now twisted with rage.

"I guess the truth hurts, doesn't it?" said Malcolm, taunting him. "You are by far the most incompetent operative known to man. And, you weren't even that good of an engineer." Malcolm knew that that little barb would wound his pride sufficiently to make him off balance.

Frye roared and tried to swing at Malcolm with a two-handed attack. The sword missed his head by inches, but Malcolm was able to step aside, trip Frye as he went by, and use his sword to swat Frye's hands as hard as he could. Frye yelped in pain and fell to the ground, the sword skittering away out of reach. "My patience with you is at an end, Frye. Give up and I won't be forced to kill you," Malcolm said as he advanced on Frye with his sword pointed at him.

Frye backed up along the floor and Malcolm realized a fraction too late that he had backed Frye toward Joan.

Frye must have seen the look in Malcolm's eyes because without looking, he swung his legs around behind him and knocked Joan to the floor. Before Malcolm could react, Frye had pulled Joan up by the hair and had her small derringer pushed hard under her chin. "Not so fast, Malcolm. I wouldn't make any hasty moves. Someone as incompetent as me might pull the trigger and your little lovely's brain will be decorating the ship's ceiling."

Malcolm's sword point dipped a little. "Frye, you're never going to escape. If you kill her, I will kill you myself."

Frye pulled Joan over toward the cargo doors. "Not too close or the little lady here gets a flying lesson." Frye continued to maneuver his way to the rope connecting the two ships. "How about you give me your sword?"

"What, a gun isn't enough?" asked Malcolm. Catching Frye's meaning that he meant to cut the zeppelin away from the Daedalus and his reaction to jab the gun tighter to Joan's jaw, Malcolm slowly bent down and slid the sword over to Frye.

"Very good. You are capable of learning something," said Frye. "And now, I must take my leave."

"Good God, man. Are you crazy? That zeppelin is in no shape to fly. It's just going to fall to the ocean."

"I'd rather die in the air than live forever in an English prison. No, now I must say auf wiedersehen. But before I go, let me give you something to remember me by. I hope it causes you as much pain as you have caused me." Frye pulled Joan so that she faced him and fired the derringer directly into her stomach. He pushed her away from him and towards Malcolm, grabbed the rope with his left hand, and clumsily held the sword with his right hand. Frye slashed the rope and swung out of the cargo hold as he was pulled toward the zeppelin.

Malcolm caught Joan before she could hit the floor, the blood already blossoming from the gunshot wound. She looked at Malcolm, her face turning pale. She smiled and said, "I guess it's my turn to be injured," and closed her eyes.

Chapter 37

Without thinking, Malcolm lifted Joan up and ran for the infirmary. The men stood in shock as Malcolm immediately ran to get Joan to the infirmary. Malcolm ran as fast he could, running over a few crewmen who had the misfortune to get in his way. After what seemed like an eternity, he stumbled into the infirmary. "Dr. Jenkins!" he shouted. "Dr. Jenkins! Get out here right now!"

"Who the bloody hell is yelling at me in my own infirmary?" Dr. Jenkins said as he came from behind a curtain. He saw Malcolm holding Joan's body and the blood coming from her stomach, and his demeanor changed instantly. "Quick, lay her over on this table," he said. "I need to examine the wound. What happened?"

"That bastard Frye. Shot her at point blank with her small derringer."

"Did you get him?" asked the doctor.

"No. The bastard got away. Is she going to be alright, Doctor?"

"I don't know yet. I'm going to have to operate to see what sort of damage occurred and how much bleeding there is. Orderly, get prepped for surgery!"

"Is there anything I can do?" said Malcolm.

"The best thing you can do is run this ship. I will call you the minute I know something."

"But..." Malcolm protested.

"No buts," said Jenkins. "Don't make me pull rank. Medical matters are the one place where I outrank you."

"Very well," Malcolm said, knowing he wouldn't win this battle. "But you better radio me the moment you're done operating or I'll have you cleaning bedpans for a month!"

"Fine. I'll call you as soon as she is out of the operating room."

Malcolm left the infirmary and wandered to the bridge. Absently, he listened to the damage reports: some structural damage, but nothing that would prevent them from making it home; casualty reports: no other major injuries; and current situation: they were nearly sixty miles from the ambush point and no sign of pursuit from the other zeppelins. Malcolm just nodded and said nothing. Saxon had made arrangements for the German prisoners. Trying to find the officers better quarters had been challenging, but he had convinced several of the Daedalus junior officers to share quarters. Malcolm nodded and said, "Wait! Their captain should have Frye's quarters."

"A capital idea, sir. I'll make it so," he said. He paused for a moment. "Are you alright sir? How is she?"

"I don't know; the doctor wouldn't let me stay. I'm... I don't know how I am."

"I have everything under control if you need to step away."

"No, no," said Malcolm, shaking his head as if to clear away the cobwebs. "I should make myself useful and carry on. She'd expect that of me. Thank you though, Charles."

"Very well, sir. But if you need to leave..."

"I will take you up on your offer. Just not now. I need to be busy," Malcolm said.

"Understood, sir."

Malcolm threw himself into the ship's business. He talked with the navigator and they plotted a course for Britain. The navigator estimated that they had another three days before they would arrive in Britain. When the course was set, Malcolm left the bridge and went to help Mr. Preston who had pressed Professor Zhukovsky into service to help with damage control. Malcolm listened to the two men's plans for repairing the critical areas of the ship. The balloon superstructure had suffered deformation during the firing of the spaceship's engines and that was the primary concern. Although it was not

The Reluctant Captain

an immediate danger, all agreed that anything that could be done to help the situation would be welcome.

Malcolm looked at his pocket watch. It had been over three hours since he left the infirmary and still no word. He thought about going to the infirmary, but thought better of it. He went to Mr. Holmes' cabin. He was sure he had heard the news, but Malcolm thought like he should say something. Malcolm knocked on the cabin door and waited. There was no answer. Malcolm assumed that Holmes must have gone to the infirmary.

Malcolm continued on to the radio room where he made his report to the Admiralty. Now that there was little fear of German pursuit, Malcolm felt safer about breaking his self-imposed radio silence. The Admiralty ordered the Daedalus to make best time to RNAS Longside, not far from Aberdeen, for repairs. The Admiralty would debrief Malcolm and his officers, and the dignitaries aboard the Daedalus would be sent home. Once the Daedalus was repaired, it would return to its base at RNAS Kingsnorth. Malcolm was glad that they had been ordered to make for Longside, as it would shave a day off their flight. And if he managed to get off base, he knew several excellent whisky distilleries not far from Aberdeen. Before he left, he radioed the new course to the bridge with orders to make best possible speed.

Malcolm wandered until he came across Frye's room. Two guards were standing outside so Malcolm surmised that the German captain had taken residence. Malcolm saluted the guards and knocked on the door. "Come," came the voice from within.

Malcolm opened the door with the guards following. "I'll be fine," Malcolm said. "Stand at your post and if there is any trouble I'll let you know." The guards looked at each other, hesitating for a second, but they saw the look Malcolm gave them and left.

"I trust the accommodations are adequate," Malcolm said.

"I am your prisoner," Captain Mathy replied. "This is luxurious."

"I'm Captain Malcolm Robertson," Malcolm said, offering his hand. "Please call me Malcolm."

"I'm Captain Heinrich Mathy. Please call me Heinrich," said Mathy. "Malcolm, thank you for rescuing my men. The ship can be replaced, but not so her men."

"I had intended to get away without necessarily destroying any ships," said Malcolm.

"That was a masterful bit of strategy. How long have you been captain of this ship?" Mathy asked.

"Only a few months, actually," said Malcolm.

"You must be having fun with me. Surely you are joking!" he said.

"My last post was chief engineer, actually. I became captain after we lost most of our bridge crew."

"You are a formidable enemy. I hope someday to have the honor to do battle with you."

"Frankly, I've had enough death and battles for a while," Malcolm said. He became quiet, thinking about Joan.

"You are worried about the woman. Was she your wife? Lover?" asked Mathy.

"Yes. Lover, I mean." said Malcolm. He fell silent.

Captain Mathy rose and went to the top drawer of the dresser. He pulled out a bottle and found two glasses. "Here, it seems the former inhabitant of this room smuggled some Russian vodka on board." He read the label. "From the looks of it, good vodka as well." He poured two measures and handed one to Malcolm. "To your lady's health!"

"To Joan's health!" Malcolm returned the toast. The vodka burned as it went down and once the fire burned out, Malcolm felt more relaxed. Mathy poured another shot for each of them. "Your turn to make the toast," said Mathy.

"Alright. Um..." Before he could think of a toast, Doctor Jenkins' voice came over the intercom. "Captain Robertson, report to the infirmary immediately." Malcolm said simply, "Cheers!" and downed the shot with one gulp. "If you will excuse me, I have to go."

"Of course." He paused. "Are you going to confiscate the vodka?"

"What vodka?" asked Malcolm in a tone of mock questioning.

"Thank you. You are an interesting man, Malcolm Robertson."

"Thank you," Malcolm said as he knocked on the door for the guards to open it. He was out the door in a flash and it was all he could do not to sprint at full speed to the infirmary. But he was captain and his rank demanded a certain amount of decorum. As he got closer to the infirmary, his resolve wavered and he broke into a run. In just over a minute, he had covered half of the length of the ship and gone down one flight of stairs to reach the infirmary.

Malcolm burst into the room and saw Dr. Jenkins and Mr. Holmes sitting down, their heads hung low. "Where is she? Can I see her?" Malcolm asked. He saw that they were sitting in front a screen. "Is she back there? How is she?"

Mr. Holmes rose and turned to Malcolm. His face looked deeply lined and he looked like he might have cried. "Malcolm, I'm afraid she's dead."

Chapter 38

Malcolm felt as if his insides had been ripped from his body. His knees buckled and he fell to the floor. His eyes flooded with tears as he gasped, "No, it can't be! There must be some mistake! She can't die like that!" He stumbled to his feet and rushed toward the screen, desperate to pull it aside. He was sure he would see her lying there breathing, just asleep. Dr. Jenkins and Mr. Holmes both grabbed him and pulled him away. He fought at first, but then collapsed in their arms, the tears pouring in a torrent of grief.

The two men held him for several minutes before Malcolm had no tears left. He pulled himself up and tried to gather his thoughts. "What happened?" he asked in a tiny, scratchy voice that didn't sound like his own.

"The damage was too extensive for me to fix, Malcolm," Jenkins said. "Almost every organ in her abdomen took damage. There was too much blood loss. There was nothing I could do. If there was, I would have done it."

"I know," whispered Malcolm. After a pause, he said, "Can I see her? One last time to say goodbye?"

"Of course," said Dr. Jenkins. He moved aside and let Malcolm go behind the screen. There, Malcolm saw a body covered with a sheet. Malcolm walked slowly, still irrationally praying that he would not see Joan under that sheet. He hoped this was a dream. He slowly pulled the sheet down to reveal Joan's lovely face. His heart ripped in half at the realization that this was not a dream. He gently touched her cheek, but it was already cold. He reached down and found her hand and put it in his own. He squatted next to the table, stroking her hair.

"Joan, I would have asked you to marry me," said Malcolm. "I loved you and I didn't want anyone else. Ever. I know you would have said no, but I would have convinced you. I know. But I can't. None of my cleverness, tricks, or quick thinking will ever bring you back. You're gone, my bonnie Joan." The tears threatened to overwhelm him again. He stifled them and took a long breath. He rose, placed a single kiss on her dead ruby lips, and covered her again. He took another deep breath and stepped around the curtain.

"Do I need to notify her next of kin?" he said, dreading the answer.

"No, Malcolm. I'll take care of all of the arrangements," Holmes said. He paused for a moment. "I'm sorry for your loss. I know she meant a great deal to you."

"That she did, Mr. Holmes," he said. Malcolm started to walk aimlessly out of the infirmary.

"Where are you going?" asked Dr. Jenkins.

"I'm going to my quarters to get stinking drunk. Inform Commander Saxon that he will be in command," Malcolm said as he continued walking out of the infirmary without looking back.

The next morning, Malcolm's head hurt as much as his heart. True to his word, he drank a great deal of whisky until he passed out. It let him sleep without dreams. He feared that he would dream of Joan and the stitches would be ripped out of the wound that was his grief and it would hurt all over again. Now, everything hurt all over and Malcolm found that to be a small blessing.

The crew kept their distance from their captain and only spoke when absolutely necessary. For his part, Malcolm was glad, because he didn't have the strength to put on a show for the men as to how tough he was. He had loved Joan and he would not disgrace her memory by pretending it meant nothing to him. It had taken a very long shower, several mugs of strong tea, and a handful of aspirin to dull the pounding in his head. The sounds of the airship that usually gave him such joy were a relentless assault on his head. His stomach felt little better; he thought he would be lucky to keep down some dry toast or a ship's biscuit. He started to eat a ship's biscuit, but quickly lost his appetite as he remembered introducing Joan to ship's biscuits while they hid aboard the Daedalus.

Malcolm spent the day on the bridge. Although everyone kept his distance, Malcolm was glad to not be alone. He avoided his office where he usually spent half of his time going over reports and ship business. If there was one thing he had learned in the Air Service, it was that paperwork was eternal. When he was done on the bridge, he wandered the ship. He checked on the repair work that Mr. Preston was overseeing; he was satisfied to see that Mr. Preston had some promise as an engineer. That thought made him remember Frye, and Joan's death played out again in front of his eyes in slow motion. Malcolm walked away from Mr. Preston who trailed off in mid-sentence, asking Malcolm an engineering question. Preston went to go after Malcolm, but one of the older hands pulled him back and said, "Now's not the time, sir."

Malcolm wandered and found himself at Mr. Holmes' cabin. He knocked and said, "Mr. Holmes, it's Captain Robertson. Are you in?"

"Just a moment." Malcolm waited a few seconds for the door to open. "What can I do for you?" Holmes asked.

"Can I talk to you for a moment?"

"Yes, certainly," Holmes said, opening the door. He offered Malcolm a chair and sat at his desk. Malcolm noticed that the radios and equipment were mostly packed up.

"You've packed up your equipment?" Malcolm asked.

"I made my report after we escaped the Germans. I know we only have a short time before we land at Longside. I think it best that my equipment is kept away from the prying eyes of our guests." Silence settled over the room. Finally, Holmes said, "You wanted to talk to me?"

"Yes," said Malcolm. He stopped, not knowing how to begin and not wanting to feel the pain once he did start. But he had to ask. "Have you informed Joan's family?"

"Yes, the service sent a telegram to our embassy in Switzerland and one of the staff informed her parents. She was an only child."

"It doesn't seem right that parents should outlive their children." Malcolm said. "Especially for such a needless death. If only I could have stopped Frye or just shot the bastard altogether."

The Reluctant Captain

"I'm an excellent judge of character; it's an occupational hazard. I know you are not that man. You would not take justice into your own hands."

"Don't be so sure," said Malcolm.

"Malcolm, she wouldn't want to you to become a cold-blooded murderer on her account. There was nothing you could have done. Joan knew that her job was dangerous. She was prepared to die."

"Well, I'm not prepared for her to die! Her death was so meaningless."

"Malcolm, death is meaningless. I've been doing this job a very long time. There is no such thing as a good death—especially in this business. I've lost many friends and even loved ones. Why do you think I insist on keeping my relationships on a formal level? To distance myself so I don't feel that pain again and again."

"Does it work?" Malcolm asked.

"Not one bloody bit," said Holmes. "Especially in Joan's case. She had an infuriating way of getting under your skin and making you care... but I don't have to tell you that."

"What do I do now?" Malcolm asked.

"You get up and get through the day however you can. The next day, you do the same. And the day after that, and the day after that. You keep doing it until you can remember the good times and the good outweighs the pain."

Malcolm nodded. He sat for a minute before saying, "How will you take her off the ship?"

"I have asked for an undertaker to meet us. He will bring a coffin and we'll take her to the hearse."

"I would iike to be one of those who carry her off the ship."

Holmes paused, considering the request. "Yes, I think she would have wanted that." He paused again before saying, "I'm an excellent judge of character, as I've said. I do believe that she loved you very much. If anyone could have gotten her to settle down, I'm sure it would have been you."

Malcolm blinked away the tears and managed to croak, "Thank you." He stood to leave.

"Malcolm," said Holmes. "I know it is hard now, but please don't do anything hasty like resign your commission. You are an excellent captain, whether you know it or not. I think Joan would want you to follow your calling. I think that's why she tried to push you away. She would have wanted you to do everything that you're capable of doing."

"I won't do anything hasty. Besides," Malcolm said, "I think I'm going to spend the next three months getting debriefed."

Holmes laughed. "You're probably right, Malcolm." He offered his hand. "It's been my pleasure to serve with you, even for a short time."

"Thank you. Likewise," Malcolm said, shaking Holmes' hand. "Do you suppose our paths will cross again?"

"I'm almost positive," said Holmes.

Malcolm started to leave. "I'm sorry, but may I ask one more thing? Do you have a photo of Joan? I want something to remember her."

"Yes, hold on a minute." Holmes went to one of his files and rifled through it. "It may not be as glamorous as she would have liked, but I think it captures her essence."

"Is this her official Secret Service photograph?" asked Malcolm, looking at the photograph. The stark black and white captured her beauty in a way that made her almost luminescent. Even though she wore a stern, no-nonsense expression, he could see her playfulness, her seriousness, her ferocity, and her tenderness. He blinked so that the tears welling in his eyes would not ruin the photograph.

"Yes. It's of little use now. All it would do is deteriorate in her file. I think it will do more good now."

The Reluctant Captain

"Thank you," Malcolm said, the words barely passing from his lips. He left the cabin and went to his own cabin. He found a frame in Captain Collins' effects that still had not been sent home. He removed Collins' photograph and put Joan's photo in the frame. He spent the night trying to wash the blood out of his dress uniform and all the while, Joan's photograph was near.

The next morning, he rose and dressed. His heart was still heavy, but he had a duty to do and Holmes was right—Joan would have wanted him to carry on to the end. He went to the bridge with a large mug of tea and was briefed on the ship's status. They were approximately two hours out from Longside. It wouldn't be long now and this mission would be complete. Malcolm wondered to himself how one mission could have such a profound effect on one's life. When the Daedalus had left Kingsnorth, he was chief engineer—alone, but happy. Now, he was captain— alone and wretched. In the months that this mission had taken to complete, Malcolm felt like his life had been altered irrevocably. He knew now he couldn't go back to being chief engineer and he knew he might never fall in love like that ever again. He also knew deep down that there would one day be a reckoning with Frye.

As was typical any time a ship returned from a long mission, there was great pomp and circumstance for the arrival of the Daedalus. It wasn't often that the flagship of the Royal Air Service made a trip to Longside and the base commander wanted to make the most of this auspicious occasion. Malcolm ordered the crew into their dress uniforms for the landing— some, like Malcolm's, a little worse for wear.

At almost exactly six bells that morning, the Daedalus glided to the mooring tower and landing platform. Once mooring lines were attached, the gangplank was lowered and the front cargo bay doors were opened. Malcolm stood in the open doorway in full dress at attention. The base commander, Captain Pearson, approached the gangway. Malcolm saluted sharply. "Captain Pearson, I request permission to land the HMS. Daedalus and disembark."

Pearson returned the salute. "Permission granted. Welcome home, Captain Robertson and the crew of the Daedalus." Somewhere nearby, a brass band struck up a march. As they had agreed, Captain Pearson first took custody of the German prisoners. As he was marched by, Captain Mathy tipped his hat to Malcolm. Then, the guests aboard the Daedalus came down and were greeted personally by the base commander. Each was to be put up in a small house until transportation could be arranged. Finally, the crew marched out and assembled on the landing pad. Malcolm knew he would be expected to say something and he reminded himself to keep it brief because everyone wanted to start liberty as soon as possible.

"Lads, first, I want to thank you all for putting up with a green captain. I think you all are the finest crew in the whole Royal Air Service!" A cheer went up from the ranks. "I'm going to dismiss you so that you all can enjoy some much-needed liberty. But before I do, I just ask that you take a few minutes to remember those whom we lost on this voyage. Drink a toast in their name or say a prayer for them. Just a simple remembrance is all I ask. Now get out there and enjoy that liberty. Crew dismissed! Except for you, Commander Saxon."

"What is it, Captain?" he said, looking a little concerned.

Malcolm handed Saxon a telegram that had arrived on the Daedalus early that morning. "It seems that you and are I to be whisked away to London for an extensive debriefing. Pack to be gone quite a while. Fortunately, we don't have to arrive in full dress."

Saxon read the telegram. "Aren't we the lucky ones?" he said. "I supposed I'd better pack. What time do we leave?"

"As soon as you can pack. I have one more thing to do before I go," Malcolm said.

"Oh?" Saxon asked. "Oh!" he said as he realized what had to be done. "It may take me a while to pack."

"Thank you, Charles," said Malcolm.

"Is there anything I can do to help?" said Saxon.

"Other than take an exorbitant time finding matching socks? No, I need to do it myself."

"I understand," Saxon said. "And just for the record, all of my socks are perfectly matched." He turned and went back aboard the Daedalus.

Malcolm turned and saw the steam-powered hearse pull up to the entry. Fortunately, nearly all of the crew had left so there would be few eyes to witness Malcolm's grief. The three undertakers, dressed in their black overcoats and black top hats, drew a simple black coffin out of the hearse. Malcolm watched as they carried the empty coffin up the gangplank to a waiting Mr. Holmes who would lead them to the infirmary. Malcolm supposed that he should follow them, but his heart couldn't bear to see her like that again.

He knew it would be some time before they returned when a thought occurred to him. He strode out to the far end of the landing field that bordered an uncultivated field. There he saw the object of his quest. He walked into the field and picked as many bluebells as he could hold. Finally, he had a great bouquet of bluebells, but nothing to hold them together. He fished around the pockets of his dress uniform and found he had left a small piece of wire in his pocket. Malcolm chuckled because he often found odds and ends from his latest project. He wrapped the wire around the stems to hold them together. He was startled to see activity near the gangplank. He had spent more time picking the flowers than he had realized. "Wait!" he yelled and ran at full speed back to the Daedalus.

His yell attracted the attention of Mr. Holmes, who appeared to direct the undertakers to stop. They gently set down the coffin and waited for him to arrive. Breathlessly, Malcolm ran up the gangplank. "Here, I thought she should have flowers," he said between gasps. He gently laid his bouquet on the coffin. "I'm ready," he said.

"Nonsense, catch your breath," said Mr. Holmes.

"No," said Malcolm, still breathing hard. "If I wait until I catch my breath, I may not be able to do it. I'm ready."

"Very well." Mr. Holmes nodded to the undertakers. The party reached down and lifted the coffin. It was heavy, but at this moment it felt much lighter than Malcolm's heart. In slow, methodical, measured steps, the group carried the coffin to the hearse. They stopped at the rear of the hearse and lifted the coffin to the waiting metal rack. Tears filled Malcolm's eyes, making it difficult to see, but he did his duty. When the coffin settled in the rack, there was a click as latches held it in place. Malcolm heard the whoosh of the pneumatics as the coffin slowly slid into the hearse. Malcolm's bouquet of bluebells lay on top of the coffin as it slid into the darkness of the hearse. Malcolm thought that the only time he had every given her flowers was for her funeral. When he heard the door shut, he turned away and walked back to the Daedalus, desperately trying to control the sobs that threatened to spill out of him.

He kept control until he reached his quarters and shut the door. The sobs leapt out and he could control them no longer. And he didn't want to control them. He collapsed in his chair and let the grief pour from him. He cried for long minutes until he had no tears left. He sat with his face in his hands, mentally depleted. He knew he had to get ready to leave for London. There was much unfinished business, but all Malcolm could think of was Joan. It seemed so unfair that she should die like that. And then Mr. Holmes' words came back to him from last night. Death is unfair and arbitrary. He knew deep in his heart that Joan wouldn't want him to crawl up in a ball. She was a fighter. He knew in his heart of hearts that he was, too. But today, the enormity of what had happened came crashing down on him and he felt like he didn't have the strength to resist. Let someone else take it for a bloody change! Why do I have to be the one who bloody well has to have the world on his shoulders? he thought bitterly.

He took a deep breath. He couldn't give in to self-pity. Joan would not have wanted it and neither did he. He took another deep breath and rose to pack his things into his footlocker. He packed the captain's log, his clothes, the bottle of whisky from the doctor, and on top of it was the photograph of Joan. He closed the locker and since there were no crewmen aboard, he dragged the footlocker out of the room and down the hall.

He stopped as he reached Joan's cabin. He hesitated a moment and opened the door. Malcolm was relieved to find that it was empty. All of her personal effects had been removed, and the bed had been stripped and remade. It looked like any other junior officer's room. He thought for the briefest instant he caught a whiff of her perfume, but decided it was a trick of memory. He closed the door and dragged the footlocker through the ship and down the gangplank.

Malcolm found Saxon waiting for him at the gangplank and a large steam car waited for them both. When the footlockers were stowed, the two men were shown to the back of the car. The steam car sped away from the base. Malcolm turned his head to watch as the Daedalus began to slowly shrink from his view. They quickly made the short trip to Aberdeen where they were handed two tickets for an overnight train to London. Malcolm and Saxon boarded the appointed train and found their sleeper car.

Once the train was underway, Saxon said, "Sir, permission to speak freely."

Malcolm smiled, "Charles, I'm not sure that rank applies here. Please speak freely. And call me Malcolm."

"Alright, Malcolm. I think you need a drink. In fact, I daresay you need many of them. I confiscated what was left of a bottle of vodka from the German captain. It appears to be very good."

"Oh?" said Malcolm, feigning ignorance.

"It might have been Frye's," he said. "The captain said he found it in his quarters."

Saxon stood up, opened his locker, and fished out the bottle. He found two glasses and poured two very generous portions. "To the Daedalus and all she's done to and for us!"

Malcolm chuckled. "To the Daedalus and all she's done to and for us!"

Malcolm couldn't have thought of a better toast.

Chapter 39

As Malcolm and Saxon disembarked at King's Cross the next morning, Malcolm caught sight of a group of naval personnel waiting near the tracks—two officers and four Royal Marines. Malcolm whispered to Saxon, "That doesn't look like a particularly welcoming reception," nodding towards the group.

"I should say not," whispered Saxon. "Do you think they'll clap us in irons?"

"I doubt it, but one never knows; it is the Admiralty," said Malcolm. "No use putting this off." He sighed as he took his trunk and headed toward the group. With Saxon following behind, Malcolm approached the group. As he got close, the officers and marines saluted. Malcolm and Saxon returned the salute.

Before Malcolm could say anything, one of the officers said, "Captain Robertson? I'm Lieutenant Tucker. I'll be your liaison while you're at the Admiralty. Let us take your trunk." Before Malcolm could object, one of the Marines had hefted Malcolm's trunk and began walking off. "This is Lieutenant Brandon. He will be your liaison, Commander Saxon. Would you follow us? We have cars waiting."

Malcolm and Saxon exchanged a glance, wondering why two cars were sent when one should have sufficed. As they followed the lieutenants through the crowded train station, Malcolm could not help but feel the almost ominous presence of the marine who stayed close to Malcolm at all times, as if to grab Malcolm if he were to suddenly bolt. For a brief moment, Malcolm toyed with the idea, just to see what would happen, but the no-nonsense look on the marine's face told Malcolm that it would be a very painful idea. Upon exiting the station, two cars were waiting and Malcolm could see that their trunks had already been loaded. "This way," indicated Lieutenant Tucker. Saxon started to follow Malcolm when Lieutenant Brandon indicated the other car. "This way, Commander Saxon." Malcolm and Saxon once more exchanged glances and went to their respective cars.

As Malcolm settled in the back, one of the marines squeezed in next to him while Tucker sat in the passenger seat and the other marine drove. Malcolm tried to portray an attitude of calm, but he felt anything but calm. "Is this your first time in London?" asked Tucker.

"What? No, I've been here a few times," Malcolm said. Taking a deep breath, Malcolm said, "May I ask what is going on? Where are we going and why are armed guards escorting me? Am I under arrest for something?"

"You are not charged with anything," said Lieutenant Tucker, "but the Admiralty wishes to understand the circumstances of your mission—particularly since a number of officers were killed and the ship was heavily damaged. The Admiralty feels it would be best to question each of you separately before any decisions are made."

"Decisions? Such as?" asked Malcolm.

"Captain Robertson, I'm sure there's nothing to worry about," said Lieutenant Tucker. "This is merely a precaution." Tucker smiled, but Malcolm did not find it reassuring. Malcolm turned and looked out the window, preferring to watch the sites of London slide by as they headed to Whitehall and the Admiralty building. Malcolm had never been to the Admiralty and was in awe at the size of the building. Nearby, construction had begun on another building. "That's going to be Admiralty Arch," indicated Tucker. "It will span the mall, giving us additional office space. It's a few years off from completion, but I believe it will be a beautiful building." The car slowed. "Here we are," said Tucker. "Your home away from home for the foreseeable future. If you will follow me," Tucker said after they left the car. Before Malcolm could say anything, the lieutenant continued, "The corporal will take your trunk to your room. I'm afraid you're needed for your first meeting."

Malcolm was led inside—again with one marine close on his heels—and through a labyrinth of halls and stairs until he was ushered into a room. The room was very simply furnished, containing a chair, a desk and behind the desk, a serious looking man that Malcolm immediately recognized as Admiral Beatty. "Shite, this is not good," thought Malcolm. He immediately stood at attention and saluted. Beatty perfunctorily returned the salute. "Sit, Lieutenant Commander Robertson," he said, indicating the chair. "Lieutenant Commander, not Captain. This is definitely not good," Malcolm thought. Malcolm sat and placed both hands on his legs to try to pretend he was not intimidated or scared.

"Lieutenant Commander Robertson, I've read your report with great interest. Let's begin with the morning of the explosion on the Daedalus. Please tell me in the greatest detail possible what occurred that morning."

Malcolm swallowed hard, took a deep breath, and detailed the trouble with the engine, his summons to the bridge, the repair of the main engine, and his attempt to get to the bridge when the bomb detonated. Before he could continue, Admiral Beatty cut him off. "Is there anyone who can corroborate this story?"

"Yes, sir. Commander Saxon brought me the message to report to the bridge and the engineering crew on duty at the time can vouch for both the problem and Commander Saxon's visit."

"I will corroborate that with Lieutenant Saxon," he said with an extra emphasis on the word lieutenant. "How do I know that you did not intentionally damage the engine as an excuse to not be on the bridge when the bomb exploded?"

Malcolm felt his temper rise and took a deep breath before responding, knowing that his career may very well be on the line. "I would estimate that it would take several hours for the sugar that was put in the fuel to work its way into the engines. At that time, I had turned in for the night and did not leave my quarters until 0600 hours, sir."

Admiral Beatty nodded. "I understand that there was bad blood between you and Commander Bromley. I understand that he had you tried for insubordination—for which you were acquitted—and as a result of your testimony, he received an official reprimand. Is that true?"

Malcolm again took a deep breath, thinking carefully about his answer. "It is true, Admiral, that we did not have a great personal relationship, but he was my superior and as such, deserved my respect and obedience."

"And yet, you went on record to object to a direct order?" asked the Admiral.

The Reluctant Captain

"I did so only because, as chief engineer, I felt his order would place the ship and the mission in jeopardy. I felt it was my duty to let him know in the strongest terms possible that his orders might damage the ship."

Beatty nodded to himself. "Tell me about your relationship with Lieutenant Matthew Frye. You are friends?"

"We were friends," Malcolm said with a hard tone of bitterness entering his voice. "I have nothing but contempt and loathing for that cowardly traitor."

"Because of the death of Miss Joan de St. Leger?" asked the Admiral. "It has been documented that you were fraternizing with her both on and off the ship."

Malcolm's anger flared and he suddenly stood up. "Yes, Lieutenant Commander Robertson?" asked a bemused Beatty. "Did you want to say something?"

Malcolm swallowed hard, trying to push the anger down. "No, sir," Malcolm said through a clenched jaw as he sat down.

The questioning continued for the rest of the day without a break. Malcolm was hungry and thirsty and by the end of the day, he could barely think. Eventually, Admiral Beatty had enough and Malcolm was escorted to his room—or cell, as he figured. Although the door was unlocked, a guard was posted down the hall and if Malcolm stepped in the hallway, the guard was there to escort him to the water closet. Malcolm was disturbed to find that both his log and Joan's picture had been removed from his trunk. The guard brought meals that Malcolm was quick to note never required a knife or even a fork.

The days after continued much the same as his first. Malcolm faced hard questions before a number of admirals and captains. At first, the questions were focused on the explosion on the Daedalus, his relationship with Frye, and his relationship with Joan. Malcolm did his level best to answer with the same truthful answers he had given Admiral Beatty, and he was not provoked into answering in anger. Gradually this line of questioning diminished, and they focused on the mission itself and the recovery of the object. As the line of questioning changed, so did the questioners. Malcolm recognized several of the officers as ranking staff of the Royal Naval Engineers who were interested in understanding how Malcolm had modified the Daedalus to take advantage of the Martian technology. The engineers wanted to know how the crew had made their escape, how they were able to activate the technology, and what was the capacity of the energy weapons.

After two weeks of intensive questioning, Malcolm received orders with his evening meal to report the following day in his dress uniform before the Admiralty staff. Malcolm barely touched his food that night and slept little, thinking his career was over. He was mostly angry; he had done everything within his power to save the men of the Daedalus and return the ship. What more could they possibly expect of him? Malcolm decided that if he was going to receive a court-martial, he would give them a piece of his mind as he figured he had nothing left to lose.

The next morning, Malcolm made sure his dress uniform was in immaculate shape and allowed the guard to escort him to the meeting with the Admiralty. He was lead into a large room and stood before a long table where the most senior staff of the Admiralty was seated. Malcolm saw Admiral Beatty and was shocked to see First Lord McKenna was presiding. Shortly after he arrived, Saxon joined him, also in dress uniform. "Is this the firing squad?" whispered Saxon.

"It appears so," whispered Malcolm.

First Lord McKenna knocked a gavel on the table to get attention. "Thank you. We are here today to discuss the results of our inquiry into the Tunguska Affair. Lieutenant Commander Robertson, as Acting Captain of the Daedalus, do you take full responsibility for your actions for the time you were captain?"

"I do, milord," Malcolm said.

"If it please your lordship, I must take responsibility for the Daedalus falling into the hands of the Germans," said Saxon. Malcolm turned to object. "You can't take responsibility for that, you were dead at the time."

"Very well. Before we begin, do either of you have anything else to add?"

The Reluctant Captain

"Milord, I would like the record to state that I did everything in my power for king and country. I would make the same choices again if offered the chance and if I am to be court-martialed, I'd go knowing I did nothing less than my best."

"And I stand with Malcolm—I mean Captain Robertson," said Saxon. "I can't think of a finer captain in the Air Service or anyone who could have done more than Malcolm. If anyone is punished, it should be me for allowing Frye to commandeer the ship."

"No, Charles, you can't take that blame on yourself. We were all duped. I should have put it together sooner..."

Lord McKenna pounded his gavel. "Gentleman! Enough! There is plenty of blame to go around for Frye's infiltration. If that is all you have to say, may we continue?"

Malcolm and Saxon nodded silently.

"Very good. It is the finding of the Admiralty that as a direct result of the actions of Lieutenant Commander Malcolm Robertson and Lieutenant Charles Saxon," Malcolm steeled himself for what must come next, "that the Admiralty promotes Lieutenant Commander Malcolm Robertson to the rank of Captain and Lieutenant Charles Saxon to the rank of Commander." Malcolm's heart leapt into his throat. He wasn't court-martialed? He was sure that it would happen. "In addition, for the gallantry and bravery displayed, we award Captain Malcolm Robertson the Conspicuous Gallantry Medal and the Victoria Cross. We also award Commander Charles Saxon the Conspicuous Gallantry Medal and the Distinguished Service Cross for his role in leading the escape from Königsberg."

First Lord McKenna rose and approached the two officers. He pinned the new ranks on each man, followed by their medals. "Congratulations and well deserved," he said. One by one, the members of the board came forward, first saluting and then shaking hands with the two officers.

When the staff had settled in their chairs, First Lord McKenna continued. "Captain Robertson and Commander Saxon, you have both performed exemplarily under the most trying circumstances. It was our unanimous decision that the two of you personify what we want from our Air Service officers. For the time being, you will be attached to Admiral Beatty's office. Please see him at the conclusion of this meeting to arrange your lodging.

"I must remind you both that your mission to Tunguska and the resulting recovery of the Martian spaceship is highly classified. Although your official record will reflect your promotions and commendations, the details of both will not be included in your official records.

"Again, I cannot emphasize how grateful we are for the return of the Martian spaceship. Once the ship has been analyzed, we expect it to provide a leap in technology greater than the invention of the printing press. You have the thanks of the Admiralty, and dare I say, the nation. I hereby bring this inquiry to a close," First Lord McKenna said as he banged his gavel.

One by one, the senior leadership of the Admiralty filed out of the room, save Admiral Beatty who approached Malcolm and Saxon. They both snapped to attention and saluted the Admiral. He returned their salute and offered his hand to Malcolm. "At ease, gentleman. If we're going to work together, I can't very well have you standing at attention all the time. Congratulations on both your promotions and commendations. They are well earned and, might I add, came at some cost," he said, looking at Malcolm. "I look forward to working with both of you on airship technology and tactics. In fact, I requested that you be attached to my staff."

"Permission to speak freely, sir," Malcolm asked. Beatty nodded. "Why did you request us? During the questioning, I was sure you were going to court-martial me."

Beatty chuckled. "Yes, I suppose it might appear like that. I needed to take your measure. I respect a man who has both the convictions to threaten to strike a superior officer and the wisdom not to do so. It shows you have both passion and discipline. But I do hope that it doesn't happen again."

"No, sir," said Malcolm.

"Very good. I've made arrangements for you to have flats near the Admiralty while you are on my staff. My assistant, Lieutenant Bowles, will take you to your flats so you can get settled. Report to my office at four bells tomorrow." Beatty saluted and, pausing only long enough to receive the salutes from Malcolm and Saxon, strode out of the room.

Malcolm and Saxon looked at each other and both burst into laughter. "I thought for sure we would be court-martialed after that interrogation,' said Saxon when he stopped laughing.

"I thought so as well. Shall we find Lieutenant Bowles and check out our new quarters? I hope that they are less Spartan than our current quarters," Malcolm added. The two officers walked the halls of the Admiralty, eventually finding Lieutenant Bowles. The young lieutenant summoned a car and Malcolm and Saxon were taken a few blocks from the Admiralty to an unassuming building. Lieutenant Bowles showed them their flats and Malcolm noticed that their trunks had already been delivered. Each man had a simple two-room apartment that was modestly furnished, but to Malcolm, it seemed luxurious compared to the cell at the Admiralty. Lieutenant Bowles left the two to unpack. Malcolm and Saxon made plans to meet for dinner and both settled into their new quarters. Malcolm opened his trunk and was happy to find that the photo of Joan had been returned to his trunk. As he picked up the picture, the pain of her loss began to overwhelm him once more. The questioning of the last two weeks had brought back her death over and over again, but he pushed his feelings aside because he didn't want to give his interrogators anything to hurt him. But, in the quiet of the flat, the feeling and the tears came flooding back.

Chapter 40

Malcolm and Saxon spent the next month with Admiral Beatty and the staff of the Admiralty discussing the technology of airships and how they might influence tactics. Malcolm explained the thought process he had used to elude the German zeppelins as well as analyze their capabilities and weaknesses. They gave their opinions about the role of the heavier airplanes that were starting to appear in the Air Service—Malcolm seeing them in an escort role for the airships, while Saxon felt that they could be used like submarines to threaten the larger airships. Malcolm and Saxon spent their evenings eating meals at a nearby pub as neither of them could do more than boil water for tea. Saxon proved to be a master of darts, while Malcolm was the undisputed king of shove ha'penny.

And as Mycroft had promised, Malcolm found the pain beginning to slowly diminish from a white-hot stabbing pain to a low ache. Malcolm found himself settling into a rhythm of long days analyzing tactics and technology at the Admiralty, with evenings spent at the pub in discussion and friendly competition with Saxon. The nights alone in the quiet flat slowly became more bearable.

At the end of the month, Admiral Beatty summoned Malcolm and Saxon to his office. "I've been informed that the repairs of the Daedalus are nearing completion. The Admiralty has instructed me, against my own wishes, that the command of the Daedalus is yours if your wish."

"We do, sir," said Malcolm and Saxon simultaneously.

"I had rather hoped that selfishly, I'd be able to keep you for myself. But I understand the desire to command your own vessel. I, too, look forward to the day when I can get out from behind this desk and return to the bridge."

"I wish to thank you for everything you have done. I believe that your analyses over the last month will have a beneficial impact on the Air Service for years to come. And it is now my pleasure to give you liberty until you report to take command of the Daedalus at Kingsnorth in two weeks. Please feel free to continue to use your flats until you report to Kingsnorth."

The Reluctant Captain

Beatty rose and shook their hands. Malcolm and Saxon saluted, left the Admiralty, and immediately went to the pub near their flats.

"What are you going to do?" asked Malcolm.

"I think I will visit my family. I have not seen them in some time and they are nearby. You?" asked Saxon.

"I think I'm going to avail myself of the opportunity to explore London. I've never spent much time here and there is much to see. It's a long trip back to Kilmacolm and I feel like I'll get there and have to turn around and come back. Also, I want to spend some time alone."

"Are you alright?" asked Saxon. "Do you want me to stay?"

"No, Charles. I'm fine. Well, maybe not fine, but I'm healing. Go, enjoy your family."

"You wouldn't say that if you knew my family," Saxon said. They spent the evening eating, drinking, and enjoying their last games of darts and shove ha'penny.

The next morning, there was a knock on Malcolm's door. Malcolm opened it to see Saxon in a sleek suit. "I'm off, Malcolm. Are you sure you don't want me to stay?"

"I'm fine, Charles. Really, I'm fine."

"Very well, Malcolm," said Saxon. He offered his hand to Malcolm. "Take care, Malcolm. See you at Kingsnorth."

Malcolm shook Saxon's hand and said, "Thank you, Charles. Take care yourself."

Malcolm spent the next two weeks exploring all that London had to offer. He saw Westminster Abbey, St. Paul's Cathedral, and he walked beside the River Thames. He spent days exploring the British Museum, fascinated by its collection of antiquities. Some days, he simply sat at Hyde Park and watched the life of the city ebb and flow around him. He spent his evenings reading an ever-increasing pile of books he purchased at the various bookstores he encountered in his travels.

The two weeks flew by quickly and Malcolm realized that he needed to pack for his trip to Kingsnorth the next morning. In the middle of packing, there was a knock at the door of his flat. Suspicious, Malcolm found his service revolver and went to the door. "Yes, who is it?"

"It's Mycroft Holmes, Captain Robertson. May I take a moment of your time?"

"Yes," he said as he unlocked the door and hid the revolver behind his back. Mycroft Holmes swept into the room with his usual disregard. "I understand you leave for Kingsnorth tomorrow?" Malcolm raised an eyebrow. "Oh, come now, Captain Robertson. I am in the Secret Service. What use would I be if I didn't know your orders?"

"Yes, Mr. Holmes. I leave tomorrow morning. I'm just getting packed."

"Congratulations on your commendations. Truly deserved."

"Thank you, sir. But I'm sure that you didn't come all this way to see me to wish me congratulations."

"No, I did not," he said, fiddling with his hat. "I wanted you to know that Joan was buried in Highgate Cemetery, on the west side. I think you should pay her a visit before you leave. I think she would like that very much."

"Oh," said Malcolm. He had assumed that her family would wish her buried in Switzerland. "She wasn't brought home to be buried in Switzerland?"

"No," said Holmes. "She was very insistent that she remain in London."

"I see," said Malcolm. He couldn't help but think there was something else about this visit.

"Well, I've said my piece. It's a wonderful afternoon for a walk outside. Goodbye, Captain."

"Um, goodbye, Mr. Holmes."

The Reluctant Captain

And as quickly as he swept in, Mycroft Holmes swept out, leaving Malcolm standing in the doorway. That was very peculiar. Did he really just come here to tell him that she was buried in Highgate Cemetery or was there some ulterior motive? With Holmes, he suspected the latter, but for the life of him he couldn't figure out what that would be. Malcolm decided that he should find out. He dressed in a civilian suit, but carefully concealed his service revolver. He took the underground to Highgate station, thinking that it was near the cemetery. It turned out to be a long walk from the station to the cemetery. On the way, he passed a woman peddling flowers and purchased a large bouquet.

Holmes had been correct; it was a nice day for a walk. Malcolm reached the cemetery on the hill and went to the west cemetery. He followed the windy path that continued farther up the hill, amazed at all of the mausoleums and ornate headstones—some containing statues, while others were very simple. Many were covered with ivy that seemed to grow from everywhere. He kept walking until he reached a place where the headstones looked less weathered and he began to search. For over an hour, he walked through the gravestones and then he saw it.

In a secluded corner, under the shade of an oak tree, he found a pillar topped with a draped urn done in white marble. He knew in a moment that it must be Joan's because it reminded him of her: beautiful, pale, and strong. He walked slowly to the grave. The feelings that he had ignored in the last two months by keeping himself busy were bubbling up. He began to feel that all too familiar pain in his heart and it felt like he was watching her get shot all over again.

He was close now and could see her inscription: "Joan de St. Leger". It was true, she was here. He fell to his knees and started to cry—crying for the loss, the waste of such a beautiful life, and the times that they would never spend together. Minutes passed and all he could do was let the tears flow. Finally, he blew his nose, took a deep breath, and pulled himself together. He looked down and realized he was still holding the flowers. "Here," he said. "I brought these for you. I never had a chance to give you flowers before, so I thought I'd make up for that. I hope you liked the bluebells; they were all I could find at the time."

Malcolm jumped when a woman's voice said, "You must have loved her very much."

Malcolm jumped to his feet, whirled, and saw a woman dressed in grieving clothes. She wore a long, black dress and a small hat with a black veil that hid her face. Malcolm could see her black hair was held in a snood, although he thought he saw ringlets curling next to her face through the veil.

"I'm sorry," she said with a very slight French accent. "What I saw was very touching and I wanted to say I'm sorry for your loss."

"Thank you," Malcolm said apologetically. He turned to look at Joan's grave. "I loved her very much and I never got a chance to tell her how much I truly loved her."

"I understand your pain," she said. "I, too, lost someone dear to me. He was a captain of an airship."

"What a coincidence. I'm an airship captain. Perhaps I know him?" Malcolm asked, although he could not remember hearing of any captains, other than Captain Collins, who had perished recently.

"You might. I am Charlotte De Marnier," she said, offering her hand.

Malcolm took the black-gloved hand and kissed it respectfully. "I am Malcolm...." His voice trailed off as he looked up at her. She had removed her veil and Malcolm caught her eyes. They were brilliant emerald green, like Joan's. No, not like Joan's. They were Joan's.

"Joan?" he whispered. There was almost an imperceptible nod. "But, how?"

"Joan was shot in front of many witnesses so there would be no question of her death. Joan's identity as a spy for the Secret Service was obviously known. And then there was the matter of that ridiculous Captain Robertson. Joan knew it was only a matter of time before someone might hurt him to try to get to her. When Joan awoke from the operation, she knew that she had to die. She convinced Dr. Jenkins and Mr. Holmes that everyone must be convinced that she had died, especially that young captain. If everyone saw his grief, there would be no doubt that she had, in fact, died."

Malcolm's relief had now turned to anger. "You let me think you had died! I carried your coffin. You made me feel like every good thing in my life had turned to shite! I think if you weren't already dead, I'd kill you myself!"

He turned from her and leaned against her gravestone for support. How could she do that to him? He felt her touch and part of him flinched. But another part welcomed the touch.

"Don't you see, Malcolm. I had to do it. Not just for me, but for you."

"For me? What could I possibly have gotten from your death?" he yelled.

"Two things. I told you that I could never marry you and I meant that. In part, I did it to protect you from yourself."

"You mean to protect yourself. You were scared that you might love me in return and you were too afraid to commit to marriage."

"That's not true!" she responded, although the fact that her cheeks reddened when she said it gave him reason to believe he wasn't far off the mark.

"The other reason," she continued, "is that I have a great number of enemies. Enemies that would have no reluctance to capture, torture, or even kill you if they thought it might draw me out. And they would be right. I would have done anything to keep you safe. That's why I knew Joan de St. Leger had to die."

They stood silent for a long time. Finally, she moved to Malcolm and reached for his hand. "I loved the bluebells."

"What? " Malcolm said.

"I said I loved the bluebells. They are the most precious flowers that anyone has ever given me."

Malcolm turned, "Thank you, I…"

She put a finger to his lips, "The problem with you is you talk too much." She pulled him close and kissed him hard. After a moment, he relaxed into the kiss and they stayed that way for a long time.

"I leave tomorrow for Kingsnorth. I don't know when I'll be back," he said.

"I leave tomorrow for France. I don't know when I'll be back," she said, mimicking his tone.

"Then perhaps," he said, "we should return to my flat and make up for lost time." He held his arm out in a gentlemanly pose.

"I would like that very much," she said as they strolled down through the cemetery, arm in arm.

THE END

Made in the USA
Charleston, SC
13 March 2015